IN THE
SHADOW
OF A
QUEEN

IN THE SHADOW OF A QUEEN

BASED ON A TRUE STORY

HEATHER B. MOORE

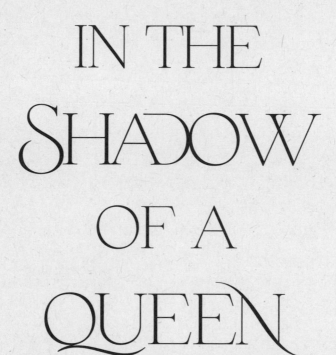

SHADOW
MOUNTAIN
PUBLISHING

© 2022 Heather B. Moore

Visit us at shadowmountain.com

This is a work of fiction. Characters and events in this book are products of the author's imagination or are represented fictitiously.

Library of Congress Cataloging-in-Publication Data
CIP on file
ISBN: 978-1-63993-050-0

Printed in the United States of America
Lake Book Manufacturing, Inc., Melrose Park, IL

10 9 8 7 6 5 4 3 2 1

Dedicated to my ancestors who emigrated from the United Kingdom:

Henry Druce & Harriet Jinks, England, 1846

Ann Blows Gilby Rideout, England/Ireland, 1850

George Shields & Jane Cardy, Scotland, 1853

Philip Pugsley & Martha Roach, England, 1853

Nimrod George Soffe, England, & Mary Ann Harris, Wales, mid-1850s

Francis James Polkinghorne Pascoe &
Margaret Maria Husbands, England, 1860

QUEEN VICTORIA & PRINCE ALBERT
FAMILY CHART

King George III
1738–1820

MARRIED

Charlotte of Mecklenburg-Strelitz
1744–1818

Edward, Duke of Kent
Third son of King George III
1767–1820

MARRIED

Princess Victoria of Saxe-Coburg-Saalfeld
Duchess of Kent
1786–1861

Alexandrina Victoria
Queen Victoria
1819–1901

MARRIED

Prince Albert of Saxe-Coburg and Gotha
Prince Consort
1819–1861

Ernest I, Duke of Saxe-Coburg-Saalfield
1784–1844

MARRIED

Louise of Saxe-Gotha-Altenburg
1800–1831

Victoria (Vicky) Princess Royal, later Empress of Prussia *1840–1901*
MARRIED
Frederick III King of Prussia & German Emperor *1831–1888*

Albert Edward (Bertie) Prince of Wales, later King Edward VII *1841–1910*
MARRIED
Alexandra Princess of Denmark *1844–1925*

Alice *1843–1878*
MARRIED
Ludwig IV (Louis) Grand Duke of Hesse-Darmstadt *1837–1892*

Alfred (Affie) Duke of Edinburgh & Saxe-Coburg-Gotha *1844–1900*
MARRIED
Marie Alexandrovna Daughter of Alexander II *1853–1920*

Helena (Lenchen) *1846–1923*
MARRIED
Christian Prince Christian of Schleswig-Holstein *1831–1917*

Louise *1848–1939*
MARRIED
John Campbell Ninth Duke of Argyll *1845–1914*

Arthur Duke of Connaught *1850–1942*
MARRIED
Louise Margarete Princess of Prussia *1860–1917*

Leopold (Leo) Duke of Albany *1853–1884*
MARRIED
Helena Princess of Waldek and Pyrmont *1861–1922*

Beatrice (Baby) *1857–1944*
MARRIED
Henry Prince Henry of Battenberg *1858–1896*

AUTHOR'S NOTE

My interest in royal families dates back to the 1980s when I began reading about Queen Elizabeth I. Monarchies have always fascinated me. Queen Victoria became of particular interest to me when I learned more about her five daughters and the contributions they made to women's causes throughout Europe by establishing schools and founding charities. Not only that, but her daughters also became the voice of the Crown. Queen Victoria relied on them to serve as her private secretaries while she battled with severe depression and kept her eldest son—and heir—at arm's length.

More specifically, Princess Louise interested me because she deviated from the traditional path of royals during her era by marrying a commoner and pursuing the masculine career of a sculptor. One might consider the modern embodiment of Princess Louise to be Princess Diana, who was also committed to the downtrodden and redefined what it meant to be a royal.

Princess Louise Caroline Alberta was named after both of her grandmothers. *Louise* for Prince Albert's late mother, Princess Louise of Saxe-Gotha-Altenburg. *Caroline* after his step-grandmother, Caroline Amalia of Sax-Gotha. And *Alberta*, after her father. Sadly, Prince Albert's step-grandmother passed away a month before Louise's birth, and with the continent in the throes of revolution, Louise's birth on March 18, 1848, came at a precarious time.

In early 1848, Europe was in upheaval with the forced abdication of the Hapsburg Emperor in Sicily, the February Revolution in France, the disruption of trade to England and the resulting severe unemployment and threatened revolt, the rise of Chartists in connection with the Irish rebellion, and the German Revolution, which led to the fall of Berlin. Thus, Princess Louise, at the young age of eight days old, was whisked away from London with her family to seek refuge at their holiday home, the Osborne House on the Isle of Wight (Wake 15–18).

Louise was the sixth child to her parents, but she was not the hoped-for male baby. With two older brothers and three older sisters, she quickly established her place in the family as a beautiful baby. She was "extremely fair with white satin hair; large long blue eyes and regular features: a most perfect form from head to foot" (Longford 7). As she grew into a young woman, Louise would never lose the label of *beauty*, so it was through her talents that she made her value known.

These talents included music, language, drawing, painting, and sculpting. Her work is still on display today, such as the full-sized statue of Queen Victoria erected in 1893, near Kensington Palace, and the memorial sculpture for the Boer War, displayed in St. Paul's Cathedral in London.

Louise grew up with the privileges of a royal princess as well as the burdens of being sheltered by the system her parents had put into place, guided by her father, Prince Albert. She was a lively child, but like all her siblings, her life completely changed in December 1861 when her father died. Louise's mother, Queen Victoria, went into deep mourning for years and continued to wear black for the rest of her life. It wasn't until seven years later, when Queen Victoria determined it was time for Louise to marry, that she let her daughter officially come out of mourning.

Princess Louise's life has been studied and written about by many talented historians. I've included a selected bibliography at the end of the book as well as chapter notes to highlight these sources and provide additional details. In my early research, I came across claims of scandal surrounding Louise, other members of her family, and Lord Lorne. These are also addressed in the chapter notes.

Princess Louise might have been a member of the most prestigious royal family of her time, but she took a step back from glitter and glamour and found ways to positively impact the lives of others, even when the climb was straight uphill. She had a queen for a mother, and Louise's voice was often strictly controlled and limited to what was considered acceptable for the era. Yet she managed to carve out a fulfilling life and push through barriers in order to achieve her hopes.

HISTORICAL CHARACTERS

ROYAL FAMILY
Queen Victoria
Prince Albert
Princess Victoria, Princess Royal (Vicky)
Prince Albert Edward, Crown Prince (Bertie)
Princess Alice
Prince Alfred (Affie)
Princess Helena (Lenchen)
Princess Louise (Loosy)
Prince Arthur
Prince Leopold (Leo)
Princess Beatrice (Bea)

ROYAL RELATIONS
Princess Alexandra of Denmark
Princess Charlotte of Prussia
Prince Christian of Schleswig-Holstein-Sonderburg-Augustenburg
Uncle Ernest, Duke of Saxe-Coburg and Gotha
Uncle Leopold, King of the Belgians
Prince Ludwig, Grand Duke of Hesse-Darmstadt
Princess Victoire, Duchess of Kent and Strathearn
Prince Wilhelm II of Prussia (Willy)

ROYAL HOUSEHOLD
Fräulein Bauer
Archie Brown
John Brown
Lady Caroline
Lady Jane Churchill
Elizabeth Collins

Reverend Robin Duckworth

Lady Ely

General Charles Grey

Sybil Grey

Madame Hocédé

Doctor William Jenner

Mary Lascelles

Henry Ponsonby

Lady Ponsonby

Marianne Skerrett

Walter Stirling

Mrs. Thurston

ARGYLL FAMILY

George Campbell, Eighth Duke of Argyll

Elizabeth Sutherland, Duchess of Argyll

John Campbell, Marquess of Lorne

JOHN CAMPBELL'S SIBLINGS

Lord Archibald Campbell

Lord Walter Campbell

Edith Percy, Duchess of Northumberland

Lord George Campbell

Lady Elizabeth Clough-Taylor

Lord Colin Campbell

Lady Victoria Campbell

Lady Evelyn Baillie-Hamilton

Lady Frances Balfour

Lady Mary Carr Glyn

Lady Constance Emmott

OTHERS

Lord Ailsa

William Beauclerk, Duke of St Albans

Edgar Boehm

Josephine Butler

Lord Coke

Susan Durant

Lord Henry Fitzroy

Lady Gladstone

Lord Gosford

Lady Granville

Lord Granville

Lord Albert Grey

Lord Hatherley

Lord Ronnie Levenson-Gower

Colonel McNeill

Henrietta Montalba

Lord Rosebery

Lord Stafford

Henry John Temple, Lord Palmerston

Mary Thornycroft

PART ONE

1861–1862

CHAPTER 1

"Until today I have been unable to write my Journal, which I shall now take up where I left off, though not before I have expressed by heart, felt thanks for God's merciful protection again on this occasion, & for being so particularly well.— I shall never forget all I suffered from the night of the 16th to the 17th. Dearest Albert was all loving kindness & thoughtfulness. I felt a little better when I got up, & then I saw Clark. Suffered all the morning, nevertheless I saw dear Victoire for a short while. Continued slightly better in the afternoon, & Clém came & sat with me. Went to bed, fairly well, & was awake at 2 on the morning of the 18th, a fine large girl being born at 8. Felt so thankful all was well over."

QUEEN VICTORIA'S JOURNAL, APRIL 2, 1848

MARCH 1861
LOUISE, AGE 12

Loo Loo!" Leopold called as he burst into the room. "Guess what's happened?" He skidded to a halt, shifting the Aubusson rug next to the desk where Louise sat. "Papa said when the sun comes out, we can play games. Can you play with me, Loo Loo?"

Her seven-year-old brother's blue eyes were round, his breathing scattered, but he grinned. The nursery maid Mrs. Thurston was steps behind him, her hair askew beneath her white cap, perspiration a fine sheen above her upper lip, and her reprimand ready. "Prince Leopold," she began, "you are not to run—"

"Yes, I'll come with you." Louise held out her hand to her brother.

The steady drum of the rain outside Windsor Castle had slowed four or five minutes before, gradually decreasing until the ticking clock outpaced the sound of raindrops. Perhaps at almost thirteen, Louise was too old to join in with the younger children, but children's games were preferable to German lessons. Besides, Fräulein Bauer already looked irritated, which made Louise inordinately pleased. The teacher's eyes narrowed, and the wrinkles about her face deepened, much like a prune.

Leopold grasped her hand and tugged, his laughter bubbling up.

"Surely, His Royal Highness meant *after* German lessons," Bauer said.

Louise ignored Bauer and hurried out of the room. If there was one thing that brought Louise joy in life, it was to see Leo happy. His health was fragile, and he didn't have many good days. Running wasn't allowed because then he could fall, and if he fell, he could get injured, and if he was injured, he could start bleeding. And never stop.

Leo had been diagnosed with hemophilia after ominous bruises had formed all over his body as an infant. Mama was so protective of him that he wasn't allowed to run or jump or ride horses. Sometimes he missed their family holidays to Balmoral or Osborne because of his health.

As they hurried down the long corridor lined with gilt-framed paintings, their footsteps muffled by the thick Axminster carpets, Louise noted the particular smell of Windsor Castle. Furniture polish and flowers—*old* flowers, Leo had claimed once. And lavender in every room, as ordered by the queen.

"Arthur!" Leopold shouted. "She said yes!"

Arthur appeared at the top of the stairs, his grin matching Leo's. At eleven, Arthur was sturdy compared to Leo, but their enthusiasm was well matched this afternoon. Since Leo often suffered with nosebleeds in the middle of the night and he didn't want to stay in the nursery with little Beatrice, Mama had allowed him to sleep in Arthur's room.

Arthur led the trio, his pace brisk and confident as they stepped into Papa's study. Their father, Prince Albert, was alone, which was excellent.

Interrupting adults was never allowed, and so now there would be no waiting.

Papa lifted his gaze from the papers upon his mahogany desk. His dark sideburns were threaded with some gray, and his blue eyes seemed tired, but they warmed at the sight of his children. Beyond him a cheery fire crackled, though it did little to heat the high-ceilinged room.

"Well, what is this?" Papa asked.

His Royal Highness, Prince Albert of Saxe-Coburg and Gotha, was the opposite of Mama in many ways. He knew every detail about each of his children—nine in all—and he managed their tutors and activities. This year, though, he'd been ill more than once, and he frequently appeared overtired.

"The rain has stopped," Leo pronounced, his chest puffed like a robin's.

"So it has," Papa said. "Shall we go outside then? I think we have visitors as well."

Leo cheered, and Papa chuckled.

Visitors meant other children from peerage families. As they followed after their striding father, Louise said to her brothers, "What about prisoner's base? Leo can be the prison guard."

Arthur scrunched up his face. "That game is too fast for girls."

Louise huffed. "You must be too scared to play with me."

Arthur's face flushed. "I'm not scared, Loosy. You'll see when *my* side wins."

Louise didn't care who won. Losing against Arthur and hearing his ribbing for days was still preferable to Fräulein Bauer's lesson. Of course she'd never tell her father about her dislike for his German native language. French was just easier to learn.

They bypassed the queen's drawing room, where Mama met with government officials like the Prime Minister, Lord Palmerston. As they neared the doors that led to the East Terrace Gardens, Mrs. Thurston was waiting, with an overcoat and gloves.

"It's not cold." But Leo dutifully pulled on the warmer clothing.

"Oh, look, we already have guests," Papa said, his tone humorous.

Lord Ronnie Levenson-Gower, Lord Lorne, and his brother Archie Campbell were batting around hoops with sticks along the paths.

John Campbell, titled Lord Lorne, was the oldest of the group at sixteen, and he seemed to be taller each time Louise saw him. His blond hair ruffled in the brisk wind as he turned to see her.

"We're playing prisoner's base," Louise announced. Papa had stopped to speak to one of the gardeners.

"Louise is on my team," Archie said. "She's fast. Leo too."

She cut a triumphant glance at Arthur, who studiously ignored her.

Everyone divided and established their territories. Three against three.

Leo distracted the other team, and Archie made it through their territory. Releasing Louise from her "prison," they raced back to their side. But not before they had to detour through some trees, startling a flock of roosting rooks.

Louise stumbled and dirtied the hem of her dress, but she refused to be caught. She soon reached Archie's speed again, and they shouted in triumph as they raced ahead of John and Arthur.

They all collapsed to the ground, catching their breath.

"Your birthday is soon, Princess Louise," Archie said.

In three days it would be her thirteenth birthday. "Yes, we're having a children's ball. Who's coming?"

"I am," Archie said immediately.

"Me too," Leo added.

Everyone laughed because they would all be attending the children's ball at Buckingham Palace.

"Albert!" Mama called from behind them.

Louise turned to see the queen standing at the edge of the terrace. Her blue eyes were sharp, and the ringlet loops of her hair styled about her ears bobbed as she looked about for Papa.

Louise's stomach tensed. Had Mama found out that Louise had left

Fräulein Bauer and Leo had run in the hallway? Would she be scolded for staining her dress?

Papa stepped into view. "What is it, Gutes Fräuchen?"

"The Russians are still demanding landing rights in Tsushima . . ." Papa had nearly reached Mama when she added, "We cannot support this."

Louise stared after her parents as they disappeared inside the castle.

"Where is Tsushima?" Leo asked.

"Japan," John answered.

Leo's brow dimpled. "*Russia* wants to take over Japan?"

"No one knows *what* the Russians want," John said in a fierce tone. "They're expanding and looking for anything they can grab. They want to set up a fleet at a permanent base in Tsushima."

Louise was surprised at the vehemence in his voice as well as his apparent knowledge about foreign politics. Maybe he'd learned it at Eton. "Do you think it will work?" she asked.

John's blue eyes landed on her, his gaze direct. "The Russians are only following Britain's interests, like usual."

Britain was interested in Japan? Louise had questions about this as well, but before she could ask John Campbell anything else, several staff members exited the palace.

"We're having tea outside!" Beatrice bounced more than she walked. Her hair was a tangle of curls that had to be tamed each day. She ran full speed toward Louise, who caught the four-year-old in her arms with a laugh.

Cradling Beatrice close, Louise said, "Did you finish your lessons, Baby?"

"Yes. I can count to thirty now!"

"You're such a dear, smart girl," Louise pronounced, then kissed her sister's forehead.

Beatrice giggled.

The boys hurried to the tables on the terrace where tea was being set out, so Louise followed, supporting Beatrice on her hip. The sisters sat together, and as Beatrice prattled, Louise realized she was looking forward to her birthday more than usual. The roles had shifted in the family since her older sister Alice had become engaged to Prince Ludwig, the Grand Duke of Hesse-Darmstadt. Their eldest sister, Vicky, already lived in Prussia with her husband. And her oldest brother Bertie was in Ireland.

That left Alfred—or Affie, as everyone called him—and Helena— nicknamed the Germanized *Lenchen* by the family. But they were too caught up in their lessons to be much bothered with the younger children.

This made Louise the leader of the younger group, and the children's ball on her birthday would be delightful for all. She'd wear her newest dress and do her hair in a sophisticated style. She was contemplating which hairstyle she might try from the fashion plates—perhaps the center parting tied into a low chignon at the nape of her neck—when she heard a cry coming through an open window. *Mama?*

Louise pushed to her feet and hurried inside. She dashed through the hallways until she found her parents in their bedroom suite. Papa sat next to Mama, tears streaking her face.

"What's happened, Mama?" Louise had been in such a rush that she hadn't noticed her other siblings run after her.

Mama extended her hands, and Louise grasped one of them. "My dearests, I've received the most dreadful news. Grandmama is gravely ill."

The room grew very small, and Louise's breath went shallow, as if she'd run the entire length of the castle.

"Is she dying?" Leo asked, his tone plaintive.

"I'm afraid so, darling."

The words cut like an icicle into Louise's heart. Grandmama was dying. Princess Victoire, Duchess of Kent and Strathearn, had been the only grandparent Louise knew. Even though Louise was one of many grandchildren, Grandmama always paid her special attention.

Louise didn't hear the soothing words spoken by Papa. Tears burned hot in her eyes, and her chest hitched with every breath she took. She did not want her beloved grandmama to die. She did not want this day to exist at all.

CHAPTER 2

❦

"The dreaded day had come at last! It was gloomy, with a drizzling rain, but it cleared later.— My dear Albert came in in his black coat & scarf, he was going as Chief Mourner. . . . Embraced my dearest Husband & begged him to pray for & think of me! At 11, they all left. I heard nothing, but the carriages drive off & saw nothing. Heard that all have been so quietly & properly conducted this morning. At ½ p. 4 the sad removal from Frogmore took place, the dear remains accompanied to St. George's Chapel by Lt James Murray Col: Ponsonby, the 3 faithful maids, her steward & 2 Pages. The coffin was first placed close to Pss Charlotte's monument, & remained there watched by the staffs, till the service began.— Our 4 daughters joined me with prayers, & in reading comforting Hymns, whilst the service was going on & I felt calmed."

QUEEN VICTORIA'S JOURNAL, MARCH 24, 1861

MARCH 1861
LOUISE, AGE 13

Louise should not have been happy on the day of her grandmama's burial, but she *was* happy to see her older siblings. Vicky had arrived with her husband, Fritz, who'd recently become Crown Prince of Prussia since his grandfather had died in January. Vicky brought her two little children, Willy and baby Charlotte. And Bertie was home from the Curragh camp in Ireland, where he'd been sent to train with the second battalion of the elite Grenadier Guards. Affie was on leave from the Royal Navy.

Louise wasn't invited to the dinner with the adults, but it was a relief because Mama's sobbing only made Louise feel worse. The queen had ordered that Grandmama's rooms at Frogmore not be touched as a memory to her name.

So Louise waited in the library on the sofa next to the window. Bertie would visit and tell her all that had gone on. The setting sun was gold, splintering the gray sky into an array of colors. She imagined her drawing master, Mr. Leitch, telling her to capture the shapes first, then add in the colors.

So she did.

Sketching the clouds hovering above the trees, she thought of how her thirteenth birthday had come and gone. No celebration. No children's ball. She would never wear her birthday gown now. The palace was in mourning along with the rest of the country for the woman who'd birthed their queen. Louise's missed birthday didn't bother her since she'd rather have Grandmama back, alive and well, sharing stories about Coburg or about Mama as a little girl.

Next, Louise sketched a line of carriages, the interiors dark, much like the clothing that the occupants wore returning from St. George's Chapel. Mama had stayed in the palace since it wasn't typical for women to attend funerals, and Louise and her sisters had stayed with her, reading hymns and praying.

"Loosy," a deep voice said as her door creaked open. A tall, slim man entered the library. His hair waved in a short haircut, and he had the beginnings of a mustache.

"Bertie!" Louise dropped her sketchbook and rushed to greet her brother. Without the grieving countenance of Mama to frown at her, Louise didn't hold back on giving her brother a fierce hug. He might be the Prince of Wales, heir to the throne of England, but he was Bertie to her.

"I almost didn't recognize you when I arrived yesterday," Bertie said. His strident voice and amused eyes were already helping pull Louise out of her gloom.

"I've not changed, you buffoon." She stepped back as if to judge his appearance as well. "*You've* changed." At twenty, her brother was turning into a man, but he was still the same old Bertie. She missed him. When he wasn't at Cambridge, he lived at White Lodge in Richmond Park.

He withdrew something from his inner jacket pocket and handed it to her. Louise took the wrapped rectangular object. "What's this?"

"Not everyone forgot your birthday."

Louise smiled, although her heart hurt a little. Her birthday would always be surrounded by the memory of losing Grandmama. Louise pulled away the handkerchief and studied the book. A *novel*.

"Bertie! If Mama discovers you gave me a novel, we'll both be in trouble."

He chuckled and leant forward to kiss her cheek. "She and Papa are too busy reading through Grandmama's private correspondence and journals before they burn them. Plus, when the shop owner told me that the serialization had been published into a book, I knew my little sister would be entranced."

"Since I was never allowed to read the serialization."

"Right."

Bertie's grin made her laugh. She promptly opened to the first page and began to read *A Woman in White* by Wilkie Collins aloud. "This is the story of what a Woman's patience can endure, and what a Man's resolution can achieve." She clutched the book to her chest. "I already love it."

Bertie's eyes sparkled. "It's all the rage, you know. It published not only in *All the Year Round*, but in *Harper's Magazine* in America." He lowered his voice. "Father has read it. Baron Stockmar told me that Father sent him a copy."

This made Louise inordinately pleased. "I hope to catch a dreadful cold so that I might hide in my room and read all day and night."

"Do not jest about such things, Loosy." Bertie's brows knitted. "Your health is not to be taken lightly."

Louise scoffed. She'd been the recipient of many colds and terrible headaches. Nothing like Leo, of course. "I shall then stay indoors instead of running out into the next rainstorm."

"Good girl." Bertie winked. "Now, do you know what the best thing will be about tomorrow?"

"You'd better not be leaving."

"No, you goose. I'll be riding with you. How about it?"

Louise held back a delighted squeal. "I might be convalescing in my room." She gave a fake cough. "I feel a cold coming on."

Bertie lunged forward. "Then I'd better take that book back."

Louise darted out of his way, sprinted across the library, then perched on the window ledge.

Bertie stalked toward her, trying to look menacing, but he only looked comical. Louise couldn't hold back her laughter any longer.

He paused to pick up her sketchbook. "What's this?"

"Drawings that kept me from getting bored while waiting for you." She was about to snatch it back, but Bertie turned one page after another, holding the sketchbook toward the fading light of the sunset.

"These are quite good, Loosy. Has Mama seen them?"

"Some of them," Louise said on a sigh. "Mama thinks sketches and watercolor are the only appropriate artistic activities for a lady. But I want to try other avenues that require more detail."

"Such as?"

Louise hesitated. "Modelling."

"You aim to be the first female sculptor in the family?"

"I want to try real sculpturing—beyond modelling clay—and turn it into a sculpture of marble. I could then create a person from every angle and every viewpoint. It's not like a watercolor that's faded and abstract and only painted from one side."

"You're right," Bertie said in a soft tone. "Your watercolors are passable. But these drawings . . . are full of emotion. I can feel Leo's melancholy." He'd stopped on the sketch she'd done of Leo sitting on the stairs, his face forlorn, when he'd been left out once again due to his fragile health.

"Has Edward Corbould seen this book?" Bertie asked.

"Yes. Cobby told me to carry a sketch pad everywhere I go," she explained. "I should consider dreary evenings as my own secret drawing class and sketch everyone I can."

"He thinks you're talented then, sister."

Louise's face warmed with the compliment. Yes, Cobby had been generous in his praises, but it was hard for her to tell if the royal drawing master Papa had commissioned was being sincere. Everyone in her family was artistic—Papa in drawing and etching, and Mama in painting.

Cobby was the first drawing master who emphasized free drawing. He'd said that ideas and imagination were more important than technique. So she'd followed Cobby's advice of committing a person's likeness to paper in a hasty manner, then filling in details later.

It was as if Bertie had read her mind. "Cobby knows talent when he sees it. You shouldn't doubt a master. Now, draw *me*, standing at the window. Pining for something I cannot have."

Her oldest brother could always make her laugh. "As the Prince of Wales, there is probably not much in the world you *cannot* have."

Bertie turned his gaze to the window and struck a pretentious pose. Louise held back a giggle, then sketched out her brother's features. His wavy hair, his straight nose, his hooded eyes.

"The light is growing dim. Shall I turn on a gas lamp?"

"No," Bertie said. "I need to join the adults soon. Let me see it first."

Louise's pulse spiked as she handed her brother the sketch.

He stared at it for a long time, saying nothing.

"Well?"

Her brother blinked as if he'd been lost in thought. "I think you're going to give Cobby some competition."

Louise felt flattered, but nothing more. It wasn't as if she, a princess, could ever become a true proficient in the art world. When Helena married, Louise would become Mama's personal secretary. "I'm a princess, remember? Proper and traditional and at the behest of the queen in all things."

Bertie's eyes widened.

"I didn't mean—"

"Of course you did," he said with a wink. "Don't worry. I won't turn you in to Mama."

Still, Louise tried not to let her eyes fill with tears. Sometimes she spoke without thinking. It was one thing around her brother, but she had to watch herself with others. She didn't have an excuse like Leo, who was practically an invalid and, for some reason, lost control of his emotions during serious or tense events. The night after they'd learned Grandmama had died, Leo had laughed uncontrollably at dinner. Mama had ordered him out of the room. Louise understood her mother's distress, yet she felt sorry for Leo being taken out. They all knew he couldn't stop his outbursts.

Bertie's hand rested on her shoulder. "Don't despair, Loosy. Think of how much riding we'll do tomorrow. Alice and Affie are coming too. Oh, and Ludwig is going to join the family at Balmoral on our holiday, and you know that will put Mama in better spirits."

This did cheer Louise. Although Alice wouldn't marry Ludwig for another year, Papa was already making plans for the event. Alice had been moping about the palace since Mama had stipulated that they must wait so long to marry.

"Will Princess Alexandra be coming?" Louise asked in a coy voice. Her parents' minute study of the royal genealogical reference book *Almanach de Gotha* had produced a likely candidate for Bertie's wife. She had to be royal, she should be a German and a Protestant—or at least willing to convert—and she needed to have the demeanor befitting a future queen of England. Princess Alexandra of Denmark was a choice favorable to both Mama and Papa, although neither of them loved that she was from Denmark. Bertie was supposed to meet the princess this coming fall and decide if they were a good match. Their oldest sister, Vicky, didn't support the marriage because her in-laws' country was in conflict with Denmark.

"Not that again," Bertie said, but his tone was light. "You sound like

Mama. Scheming to make me a match. Oh, I almost forgot, Vicky said you can help put Willy to bed tonight. He's been asking for you."

Louise yelped. "He has?" She tossed her sketchbook on the sofa, scuttled out of the room, then ran to the nursery rooms.

She cracked open the closed nursery door and found Vicky inside, sitting in a chair with baby Charlotte at her breast, while Willy intently played with toy soldiers. Willy immediately stood when he saw Louise, and the pink-cheeked, blond toddler burrowed his head against Louise's legs, as his good arm clutched at her skirt. Willy had been born with a left arm that was shorter and weaker than his right arm. Vicky had been so bothered by her son's arm, that she hadn't told Mama and Papa about it for ages.

In Louise's opinion, Willy was a beautiful angel. He was only twenty-one months younger than Beatrice, and they'd all laughed when "Baby" insisted that Willy call her "Aunt Beatrice."

"You're such a big boy now, Willy," Louise declared.

He lifted his grinning face. "Loo Loo."

"Yes, that's me." She crouched. "Let's see how smart you are. What color are your eyes?"

"Blue!" Willy announced.

"They sure are. Now, how old are you?"

Willy held up his good hand and produced two stout fingers.

"Very good, Willy. You're such a smart boy."

"Mama has a new baby." Willy pointed at Vicky. "She's feeding the baby milk."

Louise's gaze slid to Vicky. Her sister looked happy, content, even though her labors had been very difficult with her children.

"Don't tell Mama I'm breastfeeding in her palace," Vicky said.

Louise wouldn't dare. She'd already heard her mother's ranting about how Vicky had chosen to breastfeed like the animals.

"I've heard it all, believe me," Vicky said. "And from my mother-in-law, Augusta, as well. She doesn't like me missing out on court events."

Willy climbed up on Louise's lap, and she held him close. She burrowed her face against Willy's soft hair and breathed in his sweet scent. Someday she'd be a mother, and she'd love every minute of it.

"Does Fritz's mother order you about, then?" Louise asked, genuinely curious. Vicky had been married for over three years. They'd exchanged letters but had seen each other only a handful of times.

"Not as much now that she's the queen consort," Vicky said.

Louise was fascinated by the change in Vicky. She'd been the pet child of Papa, educated and groomed to make a stellar marriage match. Then at age seventeen she was married to Fritz, future emperor of Papa's country.

Bertie had told her that through Vicky, Papa was exerting his political and ethical influence where possible. Papa hadn't always been respected by the British cabinet. But through years of writing memos and minutes, he had gained respect among the leaders of the country. It was no easy task to be born a royal. Expectations were high, and their lives were always on display and under scrutiny.

Louise had read some of the articles about Grandmama and how she'd been removed from the queen's household when Mama had become queen at eighteen. Now her thoughts were on dear Grandmama again, and Louise wondered if the heavy ache in her heart and the noose of worry inside would ever ease. She wanted to believe she had a pretty future ahead of her, but how could that happen if a gaping hole obstructed her path?

CHAPTER 3

"My dearest Arthur, I miss you so much; I am so glad that you arrived safely in London. I have bought you a beautiful squirting ball I hope you will like it. We took our general Sunday walk by the Dee, and we were nearly blown into it. Leopold and I are going to play with your fair. Mr. Leitch said that he misses you very much. I am going to paint you some pictures for your book and I will give them to you at Windsor. Baby speaks nearly all the day of you. . . . I will soon write to you again and a longer letter too."

LETTER FROM PRINCESS LOUISE, BALMORAL,
TO PRINCE ARTHUR, OCTOBER 13, 1861

NOVEMBER 1861
LOUISE, AGE 13

Alice swept into the drawing room where Louise sat reading. She snapped the cover of *A Woman in White* shut and set it behind her. The look on her sister's face wasn't cheerful at all—not like it had been during her fiancé Ludwig's visit. Alice's features were naturally sharp though, so it was hard to tell if she was pleased or displeased. Her black mourning dress only made her look more severe.

"I must tell you something so that you don't irritate anyone tonight." Alice took a seat opposite Louise, not noticing that her sister had been reading a forbidden book.

Louise stiffened. "Your dowry was revoked by Parliament?"

Alice's eyes narrowed. She'd been ill-spirited because her fiancé had returned to Darmstadt. "Parliament can't revoke their own vote."

From where she sat tinkering with the keys on the piano, Helena laughed. Then she quieted abruptly in answer to Alice's glare. "It was funny."

Louise grimaced. Now that Alice told her not to be irritating, Louise *wanted* to be irritating. Prime Minister Palmerston had ensured that Alice was provided the usual thirty-thousand-pound dowry, along with a six-thousand-pound annual income, even though Alice would be living in Darmstadt.

"Your fiancé has changed his mind about you?" Louise asked.

Alice scoffed. "You, dear sister, are treading on ice. One more step, and you're falling in. I'll leave, and you'll never know what's happening."

"What are you two nattering about?" Helena left the piano and sat next to Alice on the sofa. Helena was the plumpest of all the sisters, and Mama had fretted that she was not attractive. Helena was a talented pianist though, and Louise thought she was pretty enough with her wavy brown hair and amber eyes.

Alice sighed. "You might as well hear too, although I think you'll take this much more calmly than our Loo Loo." She paused. "It's Bertie."

Louise popped up from her chair. "Is he all right?"

"He's all right—physically, if that's what you mean." Alice glanced at Helena. "Word has come that he's disgraced our family."

Slowly, Louise sank back onto the seat, dread climbing up her throat. Bertie was the Crown Prince. Someday, he'd be the king of England. If there was one thing their parents did well, it was keeping their family above all scandal and speculation.

Alice took a deep breath. "While Bertie was in Ireland, a group of the Grenadier Guards officers sneaked a woman into Bertie's rooms."

Helena covered her mouth with both hands.

Louise held very still. Her thumping heart told her there was no good outcome to this story. "Did Bertie know?"

Alice gave a short laugh. "If he didn't, he knew when he walked into his room."

"Who—who was she?" Louise asked. Maybe Bertie had fallen in love . . .

"Nellie Clifden," Alice said. "She's an actress. Our brother met the woman at a party while at Cambridge, and then this past summer a group of his friends brought her to Ireland."

Louise didn't understand the intimacies between a man and woman, but she knew that they couldn't be alone together if they weren't married or it would be scandalous. Lighthearted, kind-souled Bertie surely wouldn't want to bring scandal to the throne of England. "Did he kick her out?"

"No," Alice said. "Bertie went through with the liaison."

Louise wanted to ask exactly what that meant, but Alice wouldn't tell her. Helena closed her eyes and rubbed at her temples.

"It's been months since the . . . incident," Alice continued, "but Stockmar found out and now Papa knows."

"And Mama?"

The look on Alice's face was answer enough. "She isn't telling Vicky yet. Or any of the younger children."

"What are they going to do?" Louise asked. What *could* they do? Was this serious enough for her brother to be disinherited? Cut out of the family? And then another horrible thought crossed Louise's mind.

"What about Princess Alexandra?" Helena said, echoing Louise's thoughts exactly. "Will they keep it from her?"

"I think that's impossible," Alice said. "It's not like they're engaged or there's any understanding yet, besides Papa's approval. Mama hasn't even met her yet." Bertie had met Princess Alexandra last September. Vicky and Fritz had arranged the meeting, although to avoid controversy, Bertie was said to be in Germany in an official capacity to observe military drills at Coblenz. He'd met Princess Alexandra at the Speyer Cathedral during that time. When Papa had later questioned him, Bertie had simply said he was too young to marry.

"What will happen now?" Louise felt torn between her parents' reaction and how Bertie must have felt when he realized the error of his ways. Surely, he knew there would be consequences.

"I don't know yet," Alice said. "But Papa is in the library speaking with Stockmar. Mama is fretting in her own rooms, and well . . . if there is a child . . ."

Louise couldn't hide her gasp. She hadn't thought of what it might mean if a child came from the union.

Helena was already ahead of Louise. "She would file for paternity charges."

"Correct."

The three sisters sat silent for a few moments. The siblings had been obedient to their parents for the most part. Vicky had married the heir to the Prussian throne. Alice was engaged to a prince. And Helena would take over Alice's duties to their mama once Alice married. Bertie should be preparing to bring the Danish princess to England. Yet now . . . The papers would butcher the good, wholesome view of the family unit that their parents had worked so hard to uphold.

"Let's go down to dinner together," Alice said.

Louise fetched her black shawl from the back of her chair. Mama often kept the windows open in whatever room she occupied, despite it being November, and the larger rooms at Windsor were full of drafty air. They were the last to arrive in the dining room, with its large windows on one wall and tall mirrors on the other, reflecting the coffered ceiling and Gothic-patterned carpet in crimson and maroon.

Louise caught sight of her oval face and light-brown hair in the mirrors. It was always strange to see herself in a distant mirror, almost impersonable, as if she were looking outside herself. Mama had told her more than once she was the prettiest of her daughters, but Louise hadn't taken any pride in that since Mama had handed down plenty of criticisms as well, mostly about her stubbornness. And now, Louise was quickly becoming the tallest sister, which might bring more attention to her than ever.

She scanned the dining table for her siblings. Affie was back in the naval service, so he wasn't at the castle. Leo was in Cannes, France, with the Bowater family since the doctors had recommended that he spend the winter months in a warmer climate. Helena went to sit on the other side of Arthur. His face was tinged red as if he'd stepped out of a brisk wind. Beatrice was likely in the nursery having her dinner.

Christmas was drawing closer, and that should have lifted everyone's spirits. After all, Christmas was a favorite with Papa. But last week, telegrams bearing bad news from Portugal had arrived. Papa's two Coburg cousins, King Pedro V and Prince Ferdinand, had died from typhoid. And now, this news about Bertie . . .

Not only that, but Papa's toothache had returned, and he suffered from neuralgia. Mama also fretted over his insomnia. Louise sat next to Arthur at the Pugin-designed dining table, and he gave her the smallest of smiles. She reached for his hand and squeezed it. Whatever happened, whatever the result of Bertie's fall from grace, she loved her brothers. All of them.

As the first course of Windsor soup was brought in, Mama dabbed at her eyes with a lace handkerchief. Her sniffles weren't for Grandmama tonight, as they had been over the past several months. No, this time it was for a living crisis.

Everyone ate their soup silently. When the second course was brought in, Mama picked up her fork and speared a piece of roast beef. She ate it, and so the rest of the family followed, eating only after the queen had begun.

After the first bite, she set her fork down. If Mama was finished eating, then everyone's plates would be taken away, so Louise quickly took two more bites.

"I'm not hungry," Mama declared, then dabbed her eyes.

Papa set down his fork. "Perhaps you should rest."

"I'm tired of resting." Mama's voice was hushed, yet strong enough to carry across the room as the plates were quickly cleared from the table. "Something must be done about that boy—"

"Gutes Fräuchen," Papa cut in. "I am going to Cambridge tomorrow. I will speak with him and plan what should be done next."

Mama's shoulders sagged. "You think talking to Bertie will make him into the man he should already be?"

Papa stood and held out his hand. "Come, you should rest."

All of her siblings seemed to sigh in relief when Mama allowed Papa to lead her from the room.

The food was gone, but Louise would make a trip to the kitchens later. She did it often enough that she'd learned to cook several things. Plus, she wasn't about to let her younger siblings go hungry just because Mama was too upset to eat.

The evening hours dropped into night, passing slowly while Louise stayed in her bedroom. She sat at the bay window with its nearly floor-to-ceiling glass and watched the sun set, but not even the pretty gold-and-pink sky lifted her spirits.

She moved to the white marble fireplace and stared into the dark interior, then she lifted her chin to gaze into the mirror above the mantle. With only the single gaslight she had turned on, it was too dark to see the color of her blue eyes. Finally, she sat at her library table. She didn't want to read anything though. She knew her mind wouldn't focus.

Only when exhausted was she finally able to fall asleep in her narrow bed. But her dreams were filled with angst. Bertie arguing with Papa. Alice telling everyone she was leaving Windsor for good. Leo getting locked in his room because of one of his laughing fits. Arthur, instead of Leo, waking up with a nosebleed.

Louise awakened before dawn, her head aching like someone was pressing a board against her temples. With a grim moan, she turned toward the window and the pale-gray light coming through. She wanted to distract herself from her torturous dreams. It might be days before Papa returned from his visit to Cambridge, and in the meantime, Louise had to stay busy.

She inched out of bed, moving slowly so as to not elevate the grisly pain in her head. After drawing on a brocade robe, she crossed to the writing desk in her room. She pulled out an album she'd been working on for Affie. Inside, she'd pressed flowers and autumn leaves she'd gathered this past week, and now she was making a detailed drawing of each on the page opposite. The album would remind her brother of home, no matter where the Royal Navy took him.

She turned up the gaslight, and as she worked, the outside light brightened in her bedroom, changing from grays to warm yellow. When her final illustration was done, Louise leafed back through the album. Affie would be happy, she hoped.

Next, Louise picked up a smaller book of blank paper she'd been working on for Beatrice. She'd recopied the "Old Mother Hubbard" nursery rhyme, one verse per page, and was adding illustrations to each verse.

> *She went to the tailor's*
> *To buy him a coat;*
> *When she came back*
> *He was riding a goat.*

Louise debated whether she could have the dog in the poem riding the goat while playing the flute or smoking a pipe. She opted for the flute and soon had a decent sketch of a grinning dog playing a flute while sitting on a goat.

She'd also planned to create an album to send to Cannes for Leo. He loved cats but couldn't have one. Mama was afraid that any scratch from a cat might make him bleed to death. So Louise would make him his own picture book of kittens.

Once breakfast was over, Louise found Papa in his study, standing before the desk as he shifted through papers. He looked paler in the morning light than he had the day before. She was also certain that his shoulders were thinner. She stepped inside as he lifted his gaze.

"Louise," his voice rumbled. "Now's not the time—"

"I've only come to wish you well on your journey, Papa." For some reason her throat hitched.

The lines about his eyes eased, but the darkness beneath them remained.

"Will you—will you give my love to Bertie?"

"Of course I will."

She didn't wait another moment, but hurried to Papa and hugged him around the waist. She inhaled the wool scent of his suit. He drew her in close, his exhale thready.

"Don't go if you're too ill."

He stilled. "I'll be fine, my dear. I caught a chill from attending the function in Sandhurst when it was raining."

Louise looked up at him. She swore he'd aged another year in his hooded eyes alone.

Papa touched her cheek. "I'll give Bertie your best, and—"

"Here." Louise produced a letter. "Give him this."

"Your brother will appreciate it."

"Travel safe, Papa." She moved back a few steps. She didn't want to burst into tears in front of him. He'd had enough of that with Mama. "Be well."

CHAPTER 4

"Albert arranged a surprise for the Children. In Germany the old saying that St. Nicholas appears with a rod for naughty children, & gingerbread for good ones, is constantly represented, & Arthur hearing of this begged for one. Accordingly Albert got up a St. Nicholas, most formidable he looking, in black, covered with snow, a long white beard, & red nose,— of a gigantic stature! He came in asking the Children, who were somewhat awed & alarmed,— 'are you a good child,' & giving them gingerbread & apples."

QUEEN VICTORIA'S JOURNAL, DECEMBER 24, 1856

NOVEMBER 1861
LOUISE, AGE 13

Louise reread the short note again from Bertie, who said he couldn't wait to see her again. He was still in Cambridge, and Papa had already returned to Windsor Castle. She'd heard him complain of a headache and lethargy to Mama, and she sent for the doctor, who recommended bed rest. But Papa refused to rest, pushing through his pain and fatigue.

Louise had doubled her prayers. Her entire family seemed to be in a sad state. First Grandmama's death, then Papa's cousins dying of the dreaded typhoid, followed by Bertie's scandal, and now . . . Louise could hear her father coughing from his study.

She tucked Bertie's note into her dress pocket, then moved to one of the library shelves. The day before, she'd been looking through a medical book, *Domestic Medicine*, and found several concoctions that were supposed to help cure coughing.

Taking courage, Louise left the library and headed to his study. Papa was alone, reading through something. His hollowed cheeks were frightful, and when he looked up, she saw that perspiration stood out on his forehead.

"I will make you a fever remedy, Papa."

She sensed Papa was about to refuse, but then the tired lines about his eyes deepened. "All right, Loosy. Bring me your remedy."

Before she was out of earshot, another coughing fit erupted.

Once in the kitchen, Louise spoke to one of the cooks. "Father needs a mixture for his cough. Do we have any oranges? And I need sugar, cream of tartar, and hot water."

Mama wouldn't be happy with Louise bothering the staff. Once the cook had brought the ingredients, Louise combined everything and whipped it until the drink was frothy.

She hurried back to Papa's study, but when she arrived, she heard Mama speaking to Papa.

Louise peeked inside. They stood in the adjoining private library. So Louise waited by the desk. She caught a glimpse of her mother's back as she hovered near Papa; he stood next to a bookshelf, sorting through a stack of books.

"You must listen to the doctors and rest," Mama said. "This business with Bertie has depleted your strength, and I'll not let his foolish actions ruin your health."

Papa stifled another cough. "I'll retire to bed early tonight."

Mama only sighed. "Rest now, dear husband. This can all wait for another day."

"It *cannot* wait," Papa said, his voice firm. "The United States needs to know that we're going to remain neutral in their Civil War. If we let this slide, it's like we're supporting the Confederacy over the Union. Charles Wilkes made a grave error capturing those Confederate envoys aboard *our* mail ship."

"Albert, your draft can be done when you are well."

"The redraft on this *Trent* Affair must go out immediately, or we'll have a war on our hands. As it is, troops have been ordered to Canada and additional ships are being sent to the Western Atlantic."

"But our messages will get through to Lincoln soon enough. No one really wants a war."

"*We* know that, but the United States needs to know that too."

Louise's gaze dropped to the desk, and she saw several papers with writing, but most of the lines were crossed out. The *Trent* Affair was now in all the papers, and right in the middle of the ugly Civil War in America. To the side sat a half-written letter to Bertie from Papa. She didn't mean to read it, but her eyes scanned a few lines anyway: "no forgiveness can restore you to the state of innocence and purity which you have lost, and you must hide yourself from the sight of God."

The words were stiff and full of censure. Despite Papa's visit to Cambridge, he was still advising Bertie about his soul and duty to God.

When Louise heard the shuffle of her mother's steps entering the study, Louise stepped away from the desk.

"What's this?" Mama said.

Papa was right behind her, moving slowly.

Louise held out the cup. "I've made a remedy for Papa's coughing."

Mama's brows pinched. "I don't want your father to have a concoction not approved by the doctors."

"You say you found the recipe in *Domestic Medicine*?" Papa asked.

Louise nodded, hating that her face had heated with consternation.

"That book is a sound contribution to our library," Papa said. "Dr. Buchan is well-respected by our own doctors. I will try Loosy's creation." He came around the desk and took the cup right out of her hand, then gulped down the beverage. He closed his eyes and smiled. "I feel better already."

Louise was certain he was teasing, but it brought a smile to her and Mama's faces. For once, Louise had escaped a reprimand by her mother.

"And now, I will get back to work," he said. "I promise to retire early, Liebes Fräuchen."

Before Louise could leave, Papa asked, "When is your next piano practice? I'd like to listen in."

Louise winced. With all that was going on, she hadn't been practicing regularly, and Papa was a stickler for technique. He'd rapped her knuckles more than once. "Tomorrow," she said. Maybe she could practice later today without him hearing. Get the timing down on one of the more familiar pieces.

Her father only nodded, and relief wafted through her. She wished there was something else she could do to help him. But politics never went away. At least her father had his cough remedy now.

Louise nearly skipped back to her rooms. It was raining again, so everyone was doing inside activities this afternoon, which would give her more time to work on the needlepoint she was making of the Crystal Palace. The palace was said to be one of her father's greatest accomplishments in England, and remembering great accomplishments would surely make him feel stronger and happier. She'd been working off a photograph, since she'd only been three during the Great Expedition.

"Loo Loo!" A voice echoed along the hallway before she could reach her room.

She turned as Bea ran toward her. Her blond curls flew behind her, and her cheeks were pink with exertion.

"Slow down," Louise said with a laugh. "Who are you running from?"

Bea stopped in front of her, her breath short, her eyes bright. "We're making a play for Papa. Can you help? Arthur wants me to be the woodcutter's baby. But I don't want to. There's no baby in *Little Red Riding Hood*."

"Who is Little Red Riding Hood?"

"Helena," Bea said with a pout.

"And it's all in German," Bea continued, talking even faster now. "I don't know German yet, and everyone will laugh at me."

She smoothed her sister's hair from her face. "How about I be a fairy? And if you forget your lines, I can whisper them to you."

Bea's eyes rounded. "Really? Are there fairies in *Little Red Riding Hood*?"

"There are now."

Louise grasped her hand. "Now where are you practicing?"

"It's time for your fitting, Your Royal Highnesses." Miss Skerrett appeared at the end of the hall. Marianne Skerrett served as Mama's head dresser and wardrobe woman, but she often did other errands as well. "Your sisters are already getting measured for their Christmas dresses."

"I'm the same size as my last fitting," Louise said. Besides, their Christmas dresses were not to be festive since they were in mourning for Grandmama.

But the sixty-something Skerrett had no trouble giving orders to stubborn girls. "Her Majesty wants it done this afternoon, and we don't want to give her another thing to worry over."

Skerrett did have a way with words.

"All right." Louise kept ahold of Bea's hand. "I'll talk to Arthur later."

Bea nodded, but her expression had fallen.

Louise reluctantly followed Skerrett to the dressing room. Sure enough, Alice and Helena were in the middle of fittings with the assistant dressmakers in the lavender-scented room. Bea's expression had lightened. She loved fittings, even if the dresses wouldn't have ruffles and bows. As for Louise, she didn't want to be fussed over. She'd rather create her own outfit.

"Come stand here," Skerrett said. "And hold still so I don't have to measure twice."

Helena gave a small laugh. "Holding still for Louise is like telling a filly to walk slowly."

Louise ignored her sister.

"Can I have two dresses?" Bea asked sweetly.

"One for Christmas," Skerrett said. "You'll have to ask Her Majesty about another."

"Don't ask Mama for a thing, Baby," Alice said from where she stood, holding out her arm and examining the voluminous sleeve of her nearly finished dress. Its bell-shaped skirt draped to the floor.

The mourning gray fabric of Louise's dress had a high neck and buttoned front without lace. Only the hem of her own bell skirt sported embroidery.

"Oh." Bea pointed toward the windows. "Look at the wagons."

Everyone turned to see a line of wagons approaching the palace. Louise's heart skipped at the sight of the cut pine trees in the back of the wagons. It was another tradition of Papa's. Each child received their own tree, and beneath that tree, he'd put his gifts to them.

Louise stepped away from Miss Skerrett, and before the head dresser could protest, Louise was out the door, Bea right behind her.

Giggling, Bea grabbed her hand, and then Louise swung her little sister up on her hip. "Let's go watch them unload, shall we? Then we can report to Papa that it was done right."

"Your Royal Highnesses!" Skerrett called after her. "The fitting is still not over."

"I'm the same size," Louise called back. She'd be reprimanded for this, certainly, but it would be so very worth it.

By the time they reached the front doors, the first Christmas tree was being carried into the main hallway. Bea squealed, and Louise laughed. The scent alone brought back the memories of Christmases before. The dances, the dinners, the sounds and smells, the games, and the presents. Surely Papa would cheer up and feel better when he saw that preparations were already underway.

CHAPTER 5

———— ❧ ————

"My Dear Leopold,
Although very unwell, with general depression and therefore not able to hold
a pen myself, I dictate this to Alice, to thank you for your dear little letter.
I am glad you like your games at croquet and have such beautiful weather.
Here it is cold, damp, and detestable. . . . I trust you had your pocket money,
which I have fixed at 2 nap:n [2 Napoléon coins] a month.
Goodbye dear boy,
  Ever Your affectionate Papa."

FINAL LETTER WRITTEN BY PRINCE ALBERT, DECEMBER 2, 1861

DECEMBER 1861
LOUISE, AGE 13

Papa was not getting better.

His symptoms had progressed from bad to worse.

"Gastric fever," Louise muttered to herself as she turned page after page of *Domestic Medicine*. She was in the library late in the afternoon. The icy wind outside made it impossible for any outdoor activities. Arthur had asked her to play chess, but Louise couldn't even bring herself to do that. She'd overheard the cook speaking to Eliza Collins: "Her Majesty told us that the doctor said there is no cause for alarm with gastric fever."

Louise turned the page and landed on the description of gastric fever. Symptoms were high fever, headache, stomach pain, blotchy skin, and either constipation or diarrhea. Louise continued to read, her heart thumping harder with each symptom described.

Her father was *seriously* ill.

Above the sound of the wind, Louise heard an approaching carriage. She rose to look out the window. Were they to have a dinner guest? Mama had canceled all dinners and social events this past week and had taken meals in her room.

Alice had attended to Papa when Mama had to handle government business. But Louise and her younger siblings hadn't been allowed near Papa's convalescence.

Louise blinked when she saw the man exiting the carriage. She recognized his iron-gray hair and heavy brows immediately. It was George Wellesley, the dean of Windsor, who was Mama's advisor on church matters.

Then Louise heard a familiar voice coming from the corridor. She hurried out of the library and saw Wellesley talking to her brother. "Bertie!" she breathed.

She rushed toward him, only slowing when she saw the grave look on both of their faces.

When Wellesley hurried away, she stepped forward, then wrapped her arms about Bertie. "I didn't know you were coming home so early for Christmas."

But Bertie wasn't smiling, and his blue eyes didn't have their usual twinkle. "I'm not here for Christmas, Loosy. I arrived at three o'clock this morning to see Papa."

Louise stepped back at that. "Did Mama send for you?"

"Alice telegraphed me," he said. "I had no idea the seriousness of Papa's condition until I arrived."

It was as if Louise's stomach sank to the floor beneath her. "Is he very bad?"

"When's the last time you saw him, Loosy?"

It had been a full week. "We've been kept away because of infection.

The doctor said he has gastric fever, and there is no cause to worry. So we shall all have a happy Christmas together."

Bertie's eyes slid shut, and this scared Louise more than anything. "What is it?" she asked in a small voice.

When her brother opened his eyes again, they were clear. "Gastric fever is another name for typhoid fever. Does Mama not know this?"

Louise stared at her brother. The rock in her stomach turned and turned. Typhoid fever was fatal. No one survived it. Not even Papa's Coburg cousins, who had been a king and a prince. "Are you sure?" It was a foolish question. She didn't understand why Mama would be telling everyone that Papa would recover.

With a small nod, Bertie said, "Alice wouldn't have telegraphed me if it hadn't been serious. I've disappointed Papa greatly, but I hope he can forgive me before he leaves this life."

Louise wanted to say of course Papa would forgive his oldest son and that he wasn't going to truly die. Papa was young—forty-two. People Grandmama's age died, and that was sad. But not people Papa's age. Not the husband to the queen of England. Not her own father.

Bertie grasped her hand and squeezed it.

Not until he did that did she realize tears had fallen upon her cheeks.

"I'm sorry, Loosy." His throat bobbed as if he were trying to hold back his own tears.

She wiped at her face with her sleeve, not caring about the fabric. "Is Affie coming home too?"

"He'll be notified by telegram, then he'll come."

Vicky was in Prussia—too far to come if Papa was so very close to the end. And Leo in France was also too far away.

"Can I see him?" she said in a half whisper.

"Not until Mama gives her permission."

Louise bit her trembling lip and nodded. The tears were coming faster now, and she hadn't even fully digested the news from her brother. Just seeing Bertie suddenly at Windsor had been a shock. And now . . .

she felt dreadfully ill as her stomach plummeted, her body reacting faster than her mind.

Bertie draped an arm about her shoulders. "I'm sorry to be the bearer of bad news, Loosy. No matter what happens, you always have me, all right?"

She nodded because her throat burned too hot to speak.

"Now, I'm going to sleep for a little bit, then return to the vigil."

The word *vigil* should have never been part of her brother's language that day. Bertie headed along the corridor alone. Louise felt rooted to the floor, stuck between two different times. The time before Bertie came, when she thought Papa was ill. And the time after, when she found out Papa was dying.

A sob hitched in her chest, then burst out of her. She ran. Down another corridor, then around a corner. She didn't have a destination in mind. All she knew was that she had to move because the weight of the pain filling her limbs was so great, she was sure she'd sink right into the floor like a cannon.

"Your Royal Highness?" someone called after her.

Louise kept running until she reached the doors leading to one of the garden terraces. She flung open the door and ran across the terrace. The door banged shut with the wind, and Louise kept running. The sharp cold from the wind slapped at her face, freezing her tears, and shuddering through her body, but she didn't care.

When her feet hit the damp, nearly frozen grass, she teetered off balance as she veered toward the line of trees. She didn't want to stick to a path, didn't want to be seen or found.

In her mind, almost comically, she heard Fräulein Bauer's reprimand if Louise showed up to lessons tomorrow with a sniffle. But what was a sniffle compared to the pain and agony her father must be going through?

The words of the medical book pulsed through her mind: *high fever, headache, stomach pain, blotchy skin* . . . How her father must have been suffering all these weeks. He'd been chilled when he'd stood in the rain at Sandhurst. Then he'd gone to Cambridge to visit Bertie, and the heavens had continued to dump.

"Oh, Papa," Louise whispered as she sank to her knees onto the wet ground. She could barely focus on the trees surrounding her—blurred as they were by her tears. "Poor Papa," she cried as her chest tightened, and she found it nearly impossible to breathe.

Louise clasped her hands together and squeezed her eyes shut. "Dear Lord," she pled. "Don't let Papa die. He is ever so important and needed so very, very much." Her voice broke as she repeated, "Please don't let Papa die."

Louise's breath shuddered out of her as she squeezed her hands even tighter and prayed even harder. Was God listening? Was He too busy with someone else more important than a stupid thirteen-year-old girl? For right now, she felt so very stupid. How could she have not known her own father was dying? How could she be so flippant about the things he wanted her to learn? Why hadn't she worked harder to learn perfect German as her father wished? Why didn't she practice the piano every day like she'd been asked?

Her shoulders sagged, every bit of energy leaving her body. She was a rag doll, made from leftover scraps of life, not useful at all, except to take up space. The afternoon light weakened as the sun set, but still Louise didn't move from her spot of agony. It didn't matter what happened to her. Maybe if she became ill, God could trade her for her father. He could get better. Louise wasn't needed.

She lowered her head, the weight too heavy to bear up anymore. Time tipped sideways, and she didn't know how long she'd been outside. Her hands ached from gripping them so tightly. She unclenched her hands and wrapped her arms about her torso as if she could hold in the waves of pain that kept coming. She hadn't even seen her father for an entire week. All this time, she'd been eating, reading, drawing, dreaming. All this while, Papa had been fading.

"Loosy!"

Louise was too exhausted to decipher which brother was calling for her. Maybe it was her imagination anyway, and the icy wind had finally rattled her wits.

"Loosy! What are you doing out here? Mama has sent for us, but no one could find you."

She looked up through bleary vision at Arthur. At eleven, he was broom thin. His shoulders shivered in the cold, and his lips were nearly blue. As distressed as Louise was, her brother's red-rimmed eyes told her he knew about Papa.

"I didn't know he was dying," she choked out.

Arthur's eyes filled with tears, which made Louise only want to comfort him. But she didn't even know if she was strong enough to stand.

"I didn't either." Arthur sniffled then grabbed her upper arm. "We have to go, Loosy. We have to say goodbye before . . . before it's too late."

She let her brother tug her to her feet. Sure enough, her knees wavered, and she gripped his arm to steady herself.

"You're going to be sick, and then Mama will be mad," Arthur said. "Mad at you *and* Bertie."

"She's still mad at Bertie?" Well, even Louise knew that another crisis in the family wouldn't erase the scandal of Bertie and Nellie Clifden.

"You know how Mama talks when she's upset."

Louise increased her pace to match her brother's hurried one. She finally felt the cold, its long fingers reaching to the very center of her, making her feet and hands feel like blocks of ice.

"She blames him," Arthur continued, his voice quieter now but still chattering with the cold.

"Who?"

They were nearly to the terrace, and Arthur stopped and faced her, the end of his nose pink with the cold. "Mama blames Bertie for Papa getting typhoid. The stress and worry of Bertie made Papa sick, and then going to Cambridge gave him typhoid. So you see, it's because of Bertie that Papa is dying."

Louise held very, very still as her thoughts roared into a muddle. "Papa was sick before going to Cambridge."

Arthur's jaw tightened. "I know. We all *know* that. But no one can convince Mama otherwise."

This shouldn't be happening. Papa getting typhoid was terrible enough to comprehend. But to blame Bertie for a disease that not even a doctor or medicine could cure? "Did—did Bertie say anything?"

"He only listened to Mama's rant. Stood there, not moving, not answering, only listening."

Louise swallowed over the growing bulge in her throat. "Then we will listen too." She wiped at her cold cheeks with her even colder hands.

"Don't you get sick too, Loosy," Arthur said, his tone pleading.

With a long sigh, she said, "Let's go inside. I need to change my clothing."

Being inside felt like standing right in front of a blazing hearth. The contrast in temperature and the heat upon Louise's cold limbs sent fiery darts across her skin. Her feet tingled, and her legs ached as if she'd run up all the stairs in the entire palace twice.

She dressed quickly, her numb fingers clumsy, but she didn't ask for the help of a maid. On the best of days, she didn't want help. And today was the worst of days.

Once she was ready, she and Arthur went to their parents' suite of rooms. It was fully dark now, and the soft glow of the gaslights in the corridor should have been comforting and cheerful. But they only made the night feel too quiet, too still. In the back of her mind, she realized she'd missed dinner. Had dinner even been served? It didn't matter. Nothing seemed to matter.

Her father was close to death. How could that be possible?

She and Arthur waited and waited. For hours possibly, or minutes. Time was meaningless.

When Bertie and Helena joined them in the corridor, the weepy eyes of Helena only made Louise want to crumple to the floor and sob. If all the siblings were here, that meant this really was goodbye.

When the doors finally cracked open, Alice stepped out. Her face was as pale as a tallow candle. She motioned to everyone without a word, then led the way to Papa.

The bedroom was stuffy and overly warm, something that Mama rarely allowed. She was always asking for windows to be left open. This small thing told Louise that even the queen didn't have hope for Papa's recovery.

His bed had been moved to the center of the room. In another situation, Louise might have been curious as to why. And there, the resting form of her father. His eyes were closed, and his bedclothes showed above the blanket draped over him.

Louise crowded around Papa's bed with her siblings. She heard more than one sniffle, but she didn't look at anyone but her father. His eyelids fluttered as if he were about to open them, but he didn't.

"Papa," Louise whispered. Even if she'd wanted to speak normally, she wouldn't have been able to. Her throat was too tight to give anything a voice.

Then Alice stepped close and took Papa's hand. She leaned over and kissed him. Next, Bertie did the same. Then Helena and Arthur. Louise's tears were already falling by the time it was her turn. She took his warm hand—his fingers hotter than she expected—then she bent to kiss his brow.

"I love you, Papa," she rasped.

Papa didn't respond. Oh, how she would have given anything for him to open his eyes. To declare he was over the worst of it. To announce he was on the mend. But Papa did no such thing. His eyelids fluttered again. Perhaps he'd at least heard her.

The pressure built inside her chest, and she wanted to run again. She didn't care if it was dark or cold or that she might get sick. She didn't want to be in this room—where her beloved Papa was dying.

She released his hand and stepped away, moving closer to Bertie. He rested a hand on her shoulder, and although he said nothing, she felt his comfort all the same.

Mama held a handkerchief pressed to her mouth as her watery gaze stayed focused on her husband.

"Come," Alice said. "The hour is late, and everyone must rest."

Alice escorted Louise and Arthur out of the room. Bertie and Helena stayed. Louise wasn't sure if she wanted to remain in the quiet stillness, with her insides roiling like an impending thunderstorm.

Numbly, she walked with Arthur until she reached her room. They said nothing to each other as he left. Louise stepped into her bedroom, and as she slowly shut the door and heard the click, it was like a different door had shut. One that had closed on the heart of her childhood.

CHAPTER 6

❦

"I was so very very much grieved when I heard of the death of poor dear Papa, who I loved so very very much. I got a letter from you this morning in which you said a great deal of the death of poor dear Papa, it is such a fearful loss I am so very very much grieved. . . . I hope Mama is well."

LETTER FROM PRINCE LEOPOLD, CANNES,
TO PRINCESS LOUISE, WINDSOR, DECEMBER 20, 1861

DECEMBER 1861
LOUISE, AGE 13

Louise wasn't sure if she'd slept at all. Thoughts of Papa's impending death, mixed in with the suffering he must be experiencing, plagued her mind. When the windows of her bedroom finally lightened with the pale-yellow dawn, she didn't feel any better. She hadn't been summoned, so did that mean Papa was still alive?

Perhaps he could recover from typhoid. Surely it wasn't completely unheard of?

A tap at her door drew her attention, and she sat up in bed. Bertie entered her room. His gaze was hooded, his skin paler than Louise had ever seen it.

"Is Papa gone?" Louise asked.

His nod was slow, final.

She pulled her knees to her chest, trying to cradle the pain that bloomed. "When?"

Bertie's voice scraped as he said, "Quarter past ten last night."

Her eyes slipped shut. Had it hurt him? Where was his spirit now? Could he see her?

Bertie came around the side of the bed and rested a hand on her back. "Come with me. I'll take you, Arthur, and Bea to see Mama. She'll want the comfort of her youngest children about her."

"Does Vicky know? And what about Leo and Affie?" Tears pricked her eyes as she thought about her siblings learning about Papa's fate.

"Alice has sent telegrams."

If Alice could do that hard task of sending out telegrams, then Louise could rise out of bed and comfort their mother. She scrambled off the bed and drew on a robe over her high-necked nightgown. Before leaving the bedroom with her brother, Louise said, "Arthur told me what Mama accused you of."

Bertie straightened his features. "Mama is upset."

"I know." She might only be thirteen, but she saw that Bertie's reserve was only a mask, hiding his pain. "I don't blame you, Bertie. Papa told me that he caught a chill at Sandhurst from standing in the rain. That was before he went to see you in Cambridge."

"Thanks for telling me that, Loosy." The gratitude was plain in his blue eyes. The pain of Papa's death wasn't lessened, but she hoped her brother wouldn't feel like he was to blame.

She and Bertie walked to the rooms of Arthur and Bea. When Bertie told them the news, Bea started crying immediately. Louise gathered her in her arms and carried her.

Huge tears rolled down Arthur's face, and Louise's chest hitched at the sight of her siblings' grief. She thought of the play they'd prepared for Papa. She thought of the needlepoint of the Crystal Palace she'd nearly finished. She thought of how Papa had wanted to check her piano progress.

None of that mattered anymore. Papa was gone.

Poor Mama.

Poor Louise.

Poor England.

Lady Jane Churchill, Mama's lady-in-waiting, opened the door to the queen's private rooms as they approached. Alice was reclined on a sofa, and her disheveled state made it clear she'd slept there. Helena sat curled up on one of the chairs, her eyes puffy and red. Mama was still in bed, but she was awake. Her dark hair was tangled about her shoulders, and her eyes were hollowed circles in her face. She looked a different woman—not a queen right now—but a woman who'd lost the love of her life.

Bea squirmed out of Louise's arms. "Mama," she cried and ran to the bed. Climbing up, she nestled in Mama's arms.

"Baby," Mama whispered, and new tears trailed along her cheeks.

Louise grasped one of the bedposts to keep her knees steady.

"Mama." Arthur settled on the other side of the bed.

Mama pulled him close and said in a cracking voice, "I visited you all last night in your sleep. I wanted to see the children given to me by your dear father. He loved you so very much."

A sob broke through Louise's chest. She joined Arthur on the bed while Bertie sat next to Alice on the sofa.

"It is just us now, my darlings," Mama said. "We will carry on Papa's legacy. We will follow the direction he gave us in everything." Her gaze moved to Bertie, then away. "I will need a lot of help, from all of you. Papa was a man unparalleled, and no one can ever replace him. So we will all need to be very dedicated."

Louise's chest hurt as the sobs pushed through. "Oh, why did not God take me instead?" she cried. "I am so stupid and useless."

Mama reached for Louise's hand. "Darling Loosy. We need each other more than ever now. Papa would want us to be there for each other, always. Now that I am left as your lone parent, we must never forget the goodness of your father."

Her gaze shifted to Bertie, and there was an unforgiving glint in her eyes. Louise felt it as if she'd dug a fingernail into her palm. But Mama didn't renew her accusations. Yet.

Bertie remained sitting at one end of the sofa. His expression was unreadable, but Louise knew her brother was suffering in silence. He might not climb upon Mama's bed and embrace her. He might not be curled up, sobbing, but his pain was just as deep.

"What about Christmas?" Bea asked.

Mama looked down at her youngest daughter. "I cannot bear the thought of staying here through Christmas without your dear father. We will leave for Osborne in a few days." She brought a lace handkerchief to her nose and closed her eyes.

Watching Mama grieve was too hard to bear. Louise didn't know if she felt more sorry for her dearly departed father and all that he'd endured, or for her mama, having to carry on without him.

Over the next few days, the queen determined that she would not remain in England for the funeral but would go to Osborne. Louise spent the days waiting to depart for Osborne either in her room, doing nothing, or with one of her siblings, feeling glum together. Even when the maids came in to pack for Louise, she didn't rise to help them or take over, like she usually did. The queen had ordered everyone to wear mourning clothes, and Louise realized that the last time she'd seen Mama in something other than black was before Grandmama's death.

They were to leave on December 18, but the night before at a quiet supper with the siblings, General George Grey entered the dining room. He'd been equerry-in-waiting when Mama became queen. When she married Papa, Grey became his private secretary, and now he was Mama's. Louise had always liked him—he was efficient yet friendly, and he always took time to answer her questions. When Mama was having a bad day, Grey kept things running smoothly.

"Her Majesty has changed her mind about leaving in the morning for Osborne," Grey informed Bertie, who sat at the head of the table. "She wants to stay one more day."

That was fine with Louise. She didn't feel like doing anything, any-where. One more day at Windsor wouldn't make any difference.

When General Grey looked about the table, Louise gave him a small nod. He smiled softly. She wished he'd bring around his daughter Sybil, who was close to her age. Mama didn't like her to have friends outside of the palace or do anything that wasn't with her family, so it was a bright spot for Louise when young visitors came with their parents.

"Did the queen say why?" Bertie had changed over the past few days; he was both quieter and bolder.

General Grey didn't seem put out by the question. "She said that as long as she feels Prince Albert in the room with her, she doesn't want to leave Windsor."

Bertie nodded. "Thank you."

When General Grey took his leave, Bertie looked around the table at Alice, Helena, Arthur, and Louise. "Arthur and I will stay for the funeral, and all the sisters will go to Osborne until Mama can join you."

Louise didn't know if she wanted to go to Osborne without Mama. Alice and Helena only nodded, their eyes haunted. Arthur's shoulders were stiff, and Louise could only pray he'd be all right during the funeral. Although women didn't generally attend funerals, Louise wished she could support young Arthur so he wouldn't have to bear so much.

Everything had changed now. Everything.

Bea's naturally sunny disposition had waned as of late. She'd been forbidden to run or skip or laugh in the corridors. Mama had been most strict about everyone staying completely somber, out of respect. The thought of Bea's childhood being so drastically changed sent a sad wave through Louise. She would also have few memories of Papa.

True to Bertie's prediction, Louise left Windsor with her sisters a day and a half later. Mama, swathed in black, said goodbye to them, declaring she would arrive at Osborne before Christmas. Louise had left all of her homemade gifts at Windsor to be saved for another year. The only thing she brought with her was her sketching pad and her unfinished needlepoint.

Bea sat close to her in the traveling carriage to the train station, and Louise kept an arm about her. Osborne House was on the Isle of Wight, and they would journey by railway, then by yacht. They had previously visited in the warmer months, but never in the middle of winter.

Louise felt numb during the entire trip to the Isle of Wight. When Osborne finally came into view, she remembered from previous visits how the sight of the spacious, Italian-styled white house with large windows would excite her. But now, the house that her father had carefully designed was stark and forlorn against the pale-gray sky. Opening windows to let the summer breeze in wouldn't be happening now. Not when the wind felt like ice on her skin.

"It looks so desolate," Fräulein Bauer murmured, who sat across from them in the carriage. She'd been quiet these past few days, keeping her usual comments unspoken.

This time, however, Louise had to agree with her. The trees, typically lush with green, were bare and wind whipped. The warm and colorful countryside had faded to dull grays.

Louise eyed Fräulein Bauer and made a small vow to herself. Papa would have been so pleased if Louise had been more diligent in her German studies. Vicky had learned flawless German well before Louise's current age, which was fortunate since she was now married to the heir to the Prussian throne. So Louise vowed that she'd work much harder at mastering German. For Papa.

Bea lifted her head from Louise's shoulder as the carriage slowed. "We're here?"

"We're here, Baby."

Bea scrunched up her nose. "Osborne looks so sad."

Louise couldn't have described it better herself. Once they climbed out of the carriage, Louise walked hand in hand with Bea inside and through the rooms. Alice had already instructed the staff to shroud everything in black, per the queen's wishes. Mama's instructions to all the staff and groundskeepers were to dress in black, and even the carriage wheels were to be changed to rubber wheels to keep the noise down.

Louise scanned the areas that had been designed by dear Papa—colorful walls, rich carpeting, elegant drapes, sweeping terraces, and Italian-designed gardens. Everything reminded her of him. The selection and placement of paintings. The arrangement of furniture. The two chess sets. The rooms echoed with conversations of days gone by. Leo's laughter. Bertie's teasing. Affie's clever quips. Arthur's intelligent remarks.

Louise stopped in the drawing room and gazed at the piano. Last time she'd played this piano, Papa had been listening. He'd rapped her knuckles when she kept using the wrong finger position. Louise had been annoyed back then. Now, she knew her father only wanted her to become proficient.

She picked up one of the music sheets. Settling on the piano bench, she began to play Felix Mendelssohn, with Bea curled next to her. Moments later, two staff members entered carrying swaths of black cloth. They meticulously draped the furniture, including the end of the piano.

Louise didn't stop playing though. She played slowly, methodically, focusing on the right fingering. She didn't want to make a single error. Perhaps Papa was listening from wherever he was.

CHAPTER 7

"Woke very often during the night, thinking of the sacred work to carried out at 7 o'clock. At that hour the precious earthy Remains were to be carried with all love & peace to their final resting place by our 3 sons, (for little Leopold had earnestly begged to go too). . . . Alice came to tell me that all have been peacefully & lovingly accomplished— Dull, rainy, & mild.— Took ½ an hour's drive with Alice & at ¼ to 1, we all drove down as yesterday to Frogmore, taking Baby with us. Waited a little while in the house & then walked to the Mausoleum, entering it, preceded by the Dean. It seemed so like the day at Frogmore, when Albert was so dear & loving. Everyone entered, each carrying a wreath. The Dean, with a faltering voice, read some most appropriate Prayers. We were all much overcome we knelt round the beloved tomb."

QUEEN VICTORIA'S JOURNAL, DECEMBER 18, 1862

FEBRUARY 1862
LOUISE, AGE 13

Louise opened her eyes in the quiet darkness of Mama's bedroom at Osborne. Louise was certain that the day had begun, but the dark drapes covering the windows made it difficult to tell. It was early February, but even the softening of winter and the approaching spring hadn't lifted Mama's spirits. She insisted the furniture stay shrouded and everyone dress in black. Even the pews at the local church were draped in black.

Louise or Alice slept on the sofa at the foot of her bed each night because the queen didn't want to sleep alone. Now, Louise turned over and stretched. She'd awakened more than once last night to Mama's muffled tears. The sound tore at Louise's heart every time. Mama's grief hadn't ebbed. If she wasn't teary eyed, she was fretting over the other siblings or her correspondence or the cotton shortage due to the American Civil War, which had damaged the textile industry in areas such as Lancashire.

Squinting, Louise tried to make out a sliver of light, but there was nothing. She quietly rose and crossed to the large windows. Her eyes were adjusted to the dimness, and she had no problem circumventing the draped furniture. Louise lifted an edge of the curtain to find that the sun had newly crested the horizon, though the pale gold hadn't yet reached the grounds of Osborne.

There was no activity about the grounds yet, and that was good news. It meant that Bertie hadn't left without saying goodbye. Today he'd leave for his planned journey to Palestine and the Near East. The trip had been arranged before Papa's illness, and now Mama insisted he take it. Whatever Papa had declared in the past would happen as he had intended.

Bertie didn't want to go, but he couldn't refuse Mama in this. She was adamant, and Louise suspected that the trip would give Bertie relief from her continual barbs about his scandal with Nellie Clifden and his responsibility for Papa's illness and subsequent death.

Louise released a sigh. She'd miss her brother. She missed Leo and Affie. She missed Vicky—although she was on her way to England from Prussia.

Nothing was the same anymore.

Christmas had been quiet and somber at Osborne. Louise and her sisters hadn't worn their Christmas dresses. The staff had received pictures of Papa, and the family members were given lockets of his hair. Louise touched the locket at her breastbone—she hadn't taken it off since she received it.

A carriage pulled around the carriage circle of the west pavilion. It had to be there for Bertie. She silently left Mama sleeping and went to her own room to dress. In a hurry, she didn't fashion her hair, but only plaited it.

On the way to intercept Bertie, Louise paused by the study where Papa used to sit in the mornings and deal with correspondence while the children were in lessons. It shouldn't have surprised her to see Alice in Papa's chair, but it sent a pang through her stomach.

Alice looked up. "You're awake early. Are you ill?"

It was a legitimate question since Louise had felt sick for a few days. But last night she'd felt better. "I wanted to say goodbye to Bertie."

Alice pressed her lips together, making her look thinner than she already was.

"Are *you* ill?" Louise asked. "You look tired."

Alice set down her nib pen that hovered over several documents. "Mama has assigned the political correspondence to me."

"Isn't that what Papa did?" Louise blurted out. "How can you . . . ?"

Both sisters went silent.

"Do you know how?" Louise finally ventured.

"Not exactly," Alice said with a heavy sigh. "I've been asking General Grey for a lot of guidance." She waved a hand at the cluttered desk. "I've not the talent or experience of Papa. Yet Mama keeps to her rooms most of the time, so someone has to do this."

Louise gazed at her sister. Her eyes were shadowed with exhaustion, and her usually severe chignon hung loose. "You're running the country."

Alice didn't even blink. "Not exactly, but I'm certainly representing the Crown. So many decisions, and I can't consult Mama about any of them. She turns away and cries."

Louise approached the desk and looked at some of the documents. They were filled with subjects that Louise had heard about in passing. "I want to help. Next time General Grey meets with you, may I sit in?"

Her sister's brows lifted. "You're thirteen."

"Nearly fourteen. I'll help you however I can. Helena is too weepy to aid much. Besides, I want to learn about what's going on in the country, aside from the newspapers. Mama says that half of them can't be trusted anyway."

Alice's eyes lightened. "All right. You can help me with small things. And I'm sure General Grey will be fine with you sitting in on our discussions." She rose to her feet, then stifled a yawn. "Now, let's track down Bertie."

They found their brother inspecting his luggage, looking formal and much older in his single-breasted suit, collar starched high and cravat expertly tied. He was a somber young man now and had lost much of his lightheartedness and teasing of their growing-up years. Louise hugged her brother goodbye, telling herself not to cry.

Bertie kissed Alice on the cheek, then Louise in one final farewell. "Write to me often," he said, his gaze on Louise. "I want to know what you're up to, all the good and the naughty."

"I haven't been naughty for a long time, Bertie." *Not since Papa's death,* she could have added. "I want to hear all about Palestine, and don't leave out what it's like to ride a camel."

He smiled then and chucked a finger under her chin. It was something he'd done over the years and seemed so normal, and yet, tears filled her eyes.

She and Alice stood together as they watched the carriage pull away, away from Osborne, away from family. The winter morning sparkled in comparison to the drabness inside the house. They both waved vigorously, as if the action would make him safe in every moment of his journey.

Alice tugged her shawl closer as they went back inside.

"You should rest until Mama awakes," Louise told her sister.

Alice peered at her, her usual sharp features softened. "You are becoming quite the little mother."

Louise decided to take that as a compliment. But her sister had done so much when Mama had been too heartsick to act. All the care for their father in his last days, and now for Mama, who was still so melancholy that she barely functioned. And the worst news . . . "Are you worried about your wedding? You know that Mama said it will still happen."

Alice tightened her jaw, and when they reached the office again, instead of sitting behind the desk, she curled up on the sofa. This made her look younger, like a child almost. "I wish Bertie was staying because he has more clout than me right now, even though Mama is still holding a grudge against him."

Louise sat at the other end of the sofa and drew her knees up. This was the type of conversation Alice might normally have with their older sisters, Helena or Vicky, since Louise was usually considered too young. Last night at their family dinner, Mama had mentioned postponing Alice and Ludwig's summer wedding. Alice had gone as pale as marble, and Louise had nearly choked on her food. Helena and Arthur went still, but Bertie had no such qualms. He was already in disgrace with Mama, and he decided to speak up for his sister.

"Papa planned many of the details before his death," Bertie said in a clear, solid tone. "You said we should honor dear Papa's plans for my Palestine trip. Do you not think, Mama, that we should honor our father's wishes for Alice?"

No one had moved, waiting for Mama's reaction. Would it be anger or tears this time? Louise had wanted to stand and clap. Or rush to her brother and hug him. Instead, she watched the queen without appearing to stare.

Mama's eyes fixed on Bertie, and they reddened with tears. Next she looked at Alice, who couldn't meet her eyes. "Papa did plan the wedding," Mama said, "and he wanted it to take place in July. Because Papa wished it, we will hold the wedding then."

Louise's breath left her as Alice covered her mouth to stifle a sob of what must have been relief. Mama hadn't acknowledged that it was Bertie's suggestion to honor Papa's wishes, but that was fine. At least Mama had listened to him.

Now, looking at the strained face of her sister, Louise knew that her worries weren't over.

"I miss him," Alice said.

Louise wasn't sure if her sister was speaking about her fiancé or Papa. Louise didn't ask—she just sat, waiting.

"Do you think Mama will let me wear white at my wedding?" Alice's fingers strayed to the black piping on her black dress.

"Of course." She hadn't thought about it, but now that it had been spoken, she understood Alice's concern. "At least for the ceremony."

Alice blinked, then a small smile lifted her lips. "And how long is a wedding ceremony? Twenty minutes?"

Louise's smile appeared too. "Maybe thirty? Then you'll be off to change into something black."

Alice laughed. A rare sound as of late. "I shouldn't laugh. It's a maudlin thought because the reason we're wearing black is because Papa's gone." At this, tears welled in her eyes.

"Oh, Alice," Louise said. "Just because your wedding will be more like a funeral, doesn't mean you won't have a happy marriage."

Alice wiped at her eyes. "I hope so, Loosy. I hope so."

Louise moved from her spot and hugged her older sister. Comfort from a thirteen-year-old probably wasn't much, but it was all she could offer right now. The pain of her father's death had caused so much distress in all their lives. And this summer, Louise would have a new thing to grieve over—the loss of Alice to her husband. They would live in Darmstadt, in the state of Hesse, Prussia. She'd become another distant sister, just as Vicky was.

February passed like the slow tick of a clock that hadn't been wound properly, interrupted only by the arrival of Vicky and her children. Their childish antics provided relief from the heaviness of the house. The only place at Osborne free from Mama's suffering was the nursery.

Lessons had also resumed, and the French governess, Madame Hocédé, brought in a couple of books one day. Louise and Helena were going over their French lesson, and both were intrigued by the new books.

"What's this?" Louise asked.

"*En Français, mademoiselle,*" Madame Hocédé was quick to say.

"*Quels sont ces livres?*" Louise asked.

Madame Hocédé explained that she'd gotten ahold of two novels, newly released, but they were only to be read during free time.

Louise immediately reached for one and opened *East Lynn*e by Ellen Wood.

Helena folded her arms. "Mama won't approve."

The faint flush to Madame Hocédé's cheeks was the only indicator that Helena's reprimand stung. "You girls have been through so much," Madame Hocédé said in French. "A bit of a break will only do you good. If you want to borrow one, you are welcome to it."

"I'll take both if you don't want one," Louise told Helena.

"Take them both." Helena bent over her paper and continued conjugating French verbs.

So Louise did and enjoyed reading them late into the night.

When March arrived, with gales and wind and more cold, Mama announced that they'd be returning to Windsor for a short time. On the fifteenth, the foundation stone would be laid at the mausoleum at Frogmore, and Mama needed to be there.

Returning to Windsor, after months of absence, brought pain. The last time Louise had been there, it had been the week of her father's death. Now, the place felt foreign, remote, different. Per Mama's orders, the furniture had been swathed in black cloth. The palace staff wore black armbands on their sleeves. And everything was so quiet.

Louise found Alice in Papa's study the day after the foundation stone had been laid. She and Alice had a sort of rapport now, and Alice didn't shoo her away but let her linger and even answered questions. Since her father's death, Louise discovered that politics interested her, more so than ever before. Maybe her intrigue was in honor of her father, who had always sought and made suggestions for improvement.

"Writing another letter?" Louise sat on the sofa as Alice dipped her pen into ink, then scratched on a thick piece of paper.

"To Major Elphinstone on behalf of Leo," Alice said without looking up. "From Mama."

Louise straightened at this. "Oh?" She missed her little brother fiercely. Major Elphinstone had been in charge of Leo's care these past winter months.

"Mama wants Leo to understand that he's returning to a house of mourning." Alice's voice was matter-of-fact, but Louise heard the disapproval in it.

"Does Mama think he'll laugh too much?"

At this, Alice lifted her gaze. The return to Windsor hadn't given a healthy color to her cheeks. No, Alice seemed thinner than ever. "Mama cannot bear loud noise or any excitement, as you know, and I suppose that Leo will have to get used to it."

"Just as Bea," Louise mused.

Alice pursed her lips and continued writing.

The tragedy felt compounded with the change in all of the siblings' demeanor. But Bea, at such a young age, should enjoy a more cheerful childhood, right? Louise released a sigh. Leo needed to be forewarned, and Louise for one would be overjoyed to see him. Yet, she too needed to keep her exuberance about seeing her brother in check.

Louise leaned into the sofa, wondering if the heaviness in her limbs would ever fade. Her fourteenth birthday was in two days; the entire last year had been filled with heartbreak. As Alice started on a new letter, Louise slipped out of the room.

At least she could apply herself and be ready for lessons on time. She changed without summoning a maid and did her own hair. Then she headed to the classroom. But when Louise got there, she found not her French governess, but Mama sitting in the governess's chair. And her expression was far from pleased.

Louise dipped a curtsey. "Mama," she said. "Is everything all right? Is Govie ill?"

Mama winced at Louise's pet name for Madame Hocédé. Then

she held up a book. One Louise immediately recognized. "What's this, Loosy?"

Where was Madame Hocédé, and where was Helena?

"Ah, it's . . ." She squinted. "*East Lynne.*"

"And where did you get it?" Mama's voice was quiet, but stern.

"I found it, lying about." Louise bit her lip, willing her cheeks to stay pale and not blush hot.

Mama set the book down and rose to her feet. Then she crossed to Louise and stopped right in front of her. "Madame Hocédé has been unreliable. To bring this into our home is not appropriate. Ever."

Louise's heart raced with shame, but she didn't want her governess to be punished. "But . . . Govie didn't give it to me. I found—"

Mama raised her hand, and Louise went silent.

"It pains me to do this, but Madame Hocédé must be excused from service," Mama said. "I know you enjoy her teaching, and your French is coming along nicely, but this . . ." She waved a hand at the lone book on the table. "This is unacceptable and inexcusable."

Louise blinked back tears threatening to emerge. "Mama—"

"Even more contemptuous is that you have been harmed as well. You've been deceitful and have disobeyed my wishes." Mama's voice trembled. "What would Papa say if he were here?"

There was no reason to continue her lie, and once Mama mentioned Papa, the guilt that Louise had held at bay swept over her like a great ocean wave. She lowered her gaze, her knees feeling like they'd been jerked forward. "Papa would be displeased," she whispered.

Mama didn't move for a long moment, and the stillness was interrupted when Helena entered the room, followed closely by Madame Hocédé.

Louise couldn't remain during further interrogation. Without asking permission to leave, she left the classroom and went to sit in the corridor on a brocade bench.

The voices murmured from the other room. There was no protest from the governess. No argument. Tears slipped down Louise's cheeks as Madame Hocédé backed out of the room, not turning her back to the queen. She entered the corridor, and only then did her mournful gaze land on Louise.

In soft French, Madame Hocédé said, "*S'il te plaît, pardonne-moi, chérie.*"

Louise wanted to say, "I do forgive you," but instead she only nodded. As Madame Hocédé walked quickly down the corridor, the hole in Louise's heart expanded.

Another person gone from her life. How many more would leave?

CHAPTER 8

❧

Here Rose and Magnolia
Our dearest enshrine,
The prayer of the south wind
Is thine and is mine,
For Child and for Mother
Here sweetly twice isled,
Brave Seamen are praying
For Mother and Child.

EXCERPT FROM "SONG," OSBORNE, 1882, BY JOHN CAMPBELL

JULY 1862
LOUISE, AGE 14

Don't go in too far, or you'll get your clothing wet, and Mama will have one more thing to be upset with you about."

Louise laughed, ignoring her brother Leo as she waded into the lukewarm pond, scattering the summer leaves that had blown across it. Leo had finally returned from Cannes and joined the family for the summer. Reuniting with him had been wonderful, especially because he looked healthier and stronger, but they kept their joy to themselves. They'd gotten into a habit of going on sketching outings. Louise did the most sketching, since she was working on small clay models that she hoped to create into sculptures. Reading books on sculpting wasn't the same as having a master teach her though.

Leo was satisfied with collecting fossils for one of his vast collections.

Usually Arthur came, but he was getting all trussed up for Alice's wedding later that day in the Osborne dining room.

"Mama won't even notice water on black clothing," Louise called to Leo, who lounged on the grassy knoll next to the pond, on the other side of the Swiss cottage that Papa had designed for the children. "Besides, I have to change into my white bridesmaid dress."

Leo closed his eyes, his face upturned toward the sun. The morning was beautiful with clear blue skies. Louise took a few more steps, and the water rippled against her calves. The sun soaked into her hair, her clothing, warming her through. She closed her eyes as well, breathing in the fresh sea air coming from Osborne Bay.

This moment, right here, would be the most beautiful moment of the day. Alice's wedding should be beautiful, but the ceremony would be so small, and in a converted dining room at that. The day would be bittersweet.

"Loo Loo," Leo said. "We should go back. Mama won't like—"

"I know." Louise snapped her eyes open, feeling irritation arise. She sighed, releasing the frustration in a slow breath. "You're right."

She walked toward the bank as Leo slipped on his shoes, then stood and brushed off his clothing. He held out his hand to Louise, already a gentleman.

Louise slipped on her shoes without bothering to dry off her feet. Her shoes could air out later. Her pulse thrummed in anticipation of returning to the main house. Despite the summer's warmth and the riotous color of foliage surrounding the house, Osborne was still solemn inside. Still draped in black. Still hushed. Still grieving for dear Papa.

Louise knew she would be sorry about her father for the rest of her life, but she also wanted to live a life. Not tiptoe every day around Mama and her outbursts.

They entered Osborne through one of the side doors to avoid as many of the visiting guests as possible, but they didn't escape everyone.

"There you are," a male voice spoke as Louise and Leo turned to head up the stairs.

Louise slowly spun around.

Bertie stood there, dressed in a dark suit, his skin still glowing with the bronzing he'd acquired in the Middle East. His tawny colored hair was nearly golden, and his blue eyes snapped with interest.

Leo was smart and continued up the stairs, disappearing at the top.

Bertie crossed to Louise, and she stood still, even though she wanted to follow Leo. "You've been ignoring me these past few days."

When Bertie had returned home, everyone listened rapturously as he spoke of his experiences. Of course, those were shared when Mama wasn't present. She was only interested in the fact that he'd completed his education and should be ready to take the next step in life—marriage.

During Bertie's storytelling, Louise had felt separated from her brother. They'd been so close previously, but he'd returned from the Middle East a different person. He was more serious, more introspective, more like . . . Papa. He wasn't her laughing, teasing Bertie, the one who stirred up the room at every turn.

"I've been busy," Louise said. "I had to help with many things . . ." Her voice trailed off, and she could see her brother wasn't convinced.

"What's wrong, Loosy?" he asked. "What's got you so troubled?"

Her eyes burned with tears. How did Bertie do that? See past what she allowed others to see? "Everything's changing. Again."

Bertie's brows drew together. "Alice is getting married, yes, and what else?"

Louise huffed out a breath and looked away, her gaze focusing on the polished banister.

"Helena is now confirmed and has left the schoolroom. That leaves me with Leo and Bea. Helena will replace Alice as Mama's personal secretary, which means she'll know everything, and I'll know nothing."

Bertie stepped closer, his eyes intent on hers.

"Arthur leaves in a few months for his own establishment at Blackheath, and you . . . You'll probably marry Princess Alexandra soon."

Bertie held up a hand. "I'm not marrying anyone anytime soon. You still have me, Loosy."

Louise peered up at her brother. "It's only a matter of time. Mama told Helena that we're traveling to Germany so Mama can inspect Princess Alexandra before she gives approval for you to propose."

Bertie lowered his head and exhaled. "Mama expects me to propose to someone I've met once?"

"Papa approved of her."

There was nothing more that Louise needed to say. Her heart wrenched for her brother. "Is she horrible, Bertie? Unbearable? Impossible to look upon?"

"No," Bertie said with a half laugh. "She's pretty and accomplished and, of course, the right amount of royal . . . it's just . . ."

"What?"

The name of Nellie Clifden hung between them, but neither spoke the name. The scandal seemed like a lifetime ago; everything that happened before Papa's death was in the distant past, only a faint string of memories.

"Princess Alexandra will be a lovely wife, and I'll be fortunate to have her." He smiled, then teased, "*If* she accepts my proposal."

"The moment you viewed her photograph, you declared that you'd marry her at once."

"That I did." Bertie winked. "A wife should be, at the very least, pretty to look upon."

The teasing fell flat because they both knew his marriage could soon be a reality. And his smile wasn't completely jubilant. The same joy was missing in all of them now. Nothing would ever be the same. None of them could ever go back.

"Besides," Bertie said in a quieter tone, "Affie doesn't think I should marry a Dane. Vicky and Fritz can't openly support the union because Prussia isn't on friendly terms with Denmark. Uncle Leopold disapproves of me marrying a Danish princess. Even Uncle Ernest argued with Papa over it and wants me to marry a Prussian."

Her brows shot up. She knew most of this, but not about Uncle Ernest's objection. "Uncle argued with Papa?"

Bertie's chin dipped. "I saw one of the letters between them. And you know how Mama feels about the royal Danes."

"I don't," she admitted.

His eyes gleamed. "Mama thinks the entire family is scandalous. So, you see, marrying someone whom so many are opposed to is very intriguing, indeed."

At this, Louise almost laughed. But she didn't want to draw any attention from the staff. Voices could be heard in one of the other rooms, and it sounded like someone was asking for Louise.

"You'd better go," Bertie said in a conspiratorial whisper.

She hurried up the stairs, and Helena stepped out as Louise reached the door.

"There you are." Helena was already dressed in her white bridesmaid gown that matched Louise's. It was strange to see her sister wearing something other than black or gray.

"I'm here now." Louise brushed past her sister into the room that had once been bright and cheery, but now was drab with black drapery over the furniture. Bea sat primly at one of the small tables, playing with one of her dolls.

Her white dress of flounce and lace, with the royal blue trimming, made Beatrice look older than her five years. "You look so grown up, Baby."

Bea scrunched her nose. "I can't be the baby anymore since Willy and Charlotte are younger than me."

"That's right," Louise said. "You're an aunt. So very, very old."

Bea tilted her head, as if she didn't know if Louise was being silly, or not.

"Our dresses match," Bea said.

"So they do," Louise said.

Miss Skerrett approached and began to undo the buttons at the back of Louise's black dress. No one commented on the wet hemline; perhaps they didn't notice. Once Louise was dressed again, Skerrett set about doing her hair, parting it down the center, and pulling it back into a chignon, then adding a royal blue ribbon.

The hour was nearing one o'clock when Louise joined her sisters Helena and Bea, as well as Ludwig's sister, Princess Anna. Vicky hadn't come because of her third pregnancy.

When they reached the bottom of the stairs, Alice joined them, wearing her lovely white wedding gown that had taken months to create. The fabric was overlaid with lace and hemmed with a garland of orange blossoms. Her veil fell from a floral crown, and diamonds sparkled at her neck and wrists.

Louise smiled at Alice, but the smile she gave in return was more sad than happy. They were all sad to have a wedding without dear Papa.

Uncle Ernest approached, tall and elegant in his dark clothing, his bearing and looks reminding Louise of Papa. He extended his arm to Alice, since he was giving the bride away, then walked slowly with her toward the dining room.

Louise kept a firm grip on Bea's hand since she was already trying to twirl in her new dress. They entered the dining room behind the bride and Helena. Inside, mostly family was gathered. Ludwig's family had come—the Cambridges and Hesses. There were a handful of ministers, bishops, and other officials from London. Everyone had been required to wear mourning colors, the men in black evening coats, gray trousers, and black cravats, and the women in gray or violet gowns.

Mama had styled Ludwig as a Royal Highness, which would only be recognized in the United Kingdom. Everywhere else, he was a Grand Ducal Highness. Sometime after the wedding, the queen would make him a knight of the Order of the Garter.

Mama wouldn't arrive until right before the ceremony. Louise had overheard her complaining that she didn't want everyone staring at her or feeling sorry for the new widow.

At the altar, Ludwig waited. He was a handsome man, tall and slender, with light-brown hair that was wavy at his temples. Ludwig stood below a painting of the royal family that had been done in 1846, when Alice was young—she sat at Papa's feet as he presided over his young family.

Louise's eyes pricked with tears. Papa was here, yet he wasn't.

Next, the archbishop of York entered. Then the queen walked in, with all her sons—Bertie, Alfred, Arthur, and Leo—flanking her.

Mama sat on a chair in the corner in direct view of the family portrait. Instead of looking at Alice, Mama focused on Papa's image.

Affie started to sniffle before the ceremony had even begun, and that didn't help Louise at all. The archbishop drew in a steady breath, then began the ceremony. Before he was finished, even he had tears in his eyes.

Louise brushed at her cheeks.

"It's like a funeral," Helena whispered. "Not a wedding."

Louise couldn't agree more. Her throat pulled tight, her chest hot, and she was making every effort not to burst into a sob as the bride and groom spoke their vows. The words were beautiful, yet somehow tragic all the same. Alice was marrying the man Papa had chosen for her—the man she'd come to care for a great deal—yet it was all bittersweet.

Once the vows were finished, the guests filed out of the room, quiet and somber. They gathered in the council room for a luncheon. Mama didn't join the larger group; instead she grasped little Bea's hand and hurried into the Horn Room, where Alice and Ludwig were to have their wedding meal.

Louise and Helena sat with their brothers and the other guests. Conversation about the table was stilted. The courses continued to come, but Louise ate very little.

Helena's hands trembled as she picked up her fork and took a bite of wild duck.

"Are you all right?" Louise asked in a quiet voice.

Helena kept her gaze averted as she whispered, "I'll miss Alice. Not because she's my sister but it means that I am now Mama's personal secretary, and I fear you know more about matters than me."

Louise agreed but decided to have some compassion and not say it aloud. "You'll do a fine job." Someday, she thought, she'd be the one left to assist Mama. "Besides, now that you've been confirmed, you'll be next on Mama's list to marry off."

Helena's face paled. "You've heard what Mama has said about my appearance."

Louise's throat went dry. Mama had made it no secret that while Helena was clever and amiable, her looks and figure were lacking. Louise placed a hand over Helena's. "There's more than one opinion in the world."

Instead of looking grateful at the compliment, Helena merely sighed. "Mama only speaks to me when she wants me to eat less, but food is my only comfort now." As if to prove her point, she took another bite of her meal.

"Like art is for me," Louise said softly. "Not even swimming in the pond gets rid of all the clay."

A small smile appeared on Helena's face.

Before the dessert could be served, Louise saw Alice walk past the room. She was already on her way to change out of her wedding dress. At last her sister was married and could leave the depressing place that Osborne had become. She looked across at Leo's downcast face, then at Affie's reddened eyes. Her head was beginning to hurt at all this sadness that never ended.

When Alice had changed into a black dress, the family gathered at the front of the house to bid the bride and groom farewell as they left for their honeymoon. Louise wondered if any other fourteen-year-old in the United Kingdom was waving goodbye to a newly married sister dressed all in black.

CHAPTER 9

"I was very sorry to have been prevented from spending [my birthday] with you all at home as usual— But as this year is one of mourning and sadness, it is perhaps better that I should have been away."

LETTER FROM THE PRINCE OF WALES
TO PRINCESS LOUISE, NAPLES, NOVEMBER 10, 1862

SEPTEMBER 1862
LOUISE, AGE 14

Louise gazed out the carriage window as they approached Uncle Leopold's home at Laeken Palace. Expanses of lawn were dotted by hedgerows and framed by towering trees. The palace was beautiful, and if they hadn't been in mourning, Louise would have enjoyed exploring the whole of it, including the gardens and conservatories. But Mama had made it more than clear that they were to curb their activities.

Months before Papa's death, he'd told Mama that Princess Alexandra of Schleswig-Holstein-Sonderburg-Glücksburg, daughter of the heir to the Danish throne, would make the ideal wife for Bertie. This was after Vicky had successfully matched Alice with Prince Ludwig of Hesse. Vicky had wanted a German match for her brother as well, but each candidate had major faults. Vicky had then turned her attention to Princess Alexandra and given her a glowing report, except for one serious flaw. She was Danish.

So, here they were. In Brussels. At King Leopold's palace.

The carriage slowed at the imposing iron gates, and once they were thrown wide, continued until it reached Laeken Palace. The two-story palace with its dome-topped center was impressive. They continued up the long drive, then disembarked at the base of the staircase leading to the grand entrance. Bertie had been traveling in the carriage ahead of Louise, and she tried to catch his eyes. But he looked lost in thought as he scanned the architecture of the palace.

They were all welcomed inside and then shown to their rooms where they could freshen up. Both Louise and Helena switched their traveling dresses for different gray dresses that were just as plain. Luncheon would be served soon, but first they'd be introduced to Prince Christian, his wife, and two daughters—one of which might be Bertie's future wife, and queen of England someday.

"You look pretty," Helena told Louise as they walked along the corridor together.

"You look pretty too," Louise said with a smile.

It was their own private amusement to compliment each other on their dresses, which were always either gray or black and washed out their complexions. Since Alice's marriage, Louise had grown closer to Helena. And Helena was much more open than Alice had been about her duties for Mama. Louise would feel quite prepared when her turn came, although she preferred not to think about that now. She had a future sister-in-law to meet.

The two sisters only shared smiles when Mama wasn't around so that they wouldn't vex her too much. Now, they headed down the stairs together and walked into a drawing room where everyone waited. Bertie stood in a semicircle of people who had to be Prince Christian and his family.

Uncle Leopold greeted them, then welcomed Mama as she swept into the room, her voluminous black skirt looking out of place next to the white walls and pastel-colored rug of the Coburg room. The surrounding paintings depicted the Coburg family members, including King Leopold and the queen's parents. Then King Leopold made the introductions to the Danish Crown Prince and Crown Princess.

Louise's gaze immediately shifted to the two daughters. She guessed who Princess Alexandra was before she spoke since Louise had read Vicky's letters about meeting her. Dagmar was the younger sister, and Alexandra the elder. She had fine features, a straight nose, oval face, creamy skin, and nearly black hair. Her gaze was steady, and her smile sweet.

Louise liked her immediately.

Alexandra was not at all shy or reserved but curtseyed prettily to them all, then welcomed them to Belgium. She'd worn a black gown with a high neckline as a sign of respectful mourning of the queen's husband, and Louise noticed the approval in her mother's eyes. Alexandra's English was accented, but she spoke quite clearly.

During the luncheon, Louise could hardly take her eyes off the princess. She tried to imagine how Alexandra might get along with Bertie. Surely, he found her pretty—there was no reason to doubt that. She had such an easy way and was remarkably calm. Was she not nervous at all?

She glanced at Bertie and wondered what was going through his mind.

Louise sat straighter, eating as daintily as possible, keeping all of her conversation polite. Although Mama didn't exactly warm up to the Danish royal family, she didn't seem perturbed either. Mama asked interested questions of Princess Alexandra and nodded in approval at each answer.

When the luncheon was over, Mama, Uncle Leopold, and Bertie joined the Crown Prince and his wife in the drawing room. This gave Louise and her sister time alone with Alexandra and her sister in a sitting room.

As Helena and Dagmar fell into a conversation, Alexandra turned to Louise. "I've been looking forward to meeting you ever since Edward told me about his many siblings."

Louise couldn't help her surprise. "Bertie talked about me with you?"

"Bertie? That's right, your family calls him that. You must call me Alix. Everyone who is close to me does."

This was a request Louise hadn't expected.

"And yes he talked about you," Alix said. "When we met last year, I asked him about his family. He said you are most clever and artistic and there is never a dull moment with you."

Louise nearly blushed over the compliments, but what she really wanted to know was what Alix thought of Bertie. It didn't seem prudent to ask, at least not right now. Maybe if she became a sister-in-law. Louise was more than pleased that her brother was one sibling who'd marry and stay in England.

"Tell me of your art," Alix continued.

"It's not much," Louise said in a quieter voice. "Everyone in my family paints and sketches. But I am interested in sculpture—not just creating small medallions as gifts, but busts and full-size figures."

Alix's brows shot up. "Does Her Majesty know this?"

"Not yet," Louise said. "But I love to study sculptures, and creating an entire being instead of a two-dimensional view is fascinating to me. I have only read about this kind of sculpting in books, and sometimes I'll try clay modelling on my own, but it's nothing I've shown anyone."

Alix patted her hand, a small smile on her face. "Well, I think it's wonderful. I hope to see your work one day."

And there was the lead-in that Louise could take advantage of, but she didn't. "Do you like art?" she asked instead.

"Oh, yes." Alix's eyes crinkled at the corners. "Music is wonderful too. I believe we shall get along splendidly, dearest Louise."

Louise didn't quite know what to make of this Danish princess. She was so open, so complimentary, and so self-assured.

"What is Denmark like?"

"It's cold this time of year."

They both laughed.

"If you should ever visit, I'll be your hostess. But I am also looking forward to seeing England, if it all works out." Her eyes sparkled as if she were already confident that Bertie would propose.

"I heard you had surgery on your neck," Louise said. "Does it still bother you?"

"Not much." Alix touched her high collar. "I hide the scar when I can so that I don't have to always explain it. Or perhaps I am vain."

"The high collar is much in fashion right now anyway," Louise quipped.

Alix smiled. "Correct."

Louise wondered if she would ever visit Denmark. Perhaps, if Bertie proposed. She hoped he would. The Danish princess had proved that she would be a cheerful addition to the family. This was the first time Louise felt like she was being treated as an interesting person in her own right, instead of simply one of the younger children.

All too soon it was time to go; Bertie arrived in the sitting room and invited Alix and her sister to walk in the gardens. Alix smiled at Bertie and rose gracefully.

Louise wanted to follow, to listen in, to spy on the couple in order to analyze their reactions to each other. But Bertie hadn't invited her and Helena, probably with good reason.

"It was so lovely to get to know you better, Louise." Alix stepped close and gave her a quick embrace.

Louise was surprised and flattered. She grinned dumbly as Bertie escorted the two Danes out of the room.

"Don't even think about it," Helena whispered when they were out of sight.

Louise frowned at her sister. "Think what?"

"I know you want to spy on them."

Louise raised her brows as if she were shocked at the suggestion. Then she laughed. "Of course I do, but the spying will be from our bedroom windows."

Helena sighed, but she joined Louise at their bedroom windows that overlooked the gardens. From time to time, they spotted the three walking, and Louise was inordinately pleased to see Alix's hand wrapped around the crook of Bertie's arm.

But he did not propose that day, and the following day it was time to continue their travels. Bertie remained in Brussels, while the rest of the family traveled to Reinhardsbrunn in the Duchy of Gotha, which was Papa's childhood home. The stately castle was beautifully surrounded by huge trees and a forest beyond.

Leo leaned close to her in the carriage as they traveled. "This is where Papa collected all those plants and rocks in order to start the children's museum in Coburg."

Louise's imagination was already leaping about as she gazed at the fairy-tale surroundings. As soon as they were settled into their rooms and they'd had a bit of tea, Louise went on her own hunt with Leo. It was heavenly to be outdoors in the crisp air, away from Mama's worrying and insistence that no one could laugh or make jokes.

Louise and Leo traipsed through the undergrowth, walking in and out of patches of sunlight. She'd brought a basket and filled it quicky with plants and flowers to take back to England. Bringing part of Papa's childhood to the gardens at Windsor suddenly seemed very important.

"There's another carriage," Leo said from where he'd perched on a fallen log since his energy had waned after the first hour.

Louise straightened and squinted toward the carriage but didn't recognize anything about it.

"Maybe it's a mail coach?" Leo suggested.

"Let's go." Louise was eager to know if there were any letters with news. So she picked up her basket and started for the castle. She wanted to run, but instead kept pace with Leo.

Once they reached the castle, Louise headed in through the kitchens to set her basket on one of the counters. Then she and Leo hurried to the main drawing room, where they found Mama and Helena, who'd set up a desk to keep up letters and correspondence.

"Is there any news from Bertie?" Louise burst out. Then as an afterthought she curtseyed to Mama.

Helena glanced at Mama, then smiled. A smile in the queen's presence could only mean good news.

"Bertie has proposed to Princess Alexandra, and she's accepted," Mama said in a formal tone, although there was a softening about her eyes. "The princess will come to England in November to become acquainted with our family and *our ways*."

Louise's heart expanded to twice its size. Bertie was engaged, and he'd be marrying the beautiful, intelligent, and entertaining Alix. She was so kind and gracious, and Louise didn't care if she was Danish or if her family was full of scandal.

As soon as Louise could, she returned to her room and wrote a letter of congratulations to Bertie. She wanted to write to Alix too, but maybe that was too presumptuous. Next she wrote to Affie. Surely he'd hear of the engagement before he received anything from Louise, but she wanted to assure him of how wonderful Alix was, and that he had no reason to oppose the match, even though she was a Dane.

After her two letters, she paused, wishing she could write to Papa and tell him that he'd been right, again. Princess Alexandra of Denmark was a good match for Bertie. Louise left the writing desk and moved to the windows overlooking the forest beyond. She gazed at the rolling hills, the graceful trees, the flowering bushes, the expanse of blue sky above. Is this what Papa saw many years ago when he lived here? Did he miss this place when he married Mama and took up residence in England?

Tomorrow they'd travel to the summer house of Rosenau, where Papa had been born. There, they'd visit with Uncle Ernest, and he'd show them Papa's gardens that he'd patterned the ones at Osborne after. In Germany, and in England, Papa's legacy continued.

She wanted to find something to honor her father's memory, something she could excel at—which unfortunately wouldn't be German or piano. But she could do one thing very well—art. And perhaps with instruction and practice, she could become a recognized talent. Did she dare tell Mama she wanted to be taught sculpting?

"I'll bring part of Coburg to England, Papa," she whispered. "We won't ever forget you."

PART TWO

1863–1868

CHAPTER 10

"Tho' still suffering much from the fearful heat which we endured in the railroad yesterday from Brussels till the night—I will try and write you a few lines. Your letter gave me much satisfaction all *but the dreadful Musk Smell which I must ask you not to use again for it is* really very nasty *dear; let them get you some more sweet violet powder which is so* very nice. . . . *Oh! This sweet spot is lovely and peaceful—but it is* all *the same—lonely and pleasureless—and* dreadful *without my own darling Angel!* Nothing interests or attracts me any more."*

LETTER FROM QUEEN VICTORIA
TO PRINCESS LOUISE, ROSENAU, AUGUST 15, 1863

NOVEMBER 1863
LOUISE, AGE 15

Louise must have a friend and companion whom I can trust."

Louise stood outside the queen's drawing room at Windsor, closing her eyes at the phrase she'd heard Mama repeat more than once. This time it was to General Grey, Mama's private secretary. Louise almost turned from the summons she'd received and headed back to her room.

With Helena so busy helping Mama and her older siblings hardly at home anymore, Louise was lonely at Windsor. Sometimes her loneliness felt like a living thing in her chest; other times, she buried it with busyness. But at fifteen years old, she also didn't want someone forced to be her friend.

General Grey's rumbling voice stopped Louise from fleeing.

"My daughter Sybil is about Louise's age, and she has a quiet temperament, which will nicely complement Her Royal Highness."

Louise held her breath as she listened. General Grey was the son of an earl, so that put him in the upper ranks of society. But if his daughter Sybil was quiet, that meant she would be boring, or even worse, tattle to Mama about everything Louise said or did. She wanted to have a *real* friend. One who'd be loyal to her and her alone. Didn't Louise deserve a friend like other girls her age?

"Bring her to the palace then," the queen said. "I will give her a private interview. And you said she is a quiet and obedient girl? Will she be too vexed by a strong personality such as Louise's? She asked to be trained in sculpting—a dreadful thing for a girl to aspire."

"Sybil has brothers, so she can stand her ground," General Grey spoke with assurance. "I believe she and Louise will get along well."

Grey had only been kind and patient with her. Maybe he was downplaying Sybil's attributes, and she'd be a friend Louise could enjoy without her mother's censure.

It was time to show herself. She took in a breath, smoothed her gray skirt and walked into the queen's drawing room. "You sent for me, Mama?" she asked after a brief curtsey.

"There you are, Loosy." Mama scrutinized her appearance. Beyond her, a cheery fire crackled in the hearth, contrasting with the gloomy November rain outside the windows.

Louise didn't think she had any clay dust on her after working on her sculpture—a bust of Beatrice. There might be bits beneath her fingernails, but that was almost impossible to get out. Mama had not been pleased at her practice of modelling, but she hadn't forbidden Louise either. So she had set her mind to creating something that would impress the queen.

"Tomorrow, General Grey will bring his daughter Sybil to meet you," Mama said. "If she suits us both, she will be an approved companion for you."

Louise glanced at the general, who wore a soft smile. She nodded to him, then said to Mama, "I shall like that very much. Thank you, Mama."

The queen tilted her head. "Now, there is another matter. Helena tells me you are spending all hours in the library reading the newspapers."

It was true. Since Alix's father succeeded to the throne as King Christian IX, Louise had been reading everything about the conflict between Denmark and Prussia over the duchies of Schleswig and Holstein. Mama and most of the family were definitely supporting Vicky's father-in-law, King Wilhelm of Prussia, and that dreadful Chancellor Bismarck. Mama claimed that Papa would have supported Prussia, and so would she. The royal family had become divided, so much so that the queen had forbidden political talk when everyone was together.

Louise knew better than to argue with Mama since she'd take it as a personal attack on her late father. But now, her mother was scrutinizing her.

"I hope you haven't gotten it into your head to support the Danes."

That was exactly what Louise had done, in her heart. "I find politics interesting, that's all."

She'd never get in the middle of Bertie and Vicky's arguments. Lately Alix had retreated and preferred her own company when politics were brought up. Louise had found her crying once, and Alix had waved it off as a result of her pregnancy.

Louise was excited to be an aunt again, this time to the heir of her brother. She'd been excited when Alice had her first baby at Windsor last April, but there was something special about the next heir to the throne being born. Alix was due in a few months, and the entire country was eager with anticipation. The newspapers reported on her condition, as well as the tension between Denmark and Prussia, both with equal fervor.

When Louise was dismissed, she hurried back to the art room. She slowed her step when she heard four-year-old Willy's voice coming from the nursery above. He didn't sound happy. She went up the stairs to find her nephew throwing books. His wailing in German might have been comical if he hadn't been so upset.

His nursemaid, Eliza Collins, was muttering and picking up the books as they hit the ground.

Vicky had referred to him as a willful child more than once, but Louise hadn't ever seen him this upset. Vicky had three children now: Charlotte was three, and baby Henry was just over one.

"Willy," Louise said. "Do you want to play a game with me?"

He paused long enough to look over at her, and Louise held out her hand. "Come," she said in German. "I have the best game, and I know you'll love it."

Willy hiccupped and wiped his nose on his sleeve.

"Prince Friedrich needs his nap," his nursemaid said.

"Oh, that can wait," Louise replied in German, and before the nursemaid could complain again, she and Willy left the nursery, hand in hand.

"Now," Louise said in a lowered voice. "On rainy days in England, we have great fun playing hide-and-seek. Have you ever played before?"

"Beatrice said I'm too young to play."

"Well, that was on your last visit," Louise said. "You are grown up now and can play with us."

Willy's tears turned to smiles, and the sight warmed Louise from the inside out.

In a short time, Louise had rounded up Leo and Beatrice. Louise wished there were other visiting children about, but four would have to do.

"Now," Louise said. "We must not touch any vases or any sculptures or paintings. Part of the game is to keep your hands to yourself as you hide, all right?"

Willy gave an emphatic nod. "All right." Then his lower lip trembled. "Do I have to hide by myself? I don't want to."

Louise squeezed his hand. "How about I hide with you?"

He nodded, blinking back tears.

"I'll count first, and you two go hide." Beatrice turned toward a wall beneath a painting. "One, two, three, four, five . . ."

"Let's go this way," Louise whispered to Willy.

His eyes rounded, and he followed her, gripping her hand. Louise turned a corner, then hurried through a gallery and stepped into an alcove. "We can't shut the drapes all the way or it will be too obvious. So we need to keep very still and breathe very quietly. Can you do that? Starting now, no talking, all right?"

"Yes." Willy covered his mouth.

Louise bit back a smile and covered her mouth too.

"Forty-five!" came Beatrice's voice.

Louise and Willy's gazes connected as Beatrice searched for them.

When Bea drew back the drape and said, "Found you!" Willy squealed and begged to play again.

Playing with Willy was a fine way to pass the cold winter day. In a few weeks' time, it would be the second anniversary of Papa's death, and Mama still treated life as if they were in full-time mourning. She hadn't opened Parliament's recent session, and Louise had also read of the disgruntled public opinion of a monarch who was staying hidden away for so long. A year was traditional mourning, but *two* years?

Helena dealt with the complaining correspondence, and General Grey kept most of the negative press from Mama. But the queen didn't realize how much Louise knew.

The following day, Sybil Grey arrived at Windsor, and Louise met her in the drawing room. Sybil had pretty eyes with a gleam of warmth, a long straight nose, and rosebud lips. A few inches taller than Louise and slighter in build, Sybil was acting demure in their parents' presence, but Louise could see the humor in her eyes. Louise promptly decided that she liked her. Once General Grey finished his introductions and left the drawing room, Louise quizzed Sybil.

"Are you supporting the Danes or the Prussians?"

After a quick glance at the doors, Sybil said in a matter-of-fact voice, "Danes." She hesitated. "Unless you can persuade me otherwise, Your Royal Highness?"

Louise held back a laugh, but inside she felt as if the sun had burst.

"If you'd said Prussians, then I would have had to do some persuading." She joined Sybil by the hearth and linked arms. "Come, let's go to the library and read the newspapers."

Sybil's eyes lit up. Perhaps she would be a true friend indeed.

In the library, Louise spread out the newspapers, scanning the headlines until she came upon news about the Danes and Prussians. "See here," Louise pointed to an article. "The Prussians are most upset at the succession of Christian IX to the throne of Denmark." Who was Alix's father.

Louise read the article alongside Sybil. "King Christian has signed the November Constitution, which means that he's declared Schleswig to be part of Denmark."

Sybil looked up from the newspaper, her eyes rounded. "That can't be good."

"No. Prussia is saying that it's a violation of the London Protocol of 1852." The growing pit in her stomach told her that war would be imminent. "Prussia isn't going to allow that."

Sybil shook her head and released a sigh. "Your family will be on both sides of the conflict."

"We've been there before," Louise said in a quiet voice. She turned to the next article, which had more updates on the American Civil War. Knoxville, Tennessee, had been under siege for two weeks now.

"Oh, this is what I wanted to read," Sybil said. "I heard my father discuss it." She pointed to a section of the newspaper that held the title "The Gettysburg Address."

Both young women read it in silence.

"So much death in war," Louise said.

"And more wars on the horizon," Sybil murmured.

Slowly, Louise turned to the next page.

"I didn't think you'd be so interested in politics."

Louise lifted her head. "What did you think I'd be interested in?"

Sybil shrugged. "Clothing and jewelry."

Louise looked down at her drab dress. She wore no jewelry today, although she'd been allowed to wear pearls last March for Bertie and Alix's wedding. "Well, we are still in mourning, so although I'm very interested in clothing, I don't have much say over it."

Sybil nodded. "I am very sorry about Prince Albert."

"Thank you," Louise said. "We all are, but . . ." She bit her lip and stopped talking before she said too much.

"But what?" Sybil asked innocently.

"I don't think I'll ever see Mama happy again, that's all."

With a nod, Sybil said, "It is a very hard thing for everyone, I am sure."

"I've read the newspapers that criticize Mama for how she keeps so much to herself and won't go into public," Louise said in a quiet voice. "They are questioning her ability to rule."

Sybil didn't seem shocked at Louise's words. "Her Majesty has been queen since the age of eighteen, and she has always found a way to rule the country. Sometimes it's through advisors or secretaries who can make the hard decisions when she feels incapable. But her heart is always with England."

Louise stared at her new friend with admiration. "I can see that you are your father's daughter."

Color spread to Sybil's cheeks. "Perhaps you'll be able to go out more soon. At least by your confirmation."

"That feels like ages away."

Sybil laughed. "That's what I told my mother this morning when I was complaining about something."

Louise found herself smiling. "What were *you* complaining about, Sybil Grey?"

Sybil's eyes twinkled. "Oh, everything I could think of."

Louise laughed and then lowered her eyes, wondering what she could tell someone like Sybil. Very little, probably, but she already knew her political secret. "Laughter and jokes or any silliness bothers Mama. She's still grieving Papa, you see."

Sybil gave a sage nod. "I understand. It can't be easy to lose a husband for any woman, and especially a man such as your father. He was so talented and intelligent."

Louise straightened, warmth spreading through her. "He was, wasn't he?"

With a small smile, Sybil said, "My father says that your father is one of the greatest men to ever live in England."

"The older I get, the more I realize the same," Louise confessed. Her eyes burned as she thought of Papa's last months or, really, his last couple of years when he'd been ill so much. But no matter how ill he was, he persevered. She moved her gaze back to Sybil and found the girl watching her. "I'm so tired of wearing gray."

Sybil's brows shot up.

"The entire household is required to remain in mourning, you see."

"I did see that," Sybil said. "The papers are full of it. In fact, I didn't know what to expect when I saw you."

"Oh?" Louise was intrigued now. "What did you expect? Please tell me."

"Well . . ." Sybil's lips twitched. "Perhaps I shouldn't say. I don't want to offend Your Royal Highness or anyone in your family."

Louise impulsively reached for Sybil's hands and grasped them. "You must tell me now. That's an order."

Sybil stared at her, then snorted and laughed.

Louise laughed too.

At the same time, they covered their mouths to hush themselves, but that only made them laugh harder.

"Please, we must stop," Louise said on a gasp. "Mama has spies everywhere, and they will report that we are too cheerful. She won't like that."

Sybil sobered immediately and withdrew her hands. Looking about the room, she whispered, "Spies? At Windsor?"

"Not the cloak-and-dagger type," Louise said. "But every staff member reports the activities of me and my siblings to Mama with complete fidelity."

Sybil's eyes were as round as teacups.

Louise leaned against the chair like a wilted rose. "And so will you, I assume. You're the queen's subject too."

"I won't tattle on you," Sybil said with surprising fierceness.

Louise shrugged. "Everyone does. Mama warns every new staff member about me. Lady Caroline was told by another lady-in-waiting, 'Her Royal Highness seems to be rather naughty, with a mischievous will of her own.' But fortunately for me, Lady Caroline ignored the talk, and we're great friends—at least as great of a friend I can have with Mama knowing everything. So you could say that I have no real friends. *Companions,* Mama calls them."

"Let's be friends, Your Royal Highness, true friends. I'll be true in every way."

Louise scrutinized Sybil Grey. Only truth and sincerity were in her gaze. Her art tutor, Mr. Edward Corbould, had taught her to look for truth, so she was well practiced at it. "If we are to be *true* friends, then you must come to tea with me tomorrow to visit poor Alix. She's laid up with her pregnancy and doesn't feel well."

Sybil's mouth opened, then closed. "Alix? You mean the *Princess of Wales?*"

"Yes," Louise said. "She's my favorite sister-in-law—well, my only one right now, but she's a favorite all the same."

"I'd love to," Sybil said. "Do I need to get permission from the queen?"

Louise sighed. "I'll ask her permission, but we must plan on it. Mama respects your father very much."

"If I had known this morning that I'd be friends with Princess Louise and be invited to tea with the Princess of Wales, I would have pinched myself and told my father to commit me to Bedlam."

"Neither of us are going to Bedlam," Louise said with a wink. "At least not today."

CHAPTER 11

—❧—

"The little statuette is really admirably modelled, and I strongly advise you to continue taking lessons with Mrs. Thornycroft as you certainly have great talent in modelling, and may perhaps become some day an eminent sculptress."

LETTER FROM THE PRINCE OF WALES
TO PRINCESS LOUISE, SANDRINGHAM, NOVEMBER 10, 1863

DECEMBER 1863
LOUISE, AGE 15

The next few weeks were busy with Christmas preparations at Windsor, although on a much smaller scale than when Papa was alive. Bertie and Alix were also staying at Windsor during the Christmas season, with Alix nearly seven months pregnant. For Christmas gifts, Louise had spent hours and hours sculpting a small statuette for Alix. There were many imperfections, but Louise was determined to show Mama that she had the talent—and all she needed was proper training. For Sybil's Christmas gift, Louise spent her spare time hand-illustrating a Sir Walter Scott poem they both liked—"Lucy Ashton's Song."

After the holidays, the queen again took Louise, Helena, and Beatrice to Osborne. The trip was brightened for Louise because Sybil was joining them, along with her father. Sybil was officially Louise's closest friend. They'd confessed many things to each other and had sworn to be each other's confidantes. Sybil had been true to her word and hadn't divulged any confidences Louise had shared with her. They had tea together often, and when they couldn't be together, they wrote letters.

Louise planned to show Sybil the latest sculpture that she'd been working on. Mama still didn't fully approve of Louise's hobby, but since the queen had commissioned female sculptors, such as Mary Thornycroft and Susan Durant, to produce work for the royal family, Louise held out hope.

When Sybil was shown into the music room where Louise was practicing the piano, she stopped the piece she was working on. "Come with me right away."

Sybil was well used to Louise's habit of skipping formalities and getting straight to the point. They walked through the long corridors until they reached one of the galleries. There, Louise stopped in front of a marble sculpture of an arm and hand.

"Do you know whose hand this is?" Louise asked Sybil.

Sybil made a great show of studying it, so exaggerated in fact that Louise had a hard time keeping a straight face. "Princess Beatrice?"

"No," Louise said. "It's me as a baby. And the woman who sculpted it is coming to Windsor once we return to be my tutor since Leitch teaches only painting and drawing."

Sybil stared at Louise. "Today is not All Fool's Day, is it?"

Louise grinned. "Mama suggested it. I created a small statuette for Alix's Christmas gift, and Mama was impressed. So now I've begun a small sculpture of Beatrice, and Mama says she is pleased with the progress."

"Who is this sculptress?" Sybil asked.

Louise grasped her friend's hands. "Prepare yourself. She exhibited at the Royal Academy and then the Great Exhibition in 1851."

"Mary Thornycroft or Susan Durant?"

Louise loved that Sybil knew the sculptresses' names. "Susan Durant. I want to be everything like her. Creating real art that will last centuries."

At this, Sybil raised a brow. "You're a princess, and you barely have time with all your lessons and public duties."

"What public duties?" Louise released Sybil's hands. "Mama keeps me home. We're at Osborne more than we're at Windsor. When Helena leaves, I'll be relegated to keeping her correspondence. We never go anywhere since we're still in mourning. Mama won't even open Parliament next month, and again the papers are full of criticism about that. And you know I am in no rush to marry at such a young age like my sister Vicky did. So I have time to sculpt. Although marriage will be freedom in comparison to becoming Mama's secretary."

To her credit, Sybil never joined Louise in any complaints about her mother. "When we are married, our children will be the best of friends."

"Of course they will. Now, let's go riding. You can borrow something from me."

"It's rather cold outside," Sybil said, but her eyes were bright.

"But not raining," Louise said. "Besides, I have Mama's permission."

Sybil didn't comment because they both knew what had happened when Louise had taken Lady Caroline, her mother's maid of honor, out riding without getting permission first from the queen. Louise had been punished, and she dared not take a guest riding again without permission.

Once they were saddled and riding along the paths that cut through the grounds, elation sifted through Louise. There was no other feeling of freedom that compared to riding a horse, high off the earth and surrounded by nature. Even with a groomsman following, it was still a delicious waft of freedom. Only when she was deep into one of her art projects did she feel such joy as she did upon a horse. They kept a mild pace, and the cool air threatened rain, but not until the clouds darkened did they turn around and head back.

After they dismounted and walked from the stables to the house entrance, Louise noticed a messenger hurrying to the front doors.

Foreboding swept through Louise. "Something's not right. There must be news from London."

She and Sybil reached the front doors just as the messenger left. Louise grasped Sybil by the hand, and they hurried inside to find Helena and Mama in the library.

"What is it?" Louise said.

For once, she wasn't told that it was a private matter.

"Alix is having labor pains," Helena said as Mama paced the room.

"It's too early," Mama pronounced without pausing in her pacing. "The baby can't survive this early."

Alix was only seven months pregnant. Louise blinked against the hot tears threatening to fall.

Sybil moved out of the room, whispering something about returning to her cottage. Louise didn't have the energy to respond. Her thoughts were numb, cold, and forlorn. Poor Alix. Poor, dear, sweet Alix, who had only been a friend to her. Who had charmed the city of London and the entire nation when she'd traveled from Denmark to marry the Prince of Wales.

"Shall we go to her?" Louise asked.

Mama stopped and looked over at her as if only just realizing Louise was there. "The labor might stop." She closed her eyes and exhaled. "Babies are a messy business."

Something washed over her mother's face. Pain mixed with regret, or was she remembering her own labor pains?

When Mama opened her eyes again, her expression was set in stone. "It's all those late nights of Bertie's, and Alix trying to keep up with him. Imagine, a heavily pregnant woman going to balls and parties. It's indecent."

Louise had no answers. She'd thought Alix so modern, lively, and charming. But now she found herself agreeing with Mama. When the Princess of Wales announced her pregnancy, the entire country was thrilled. Alix hadn't worn a maternity corset or abdomen belt and openly paraded her condition. She felt no need to take advantage of the current fashions and add decorations to her dresses, such as silk flowers or frills, to detract the eye from her growing body.

Mama continued her pacing, and Louise sank onto a chair. She could do nothing to help Alix except pray. And wait.

The hours came and went, and more news arrived. Alix had been at Virginia Water watching ice hockey when the labor pains had started.

"Imagine. A pregnant woman sitting in a sledge watching ice hockey," Mama huffed, wringing her hands. "It's no wonder she went into labor early."

Her voice faded away as her attention was caught by the sound of a rider arriving at the house. "If it's news about Alix, bring it to me right away."

Helena nodded and hurried out of the room. By the time she returned, her face was flushed, telegram in hand.

The queen took it from Helena and scanned it quickly. She lifted her gaze. "Alix has delivered a son, and he's alive. But he's only four pounds." She sank into a nearby chair. Relief mixed with apprehension crossed her features.

Mama brought her handkerchief to her mouth as if to school her emotions. "God willing, he will be a fighter." She turned to Helena. "We will go to Windsor right away."

Louise rose from the sofa. "Can I come with you?"

Her mother didn't even hesitate. "No, Loosy. I don't know what we'll find."

Louise tried not to let tears form, but they did anyway. Left again. She had to think upon the fact that she was an aunt again, and this time to a child of Bertie's. That was something to be happy for.

The following morning, after a night of restless sleep, Louise rose to find that Mama and Helena had already left Osborne.

It was weeks before Louise returned to Windsor. During the wait, she and Sybil read everything in the newspapers they could find. None of the palace doctors had been present at the birth, and there'd been no cradle or infant clothing ready. They had to get a cloth from elsewhere to swaddle the baby.

Once they returned to Windsor, Louise asked Mama for permission to visit Alix and the baby at Marlborough House.

"You may take Helena with you," Mama said. "After your lessons."

After her lessons, Louise headed to the kitchens to put together a basket of goodies to take to Alix. Surely she'd need her strength. When she arrived in the kitchen, she found the kitchen staff huddled over the newspaper.

"What is it?" she asked as she approached.

The staff quickly straightened and moved away. Louise scanned the front page announcing the birth of Prince Albert Victor, still newsworthy even weeks after. The title dubbed him "Prince All-but-on-the-Ice."

Louise bit the edge of her lip. She wasn't sure if she should laugh or complain about the headlines being disrespectful to a new mother and the royal baby. There was no way around the truth.

She met Helena at the front doors, and a carriage took them in the drizzle to Marlborough House. The house had originally been built for Sarah Churchill, Duchess of Marlborough, a confidante of Queen Anne. Now, the house had been enlarged with added rooms on the north side. They arrived at Marlborough House and were rushed inside since the spitting rain had begun in earnest.

A maid took their cloaks, and then the housekeeper led them to the private quarters of the Prince and Princess of Wales. Entering the bedchamber, they found Alix elegantly dressed, sitting on her sofa.

Her smile appeared. "Helena and Louise, it's so good to see you."

Both women bent to kiss their sister-in-law, and Alix grasped Louise's hand. "Hello, my little pet."

Louise loved the nickname. "We've brought you some goodies." She set her basket on the side table. "How's the new mother?"

Alix's smile was light, but that didn't diminish the tired lines about her eyes. "I am well. The little prince is well too."

Louise stepped up to the cradle. Helena had already bent over it. Inside was the sleeping prince. With every breath, he made a small cooing noise. Louise wanted to scoop him up and kiss his cheeks, but he was so small, so fragile.

Besides, a nursemaid hovered nearby, looking as if she'd have no problem giving a royal visitor a reprimand. Louise touched the tiny clothing of the baby. "I'm your Aunt Loosy," she said. "Can you say *Loosy*?"

"There you are," a male voice said behind her, and Louise turned as Bertie strode into the room. "I thought I heard voices." His blue eyes glowed with delight. "You've met Prince Eddy, I see."

Louise laughed. "Already a nickname."

"Of course." He leaned down to kiss her cheek, then Helena's. "We wanted to name him Prince Louise, but Alix wouldn't hear of it."

"Oh, Bertie, we never discussed such a thing," she drawled.

He crossed to the sofa. "How is my wife?"

She smiled up at him, and something in Louise's heart tugged. They were a wonderful match, and she was grateful every day that Alix agreed to marry her brother. Louise was determined to ignore the gossip that said her brother wasn't faithful to his wife. Bertie was good to Alix—this Louise could see. Gossips should mind their own business.

"So, what will it be today?" Bertie straightened and rubbed his hands together. "Should we take Prince Eddy out for a stroll? Perhaps to the theater and introduce him to Italian operas?"

The women laughed.

"No? Well, then, I suppose I'll let you rest and recover. Eddy will be out of leading strings soon enough, and we have a lot to teach him."

"He's not even *in* leading strings yet," Alix said, her smile tender.

He only chuckled, then said to Louise, "Stay a while. Have tea with us. Move in. I'll set up your own art studio. Helena can send you letters with Mama's instructions."

Another tease, but it warmed Louise. "I'll stay for tea, how about that? And then come back tomorrow."

Tea was sent up to Alix's room, and Louise settled on the sofa with hers after the nursemaid had been dismissed. Helena pulled a chair closer to the cradle and spent her time gazing at the tiny baby.

"She'll like the break." Alix picked up a scone. "Thank you for coming and for your basket of goodies."

"You're welcome," Louise said. "I wish I could do more, and I hope that Eddy will grow to be healthy and strong."

Alix nodded. "So do we. I certainly didn't expect him so early." She waved a hand. "Oh, I know what everyone is saying in the papers, and I can only imagine what your mother thinks."

"She's never quiet about her opinions," Louise said. "But underneath it all, she was worried about your early labor, and now she's happy about Eddy and your recovery."

Alix nodded, but she didn't smile. "Now that we have an heir, I suddenly feel exhausted."

"You did just give birth."

"I know, and this will pass, but it's a deeper exhaustion." She sipped at some tea, then leaned back on the cushions and closed her eyes.

"I should let you rest and send the nursemaid back in."

"No." Alix reached for her hand. "Stay and talk with me. Tell me that my son will be healthy and that life will be wonderful. Tell me that the newspapers will be kinder to my family now."

Louise's throat felt strangely thick. She wasn't sure what Alix was wanting to hear, since her son appeared healthy and her life was wonderful.

"Did you know that more than eighty thousand people gathered to cheer on your procession when you arrived in England?"

Alix's mouth lifted on one side. "Who could even count that high?"

"Someone figured it out, I suppose." Louise shrugged. "I was so upset that I wasn't allowed to be part of the greeting party, so I read every bit of newspaper in the days following."

"Oh?"

"Did you know the archbishop of Canterbury had told Mama that your wedding date had to be moved because weddings weren't supposed to be held on Lent?".

At this, Alix looked intrigued. "I didn't know there'd been a dispute. When the queen didn't allow most of my relatives to attend the wedding because she considered them scandalous, I gave up hope that she'd be on my side for much else."

"The dispute was reported in the papers," Louise said.

"Papers you weren't supposed to read," Helena cut in.

Louise only shrugged. "I hear about things one way or another, and now I'm plenty old to read the papers—no matter which scandal is being reported."

Alix gave a sage nod.

Even now, Louise could see the day of Alix's arrival in her mind. Although she, her sisters, and Mama had waited at Windsor for Alix's arrival, from the palace windows, Louise had seen the roads of Windsor decorated with banners, lanterns, and riots of color from the flowers.

One detail had stood out. "Remember those children from the British Orphan Asylum, who had banners of welcome written in Danish?"

"I remember the banners," Alix mused. "I was very touched."

"And when you were married, I got to wear a white dress, trimmed in purple. Mama let me wear the pearls that my grandmama, Louise of Coburg, bequeathed to me."

"Your namesake. And you looked beautiful that day, my pet," Alix said. "You look beautiful every day."

It was a compliment that Alix gave Louise often. Sometimes it made her feel self-conscious, but today it only made her love her sister-in-law more.

"It all feels so long ago," Alix said, her smile impish. "Your words are bringing it all back."

Helena began to softly hum to the baby. Neither sister was in a hurry to leave and return to the demands at Windsor.

So Louise continued. "Even though it was a rainy March day, the crowds still came out. We'd been in mourning so long, it was like a new day had arrived, and we had something to celebrate at last. There were flowers everywhere, banners and bunting decorating shops and homes. Much was said of how Bertie ran to greet you at the pier."

"He was late—that's why he ran."

Louise shrugged. "It was still romantic. Bertie running to you and kissing you in front of everyone."

Alix's tired eyes dimmed a bit. "What else?"

"You were a hero for disentangling that horse from your carriage wheel."

Alix waved her hand. "Poor horse."

"London fell in love with you at that moment."

"Thank you, my dear Louise," Alix said in a soft voice. "Thank you for reminding me."

CHAPTER 12

"Poor Leopold has rheumatism in his leg, and it was very much swollen yes-terday. . . . He must be carried up and down stairs, the doctor says it comes from wearing the kilt in such cold weather, but Mama does not think so, poor little boy he says it hurts very much."

LETTER FROM PRINCESS LOUISE
TO PRINCE ARTHUR, WINDSOR CASTLE, NOVEMBER 1863

FEBRUARY 1864
LOUISE, AGE 15

Beatrice squirmed on the chair positioned in the center of Louise's art room.

"You just had a break," Louise said. "Can you hold still now?"

Beatrice pushed her mouth into a pout. "You already drew me three times. Why do I have to sit here while you model the clay?"

Louise made an exaggerated shape on the clay model, so that the girl's lips protruded too far. "This is what your bust will look like if you don't stop making faces. Do you want this to be in marble, forever and ever?"

Beatrice narrowed her blue eyes as if she really had to consider that option.

"Ten more minutes, then we'll be done for the day, all right?"

Beatrice sighed and then held perfectly still for three minutes.

Perhaps Louise needed an older subject, like one of her brothers. Surely Arthur or Leo would have more fortitude than a six-year-old.

94

After Beatrice left to find something more entertaining, the energy seeped out of Louise, and she found Helena and Mama in the drawing room discussing the gifts they wanted to send for the new prince.

"Can I help?" Louise asked when the royal drawing master, Mr. Edward Corbould, presented a list of suggestions to the queen. "I could do a sculpture of the baby's hand."

All three gazed at her, and she swallowed. Mama had liked her statuette of Alix, and besides, Susan Durant was coming later today for their first lesson. Louise hoped to be a master in no time.

"Perhaps Her Royal Highness can help me in the design of whatever it is we agree upon?" Mr. Corbould suggested.

"Perhaps I can create a christening cup fashioned after Prince Albert in medieval armor, such as in my painting. It would be a statuette in the shape of a cup."

Mama's brows tugged together. Her mother wouldn't turn down any work connected to their beloved father. Mama gave her regal nod. "Very well. I think that will be a nice gift for the prince."

Louise held back a grin, tamping down her elation. She couldn't wait to tell Sybil. But first, she was to have a lesson with Susan Durant.

When the sculptress was shown into the art studio, Louise stepped forward to greet the woman. The artist surely had a lot of work to do. Yet she was here to instruct Louise.

"Show me something you've done, Your Royal Highness."

Louise showed her the clay model that sat unfinished. As Susan examined every detail of the model, Louise clenched her hands behind her back, hoping that the news was good. The clay rendition wasn't quite as detailed as other sculptors might have created. But Louise hoped that Susan would think she was talented enough to train.

Susan straightened and turned her sharp eyes on Louise. "You've not trained with anyone else?"

"I've had art tutors in drawing and painting, but no one to teach me modelling."

Susan's brows lifted. "You have done a commendable job, Your

Royal Highness. You have a good grasp of shape and composition already. I can help you advance, of course. It will be a privilege to teach you."

"Thank you."

Susan dipped her chin. "Well, how much time do we have for our lessons?"

"Mama said one hour. She doesn't want sculpting to consume me, and I must give due attention to other things."

"A princess is kept very busy, I see," Susan said with a wink. "Then we shall start with a medallion portrait. Who shall we choose?"

"I have plenty of sketches of Beatrice." She was the most accessible sibling.

"Very well." Susan slipped on an apron over her clothing.

Louise did the same, then watched Susan open the case she'd brought. Inside were several sizes of chiseling tools. "First, you must be able to identify the instruments we'll be using."

She took out a chisel with a round-point end.

"The point chisel," Louise said immediately.

"Very good. And this?" Susan held up a chisel with a flatter end and a divot dividing the end. "This is a tooth chisel."

Louise took the tool and turned it over in her hands. It was lighter than the point chisel.

"Do you know what this is?" Susan held up a rectangular metal piece with dozens of grooves in it.

"A rasp."

"Correct," Susan said. "It can smooth out and refine the planes."

Louise nodded. Identifying the tools was easy enough since she'd been reading everything she could about modelling.

Susan lifted a thin slab of marble from the bottom of her case. "This marble might be thin, but it's very strong, so don't be afraid to put strength into your work."

Susan showed Louise how to rough out the larger areas they would chisel away later. "Now you try."

Louise held a point chisel in one hand and a hammer in the other. She pounded a few times.

"Harder and with more deliberation," Susan instructed.

The pounding reverberated in her ears, and each hammered stroke sent a zing of accomplishment through Louise.

Susan moved in to work in tandem. After only a short time, the form was already taking shape. Louise couldn't stop a smile of triumph from crossing her face.

"Excellent work so far." Then Susan picked up the tooth chisel. One end had a long divot. "This chisel creates smoother definition and can also remove the marble quickly."

Occasionally, Susan directed the position of Louise's hand. "If you chisel straight into the stone, you'll get a different texture than going in at an angle."

Louise tried both, noting the difference. She looked again at the sketch of Beatrice she'd set on the next table over, then made an adjustment.

The hour ended much too soon, and a maid arrived to announce tea.

As they left the art room, Susan said, "I noticed the staff is still wearing their mourning armbands, and you are still dressed in mourning colors."

"Mama insists," Louise said. "She doesn't want anyone to forget our Papa."

"Of course not."

"I hope Mama is feeling generous today because I have something to ask her. It's almost my sixteenth birthday, you know."

Susan smiled. "What a wonderful year for a girl. You'll be completing your education and organizing your wardrobe for all the social events that will start when you come out."

Louise released a happy sigh. "Seventeen will be so much better than sixteen. My friend Sybil and I have so many plans already."

Susan gave a short laugh. "I have no doubt. A princess and her best friend. What a time it will be."

Louise felt like she was walking on clouds when she entered the dining room. Leo greeted Susan, and she was then introduced to everyone else. Mama was quiet, but that didn't dampen Louise's spirits. Mama frequently took tea at the Frogmore gardens, where she said it was peaceful, but today's weather was too chilly to make the trek.

After tea was finished, Susan was excused for the day. Mama gave Helena several tasks, and everyone else disappeared, while Louise lingered.

"Mama, I have a question. I know that we won't have a children's dance for my sixteenth birthday since the ballroom at Buckingham Palace is still closed, but what about my seventeenth birthday? It will be my come-out ball."

Her mother's shoulders stiffened as she pet her dog, Looty, the first Pekingese in Britain. "The ballroom will remain closed, and I have no intentions to open it."

"Not even next year?" How could her mother predict such a thing? But the dread growing inside told Louise that it could very well be predicted.

"One lesson in sculpting, and you've forgotten your place and your duty, Louise." Mama's tone was mild yet firm. "There will be no coming-out party. You'll be confirmed and allowed to attend some events, but what will it look like if we open the ballroom and celebrate like we've not had a great loss in our family?" She looked up at the ceiling as if dear Papa were looking down upon them from his high heavenly perch.

Louise pressed her lips together. They had had a great loss. Over *two* years ago. But her mother's eyes were tearing up now, and Louise felt like crying too. Although for a different reason.

Perhaps she *was* a selfish, useless creature.

When Louise's sixteenth birthday came and went with little fanfare, she determined to not be bothered by the lack of celebration. A few gifts from her family were more than sufficient. She was becoming a young lady now, and she needed to rise above childish wishes. She determined to look forward to her confirmation.

But even that had to be put off. In the autumn months, they traveled to Balmoral, where Leo developed rheumatism in his leg. It got so bad that Leo had to be carried up and down the stairs. Louise felt terribly sorry for Leo, and she visited his bedchamber as often as possible to read to him or ease his ailments.

Mama had told Louise more than once not to fret so much over Leo. He didn't need to be coddled, but Louise couldn't stand to see her brother suffering with a swollen leg. Every spare moment, she spent with him.

"Try this poultice," Louise said in a cheerful voice. It was late afternoon, tea was over, and everyone was attending to their various tasks. Her task, Louise had decided, was her brother's health. "I read about the mixture in a book, and it will help you sleep better."

Leo only nodded. He was so very quiet when he didn't feel well, but Louise could see the gratitude in his eyes.

She carefully applied the poultice, then covered his legs with a heavy rug. Mama insisted that her brother wear kilts at Balmoral, no matter how cold the weather was. Louise wasn't a medical expert, but she didn't think Leo feeling cold all the time was good for his health. He'd been sent away for the winter to France when he was younger. Had Mama forgotten?

"Good afternoon," a voice said.

Louise looked up to see Dr. William Jenner and his medical assistant enter the room. No one asked her to leave, so she remained as Jenner performed his examination.

"What's this?" he asked when he saw the way Leo's leg was wrapped.

Louise explained the poultice, then said, "He's so much more content when he's warm." She shivered involuntarily, as if for emphasis.

The doctor gave a brief nod. "He would do better if he was more warmly clad. Wearing a kilt all day when the weather is cold only makes his rheumatism worse."

"Have you told the queen?" Louise asked. What a simple solution. Leo didn't like being cold anyway; none of them did.

The doctor didn't answer right away, but instead glanced at his medical assistant.

"The queen already knows?" Louise pressed.

The doctor nodded.

Louise didn't know what to say. Her mother's stubbornness was beyond reason sometimes. But Louise couldn't show that displeasure in front of the doctor and his assistant. It wouldn't do Leo any good either. Maybe having him in bed was the best thing until they left detestable Balmoral.

Louise did know one person she could talk to, but the talk would have to be in the form of a letter. When the doctor left, Louise settled at Leo's writing desk and wrote to Sybil. Then Louise pulled out another piece of paper to write to her brother Arthur. If Louise couldn't tell her mother mistakes were being made with Leo, she had to tell someone.

Soon, however, Louise had to give up nursing Leo because she began to feel ill. She'd had a headache off and on, but now her headache was fiercer than Louise had ever experienced. Even light hurt her eyes.

"Are you feeling better?" Helena whispered in the darkened room where Louise was trying not to think of anything.

"No," Louise said.

"It's so dark in here," Helena continued in her quiet voice. "Are you sure you don't want a little light? Perhaps you can read some?"

Louise would have shaken her head, but her head hurt too much. Besides, her neck hurt too. Her temperature had risen high enough that Mama had sent for a London doctor.

"Is the doctor here?" Louise asked, pain lancing every forced word.

"He is." Helena moved, her skirts rustling, but Louise still didn't open her eyes. "He's coming in soon, and I'm afraid he'll need some light to see."

Louise licked her dry lips. "I know." But she dreaded it.

When the door next opened, bringing with it a dash of cooler air,

Louise moaned at the light that followed. Someone had drawn open the drapes.

"I'm sorry," Helena murmured.

Another voice, this one male, said, "I'm Dr. Sieveking, Your Royal Highness. And I'll ask you questions that you only need to answer with yes or no. Do you understand?"

"Yes," Louise whispered.

The doctor asked about her nausea, her breathing, her muscle and joint pain, any rashes, her headache, her stiff neck, and how much she was sleeping.

"I sleep whenever the pain allows me to," Louise said in reply to the last query.

The doctor checked her temperature, then he felt the pulse in her wrist. Murmured voices rose and fell, and then Helena's spoke clearly.

"I shall tell the queen."

Footsteps left the room. Louise wanted to open her eyes, wanted to ask her own questions, but the effort was too great. "What . . . is wrong?" she managed.

The doctor didn't answer until the drapes had been drawn closed again. "You have meningitis complications."

Louise knew enough about medical conditions to know that meningitis could be very serious, and with the way she was feeling, she was certain death would soon follow.

CHAPTER 13

—⟡—

"Lenchen and I are going to a ball this evening at Bertie's, being their wedding day [anniversary] it will be very nice, it is my first ball. . . . I envy you having been to Naples, such a beautiful place, I should give anything to see it. We have such dreadful cold weather here again we had a snowstorm two days ago but none lay on the ground, it must be charming weather with you now."

LETTER FROM PRINCESS LOUISE
TO PRINCE ARTHUR, WINDSOR CASTLE, MARCH 10, 1865

DECEMBER 1864
LOUISE, AGE 16

To her relief, Louise did not die of meningitis. But the headaches and fatigue lingered well into the new year. After two months of convalescing at Balmoral, Mama insisted they return to Windsor.

The train journey had been agonizing. Louise had been taken off the train in Carlisle to sleep in a regular bed, and the rest of her family had continued on to Windsor. Finally, she was able to join her family, and December brought some reprieve from the pain.

January arrived, and the family returned to Osborne. Much to Louise's relief, her mother had agreed that she was well enough to be confirmed. Not as her siblings had been—their confirmations had been royal occasions—but in a quiet family affair. But Louise was satisfied that there was to be something. Canon Prothero of Whippingham had been instructing her these past few weeks when she felt up to it. And on the day that he examined her for an hour in the presence of the queen, she had been able to go through the catechism and recite and explain the Creed. The rest of the day had been spent studying the Bible in her room, even though Bertie and Alix had arrived to be part of the ceremony that would take place the next day.

Alone in her room, she'd read only her favorite parts of the Bible, and only let herself be distracted a handful of times as she thought of the dress she'd get to wear. Not one of mourning but one of white silk.

Louise slept little the night before, and when the time came to dress in the morning, she did so with demure patience. But inside, her stomach was dancing with nerves. Would she forget her rehearsed answers to the archbishop of Canterbury's questions?

Once Louise was ready, she stood before the tall mirror. Her white silk dress was nearly blinding in the midday light that sparkled through the windows. Wide bands of swan's down trimmed the cuffs and hem. She wore no jewelry—that would be gifted to her later by Mama.

She lifted her chin and met her gaze head-on. Her illness had made her weak—the Louise looking back at her was thin and pale—but also more determined to follow her desires to become a talented and notable sculptress.

What if she had died? What legacy would she have left the world? She would be known as the fourth daughter of Queen Victoria and Prince Albert, but what else? It was time to move forward in her life.

Louise met Mama at the palace doors, and they traveled together to Whippingham Church. Mama was in her usual widow's black, a sharp contrast to Louise's white dress.

Once they arrived at the church, they walked in to find the guests already present. The Greys were seated in the pews, as well as other courtiers, including the Osborne staffs. So many familiar faces. Mama sat with the rest of their family in a semicircle in front of the altar, while Louise stood, trying not to look too nervous.

The archbishop of Canterbury began with the confirmation questions, asking about her commitment to the faith. Louise answered in a clear, confident tone she didn't feel, but she was able to recite the words perfectly. Next, the archbishop delivered the confirmation charge, including advising her that "a meek, a quiet, and a submissive spirit is the spirit that will please God the most."

Louise almost smiled, sure that the queen had dictated the archbishop's words, and the next ones only confirmed it.

"As a young woman and representative of the royal family, you must take this warning to heart. When you are surrounded by the splendor and luxury of a court, you will be in danger of being fascinated by its witchery and tempted to set your heart on the pleasures of the world."

Louise bit back a smirk. Did the archbishop not know what a protected life she led? She might be argumentative and stubborn and have a great love for the masculine art of sculpture, but she was no indulgent courtier. The back of her neck prickled as she thought of Bertie and Alix—but mostly Bertie. His life was large and colorful, much to Mama's consternation. What must he think of the archbishop's admonishments?

But Louise didn't have time to analyze further because the final words had been said. After congratulations from those in attendance, Louise found herself back at the palace and walking with her mother to the Blue Room—the bedroom where Papa had died.

The Blue Room remained unchanged since the day of his death, save for the added paintings of angels on the ceiling and the commissioned bust of Papa that stood between the two beds. Even now, fresh flowers and memorial wreaths sat upon each bed. His dressing gown and daily clothing were laid out each evening. Louise gazed at the glass on the bedside table that had been used to take his last dose of medicine. In the corner stood his writing desk that still had his pen atop the blotting book.

As they paused in the center of the shrine, Mama brought a handkerchief to her eyes. "Since Papa isn't here to do the honors, I shall take his place. The last child he had the duty of choosing confirmation jewelry for was Helena. So you will have to be satisfied with my choice."

Louise nodded.

Mama crossed to the bureau, where a velvet box rested. Opening it, she drew out a diamond necklace. "Come here, child."

Louise obeyed and lowered her head as Mama clasped the diamonds about her neck. "In the name of the Victoria and Albert Order, I present this necklace and earrings."

Next Mama fastened on the earrings. Next to the bureau, the mirror above the mantle showed Louise that the diamonds were ethereal. Despite the complicated relationship Louise had with her mother, at this moment, with the two of them alone together, she felt like they had the same heart and mind. They missed the same man. They wanted the same good to come of things. They had similar hopes in many cases.

"Thank you, Mama." Louise bent to kiss each of her mother's cheeks. "I shall wear them with honor."

Mama grasped her hands then and held tight. "You look lovely today, Louise, but remember the archbishop's words, and don't forget yourself."

"I won't," Louise murmured.

"We will have the customary reception that will count as your formal debut into Society," Mama said. "But all other social events will be relegated to ones that you attend with me, unless you go to a family ball with Helena. I can't have my daughter taking risks like other young women who find themselves in compromising situations."

Louise nearly had to bite her tongue to stop herself from countering her mother. She was wearing a beautiful confirmation gift, and she didn't want to sour the moment. Besides, at least she'd be able to wear a debutante gown.

And she did. She was allowed the customary debutante ballgown made of swaths of tulle with a long train. The bodice of the dress was made of silk, and the short sleeves left her sloping shoulders bare. In addition to wearing white feathers in her hair and carrying a white fan, she wore her confirmation gift of diamond earrings and the triple-row pearl necklace.

Her life had officially progressed to the point when she was expected to accompany Mama to the next Drawing Room. It was the only court affair that Mama had continued to adhere to throughout her mourning.

The Drawing Rooms took place at three o'clock in the afternoon in the throne room at Buckingham Palace. This formal court function allowed young women to officially enter Society with the blessing of their sovereign. During the first one that Louise attended, she stood with the other royals in line and tried not to gawk at the procession of young women. They were dressed in all-white ballgowns, long trains of fabric, complete with plumes of feathers atop their heads, plus tiaras with long white veils. Louise noted the hopeful eyes of the young women, the stern expressions of some of their mothers, the panicked expressions of the rest. So much work and effort had been put into one occasion, to be seen by the queen—a once-in-a-lifetime event—then to leave Buckingham Palace, likely to never step foot inside again.

Louise tried not to react to the sight, but it was very difficult to keep any laughs or smiles to herself. She had to focus on Helena and mimic her more serious demeanor. Standing about for hours and hours wasn't particularly entertaining. In fact, after the first Drawing Room, Louise started to dread them. Still, Louise had to try to not be envious of the young women in Society who, unlike her, looked forward to a full year of social events and balls. Although Mama had said she could attend a ball once she passed her seventeenth birthday.

March, and her seventeenth birthday, finally arrived, and Louise prepared to attend her very first ball, celebrating Bertie and Alix's wedding anniversary at Marlborough House.

"Your hair isn't finished yet." Helena came into the library where Louise was watching out the window.

"I'm waiting for Sybil."

"Because?" Helena prompted.

"She's going to tell me which style looks best. Ringlets or pinned knots?"

"Mama will have to approve still."

Louise bit her lip. "I know, but it will be nice to have a second opinion." Truth was, she was nervous. This would be her first public event without Mama since Papa's death, and everyone around her would be looking at her in a new light. Now that she was seventeen and confirmed, she was considered adult enough to attend a ball. Sybil was still too young to attend and wasn't considered "out," but she wanted to see Louise all dressed up.

She hoped her headaches would stay away. One slip in health, and Mama would rescind future social events.

"There's her carriage now," Helena said. "Who knows, perhaps you'll meet your future husband tonight."

Louise scoffed. "*You're* next in line, and Mama won't even hear of you leaving the nest. No one can replace the hard work you do for her."

"She said that about Alice, and somehow, I'm sufficient now."

Louise peered at her older sister. Helena was the more intelligent and efficient out of the two of them. "Of course you're sufficient, and you can soothe her worries."

A small smile flitted across Helena's features. "I can placate her, that's all. I had to learn it, just as you will have to learn it. I'm not going to be a spinster, living at Mama's side for the rest of my life."

Louise shouldn't have been surprised, but she was. Helena was always so quiet, so obedient, so . . . unassuming. But she looked elegant in her violet dress, which was considered a mourning color, and surely she'd turn the eye of more than one man tonight. Not that Mama would allow Helena to marry a single one of them. Not if they didn't meet the queen's requirements—a husband of royal blood, Protestant, healthy, and with an independent fortune.

"You know you'll have to look outside of the country, unless you want to marry a commoner," Louise teased.

Helena didn't laugh. "Mama would never allow that. Whatever prince I choose will also have to agree to live in England so that we might be close to Mama."

Louise frowned. "She said that?"

"She's quite set on it."

Louise exhaled. Vicky and Alice both lived outside of England, and Mama had voiced her displeasure more than once that her daughters had to move away from home. It was their royal duty to spread their political influence across nations. But at the center of it all was a mother who missed her children. No matter how complicated she might be sometimes.

"Well, in that case, you can marry but live in England," Louise said. "So close, in fact, that you can continue helping Mama."

"While you do *what*?" Helena said with a wry smile. "Sculpt all day?"

"Perhaps." Louise shrugged. "Other women do it, and their work is displayed at the Royal Academy. Besides, Susan Durant believes my talent is promising. She's wholeheartedly on my side to continue training. Perhaps even at the National Art Training School."

Helena's brows arched. "A *public* institution? You can dream about that, Loosy, but don't set your sights on it."

Too late, Louise thought, because she already had. Convalescing for months at a time, with nothing to do but think deeply, had led her to some decisions. She wanted to develop her artistic skills as far as her mind would take her. And that would require more than the occasional tutoring. Convincing Mama would be a major task, but Louise was willing to be patient.

Sybil was shown into the library.

"What's this?" she said, entering in a sweep of green skirts. The day that Sybil came out would be gossiped about in the newspapers, for she was a pretty picture, even in a regular day dress. "You're planning a future without me?"

"Never without you." Louise stepped to her friend and grasped her hands. "Now, come with me. I need your advice on my hair."

Once Louise was happy with her coiffure and Mama had given her final approval, which included a very nice compliment, Louise said goodbye to Sybil.

Helena and Louise, accompanied by Lady Jane Churchill, climbed into the carriage that would take them to Marlborough House. Evening had descended, turning the gray sky into dark velvet. On the way, Louise went over in her mind the attendees who Alix had told her would be coming.

The glittering gaslight spilling from Marlborough House and the line of carriages waiting to unload their passengers sent a thrill through Louise. She clasped her hands together and leaned close. "I hope I remember the dancing steps."

"You're a better dancer than any of us," Helena said immediately. "Even if it has been ages since we've had a children's ball. Just remember you can't dance the waltz or it will hit the gossip pages."

The words sent a pang of memory through Louise. The last children's ball was canceled because of Grandmama's death. Nothing had ever been the same again, and Louise's childhood of happy things felt more and more distant.

"Ready?" Helena's words cut through Louise's maudlin thoughts.

Louise swallowed against the weight that had started to build. "Yes." She followed Helena out of the carriage, handed down by a footman. She thanked him, but her attention was captured by the billowing skirts of the women and tailored jackets of the men entering the house ablaze with light.

Above the general chatter, the stamping of horses' hooves, and the rustle of silk and satin, Louise heard the soaring music of a quartet. The melody floated into her heart and lifted her feet as she walked with Helena to greet the hosts for the evening—the Prince and Princess of Wales.

Alix was all smiles, and her complexion glowed, making her look ethereal. She was pregnant again, and despite Mama's comments about pregnant women not attending balls, here was Alix. She didn't even appear to be wearing a maternity corset.

Inside Marlborough, the gaslight created a glittering halo about the room. Dancers populated the center of the ballroom, moving in sync to the steps that Louise could do with her eyes closed.

Heads turned, whispers were spoken, and Louise knew some of them were about her. But she didn't mind, not right now. She was here. She was out. She was an adult woman. At last.

She wouldn't be dancing with anyone new and exciting. Everyone who asked her was an acquaintance and a member of the royal line. It wasn't so bad to be partnered with an older man, one of the cabinet ministers, was it? Or with one who'd apparently not danced in a while? Louise felt like she was a step and a half ahead, but she tamped down her frustrations with her dance partners and decided that she should be happy to be at the ball in the first place.

Her eyes caught Helena's, who was dancing with an aged ambassador Louise couldn't remember the name of. The two sisters' gazes caught, and Louise was sure that Helena was about as unexcited with her dance partner as Louise was with hers.

The supper dance was next, which Louise and Helena both had to sit out. Royals weren't allowed to dance the supper dance since the dancers were to sit through supper together, and Louise and Helena had to eat supper with other royals. Louise knew she was different than most of those in attendance, but she'd never felt so different until now. Staying with her mother and siblings in their palaces and holiday homes had kept her away from seeing what she was missing.

And now she was seeing it. The gaiety, the chatter, the switching of partners, the planning of future outings—all of which Louise could never be a part of as a princess.

Loneliness was a strange thing for a young woman to feel when she had so much and was surrounded by so many.

CHAPTER 14

—◦◦—

"Dearest Arthur, I write you a line or two whilst we are still on board. I was so sad at leaving you yesterday, the last I saw of you was when you were surrounded by all those ladies and Colonel Du Plat behind you. What a quantity of people there were, but I was pleased to see that Mama did not mind it very much. . . . I have had nothing to do this morning so I have been drawing the sailors, and Leopold was delighted with them. My head aches very badly and this letter is very stupid so I give you a reason why it is so. I shall write again and tell you how *we feel after having slept* two nights *in the train."*

LETTER FROM PRINCESS LOUISE
TO PRINCE ARTHUR, HMY VICTORIA AND ALBERT, AUGUST 9, 1865

AUGUST 1865
LOUISE, AGE 17

Coburg was beautiful in August, and Louise had found many things to sketch. Mama had insisted they make another trip to Germany for a very significant meeting, plus the unveiling of a statue of their father. All of her siblings had come, and Coburg was overrun with royals and courtiers. Being away from the social events of the season was a relief to Mama, but Louise felt a bit mopey, knowing the fun that Sybil was having without her. Even though Sybil was an acceptable close friend, Mama still hadn't let Louise attend Sybil's come-out ball.

Louise sat in Rosenau—the childhood home of her father—at the bedroom window, sketching. Outside the Schloss garden was in bloom, with roses and delphiniums everywhere, burgeoning the air with their heady, sweet scents. Instead of sketching flowers, she'd been sketching the scenes from their travels on the royal yacht. Particularly the sailors. She wondered if she dared create a sculpture of a sailor. No. Not even she would be that courageous. Women sculptors were relegated to sculpting women, children, or animals. Never the male body. When she'd told Arthur about her latest series of sketches, he'd teased her about enjoying the yacht voyage too much.

"Loosy, are you going to sit around all day?" Leo tapped on her partially opened door.

Louise looked over at him. He was twelve now, and he'd been more than healthy the past few months. Nothing could make her happier.

He folded his arms and leaned against the doorframe. "Let's go on a ride together before the sun sets."

"Are you sure you're up to it, little brother?"

His eyes sparked. "I'll race you to the stables."

Before Louise could say another word, he took off down the hallway. Louise dropped her sketchbook, grabbed her shoes, and fled after him. They both came to an abrupt stop at the top of the stairs. The staff would certainly report them for running through the house. Germans were so fussy and strict. And boorish, especially the men, Louise had decided.

"Wait." Louise sat at the top of the stairs and drew on her short boots, then laced them up. When she rose, she and Leo descended the stairs with practiced calm, not raising anyone's ire with pounding footsteps.

Riding horses with Leo took her mind off the fact that tonight her sister Helena would meet Prince Christian of Schleswig-Holstein-Sonderburg-Augustenburg. He and his mother would be arriving at Rosenau this evening.

All was not well, though. Once Bertie had learned that Mama was in favor of the potential match, the family had been sharply divided.

Vicky, Alfred, and Alice were all in favor of Christian. But since the Augustenburg family was a sworn enemy of Denmark, and therefore Alix's family, that set the Prince and Princess of Wales against Prince Christian.

"Do you think she'll like him?" Leo asked Louise as they slowed their horses atop a knoll. They'd been riding slowly about the gardens and hill for over an hour and needed to return soon to prepare for the supper.

Louise scanned the little River Itz below. "It's hard to say with Helena. She wants to marry, though, and with Mama so critical of her appearance, I think she is more worried if Prince Christian will like *her*."

"Do you think she'll be picky with her decision? Or agree to the first man Mama approves of in order to have her own household?"

This was a very good question indeed. And one that went to the very center of Louise, for if and when Helena married, Louise was next in line to help Mama. And the queen's stubbornness continued to clash with Louise's own.

"Mama has made it clear that whoever Helena marries, he will have to live in England."

"That narrows the field by a lot."

Yes. Alice's husband, Ludwig, had refused to live in England, and there was no way Vicky could have brought her husband, the Crown Prince of Prussia, to England.

Above all else, Louise would like to see her sister happy. "Oh, I forgot I told Helena I'd help her dress tonight." She turned the horse around with a skilled hand. "She'll be put out if I'm late."

Leo's gaze met hers as he turned his horse around too. "She'll be surprised if you're on time, that's what."

Louise smirked. She couldn't help it if she was frequently late. There were so many things to do, and she was always running out of time.

"We're all growing up, Loosy. Soon *you'll* be searching out a husband, since Mama has reconciled herself to having Beatrice be the one to attend her in her later years."

Louise laughed. "I'm in no hurry to marry. I can wait years and years." It wasn't that she didn't appreciate the men in her life, but she'd just started to enjoy a little more freedom. Even though the court functions were all accompanied by family members, she couldn't imagine herself a wife yet and, heaven forbid, going through childbirth to become a mother.

Although Vicky had married at seventeen and had a baby the very next year, Louise felt that sort of future for *her* was ages away. Besides, she couldn't very well leave Mama when Beatrice was only eight years old.

Once they returned to the Schloss, Louise hurried to Helena's room, where she found a flustered sister.

"Where were you?" Helena said. Never mind that Alice and Vicky were both there. "Can you fix these bows, Loosy?"

"Of course." Louise's face burned as she knelt and tied the limp bows into neat formations.

"Bertie's threatened not to appear at dinner tonight," Alice said, her tone worried.

"Bertie wouldn't dare defy Mama," Vicky pronounced, always the wiser and more exacting of the sisters. "He might bluster about it all, but he'll be perfectly polite when it comes down to it."

"Well, Bertie wants his opinion considered," Alice said, "and not always dismissed out of hand."

Louise noticed the distress on Helena's face. "Let's not worry about Bertie. He'll come around."

Helena touched the diamond earrings at her earlobes. "I don't know about that. Even if he tries to make peace, it will be too late."

Louise drew in a breath. What was Prince Christian walking into?

Alice's face had grown tight, and Louise sensed that she'd talked to Bertie privately and was becoming more sympathetic to him. But what could any of them do? Mama had invited the prince and his mother. They'd be here in less than an hour.

Once Helena was primmed, laced, and ruffled, Louise went to her own room to dress. She'd be wearing something simpler, and in mourning gray, but she was happy for Helena, who'd shine tonight.

It didn't take long to get ready, so Louise went into the library until it was time for dinner. Just as she found a book to browse through, Bertie strode in, tension rolling off his shoulders.

"Have you talked to Helena about what a fool she's being?"

Louise opened her mouth, then shut it. Bertie wasn't even looking at her but had stopped at the bank of windows. Gazing out of them, he clasped his hands behind his back. "This will be a catastrophe, Loosy."

He turned then, his blue eyes piercing, but not completely focusing on her. "The London papers are already full of it." He paced to a chair, then back to the windows and folded his arms. "What will it mean if Helena marries a member of the August family? How will it affect my own in-laws and their position on the Danish throne if our family forms this alliance?"

He rushed on, not giving Louise any chance to reply. "Helena marries this prince and then what? You'll become the buffer between Mama and the rest of us. Is that what *you* want? Do you want to be the target of the newspapers that are unhappy with how Mama is neglecting her public duties? Papa's been gone for nearly *four* years. Yet, the queen is running the country through her daughters, right after they're out of the schoolroom. I am the *heir* to the throne, yet Mama refuses to include me in state affairs and has yet to ever inform me of cabinet proceedings."

Louise ignored the barbs. "You're still the Prince of Wales," she said in as calm a voice as she could muster. "You're still Mama's heir. Everyone knows and respects that."

"*Respects?*" Bertie gave a dry laugh. "They follow the queen's lead. Don't you see, Loosy? Mama will bring in a prince for her darling Helena, mandate that he live in England, then continue using Helena as a shield from the rest of the world. What do you think will happen?"

It was so obvious now that Louise couldn't believe she hadn't seen it before. "She'll take Prince Christian into her confidence and elevate him as high as she can."

Bertie nodded, his bloodshot eyes boring into Louise. "Now someone gets it!"

Louise curled her fingers tight. "Even if Mama gives him titles and property, you are still the heir, Bertie. It's your birthright. And after you, it's Eddie. No one can take that away from either of you."

For a moment, Louise thought he'd argue with her. Instead, he exhaled slowly and closed his eyes. Louise waited.

When he finally opened his eyes, he said, "When Papa died, I felt crushed with guilt." He lifted a hand. "I don't need platitudes right now. But I was convinced I would work my way back into Mama's confidence and good graces. That she would trust me again."

"You need to be patient with Mama," Louise said. "She is slow to warm up to things, as you know. Eventually she'll have a better perspective about how our family should function."

Bertie's expression didn't soften. "I used to believe that too. I used to believe that our family would be restored to something noble. Then John Brown came along and interfered all over again."

Louise released a breath. John Brown had been Papa's ghillie, but after his death, John had been brought into Mama's household as the keeper of her pony. He quickly became a personal attendant. She'd already created two medals for him—the Faithful Servant Medal and the Devoted Service Medal. It seemed that she valued his opinion more than almost anyone else's.

Bertie rubbed a hand over his face. "Nevertheless, as someday head of this family, I will do my duty tonight. I will meet Christian at dinner. I will shake his hand. Greet him as one royal to another. But I do not endorse a match between our families. From this point on, I can't be involved in family matters. I have my own family to take care of."

Louise swallowed down the emotion clogging her throat. Bertie had always taken her side in things. Life was always more lively when Bertie was around, and she loved Alix dearly. She didn't want him to make himself scarce.

He crossed to the door and rested his hand on the latch. "I fear for our future, Loosy. Your future *and* mine. Wars are breaking out all across the Continent, and there's a growing republican movement at home. The queen can't afford to hide behind stone castle walls, ignoring her people who provide her living, and playing matchmaker with a family who are enemies to my wife."

Bertie stalked out of the library, leaving behind tangible tension in the room.

Louise had seen the excitement in Helena, she'd felt the support from Mama, and she'd also seen the fear in Bertie's eyes. What would become of them all?

She waited until the last possible moment to descend for dinner; she needed the time to compose herself and to make a few decisions. It struck her that Helena had the upper hand because Mama found the match suitable. So if Helena decided she liked Prince Christian well enough, then Bertie's opinions would be left in the dust.

Leo joined her outside the library. "I heard Bertie cornered you."

"He shared his opinions," Louise said. "I agree with him, but it's still up to Helena. We know Mama will support her since she arranged this meeting in the first place."

Leo looked like he wanted to say more, but they were too public now as they walked down the stairs.

Vicky entered the great hall. Louise wished she would have brought her older children with her. Since this was a shorter trip, Vicky hadn't brought all five—just the youngest, baby Sigi.

"Well, Loosy, what do you think?" Vicky threaded her arm through hers.

"About what?" Louise would never tell her sister that her English had become accented from speaking so much German in Prussia.

"Helena and Prince Christian, of course."

Louise's ears were still burning from Bertie's declarations, and she didn't want Vicky to use Louise as part of her argument. "Helena can make up her own mind." That was true, to an extent. "If Mama is pleased, then there is little any of us can do or say."

Vicky chuckled. "Right you are, but once Helena marries, you will have Mama's ear."

Louise swallowed down the dread. Helena fielded letters from their older siblings when they were in a dispute with Mama over something. Now, Vicky wanted to be assured Louise was her ally.

"If Helena agrees to marry Christian," Vicky continued in a confidential tone, "and he agrees to live in England, as Mama will request, then that leaves you more options to marry. There's more than one eligible Prussian prince who might interest you." She tapped Louise's arm and smiled. "You'll live close to me. What fun we'll have."

Fun wasn't how Louise would ever describe Vicky. More like fussy and domineering.

Louise had been in the presence of plenty of Prussian men. Royal and nonroyal. She'd never found anything remotely "interesting" about them. They were all boorish, stiff, opinionated. Only interested in their own conversation. Not to mention Louise had to fight not to wrinkle her nose when she was around Prussian men. They smelled bad, like they'd never heard of bathing with soap and water. Plain and simple, Louise wouldn't marry a Prussian.

But right now wasn't the time to express her decided opinions on the matter. They had an Augustenburg prince to meet.

Louise and Vicky followed Leo into the drawing room where Prince Christian stood in the middle of the room with his mother. He was certainly older than Louise had expected—his hairline had already begun receding. His eyes were kind though, and perhaps that was the more important attribute.

Helena hadn't arrived yet, but Bertie and Alix were there, along with Alice and her husband, Ludwig. Affie walked in next, and introductions were made all around. Bertie moved away from the circle, keeping his hands behind his back and his face expressionless. Louise knew he was making a great deal of effort to not say anything contrary.

Then Mama entered, dressed in all black. Helena and Bea walked in at her side, both wearing gray—not even this occasion had relaxed Mama's standards of mourning dress.

Christian bowed to the queen first and responded in kind to her greeting. But his eyes strayed to Helena, and his gaze swept her appearance.

As for Helena, her blush from earlier had returned. She extended her hand and murmured a greeting. She looked so serious that Louise wanted to tell everyone a funny story to bring about the smiles again, but she was gratified to see the prince smile. And it reached his eyes, which told her it was genuine.

Could Prince Christian love Helena? Could their match be a happy one? Would Helena agree to marry him? Surely he hadn't come all this way *not* to propose, unless there was something truly off. The way they were stealing glances at each other and the smile that continued to play on the prince's lips told Louise that neither of them were opposed to each other based on appearance.

Dinner was announced, and Louise followed the group, walking with Leo. He leaned close and whispered, "Did you smell the tobacco smoke on Prince Christian?"

"Will Helena tolerate it?"

Leo smirked. "I don't know about Helena, but Mama certainly won't." He chuckled. "And marrying the daughter of Queen Victoria is like marrying the queen herself."

At the dining table, Louise had a clear view of Bertie and his scowl, which he seemed to be trying hard to conceal.

Leo came to the rescue and diffused the tension coming from Bertie. "Do you like bats?" Leo asked the prince.

Prince Christian immediately set down his wine glass. "I do. Only in the daytime though when they're asleep. I don't care much for them flying about my head."

Leo laughed.

Mama looked up from her plate, and the entire table went silent.

Leo stopped laughing, but his eyes were still merry as he said, "You must see the Rosenau bats. In the daytime, of course. This Schloss has a tall loft that's as long as the entire roof. Bats hang from the ceiling in neat rows like military men."

Louise smirked.

Helena gave Leo a murderous look. Alice and Vicky were staring at him. Alfred was clearly holding back a laugh. But Christian's smile was wide.

"Do you want to see them?" Leo pressed, oblivious to everyone else at the table. "Tomorrow, perhaps? Helena can come with us. She likes bats too."

Christian's eyes slid to Helena's.

Could she blush more than she already had? Apparently she could.

"Tomorrow would be perfect," Christian said with a wink.

At that moment, Louise knew. She couldn't explain how she knew or when it would happen. But Christian would propose, and Helena would accept.

CHAPTER 15

—❦—

"Oh, darling Bertie, don't let you be the one who cannot sacrifice his own feelings for the welfare of Mother and Sister!"

LETTER FROM PRINCESS ALICE TO THE PRINCE OF WALES, 1866

DECEMBER 1865
LOUISE, AGE 17

Despite the family's divide and Bertie's threat to boycott the potential wedding, Prince Christian arrived in England in December to visit Helena. They became engaged that night, and Louise had never seen her sister look so happy. Was it because she would finally be out from under Mama's thumb? Or because she had truly fallen in love with the man?

Bertie hadn't been the only one to complain to Louise before leaving Coburg. Alice had said her piece too, and Louise had listened but hadn't shared her opinion. Alice didn't like that Vicky's royal Prussian in-laws would be riled by the union, since it was never wise to antagonize a powerful country. Alice had also complained about Christian's age—he was fifteen years older than Helena. Her final complaint was that Helena only wanted to marry to be free of her daily tasks for the queen. This had been Louise's concern too. But when she saw how Helena blushed around Christian and how good-humored he was with her, Louise decided the pair had minds of their own to follow.

Whereas Bertie had taken a step back from the matter and stayed away from the family to prevent further discussions, Alice hadn't let it drop. She'd continued to express her displeasure in myriad letters to

121

family members. Mama had become angry enough to say she didn't want Alice to come to the wedding.

Either because of the family divisiveness or because the British press was becoming more and more critical of the queen's continuing reclusiveness, the queen decided to appear in public and open Parliament in February. Louise attended the state event, her first experience with the ceremony. She'd even been allowed to wear a white satin dress. Helena came too, and Louise felt keenly how she was being trained to take her sister's place at their mother's side.

The queen spoke to the assembly on the topic of the cattle disease of distemper that was spreading through the United Kingdom. "I have observed with great concern the extensive prevalence, during the last few months, of a virulent distemper among cattle in Great Britain; and it is with deep regret, and with sincere sympathy for the sufferers, that I have learnt the severe losses which it has caused in many counties and districts."

Louise listened intently as she scanned the faces of the audience. This was the first public appearance of the queen in years, and Louise wondered what these men thought and what they might say after the queen left. Louise hoped the newspapers would be kind and compassionate toward their queen, who continued to suffer without her Albert.

"It is satisfactory to know that Ireland and a considerable part of Scotland are as yet free from this calamity," the queen continued, her voice calm, confident, and poised.

Yet the rustling started, the serious expressions, then doubtful gazes . . . it all pulled at Louise's heart.

It had taken the full convincing of her siblings to get Mama to agree to come. Even John Brown, Mama's personal attendant, had encouraged her. It was a miracle that they all had the same conviction. And now if this all ended badly, what would happen next?

Louise glanced at Helena, who was staring straight ahead, immobile.

When the queen concluded her address, it was everything that Louise could do to hide her relief. They'd made it this far. One step at a time, she decided. Yet her stomach roiled at the thought of Helena's upcoming wedding, which would leave Louise alone to navigate all that their mother needed help with.

The newspaper fallout came when they packed up and traveled to Balmoral. Not Louise's favorite place, especially in February, when the temperatures were below freezing at night. Besides, the last time Louise had been to Balmoral, she'd been deathly ill with meningitis.

The queen's appearance at Parliament hadn't stemmed the tide of political rumblings. When they were in Balmoral, William Gladstone introduced a reform bill in the Commons, which sent everything into disarray. Mama refused to return to London, and news from abroad made it clear that Prussia and Austria were about to enter into a war over the division of the Schleswig and Holstein duchies, which meant that Vicky and Alice would have husbands on opposite sides of the conflict.

It was all out of Louise's control, so she stayed busy, trying to keep her mind and hands occupied. She sketched and painted. Sculpted small medallions and statuettes. Beatrice's bust was finished now, and Mama had been very impressed with it. This gave Louise license to add sculpting work into her weekly routines. But her work was limited at Balmoral, so she played the piano, helped Helena with correspondence, listened to the queen's worries, wrote to her brothers, walked the gardens outside, and hoped that Helena's wedding would still happen in July.

When Mama announced that she'd hired a new governor for Leo, after Sir Charles Phipps had died, Louise dreaded who it might be since there were debates going among the Highlander servants. Would it be the brother of John Brown? Archie Brown was currently Leo's valet, and if he was promoted then even more Browns would hold key household positions.

"I've met Lieutenant Walter George Stirling of the horse artillery," Mama said one night over dinner in late March. "He'll arrive tomorrow and take on the position of Leo's new tutor."

Leo looked up from his plate of food. As usual, in the cold climate of Balmoral, his rheumatism had acted up, and he had to be carried up and down the stairs. A miserable fate for an almost thirteen-year-old. He said nothing though, only nodded.

The next day, Lieutenant Stirling was brought into the receiving room and greeted Leo with a jolly, "Greetings, Your Royal Highness."

Louise noticed a genuine smile on her brother's face. From that time on, Stirling and Leo were nearly inseparable. Stirling was in his late twenties but seemed more of a friend than a tutor. Leo was fascinated with Stirling's knowledge of horses, and they could talk for hours about them.

Louise wasn't as interested, although she did love to ride, but she enjoyed seeing Leo so enthusiastic about something. Riding a horse gave Leo a freedom he didn't have when walking—especially now when he couldn't even navigate stairs on his own.

Louise rode with Stirling and Leo when time permitted, and on one outing, Stirling paid her a compliment as they rested their horses before riding back to Balmoral.

"Before coming here as tutor, I had heard that you were a beautiful young woman and the fairest of your sisters," Stirling said with a smile. "Although I never believe the gossips, in this case, I've found them to be right."

"You are blushing, sister." Leo laughed.

Louise scoffed. "I don't blush." But she could feel the heat in her cheeks. Was it because Stirling had called her beautiful or because an outsider had noticed her as something other than a little girl? She should not put too much value in Stirling's comment, but she couldn't deny the secret pleasure it brought her to think that a young, handsome, and charismatic man such as him would compliment her apart from any duty.

The thrill of the attention was cut short soon enough, though. In May, Louise developed whooping cough, and she fully blamed it on living at Balmoral. Last time she'd been seriously ill, it had been at the same place. During this illness, though, she could tolerate visitors.

Knowing that Louise loved any news on politics, Helena would bring the papers and read aloud. The London bank Overend, Gurney and Company had recently collapsed, creating a financial crisis throughout the city. And the Prussians and Austrians were building up their military forces, threatening war with each other.

Leo visited too. He glowed with stories about Lieutenant Stirling, and Louise found herself laughing, which quickly turned into coughing.

"I am sorry to make you laugh," Leo said one afternoon, but his smile was impish. "Maybe I should tell you something that's not humorous."

"Oh, I'm sure you have plenty to tell me then."

Leo's face had turned serious.

"What is it?" Louise asked after sipping from a cup at her bedside, trying to prevent another coughing attack. Early in the illness, her coughing was so violent that it would provoke vomiting. Thankfully, she was past that stage now.

"Lieutenant Stirling and Archie Brown argued the other day," Leo said in a hushed tone as if someone were listening right outside the door.

Archie Brown worked as one of Leo's personal staff as a brusher since he was strong enough to carry Leo when needed. As the younger brother of John Brown, Archie had a lot of confidence in his position as a favored Highlander servant.

"What did they argue about?" Louise kept her own voice low too.

"Me." Leo shrugged. "Archie jeers at me when he doesn't think I can hear him. He won't help with anything at night when I ask it of him. Says he doesn't work at night. He ignores me if I ask for the chamber pot, or a towel to stop a nosebleed."

Leo sometimes woke in the middle of the night with a nosebleed. And with his hemophilia, they were difficult to stop.

"What did Archie say to Stirling?"

"He blustered then went to complain to John Brown."

"Which means Mama heard of it."

Leo nodded, and both siblings fell silent. It was no secret that John Brown couldn't do much wrong in Mama's eyes. Bertie had complained more than once to Mama that there were rumors about the pair of them going around. Mama always dismissed them as if she didn't care about anyone else's opinion. She relied on John Brown for emotional support, and Louise was happy she could get it somewhere. But his wishes shouldn't be put ahead of Leo's.

"Stirling also had words with Robertson," Leo continued.

Louise sighed and reached for her cup again. Robertson was another Highlander assigned as valet, and he didn't have a soft spot for his fellow Scots. "Stirling is a military man first and foremost. Maybe that's what this household needs more of, so that things can be run in better order."

Leo nodded, though his brow furrowed in worry. "I'm glad that Stirling stands up for me, but it makes me worry too. Going against the Browns might not be a good thing."

If Louise had been feeling better, she'd have a mind to confront Archie Brown herself. He couldn't hurt her, and even though Mama would probably tell her she was out of line, Leo didn't deserve all of this trouble.

But once Louise was feeling better, she'd all but forgotten about Leo's tales of Stirling. She still spent time with the pair of them but had become increasingly involved in creating a new sculpture of Lady Jane Churchill—from start to finish, on her own.

When they returned to Windsor, Louise had Lady Jane sit for sketching. Louise spent every spare moment creating a series of different-sized clay models of Lady Jane, practicing all the techniques taught by Susan Durant.

Once the marble cube arrived, Louise measured it—knowing already it was the right size. The first cut into the marble always gave her pause. She gripped the chisel in her left hand, the hammer in her right, and made the first strike. Marble shards fell away, and Louise struck again.

Soon she was in a rhythm, broken up only when she needed to adjust the chisel or shift her position. The shapes and lines emerging sent a thrill through her. It poured satisfaction into her soul to create something beautiful out of what had previously been a flat space.

The project would take weeks, but Louise didn't mind. Every moment spent working on the bust was satisfactory. She attended some wedding dress fittings with Helena, her mind still on the progress of her sculpture. If she could impress Mama enough, then maybe she'd be able to attend art school.

When Mama complained about too much pounding coming from the art room, Louise spent any other free time reading the latest news.

"What are you reading now?" Helena asked, walking into the library. Her wedding was in a few weeks.

"A petition for women's suffrage was presented at the House of Commons," Louise said. She and Sybil had discussed this more than once, but Louise wondered what Helena would think of it. Mama was still against women's suffrage and didn't view her own sex as intelligent enough to vote or to have all the same rights as their male counterparts.

Helena sat beside her and read along with Louise. "John Stuart Mill is the leader. Who are Emily Davies and Elizabeth Garrett?"

"They brought the petition after securing 1,499 names," Louise said. "They smuggled it in with an apple seller because they thought it might be stolen or stopped."

"Did it pass?"

"It was just introduced, and nothing's been voted on yet."

Helena pointed at one line in the article. "It looks like they've printed all the names and sent it out as a pamphlet."

"What's this?" Mama entered the room. Her gaze was sharp, although she looked like she'd had another lousy night of sleep.

Louise and Helena immediately arose and curtseyed. Louise handed over the newspaper. "Women's suffrage has been brought before the House."

Mama glanced through the article for a handful of seconds, then she set the newspaper on the table. "There's no use for women to vote when their husbands are perfectly capable of representing the household. Now." She looked at Helena. "When is the next fitting for your wedding dress?"

Lately, anytime a political topic came up that made the queen uncomfortable, she deflected to plans about the wedding. As political fate would have it, neither Vicky nor Alice was able to travel to England for the July wedding since General Bismarck of Prussia had indeed campaigned against Austria, and the continent was now in the middle of the Austro-Prussian War. Bismarck hoped to make Prussia the dominant force in Europe, second only to England. But this created more strife within the family and among the siblings. Vicky's husband, Fritz, was commanding the Prussian troops, while Alice's husband was leading the Hessian troops in support of the Austrian army.

"The wedding will continue," Mama had declared when questioned by the court if the war should delay the wedding. "We will hold it in the private chapel at Windsor."

This was a big step up from Alice's wedding in the dining room at Osborne.

Helena had only nodded at the announcement, but once alone with Louise, Helena said, "Can you believe it, Loosy? I'll have a *real* wedding. Not one step above a funeral."

Louise laughed. "I'm happy for you."

Helena wiped at her eyes. "It's as if dear Papa is looking down upon us and orchestrating everything. Healing Mama's grief so that we can start to enjoy life again."

"Oh, Helena." Louise hugged her sister. "By this time next year, I'll be an aunt again with a little Helena to hold."

Helena drew away and brought her hands to her cheeks. "I don't know about that."

"It happens with married couples."

Helena smirked. "I know *that*, Loosy. I don't know any specifics . . . Well, Alice told me a few things. Mama refuses to, you know. Papa was the one to speak to our sisters before their weddings."

Louise had no information to offer. The mysteries of marriage remained unknown to her. She hoped her own marriage would be as wonderful and affectionate as Mama and Papa's had been. That was *if* she were to marry.

And if a Prussian prince was in her future, like Vicky hoped it would be, then remaining single sounded quite appealing to Louise.

CHAPTER 16

———— ❧ ————

"I am very glad that your Xmas went off well—tho' very lively it cannot have been— I wish that you could once spend it with us— how nice that would be and what fun we would have. I think you did quite right to buy pipes and cigar cases for the servants, although Sir Thomas was very much shocked."

LETTER FROM THE PRINCE OF WALES
TO PRINCESS LOUISE, SANDRINGHAM, JANUARY 2, 1866

JUNE 1866
LOUISE, AGE 18

The July morning of Helena's wedding had Louise awake early, knowing that after today, her life would change once again. She'd be at the queen's beck and call even more so, and her art would move down in priority. Although Louise was now eighteen, she hoped that discussion of her marriage would still be years away. Besides, Bea was only nine years old. Surely Louise couldn't marry when Bea was still in the schoolroom. Whatever would Mama do without a daughter as her aide?

Although Louise thought Prince Christian was a good man and good for Helena, Louise didn't think she herself could ever marry someone so old. Even Affie had said, "He is really a very good fellow, though not handsome."

Multiple people had begged Bertie to support the match. Alice had even written to him, even though she, herself, felt the same way. Mama had asked General Grey to intervene as well. So today, Bertie would be attending the wedding, and for that Louise was glad.

It was no small feat that the wedding hadn't been delayed because of the Austro-Prussian War, but it only demonstrated the queen's determination. No one in Queen Victoria's household appreciated Bismarck's aggressiveness, not even Vicky and her Fritz. Louise had jokingly said, "Helena, like Herodias, should ask for Bismarck's head as a wedding present from the king of Prussia." Everyone had been amused by her comment, but in all seriousness, Louise had decided that having Prince Christian committed to living in England would be a good thing. No more sisters living abroad with husbands who were commanders of armies.

As the sun warmed the windows, Louise dressed in a blue satin dress that would match Bea's. The satin was overlayed with tulle, trimmed in point lace, and decorated with blue and silver ornaments. Her hairstyle would be the same as Beatrice's—with a wreath of roses and a silver tulle veil. Someday, they'd be out of mourning, but until then, dressing up for weddings was a treat. She'd collected embellishments for Helena's dress as a surprise, and she headed to Helena's bedroom with a box.

Louise found Helena in her bedroom, with a handful of maids fussing over her. Alice and Vicky hadn't been able to come, so Louise and Beatrice would be the designated sister bridesmaids.

"You're early." Helena faced the long mirror, her back to Louise. Her reflection showed a nervous smile. The maids curtseyed, then left the room after Helena excused them.

"I didn't want to worry you. Not today." Louise set the box down and put her hands on her hips. "Now, turn around."

Helena turned from the mirror, and the hooped skirt of the white satin gown reflected the morning light, making her look angelic.

"What do you think?" Helena prompted. "Will I outshine everyone?"

"Of course. You make a beautiful bride."

"Even though I'm marrying an aged uncle?"

The words were spoken in a light tone, but Louise heard the pain beneath them. Helena knew the gossip like everyone else.

"Christian is nothing like our aged uncles." Louise gave her sister a fierce look. "He is mature, and that's better than some silly boy."

Helena reached for Louise's hand. "Thank you for that, sister. And I'm sorry that we won't be able to attend the socials and balls together like we used to."

Louise swallowed down the despair trying to rise like a wave. Her sister's marriage meant that Louise would attend even fewer socials, since Helena would be attending events with her new husband. But Louise wasn't envious, just a little sad. "I've brought you a surprise." She lifted the lid from the box and drew out orange blossoms and myrtle.

"For my dress?" Helena asked.

"Yes." Louise walked around her sister. "We'll decorate the skirt and the bodice. Not only will it be beautiful, but you'll smell nice too."

Helena smirked, then tears filled her eyes.

Louise paused. "What is it? We don't have to do the orange blossoms."

"It's not the orange blossoms. They're lovely. I'm . . . nervous, I suppose. About what Christian thinks of me. About the wedding night. And being a wife? A mother?"

Louise had no answers or advice for her. Helena knew more about those sorts of things than she did. "I think once you kiss him, everything else will fall into place."

Helena's face flamed. "I suppose you're right."

"Besides, women and men have been marrying for centuries, and Vicky and Alice survived."

Helena puffed out a breath. "Yes." She smiled softly. "Now, let's get those blossoms on."

Despite all the finery in the chapel, Helena still outshone the military uniforms, court dresses, and bridesmaid dresses. Behind her, eight bridesmaids held her train. Most surprising, the queen wasn't wearing solid black. She'd chosen to wear a moiré gown with silver trimming. Compared to her usual somber clothing, this dress was nearly festive.

Mama was the one to give away Helena. Even though Bertie could have done it, the queen considered it *her* duty to represent Prince Albert.

Prince Christian stood tall and erect, looking regal in his British army uniform reflecting his recent commission as a major general. He'd taken an oath of allegiance and become a naturalized citizen.

Louise caught Helena's eyes. The nervousness was still there, but there was triumph and happiness too. Helena had done it. She'd secured herself a husband. Nothing had stopped the wedding, not even a war.

The archbishop began the ceremony, and everyone focused on the regal couple. Louise bit her lip, staving off tears. She was happy for Helena, who looked beautiful. Her opal and diamond jewelry sparkled in the candlelight of the chapel. And behind Helena, the bridesmaids were equally as elegant. Christian looked proud and stoic in his uniform. Louise wondered what was going through the man's mind and what sacrifices he was making in order to come to a new country and live quite directly under the queen's reign. Perhaps his age was an advantage. If up until now he hadn't found a bride, then maybe he was also aware of time running out?

No, Louise must not think that. She had to focus on the fact that Helena and Christian were both amiable, both dedicated, and they would make this marriage a success. After the festivities, the couple would travel to Osborne to spend their wedding night there. Their honeymoon would take them to France, Switzerland, and Italy.

And Louise would take over Helena's duties. Her sister's happiness would be worth it though.

As the ceremony ended, Louise's mixture of thoughts turned into worry for the changes in her life. At least Mama was doing much better now, as evidenced by the fact that this wedding was being celebrated in an almost-normal fashion. Louise would change into her mourning clothing later that day, and the staff still wore their black armbands, but the wedding had happened.

When the wedding luncheon was over, Leo stood by her as Helena and Christian's carriage pulled away. Helena's smile and Christian's grin were enough for anyone to wish them a happy life.

Louise waved until there was no way Helena could see her any longer.

"Miss the bats?" Leo nudged her shoulder.

Louise looked at him sharply. "What?"

"I was checking to see if you were listening. No bats at Windsor."

Louise sighed. "Nothing but work for me. I don't know what Mama will do without Helena. I'm not half as clever, and I don't know if she'll ever forgive me for my Christmas presents last year to the staff."

As they walked back into the palace, Leo snickered. "You mean when you gave the male staff pipes and cigar cases, when you know how much Mama abhors smoking? Just as Papa did."

Louise elbowed her brother. "I know. Don't you think I've been lectured enough these past months? Why can't we give a gift that someone else will truly appreciate? The male staff are all fond of smoking, so why shouldn't they have something nice if they're going to do it anyway?" She dropped her voice. "Besides, I'll bet *you've* tried smoking."

"Loosy, Loosy, Loosy," Leo said under his breath, but his tone was affectionate. "By the way, dear Loosy, *you* are the most clever person I know."

"Are you trying to butter me up for something, dear brother? You want me to sit for hours playing chess with you?"

"Not particularly. But I do hope we can spend some time together today before Mama has you under her thumb."

Louise didn't even crack a smile.

"You're really that down?" Leo asked, following her up the stairs. "Helena will be back in a couple of months, then she'll be living in apartments at Buckingham Palace or at Cumberland Lodge in Richmond Park. Not far away at all."

Louise sighed. "It won't be the same, but you're right. She won't be far away. And that will make Mama happy. When she's happy, we're all the better for it."

Leo grinned. "You're a fast learner."

He'd followed her all the way to the art room. She turned to face him in the doorway before entering. "What if I make mistakes? What if I do something terribly wrong?"

Leo grasped her hand. "That might happen, but we all make errors."

She blew out a breath. "Do you want to know what will make me feel better?"

"Don't tell me. You want me to sit for you?"

This time Louise did smile. "No. Come inside and be a witness to my masterful art and see what I'm working on now."

He laughed, and they entered the room. "Well, at least I can recognize this person," he said with a wink. "You're getting better, sister. Lady Jane Churchill, right?"

Louise released a dramatic sigh. "You've always been able to recognize my work. It's nearly perfect, you know."

Leo laughed again, and Louise grinned.

"What do you really think?"

Leo walked around the half-finished bust, his limp more pronounced today. Bringing his hand to his chin, he acted as if he were in deep thought, considering the finer points of the sculpture. "It's remarkable, Loosy. But how much is your work and how much is Susan Durant's?"

"Prepare to be impressed. I started this from the very beginning and intend to finish it out completely." She tilted her head, trying to see it as another might. "Does it pass muster?"

"I've never been more impressed, and that's saying a lot."

She peered at him. "You're trying to be my favorite brother."

Leo groaned. "You mean I'm not already?"

Louise's laughter filled the room. It felt good to laugh after the sorrow of Helena moving on with her new husband.

"What's this?" a voice said from the doorway. "Am I missing out on the fun?"

Louise turned to see Stirling at the doorway. She had not seen him in weeks, so it was good to see him now. "Come in. I was showing off my talents to Leo, trying to convince him that I'm no amateur."

The dip in his brow was immediate. "You've never been an amateur, Your Royal Highness."

Louise didn't let this compliment go to her head as she had his earlier ones. Although she felt quite pleased watching Stirling admire the burgeoning sculpture of Lady Jane.

"Excellent," Stirling declared. "Excellent indeed."

Since the queen hadn't asked for Louise's presence or requested any tasks, she and Leo and Stirling spent the better part of the day together. The men chatted while Louise chiseled. She didn't pay attention to all that they said, but their conversation was a pleasant hum in the background as she focused on the good things that the future might bring. Everyone was moving forward in their lives, which gave her hope. The day spent with Leo felt almost as if they'd returned to their childhood, before the sorrow had eclipsed their lives. The mood wouldn't last, Louise knew, but how wonderful it would be if it did.

The following morning started early when Louise was sent for. She entered Mama's bedroom and found her sitting at her vanity table, having her hair arranged in its usual tight chignon. Lady Jane Churchill sat composing a letter at the desk.

The queen's sharp eyes took in Louise's appearance—she wore a gray dress and had put up her own hair.

"You looked very beautiful yesterday. Many paid compliments toward you and speculated on whom *you* might marry."

Louise tried not to narrow her eyes. Helena hadn't been gone a full day, and already words were being said about the next wedding. "I am in no hurry."

This brought a hint of a smile to Mama's face. "Good. We'll let it rest then. For now. We need to begin the thank-you notes for all those who attended the wedding, and then—"

"Now?" Louise said. "I usually ride first thing in the morning, and—"

"We'll see about riding another day. These notes are urgent. It's impolite to delay gratitude."

She could do both. Ride and write the notes. But if she rode this afternoon, it would be too hot and likely windy.

"Jane, might you finish that letter later?" Mama said.

Lady Jane immediately rose and curtseyed. Then, with a quick smile at Louise, she left the room.

With Lady Jane gone, Mama said, "Also, today will be a hard day for Leo. He might need some cheering up, but don't coddle him. He's nearly a man, you know."

Louise frowned. "Why will today be hard?"

Something like regret crossed the queen's features. "Lieutenant Stirling has been dismissed, and I've sent inquiries through John Brown and General Grey about securing another governor for Leopold. The lieutenant will leave tomorrow."

At the mention of John Brown, Louise knew exactly what was happening. She tried to keep her voice level and not let the shock show on her face, but it was difficult. "Archie has been a beast to Leo. Just because he's John Brown's brother doesn't mean Archie can treat Leo the way that he has—"

Mama held up her hand. "It is done, Louise. There is no use debating any of the finer points. The lieutenant wasn't as experienced as I'd have liked. Leo might be saddened for a short time, but in the long run, I only want what's best for my son. His health is delicate, and the utmost care must be taken."

Mama's sense of protection toward Leo was commendable, but in this case, Louise thought the queen had taken things too far. Leo was close to the lieutenant, even though he'd been a tutor for only four months. This would devastate her brother, and she herself would be sorry to see him leave. Louise swallowed back her disappointment. "None of your children care for John Brown. You know what the press says about him, and this latest dismissal of Lieutenant Stirling will only start the gossip up again. Leo should be the one we think of here, not John Brown or his brother."

Mama stood then. Her full height was still dwarfed by Louise's taller frame. "John Brown served Papa favorably as his ghillie, and if Papa wholeheartedly supported him, then I support him too."

It was an argument that never changed.

"Who is watching after Leo until you find a new governor?"

"Those who are currently in my employ," Mama said, her chin still lifted, her gaze direct. "Reverend Robin Duckworth can spend more hours instructing if needed."

Duckworth was one of Leo's instructors, and he was well liked—charming and talented in music. But was he well-rounded enough to be Leo's governor?

"Now let us get started on those notes," Mama continued as if she hadn't upended Leo's entire day.

Louise had to think of something to soften the blow. Something that would keep her brother's spirit from breaking. The hours passed slower than ever, and once Louise could escape to her bedroom, she rifled through jewelry pieces she'd made. She paused on the ornamental cross she'd started on but hadn't completed. She had another idea. Finding a silver inkstand, she polished it and carved Leo's name on one edge. Then she made her way to the library. She'd been right to search for him there.

He'd obviously been crying, but his gaze was now stoic as he sat by the window. The bright, warm day was a terrible contrast to what was happening inside Leo's heart.

"I'm sorry, Leo," Louise said, her words feeling hollow.

He sniffled but didn't turn her way.

She took a few steps closer. "I thought of a goodbye present for Stirling," she continued as if her brother weren't on the verge of more tears. She held out the inkstand. "It's an inkstand, and I've carved your name into it. I thought Stirling could remember how much you cared about him whenever he writes letters to you. We could also give him a bust of you, and he'll know how much we'll miss him."

Leo turned then and looked down at the inkstand. He picked it up slowly, his cold hands brushing her warm palm. Leo was always cold. Even in July. He sniffled again then wiped at his eyes with his other hand. "Thank you for thinking of this." His voice was halting, rough.

"Let's find a nib pen to go along with it."

Leo's throat bobbed, but he went to the library desk. In a moment, he produced a pen. "This one."

"Excellent." Louise set the pen into the silver inkstand. "Now, let's go to the gallery and look at your busts. I have one in mind."

"Wait," Leo said, his tone more solid now. "We need to write something nice. A note of some kind. Maybe a poem?"

Louise paused. "Of course. I love that idea."

CHAPTER 17

"We give on Thursday evening what is called here a 'Quality' Ball at 10 o'clock—and we shall be only too happy if you or anybody else at Balmoral like to come. You know best if Mama will allow you to come or not—at any rate I hope you will come."

LETTER FROM THE PRINCE OF WALES
TO PRINCESS LOUISE, ABERGELDIE, AUGUST 28, 1866

APRIL 1867
LOUISE, AGE 19

Louise set her hands on her hips as she scanned her art studio at Osborne. The queen had finally agreed to give Louise her own studio since sculpting took up so much space and created a mess. While Louise might have preferred a room of windows to let in the bright island sun, this room was fine, since it was hers alone. In the same corridor as her bedroom, it was easy to squirrel away from everyone else. Over the mantlepiece, she kept a copy of one of her favorite paintings—Leonardo da Vinci's *Last Supper*. She also had a row of photographs of other masterpieces by Italian painters.

With the limited lighting, Louise did her work in the daytime, and that meant juggling her duties with Mama. The past few weeks, she'd asked Arthur to sit for her so she could sketch him, then eventually create a bust to give to Mama on her next birthday. Louise wanted to impress her mother enough that she'd allow Louise to attend the National Art Training School. The bust of Lady Jane had been a success, but still, Louise needed more completed pieces.

And Mary Thornycroft was going to help her with the recommendation to Mama. At Windsor, Louise worked in a room next to Mary's, but at Osborne, the art room was Louise's alone.

"You sent for me, Your Royal Highness?" Mary Thornycroft said at the door before entering the room.

Louise looked over at her art tutor who'd been appointed to teach just this year. Mary Thornycroft was a sculptress who'd exhibited her works at the age of twenty-one at the Royal Academy of Arts. Now, Mary was in her fifties and had a husband and six children. Louise was inspired by how Mary managed family life and a profession as a sculptress, with a supportive husband. Louise was dying to know if Mary supported women's suffrage but didn't dare ask in case it got back to the queen. The rights of women voting had been debated in Parliament, and each time it was in the papers, Mama said something disparaging. When referring to a society lady who supported the vote for women, Mama had said that she deserved a good whipping.

Right now, Louise had to put all of this out of her mind and be grateful for what Mama had allowed her, and that included Mary Thornycroft's instruction.

"Come in," Louise told Mary. "I want to get your opinion on the clay model I've done of Arthur." Her brother had sat for several sittings so Louise could sketch him from multiple angles. Mama was more amenable to the time that Louise spent in her studio when it involved creating art based on a family member.

Mary clasped her hands in front of her as her gaze zeroed in on the small model. Mary's artistic focus was busts, fragments, and full bodies. She sculpted from marble or bronze, and her subjects were children and infants—since these were acceptable subjects for a female sculptor. Mama had also commissioned Mary to do fragment sculptures of her children in marble, even though those were usually reserved for funerary pieces.

Mary bent to examine the finer details. Louise had done quite a bit of work with the clay model so that when she did the larger marble version, she'd not make any irreversible errors.

"The likeness is extraordinary," Mary said. "Your talent improves with each sculpture."

Louise held back a smile. Mary always started with a compliment, then the real criticism would start. "The ears are a bit large though. Do you see how it changes the slope of the face?"

Louise didn't need to take notes. Mary was saying things that Louise could see for herself, now that it was spoken aloud.

"Overall, though, you are ready to start the full-scale model." Mary's eyes shifted to the lone window. "I wish you had more natural light in here, but that can't be helped, can it?"

The words hung between them. Louise was fortunate to have this studio to herself. "I've adjusted to the lighting."

Mary nodded. "I've sent inquiries to the National Art Training School to get some particulars."

Louise tamped down the thrill running through her body.

"There is an art certificate course with 128 students enrolled," Mary continued. "You, of course, don't need to seek out a certificate. But I think you'd enjoy the modelling classes."

Louise exhaled. "I don't dare hope, but I'm going to anyway."

Mary's laughter was soft, and she rested a hand on Louise's arm. "Hope is where it all begins, Princess Louise. No matter what happens though, it won't take away your talent, and the day will come when I won't be able to teach you anything new."

Louise let the hope soar within, ebbing into something warm and light. She moved to the table with the clay powder and began to mix in water, slowly, letting the bubbles pop as she did so. Mary joined her, mixing up more clay.

"Do you think Arthur will like this?" Louise asked.

"He'll be proud and honored." Mary's hands were swift and sure.

Louise looked from Mary, whose aged hands contrasted with

Louise's younger ones, as if the art were being passed from one generation to another.

"The queen will be pleased too," Mary said. "How could she not? Based on this small bust, I'm predicting your final will be magnificent."

"Smaller busts are much easier," Louise mused. "This one will be life-sized." Sometimes she was hesitant to fully believe a compliment. Perhaps it came from being a royal, and compliments were plenty and many times overdone.

Mary hummed to herself as she continued to mix in the clay.

Humming while working on an art project was the epitome of contentedness, Louise decided. Life should always be like this. Working on what she loved to do, content in most things, and watching the world grow and change around her.

"What if I tell Mama I want to do a bust of *her*?" Louise said. "Do you think she'll agree?"

Mary looked up, her eyes alight with approval. "I think Her Majesty will agree, especially if the work is started here at Osborne—her favorite place. Besides, everyone who comes to visit now wants to see your studio. I think the queen has found pride in that."

In the end the bust of Arthur was successful. Mama was very impressed and loved it so much when Louise presented it on her birthday in May that she recommended that it be given to the Royal Military Academy in Woolwich. After the queen had ample time to enjoy it, of course. "You have developed your talent quite nicely, Loosy," Mama had said, and Louise had glowed in that praise for days.

Another highlight came when Helena gave birth to a baby boy. They named him Christian Victor, and he was baptized in the private chapel of Windsor Castle. Although the May day was cold and rainy, it was nice to see Helena looking so happy and pretty in a lilac-colored dress. Mama wore her usual black.

Louise stood as proxy, representing Vicky as godmother, and Affie stood as proxy godfather for Uncle Ernest. Louise was happy for Helena, she truly was. Even though she missed having the freedom she did when

Helena was Mama's personal secretary, a growing little family was more important. Her eyes filled with tears when the commencement hymn—"In Life's Gay Morn, Ere Sprightly Youth"—began, which had been composed by dear Papa.

The baby prince slept nearly the whole time, swathed in the Irish lace robe that had been a gift from the queen. After the end of the ceremony and the lunching in the Oak Room, Affie took his leave of everyone. He was departing the next day to Paris, and would eventually travel to Australia. It would be a memorable trip since Affie would be the first member of the British royalty to visit Australia.

In May, John Stuart Mill had succeeded in amending the Second Reform Bill and replaced the word *man* with *person*. Louise and Sybil had pored over the article about how the amendment was defeated, losing by seventy-three votes, but Mill still considered it a victory since those who'd voted in favor had come from both sides of the House.

The rest of the year passed quickly. Louise was delighted with having another nephew close by in England, and they started calling Christian Victor "Christle." Then, Sybil became engaged to William Beauclerk, the Duke of St Albans. The moment Louise received the news, she was anxious to congratulate her friend in person and to also let her know that she'd be happy to attend the wedding.

Because Louise was royalty, and Sybil was not, she couldn't invite a princess. The princess had to invite herself as well as secure the permission of the queen. But that hadn't worried Louise in the slightest. Mama was supportive of the friendship and everything to do with the Grey family.

The June 20th wedding took place at the St. James Palace. Although Louise was now nineteen years old, plenty old enough to marry, she told herself that she wasn't ready or interested. Her days and weeks would center on fulfilling Mama's wishes and desires. And a husband would likely take her to another country. She would miss Sybil Grey too much for that. And when would she see her brothers?

The first few months of working with Mama so closely might have been full of trials and errors, but now that Mama supported her sculpturing so much, things were peaceful for the most part. Louise felt seen and heard and appreciated. She was lonely at times without the frequent company of Sybil and Helena, but art was something to look forward to every day.

Soon, Louise secured Mama's permission to do a bust of her, and they spent hours in the studio together, just the two of them, as Louise sketched and modeled the clay bust that would eventually become cast for the final life-sized version.

Mama was quiet on some days and talkative on others. On her talkative days, she spoke of Vicky and Alice the most—since they were living abroad and their communication was relegated to letters. On her quiet days, Mama complained about Bertie. Louise never quite knew what Mama would say, and once when she complained how small both Bertie's and his wife's heads were, Louise had to bite her lips to keep from laughing. She supposed her brother and his wife did have smallish heads, but she'd never thought to comment upon it.

She waited for the perfect day—one in which Mama was talkative—to show her the clay model of her likeness. The queen studied it for several moments.

"I have loved learning from Mary Thornycroft this past year," Louise said, "and Susan Durant before that."

Mama looked up. "Your talent continues to grow, and your tutors have been impressed with you."

Louise smiled dutifully, but she wasn't looking for compliments. "I'd like to get as much training as I can, and I've been thinking about enrolling at the National Art Training School, if you agree."

"That school is public, Louise, not a place royalty attends."

Louise was ready. "I understand. My brothers are allowed to pursue educations that they need, one that a woman doesn't need. This school may be public, but they also allow female students."

One of Mama's eyebrows rose. "You're a princess. You'll be followed and gossiped about. You'll not be able to go alone to a place so public as that."

Louise held her breath. Mama hadn't said no yet. "I would only attend when my schedule permits." Louise tried to keep the nervous tremble out of her voice. "Mary Thornycroft told me that the female students are in the same classroom together, and they are taught appropriate artistic methods. Only very serious artists attend, so I wouldn't be bothered by onlookers." She took a quick breath. "My loyalty is to you first and the family, as always. Art comes after, but if I am well-trained, then my art will stand up to the worst critics."

"You are thinking of Matthew Noble, I see."

Louise nodded, her breathing thready now. Noble was one of the leading sculptors of the decade who'd attempted a sculpture of the queen. His work had been condemned by the eminent art critic Francis Palgrave.

"You did tell Vicky that you thought I could alter it enough to be respectable." Louise knew this because she'd penned the dictated letter. "If I'm trained by the top instructors, what happened to Noble will never happen to me."

The softening of the lines about Mama's eyes told Louise that she was about to receive permission. "I am hesitant, but you also make a good argument," Mama said, "which is not always the case." She released a breath, then said, "I will grant permission for you to attend the training school, but only the modelling class."

Louise hardly heard the end of Mama's sentence. She leapt from her chair and threw her arms about Mama's neck.

The queen laughed. It was a beautiful sound. "You are such an impulsive child, Loosy," Mama said.

Louise drew away and untied the smock covering her clothing. "I'm nearly twenty, Mama. Perhaps I am a woman now?"

Mama's smile appeared again. "You will always be my child." She held out her hand, and Louise drew her mother to her feet. "Now, let's go to the music room. I'd like to hear you play something with a jaunty tune."

This was a change indeed. Mama hadn't asked Louise to play in a long time. Moments later, Louise was playing Mendelssohn's "O For the Wings of the Dove," and Mama stood at the other end of the piano, singing along.

Louise couldn't remember the last time she'd heard her mother sing. Surely it was before Papa had died. She was glad she had the piece memorized because her vision had blurred too much to see any notes upon a page.

Soon Leo appeared at the door with Bea, both looking surprised, but pleased, at witnessing their mother's singing. Louise sensed that Bea had no memories of their mother singing. Leo's instructor Reverend Robin Duckworth had been promoted to governor, and he was very talented in singing. So on long winter nights when Louise played in the evenings, Duckworth sang, sometimes as a duet with her or as a solo. But Mama had always retired for the evening by then.

Mama singing at last gave Louise hope that the evenings would be far less lonely and forlorn from here on out. She would be able to attend a public art school—meet other people, and learn how to grow her talents. She'd been handed a precious gift. This wasn't the end of the bad days, the trying days, but for the moment, she had reasons to revel and celebrate.

CHAPTER 18

"I cannot tell you how sorry I am that you were not allowed to come and stay here with Alix while I am at Paris, but I was afraid that there would be difficulties in the way. I saw Lenchen on Friday and she seemed very well. Both Alix and I were very anxious that you should be Godmother to our little girl, especially as she is to bear your name. The christening is to take place here (quite privately) in Alix's sitting room on Friday next."

LETTER FROM THE PRINCE OF WALES
TO PRINCESS LOUISE, MARLBOROUGH HOUSE, MAY 6, 1867

SEPTEMBER 1867
LOUISE, AGE 19

London's mugginess made Louise feel like she wore a heavy dress of wool instead of her linen frock. No type of weather could hold her back from what the day would bring. She'd been looking forward to it for months, possibly years. The newspapers had been full of her enrollment in the National Art Training School, so the queen had insisted that Louise go early, to beat the press.

The streets were quiet as Louise's carriage pulled up to the building in South Kensington. Mary Thornycroft sat across from Louise on the other bench. "Here we are."

"Here we are," Louise echoed, her pulse a fast rhythm in her neck. She was nervous, but not because she didn't think she could keep up with the classroom instruction, but because she'd spent her nineteen years surrounded by royals or courtiers. Inside this public institution would be regular people. Artists, sure, but people who weren't under the expectation of all that was royal.

She'd focus on staying open minded. Learn all that she could. Form friendships. It was all so exciting and overwhelming at once. And freeing.

The coachman pulled up in front of an unassuming, brown brick building. He opened the carriage door and handed Louise down, then Mary followed. Along the sidewalk, people were already stopping and staring. Louise should be used to the attention, but her neck felt hot.

The carriage gave away her status, but not necessarily her identity. Yet anyone who'd read the newspapers could certainly put two and two together. Louise followed Mary into the building, feeling the gazes upon her back until the door swung shut behind them.

The carpets were plain, the doorways rectangular and serviceable, and there was nothing remarkable about the ceilings. But the walls were covered in framed paintings of all types and styles. But it was the smell that made Louise pause. Paint, charcoal, clay . . . She inhaled, feeling like she'd stepped into her studio.

Since she'd arrived early, no administrator was there to meet her, so Mary simply led her to the female-school portion of the building. As they entered the corridor, Mary said, "This is the picture gallery."

The corridor was somewhat narrow, with windows on one side and classroom doors on the other. Speckled between the various classroom doors were framed works of art—everything from landscapes to portraits to abstract images. She stopped before one painting that made her feel like she'd stepped back in time a few centuries. Not another soul was about, and it was easy to get lost in the artwork. "Are all of these done by students?"

"Yes, all of them," Mary murmured. "There is great potential here, don't you think?"

"I do," Louise agreed. Some of them were truly amazing. Others looked as if the artist still had more training to do. But she loved the variety. Mostly she loved being in a place that celebrated art of all styles. A place to grow. A place to develop into her own potential.

"Come, I'll show you the modelling room."

They passed other classrooms, and with each, Louise's heart heaved. She wished she could take every single art class here, but Mama had been insistent that she was to only take the modelling class. It was a start, and perhaps it would develop into something more? She'd already begun chiseling the marble for the queen's bust, and at the rate she was going, it would take the rest of the year to complete. Louise didn't mind though. The queen had been coming out of her darkest moments, and Louise could only be happy about that, along with the rest of the country.

"This is the classroom," Mary said, opening the door.

Before entering, Louise embraced Mary. "Thank you for bringing me. You don't have to wait around. I'll meet you at the carriage after the class."

Mary hesitated, as if she wasn't sure if she should stay with Louise like the queen had suggested.

"Truly, I'll be fine." Louise waved off Mary.

Then she walked into the room and paused only a few steps in. She was entranced. The room was crowded with tables and half-finished projects. Large windows allowed plenty of light in. She walked among the tables and examined the clay models and small marble sculptures that were partially complete.

Louise stopped in front of a sculpture formed into a horse. She followed the lines and contours with her eyes, wondering how hard it would be to create this animal. Another sculpture caught her attention—that of a young boy's bust. The sculptress had begun to create tendrils of hair. "So detailed," Louise said to herself. "It's beautiful."

"What's beautiful?" a voice said from the doorway. "And who are you speaking to?"

Louise turned to see a dark-haired woman bustle inside. She tugged off her hat and brushed at something on her navy skirt as she weaved through the tables. "Ah, you've found my child. Well, not my *actual* child. I'm not even married." She laughed to herself, her brown eyes bright with humor.

Louise smiled. It was strange to have someone speaking to her and not pay any deference. Or even curb her tongue.

"Are you newly enrolled?" the young woman asked, then continued without waiting for a reply, "I know that I am frequently fog-brained when working on a piece, but I should at least notice the other students around me. Now, if we could have a few male students in our classroom, I would certainly look up more from my work. I suppose it's a good thing there aren't any."

Louise guessed this woman to be about her age. And goodness, she could rattle on. "I suppose so."

"Now, what's your specialty?" the woman continued. "Oh, don't tell me. I will guess." Her brown eyes peered at Louise closely, looking her up and down with utmost care. Her gaze paused at Louise's hands, which were, as usual, scrubbed raw to remove dried clay. She pointed at Louise's hands. "May I?"

Louise was too shocked to say no. The woman lifted her hands and turned them over.

"Strong, callused, rough. Ah. You're a sculptress already." The woman dropped Louise's hands. "What are you working on now?"

"A bust of my mother."

The woman's smile was quick. "How wonderful. Do I know your family? I am Henrietta Montalba, by the way."

Louise committed the name to memory. Surely, this woman was one she wanted to be acquainted with—her talent and personality were both delightful. "I am Louise," she said, leaving off the princess title purposely.

"Nice to meet you, Louise. Welcome to the school." Henrietta held out her hand, and Louise shook it, still feeling bemused.

Suddenly Henrietta dropped her hand, and her face went marble white. "Oh gracious. You are . . ." She dipped into a low curtsey and bowed her head. "I apologize, Your Royal Highness. I heard that you were joining our class, but I didn't know, didn't think, it would be *today*. I should have never said all of those things, and—"

"Henrietta." Louise put a hand on her shoulder. "You are going to cramp your knees. Please stand. I find it refreshing to be treated as if I'm another fellow student."

Now, Henrietta's face was pink. "But you're *not* a fellow student, Your Royal Highness," she rushed to say. "I apologize again. I shouldn't be arguing with a princess. I should . . ." She brought her hands to her cheeks. "Oh, I don't know. Can we start again? Pretend we haven't met and the last few minutes never happened?"

Louise laughed then. "I'll not pretend because I very much enjoyed your prattling."

"It was prattling, wasn't it? My parents tell me I talk too much, especially for an artist. Whatever that means. Heavens, I'm doing it again."

Louise only grinned. "Now, Henrietta Montalba. Tell me about your work. I'm fascinated by the tendrils you've created in the boy's hair. So fine and detailed. Which chisel did you use?"

"Oh." Henrietta puffed out her cheeks. "Oh, all right. Well. This small chisel." She picked up the instrument. "It's a fine tool, only good for the little stuff, you know. My mother thinks I'll go nearsighted if I keep it up. She doesn't want me wearing spectacles because then I'll be unattractive and stay a spinster forever. I'm only twenty, but apparently that is one year away from spinsterhood."

Louise laughed again. "Then we shall be spinsters together."

Henrietta's brows went sky-high. "Oh, I didn't mean . . . You shouldn't think I was implying—"

"It is a subject that my sisters frequently remind me of. They all married before they turned twenty, and even my close friend Sybil Grey is now married." Louise shrugged. "I was hoping to meet an eligible bachelor at art school, but I'm not sure the queen would approve."

Henrietta laughed aloud at this.

The shuffle of footsteps caught Louise's attention. Two other young women had entered the classroom, their eyes wide, their mouths agape. As soon as Louise's gaze landed on them, they dipped into curtseys.

Louise held back a sigh and said brightly, "Good morning. I'm Louise."

Slowly, the other women rose, their eyes still wide.

"How many are in this modelling class?" Louise asked.

"Eight," Henrietta said in a cheerful tone. "Nine now that you're here."

Soon, others joined them, and the process was repeated. Wide eyes. Curtseys. Murmured accolades.

"I hope this doesn't happen every class session," Louise said to Henrietta. "It's quite cumbersome, and I'm truly here to learn."

Henrietta eyed Louise. "I assume you're used to protocols. Surely none of this surprises you?"

"I am used to it," Louise said. "That doesn't mean I enjoy all the formality. Did you know you're the first person I've talked to in ages who hasn't been a royal or courtier?"

Henrietta's smile flashed, and although her cheeks bloomed pink, she didn't appear abashed. "So what you're saying is that I am your first peasant friend?"

Louise grinned. "Are you a peasant, Miss Montalba?"

"Artists are always poor, so perhaps?"

Louise was about to answer, but then the instructor entered. George Watts also bowed to Louise and welcomed her with an exuberance that outshone all the other greetings that morning.

"Thank you for accepting me into your school," she told Watts. "I've looked forward to this for months."

Soon, Louise realized that the class wasn't about generalities but individualism, about creating new ideas, and not *re*-creating things. As the students worked, the instructor would visit tables and give advice and criticism. Louise had brought a sketch of her friend Sybil so that she could start on a bust as her first project. She'd do a small one since her time at home would be spent on the queen's.

The next weeks were absolutely glorious in Louise's mind. She went to the institution at varying times since crowds routinely developed, waiting to catch a glimpse of her as she entered. That was truly the only downfall of the whole experience, though. The newspapers were full of reports, most of them treading the line of fiction, of how she was managing in the modelling class.

Louise didn't mind the speculations about her talent in the newspapers. Editors questioned if her art would ever truly be comparable to a master's or if she'd be falsely trumped up because she was a princess. The words stung at first, but then Louise determined that she would just have to prove her critics wrong, develop her talent, and shine in her own sphere.

Despite any naysayers in newspaper articles, Louise enjoyed the class and her fellow students. She especially enjoyed her friendship with Henrietta. The young woman was so lively and direct—such a change from Louise's homelife. Even though the queen had begun to return to activities she'd once embraced, the palace staff still wore black armbands, and Louise wore grays and blacks. The colorful dresses of the others in her classroom filled Louise with a longing that would offend the queen if she knew about it.

"The press has taken this too far," Mama said during one of their sittings in Louise's art room. "They've made such a deal out of you being the first royal to attend a public institution."

"But it's true."

"Of course it's true," Mama said with a sigh. "I don't understand why they have to go on and on. Crowding the sidewalks to get a glimpse. It's like you've become a target now, and I need you better protected."

"I am protected." Louise was escorted to and from the school each week. Mama was overly bothered, and Louise didn't want her to be. The last thing she wanted was for the queen to withdraw her permission.

But as the months went on, Louise attended less and less. She tried not to complain, but it was difficult. She wanted the people of England to see her as a hardworking and dedicated student of the arts. If only they could understand her drive and passion for sculpting and not think she was just a princess being spoon-fed on whims and fancies.

During the weeks that Louise missed class, she wrote to Henrietta, who replied with entertaining letters. Louise discovered that Henrietta had attended some rallies on women's suffrage, and Louise read her friend's letters multiple times, then tucked them away in a safe place. How she would love to become more involved in the cause.

At least the queen allowed Louise to attend Lady Augusta's tea parties. There, Louise listened attentively to the latest news of social movements and rallies and meetings. But they weren't things she could ever share with her mother.

Any permissions the queen might have given Louise for additional outings were sharply curbed one March morning when Louise saw a rider approach Windsor at a speed that told her something was wrong. By the time she hastily readied herself and made it down the stairs, followed by Leo, the throne room was filled with government members and courtiers.

Since Mama was surrounded by her advisors, Louise approached General Grey. "What's happened?"

He faced her then, his kind eyes bloodshot. "Praise God that your brother Prince Alfred is well, but he was attacked in Australia."

Mama stood and paced the drawing room in deep conversation with John Brown.

"Who attacked him?" Leo asked. "And what happened?"

General Grey looked from Leo to Louise. "While Prince Alfred was visiting Sydney, he was shot in the back by a Fenian. The bullet missed his spine by a half inch and missed all the major organs. He will recover completely, thank the Lord."

The news was hard to comprehend. *Affie was shot?* He could have died. A half inch stood between her brother's life or his death. How was her mother up and pacing? Leo's face had drained of color, and Louise's breath had cut in half.

"We always thought the Fenian revolt was only a lot of noise," she said, "not a real threat on a royal's life."

Grey nodded. "That's what we all thought. They have strong supporters in Australia, it seems."

Louise's thoughts spun in different directions. The Fenian movement had been sparked decades ago after the Irish Potato Famine. They blamed British royalty for their plight, and the movement had grown into the demand for Irish independence. But to assassinate a British prince?

"What was he doing in Sydney?" Louise asked General Grey, if only to keep her mind from dwelling on the image of Affie bleeding in the streets. What if he'd been alone? What if that half inch had been much less?

"Prince Alfred was at a charity picnic that was raising funds for the Sailors' Home at Port Jackson," Grey said. "It was a public event, so the Irishman had no trouble getting close enough to shoot."

"What is his name?" Leo ground out. His skin had gone from pale to a mottled tone.

"Henry James O'Farrell."

Leo gave a short nod. Neither of them would forget the man's name. A man who had directly threatened their brother, their family, the monarchy.

"O'Farrell should hang," Leo said. "I'll make sure of it."

Now wasn't the time to ask Leo how he'd manage to accomplish all that, but Louise felt the same way. There was no doubt that O'Farrell had been aiming to kill.

CHAPTER 19

*"Thousand thanks for your dear letter, which gave me so much pleasure.
Thank God that darling Leo now is getting on and now is out of danger.
How easily can I understand your feelings and your anxiousness about that
darling boy! What your poor little heart must have suffered in seeing your
darling brother in such danger, and in so critical a state. How anxiously
you must have been watching his bedside and how dreadful to think how
soon and easily everything might have been over!! Oh! Sometimes one might
wonder how human beings can bear so much!"*

LETTER FROM THE PRINCESS OF WALES
TO PRINCESS LOUISE, FEBRUARY 3, 1868

APRIL 1868
LOUISE, AGE 20

As it was, Henry O'Farrell had been quickly arrested and lost
his case of pleading insanity. The man hanged before Prince
Alfred had even returned home. With the trial and sentenc-
ing out of the way, Louise virtually held her breath, waiting for Mama to
change her mind about art school. But she didn't, and Louise continued
to attend sporadically.

With Sybil married now, their time together was less frequent. So
Louise made the best of the time they did share. Through Sybil, as well
as occasional conversations with General Grey, Louise learned so much
more than reading the biased newspapers. She'd recently discovered that

a public meeting about supporting women's right to vote would be held in Manchester. And Sybil planned to attend.

"You must tell me everything," Louise urged Sybil as they had tea together the day before the public meeting. "Mama would threaten to disown me if I attended."

Sybil gave a light laugh, although they both knew Louise attending would be scandalous. Louise had gone so far as to write to her sisters Vicky and Alice and ask their opinions on women's suffrage. Both of them were supportive but also cautioned Louise about antagonizing the queen about it. So Louise stayed silent around her mother, hoping that someday she could be more involved. It was exciting to think that women, who were just as intelligent and talented as men, would be able to make their own decisions and vote. Even if the queen did support Louise's views, as a royal, she couldn't involve herself in politics. And women's suffrage was political.

"I'll report back word for word." Sybil squeezed Louise's hand. "It will surely be in all the papers too."

Louise nodded. "You might have to bring them to me. Mama has censored which newspapers remain at Windsor. She's already upset about the movement enough."

"Many are," Sybil said. "Yet educating women and giving them the right to vote is not going to threaten our country."

"It will only strengthen it. Mothers who are educated can then educate their children," Louise continued. "Girls and women who don't have the ideal life can enjoy more opportunities to contribute to our society and the development of the country. Surely the queen will have to see reason and will change her mind eventually. Did you read what Edward Fitzgerald said?"

"I can guess." It was no secret that Sybil despised the man's opinion as equally as Louise.

"He doesn't see any point in the education of women since we belong in the kitchens, minding our children, and caring for the poor."

Sybil shook her head. "We do that already, and we can accomplish even more than that. Not every woman will marry or become a mother. And not every woman has the time or luxury to give to charity. That's why women need more options and a voice."

Louise took a sip of her tea, now lukewarm. "I'm going to find a way to send my endorsement. I've written to Vicky and asked her to send a letter of introduction to Josephine Butler and let her know of my support."

"The Crown Princess did this for you?" Sybil asked in a dubious tone.

"Vicky is quite forward thinking, you know," Louise said. "Besides, she has a prominent position in Europe; and I hope that Mrs. Butler will come to realize that not all royals are against women's suffrage."

Sybil didn't congratulate Louise as expected. "You are taking a great risk, my friend. Please tread carefully."

The words might have been ominous and pricked at Louise's loyalties to Mama, but if no one ever changed viewpoints, then change would never happen.

On the day that a letter arrived for Louise, from the esteemed Mrs. Josephine Butler, Louise hurried to the privacy of her bedroom to read it. Mrs. Butler declared that she was honored to have the support of the princess. Over the next weeks, Louise enjoyed their written exchanges immensely. Mrs. Butler even sent Louise a copy of her book, *Women's Work and Women's Culture*.

She should have known that Mama and her other siblings would find out sooner rather than later.

"What is this?" Mama demanded one morning in early May, holding up a letter the moment Louise entered the room she'd been summoned to.

From the doorway, Louise could see which letter it was exactly— one from Josephine Butler. Louise had eagerly accepted the call to support the rescue work of prostitutes in Liverpool. The women were being given a second chance at life. Clothed and educated and established at skilled positions where they could support themselves and their families without resorting to immoral deeds. She'd agreed to write fundraising letters on behalf of Mrs. Butler and spread the word at various teas.

"That is my private correspondence," Louise said at once, then realized she should have bit her tongue.

"Nothing is private when you are the daughter of England's sovereign." Mama's eyes flashed. "You know this, Louise. And helping this . . . woman—Mrs. Butler—with her distasteful work is no duty for a princess."

"Those women need help, desperately," Louise said, her voice rising despite herself. "They have not chosen this life, and they deserve a second chance and the grace of God too."

Mama didn't speak yet, yet sometimes her silences were harsher than her words. Louise was too young to remember the time that Mama and Papa wrote letters to each other for weeks when they weren't speaking to one other, yet she'd heard about it.

"I understand your passion and sense of wanting to help those who are destitute," Mama said finally, her patient tone surprising Louise. "But I cannot have my daughter, a princess, associated with these suffragettes. The royals champion worthy causes but avoid political matters, especially ones that center on women who have degraded themselves."

Louise's chest heaved as she stared at her mother. "And what about women who want to vote? Women who want to have a profession? Women who are equally skilled in mind and body and can accomplish the same things as men?" She was proud of herself for keeping an even tone.

"If you are speaking of a woman becoming a doctor, I cannot support it," the queen said. "Women are feminine, pure, and delicate. A woman does not need to learn anatomy and perform surgeries."

"Not even to save a life?"

The queen pressed her lips together. "Our lives are in God's hands. I might be a female sovereign, but I must support the proper order of society."

"What about France? Are they heathens for allowing women to obtain doctor training?"

The queen set down the letter on her writing desk and clasped her hands. "In all things, daughter, whether public or private, *you* represent the monarch. You represent *me*. I've asked you to stay clear of the likes of Mrs. Butler, and so you must."

It was a command, an order. Not only from her mother, but from the queen, whom Louise was allegiant to.

The queen wasn't finished. "As the monarch, I need to set the example for how proper women must conduct themselves. I expect my own children to do the same. Now, I know you have a book that you've borrowed from Mrs. Butler. It needs to be sent back immediately."

Louise exhaled slowly. If women could be nurses, they should be allowed to train as doctors. "I will cease my correspondence with Mrs. Butler, and I will return the book." There were other issues to champion, and it would take time to change Mama's mind. As well as that of the rest of the country. Change didn't happen overnight, Louise reminded herself.

Perhaps she could discuss her views with Alix. She hadn't been happy when Louise sided with Helena over marrying Prince Christian, but the passing months had dissipated that family issue, and Alix wasn't steeped in the British culture of repressing women's rights.

In recent weeks, Louise had heard of Elizabeth Garrett, who was the first female practicing doctor in England. Of course, Garrett had trained in France. With Emily Davies, she had brought the women's-right-to-vote petition to Parliament. Louise had heard of Garrett through mutual acquaintances, including Mrs. Butler, as well as Lady August Stanley.

Mama seemed content as they began the day working through correspondence. They followed that by another sitting together in Louise's art room.

But Louise's mind would not settle. She had to obey the queen as her sovereign, but could Louise not have her own opinion? The world outside of England was changing for women, and Louise wanted to be a part of championing those changes in her own country. A plan began to form in her mind, one that she wouldn't even share with Sybil. There was too great of a risk that it would be discovered with the Greys' close connection to the queen.

The day of her plan arrived, and the weather was sunny and warm, which bode well. Louise took one of her ladies-in-waiting, Emily Cathcart, with her into London on a superficial errand. As the carriage approached Upper Berkeley Street, Louise rapped on the carriage roof, signaling the driver to stop.

When he did, Louise and Emily climbed out of the carriage and walked up to the doorstep of number twenty. Louise knocked on the door. Perhaps it was brash to show up at the woman's home, but it was the only way Louise could think of to meet her.

When a parlor maid answered the door, Emily asked, "Is Miss Elizabeth Garret at home?"

The parlor maid dipped into a curtsey, likely noticing the fine clothing of Louise and Emily.

"I am Emily Cathcart," Emily continued smoothly, "and this is Her Royal Highness, Princess Louise."

At this, the maid's mouth dropped open, and she said in a rush, "Come in and be seated, Your Royal Highness. I will fetch Miss Garrett from her consulting room." Then she led them up the stairs to the front drawing room.

In another circumstance, Louise might have told her to not be so fretful since the visit was unannounced, but she wanted to get off the street as quickly as possible. She didn't want any passersby to recognize her. The queen would not be pleased to discover this adventure through the newspapers. And if Louise could help it, she'd keep this visit a secret until her grave.

Louise wasn't about to sit in the parlor and wait, so she continued past the room and into the adjoining one just as the parlor maid announced, "Her Royal Highness, the Princess Louise."

Louise stepped into a room that was far from tidy to find a woman standing on a step stool, hanging wallpaper. Her hair was in a loose pompadour, and the fine lines about her eyes were gentle. Those eyes were currently about as wide as door knockers. "Y-your Royal Highness," Elizabeth Garrett stuttered. "I apologize for my state."

Louise waved a hand. "It is I who must apologize for the unexpected visit. I have heard much about you and your work, and I'd like to hear about it firsthand."

Elizabeth moved off the step stool and smoothed the dirty apron she wore over her modest clothing. "I'll answer anything you'd like to hear about, ma'am. Please, let's move into the parlor. The chairs are less dusty in there."

Louise only smiled. Piles of books sat on nearly every surface, including the chairs, and stretched across the long table was an articulated skeleton. "I don't mind dust," she said, but she and Emily walked with Elizabeth into the parlor.

For the next hour, Louise plied Elizabeth Garrett with questions about her education and experiences working as a doctor in England.

"I must say that there are those who refuse to accept treatment because of my gender," she said. "My circle of influence is quite small compared to what it might be for a male doctor. But I am content in my work, and I'm fascinated with learning as much as I can."

Even in the parlor, books were stacked about. This did not bother Louise in the slightest. In fact, she was tempted to borrow a few and return them later, but the queen would surely discover such an act.

"I wish there were a way I could support you more," Louise said. "As the times change and progress is made, I will have more freedom to do so."

"You are very generous," Elizabeth said. "I appreciate your visit, and it's an honor to speak with you."

"And you as well, Miss Garrett." Louise paused. "As tempting as it might be, please do not speak of this meeting to anyone. The queen would not approve. It is nothing personal, you see, but she is very tradi-tional in her views."

"I understand," Elizabeth said, her smile bright. "I won't say a word, and I'll make sure my staff keeps quiet as well."

Louise believed her, so she was surprised when the queen found out anyway. The driver of the carriage must have said something.

Mama entered Louise's studio the following afternoon, already dressed for a dinner that would include dignitaries. Louise immedi-ately stood and curtseyed. But the high color on the queen's cheeks told Louise this was not a trifling visit.

"Your errand yesterday will not happen again," Mama said. "You know my feelings about women such as Elizabeth Garrett. I'll not have my own daughter visiting homes of the working class."

Louise wanted to ask how Mama had found out, but did it really matter? She clasped her hands tightly behind her back, sending the pulse of her frustration into them.

Mama's eyes trailed over Louise's clothing, which was covered in an apron and dusty from sculpting. "I think it is time that you settle down and marry."

PART THREE

1869–1871

CHAPTER 20

"I would only say I wish you all the happiness which I am sure you do not completely get at home and recommend you to take my advice and not forget Albert of Prussia. He is good and excellent, clever and rich, wishes it himself and I think would make you happy."

LETTER FROM PRINCE ALFRED
TO PRINCESS LOUISE, DEVONPORT, NOVEMBER 1, 1868

JANUARY 1869
LOUISE, AGE 20

Her husband must agree to reside nearby," the queen told Bertie and Alix.

Louise stared out the window of the drawing room. The January rain had stopped about an hour ago, but the gloom of the late afternoon still clung to the bare trees outside. Louise was half listening to the discussion over her future. Well, _debate_ might be the more accurate word.

Her mind was on her recent viewing of Edgar Boehm's equestrian statuette of a lady. Boehm's work had become all the rage in England. She'd met him earlier in the year when he'd come to Osborne to create an equestrian statuette of her. Louise had been entranced with his work ever since, and Mama had agreed that she could take some lessons from him. His insistence on paying attention to details such as drapery and trimmings in clothing had intrigued her. As well as his skill modelling in bronze, something that she hadn't tried yet.

"My eldest brother, Frederick, would be a wonderful match for

Loosy," Alix said, drawing Louise's half-hearted attention. This wasn't the first time she'd suggested her brother, who was now the Crown Prince of Denmark.

Mama had opposed the suggestion each and every time. "Louise won't be living in another country. If she marries Prince Frederick, she'll spend the rest of her life in Denmark."

At this, Louise looked over at her sister-in-law. As always, she looked beautiful and fragile; her health was declining more each year. She'd managed to have four children so far. Louise could see that Alix wanted to argue that living abroad was to be expected for a royal because a woman should live and raise her children where her spouse reigned.

But it was Bertie who surprised Louise when he spoke up about the Danish Crown Prince. "Louise would be well-suited to the Danish court, Mama. The informal, quiet family life of the king will carry over, and I think our sister would thrive in such an intimate setting."

Mama wrung a lace handkerchief between her fingers. "Regardless of whether Louise will suit them or not, it will not suit *me*. I don't want *all* my daughters living abroad, under the roofs of foreigners. Helena's husband moved here, and there's no reason Louise can't find a husband to do the same."

Alix gazed into the cheery fire in the hearth, her back very, very straight.

Bertie persisted. "Beatrice will take over as your personal secretary when the time is right, and you've already declared that *she* will not marry."

"Hush," Mama said. "I don't want word of *marriage* to get back to Beatrice. Don't bring it up to her. If she gets anything into her head about marrying, or that she'll be allowed to marry, then I'll be left with no one."

Bertie's expression remained tight as if he knew it was fruitless to argue with the queen.

"And no more mention of Prince Frederick around others," Mama continued. "I'm still upset about the newspaper reporting on their rumored engagement last year." Last summer, the Danish newspaper *Dagestelegraphen* reported on Louise's supposed engagement to Frederick. This was quickly refuted the next day by the *Times*. Louise had never discovered how the rumor was started in the first place.

Alix rose to her feet at that, using her cane that she'd come to rely on since her recent bout with rheumatic fever. "It's getting late, Bertie."

Bertie nodded, then turned again to Mama.

She didn't even meet his gaze. "You may go," she said with a wave of her hand.

Ever the dutiful Prince and Princess of Wales, each of them crossed to the queen and kissed her cheek. As Bertie and Alix left the room, Mama released a sigh. Yet before she could say anything, Bertie returned.

"Alix's brother will be visiting her next week. It might be good to at least have Louise meet the man." His gaze shifted to Louise. "Then she can make her own judgement."

Louise stared at her brother. Had this visit been planned by him and Alix in order to arrange an introduction? She didn't know what she thought or felt . . . She didn't want to live in Denmark either but had let Mama take on that argument. It wasn't like Frederick was German though—that would have been a resounding *no* for her.

Alix watched from the doorway now. She was the dearest sister-in-law. How could Louise say no without at least meeting the Crown Prince?

"I will meet him," Louise said before Mama could argue. He was royalty after all, and like her siblings, she'd have to marry someone royal. It may not be realistic to count on finding another prince, such as Helena's husband, who'd agree to live in England.

Mama's brows raised, but her pursed lips said everything that she wasn't. Finally, the queen replied uncommittedly, "We shall see, Bertie."

This was leagues better than a no, so Bertie smiled and again kissed Mama's cheek. With that, he and Alix left, leaving Louise feeling strangely exhausted.

"This letter came today." Mama reached for a letter on the side table that Louise hadn't noticed earlier.

"Who is it from?"

"The queen of Holland." Mama unfolded the pages. "You can read it yourself."

Louise settled next to Mama and took the letter. She scanned the words, moving past the beginning pleasantries, until her gaze landed on the suggestion of Louise marrying her son, Prince William of Orange. Louise lowered the letter. "Wasn't Prince William considered for Alice?"

"Yes, he was," Mama said. "Don't worry, dear Loosy. You'll not have to endure a marriage to that man. If he wasn't suited for Alice, he's not suited for you either."

Relief settled over Louise. At least she and Mama agreed on that point. Louise didn't want Alice's castoff.

"But there are other princes you might consider," Mama said. "Thirteen in total who are unmarried, single men."

"Thirteen?" Louise asked with a frown.

"Well, seven out of the remaining thirteen are eligible."

Louise knew her mother's strictures for eligibility. Her husband had to be Protestant, healthy, and independently wealthy. "And which ones are willing to live in England?"

At this, the queen looked up at the ceiling as if she needed to consult with the heavens. "One, according to Vicky." She directed her gaze at Louise. "You must know that I'm not happy how Vicky has gone behind my back to make inquiries about him and send you letters with her recommendations and compliments. She's even pulled Alice to her side."

Louise knew exactly who the prince was now, and she told Mama what she'd told both Alice and Vicky. "Prussian men smell, and they're rude. Not to mention so very tall. Prince Albrecht of Prussia is no different." She was pleased to see that Mama was upset over her sister's meddling—because then it would lessen the pressure on her to consider such a brute. Why couldn't a royal prince be charismatic, attractive, and interested in art—a man like Edgar Boehm? Even now, Louise could picture Edgar's dancing blue eyes, feel his enthusiasm, and marvel at his insights and talent. What would it be like to marry a man with so much personality and charm?

The queen cleared her throat. "Vicky thinks that Prince Albrecht will agree to live in England."

All images of Boehm faded, and Louise shot to her feet. Had it come to this? The only prince everyone agreed upon was a Prussian? The man was huge. Taller than General Bismarck, who was said to wear the largest-sized helmet in the Prussian army. Louise paced to the window as her mother spoke.

"Vicky says he is good looking and very nice," Mama said. "He has a fortune as well, so you won't need to rely on Parliament giving your husband any sort of allowance."

More like *persuade*, as the queen had done with Alice and Ludwig. Louise turned to face her mother. "And you would approve the match if he agreed to live in England?"

With a slow nod, Mama said, "I would have to meet him to decide. But out of the seven eligible princes, he is the most logical match."

Was this Prussian prince her only choice? Louise rubbed her fingers into her temple. "I will think about it," she finally said. "I suppose meeting Prince Frederick will help me make up my mind."

Mama made no further argument for or against either man, and for that Louise was grateful. She didn't know which was worse—moving to Denmark or marrying a Prussian.

A week of anticipating the meeting had Louisa thumbing through the *Almanach de Gotha* more than once as she studied more about Denmark and the actual distance from England. She'd have to learn Danish, and her children would be Danes. Everything that she was would be devoted to a royal court that she hadn't been born into— which begrudgingly led her to the same conclusion as Mama. Prince Albrecht was the best candidate—if he agreed to move to England.

On the appointed evening with Prince Frederick, Mama said she would meet Alix's brother another day, which only demonstrated her dislike for all things Danish. So Helena and Christian came with her, so Louise wouldn't feel quite so much on display.

As Louise alighted from the carriage in front of Marlborough House, all lit up, she swallowed back her trepidation. Frederick was probably perfectly nice if he was anything like his sister. Besides, how else was she going to decide about the prince unless she met him?

As she walked into the grand hall, Alix was the first to greet her. Next to Alix was a man who had to be her brother. "Welcome, dear Louise, I'd like you to meet my brother Frederick."

Louise turned to the man.

Prince Frederick was lighter haired than his sister and five years older than Louise, which made him seem so much more mature. His mustache was thin, and his hair even thinner.

He grasped her hand and greeted her in a thick accent.

Louise smiled. "It's so lovely to meet you."

She fully expected him to say some other pleasantry, but he dropped her hand and said something to Alix in Danish.

Louise was trying to decide if that was rude when they were all ushered into the dining room.

He and Alix conversed in Danish throughout part of the meal, and Louise had no hope of keeping up, even though she'd learned a bit from Alix over the years. Louise's gaze connected more than once with Helena's. She looked as frustrated as Louise felt.

When Prince Frederick did speak to Louise, he didn't exactly look her in the eyes. And she was too caught up with deciphering his heavily accented English. She could see the similarities between Alix and her brother, and those were endearing. They shared lighthearted stories that made them both smile and laugh, but Louise could understand very little.

"What do you think of Frederick?" Alix asked, linking their arms later in the evening after Louise had made her goodbyes to the dinner party. "He's handsome, no?"

"He's handsome," Louise conceded, although she wasn't sure if he was handsome to *her*. If he had been, wouldn't she feel at least a small bit of attraction?

"And so witty," Alix continued. "His stories are amusing, don't you think?"

Louise couldn't remember laughing at anything he'd said in English. Perhaps his humor was only in Danish. "You have a fine brother, Alix. Thank you for introducing us."

"Oh, no you don't," Alix said in a fierce tone. They were alone now in the corridor, and Alix faced her. "Tell me what you *really* thought and if you can picture yourself married to Frederick."

Alix's expression was so imploring, but was it fair to give her sister-in-law false hope? "I don't think I'm ready to marry," Louise said. "This isn't about anyone else—just me. I know that Mama thinks I am, but I'm not sure. And I want to be sure."

With a tremble to her voice, Alix said, "I understand, dear Loosy. It's quite a decision, after all." She leaned forward and kissed Louise's cheek.

On the way home, Louise wondered if she'd done the correct thing. Upon arriving, she went immediately to the queen's rooms and reported on the evening.

Mama was settled in her reading chair with her diary and her dog, Looty. "So you've delivered the news directly to Alix?"

"Yes," Louise said. "I don't think her brother will be much heartbroken. There wasn't any sort of affinity between us."

Mama closed her diary. "Then will you consider Prince Albrecht?"

Louise closed her eyes. "I don't know." She would be disappointing many people if she set aside Albrecht. Less so with Prince Frederick. Only Alix would be disappointed.

"Sleep on the matter, Loosy," Mama said. "The world always makes more sense in the morning."

Louise was grateful for the advice because it was what she intended to do. That and beg for Sybil's advice. She was a married woman, and perhaps she had more insight because of it.

Once Louise was back in her room, she penned a note to Sybil, asking her to visit at her earliest ability. Louise needed someone to confide in. Her dog, Frisky, a terrier who was loyal to the core, hopped up on her lap and nudged Louise's hand to get her to pet him. "What? You want some attention?" she asked her dog. "You don't want to visit Germany with me, do you? The Prussian courts are so formal, so stiff, so backwards. Not to mention speaking German."

When she and Sybil met the next day, Louise was bursting with the news. As they walked the grounds of the palace, both cloaked in long wool coats, Louise told Sybil of meeting Prince Frederick VIII of Denmark. Then she shared the basics of the queen of Holland's letter about her son, and finally, she spoke about Prince Albrecht. The most logical choice.

"But I don't want to be logical," Louise said. "I mean, I do. Marriage is much more than friendship and attraction. It's a life spent together. Blending families. Raising children. Attending events and holidays together. Finding common ground—"

"Prussia?" Sybil cut in. "You're not going to pack up and move to that dreadful place, are you? You'll have to speak German and teach your children all those formalities like heel clicking and bowing to everyone."

Louise linked arms with her friend. "No. Mama will insist that he move to England if we marry. My children will be taught German, but English will be spoken in our daily activities."

Sybil gave Louise a side-eyed glance. "He is very tall."

"Yes." So her friend had heard about his size. "He is."

The two friends fell silent again. Then at the same time, Sybil said, "You could wait," and Louise said, "I could wait."

Sybil smiled. "It would be wise, the more I think about it. My father refused my William's proposal at first. After some time, it seemed right, when early on, it didn't."

Louise nodded at this. Sybil had a good marriage. She was happy with her husband, and she hadn't been too hasty in her decision.

"Alix sent me a note this morning," she told Sybil. "I thought it would be full of disappointments since I wasn't interested in her brother. Instead, she told me I shouldn't let so many others guide me. I'm sure she's referring to Vicky and Alice, but mostly Vicky. She's the one who will be most upset when she finds out I want to delay marriage."

Sybil nodded. "She was married at seventeen—so young."

Both women mused over this.

"Alix was very sweet and diplomatic though," Louise said. "And if my dear sister-in-law and my best friend are in agreement, then I shall tell Mama that I'm not ready. It will be reason enough for Prince Albrecht and hopefully won't damage his Prussian pride."

Sybil covered her mouth to stifle a laugh. "I am sorry. I don't mean to make light of any of this."

But Louise smiled. "I feel relieved, more so than I expected. Since Mama wants me to remain in England, and I daresay, I'm not opposed to doing so, perhaps I won't marry."

Her shrug of nonchalance covered up the fact that Louise had, in fact, started to entertain the notion of marrying and having a family of her own. Three years ago, she would have pushed that desire away easily. But now . . . with four of her siblings married and having babies, Louise felt left out. Significantly so. But it wasn't something she was about to admit to anyone, except to herself.

CHAPTER 21

❧

"My thoughts have been a great deal with you my sweet Louise, and I have been wondering how things have gone on since I left, and hope they have not again been teasing you dear, like the last day I saw you when you looked quite worn and sad!! Pray don't let yourself be guided by so many!!! But better go straight about that kind of thing to your Mama. I am sure she would not then misunderstand you, and she surely would give you the best advice—don't ever believe that she would think first of herself in such a case as this!!! Those who tell you that, give you the very worst of advice, and don't either do any good by it but harm you! So pray Darling, follow my advice, and listen to a sister who, God knows, means well and loves you very much."

Letter from the Princess of Wales
to Princess Louise, December 14, 1868

APRIL 1869

LOUISE, AGE 21

The queen's fury could be felt throughout the palace. Vicky had written that Prince Albrecht had refused to consider Louise on account of the queen's insistence that he reside in England. So Mama had penned a quick reply that Louise was not interested in marrying at this time, to him or to anyone else.

The interchange of fierce letter writing had only one result. Louise was out of princes to consider marrying. Spinsterhood would be for her.

"Loosy," Mama's voice cut into her drifting thoughts as she sat in the library.

Louise rose to her feet, displacing her dog, Frisky, and curtseyed as her mother walked into the room.

The queen carried the well-worn *Almanach de Gotha*. She set it down on the side table, then settled on a sofa. "We are out of royal options for your spouse."

Louise stiffened. Yes, this was true, but to speak it so plainly sounded harsh.

"Therefore . . ." Mama waved at Louise to sit. "We might consider a commoner."

Disbelief vibrated through Louise as she sat. Frisky settled on her lap, and she absently stroked his soft fur. Was the queen saying . . . No. It couldn't happen. Royals didn't marry commoners.

"He would have to be independently wealthy," Mama said. "From a very respectable family. And . . ." She lifted her chin, her eyes focused right into Louise's soul. "You would have to approve of him too."

Louise's thoughts tumbled. "A . . . nonroyal?"

"A duke, maybe, or a marquess," Mama said. "Or the heir to such a title. Not any position lesser."

Louise was familiar with the peerage of England—the dukes and their heirs apparent. Maybe she didn't know each and every one, but now she planned to scour all the information she could about them.

"We will need assistance in this," Mama continued. "It won't do for the entire kingdom to know of our pursuit. I will employ trusted advisors."

The only one Louise completely trusted was General Grey, but while Sybil was still a close friend, Grey had recently been ousted from the innermost circle of the queen since he'd pressured her too much to return to public appearances.

"I cannot go into Society myself, as you know," the queen said. "And it's unseemly for you to do so as an unmarried woman without me. But I'll give permission for you to attend a few more events so that you can begin to meet eligible . . . candidates. You will come out of mourning so that you can be appropriately attired."

The information was almost too much to take in.

"Do you have certain noblemen in mind?" Louise ventured to ask.

"Gerald Wellesley and Earl Granville will be sending me recommendations," Mama said, "and I will pass them on to you. Since this is such a delicate matter, I don't want there to be a public fuss about it, or we'll suddenly have too many opinions and offers to wade through."

Louise couldn't argue with the queen's choice of advisors. Especially Earl Granville, who was related to most of nobility and knew the best and worst about everyone. That would all come in useful when sorting names.

Was this really going to happen? Instead of settling for spinsterhood, would she marry a member of the peerage? Someone whom she could relate to, speak to, and have much more in common with?

A smile tugged at her lips as Mama continued detailing her requirements and qualifications that would have to be met. Of course, Louise eagerly agreed to each and every one, because at the end of it, *she* would be able to choose the man.

Over the next few days, Louise was barely able to focus on any of her tasks. She continually made spelling errors in the queen's correspondence and had to start letters over. She sketched and sketched, forgoing the more laborious art projects she was in the middle of. She increased her walking about the grounds, not caring about the damp or the cold.

But as the weather warmed, the charm and novelty of finding a husband began to wear off. Matching Louise with a commoner had only complicated the process a great deal more.

Louise returned to her sculpting. The day she finished Mama's marble bust, Louise found the queen with her collection of dogs in the library.

"If you're not busy, Mama, I have something to show you."

Mama didn't ask any questions. She merely followed Louise to the studio, dogs trailing.

Louise had cleaned everything off the table in the center of the room so that the bust would be on full display. Her throat felt thick as Mama walked around the table, gazing at the bust from all angles.

The minutes were the longest of Louise's life.

When Mama turned, her hands were clasped together, her eyes teary. Louise could hardly take a breath.

"It's exquisite, darling Loosy," Mama said in a trembling voice. "We shall send it to the opening of the Royal Academy at Burlington House. Everyone should have the privilege of seeing your work."

Louise's eyes filled with tears, and she wasn't sure if she was laughing or crying or both. She hugged Mama, then ran to tell Leo, who was somewhere studying.

The May day arrived when Louise traveled with her family to Burlington House. It was surreal to stand before her creation and to have others admire and appreciate it.

Leo had insisted on coming, but he wasn't admiring the bust. No, he was more interested in observing the other patrons. "Maybe your future husband is here, right now," Leo whispered in Louise's ear.

She discreetly elbowed her brother in the ribs. Not too hard because bruising Leo could still lead to dire health troubles. Leo knew about the hunt for a husband among the commoners. It was Bertie who Louise dreaded finding out, though it would be Mama who would battle with the Prince of Wales. Maybe he'd be all right with it once he realized Louise had arrived at a dead end. After all, she was his favorite sister—he and Alix had even named their third child Louise Victoria Alexandra, Princess Royal, after Louise.

But her hopes about Bertie were soon dashed. He might not have been perfect in manner and morals, but his views were stalwart in tradition.

"We've invited the Marquess of Lansdowne to dine with us tonight," Mama said to Bertie as he paced the Windsor drawing room on an early July day. He'd just been informed of the queen's hunt for a nonroyal.

Bertie spun on his heels, his face a mottled red. "This is absurd. Do you not realize that? Louise is the daughter of the queen of England, and you would hand her off to some . . . harebrained, two-bit *commoner*?"

Louise sat fanning herself on this unusually muggy day. The heat might be unbearable, but at least the knot in her stomach was loosening. With Bertie knowing Mama's plans, soon everyone in the family would know. Her eldest brother was always the most vocal about his disapproval, and since he was the next in line to the throne, he considered his word as weight. Tonight, Louise would be meeting Henry Petty-Fitzmaurice, the fifth Marquess of Lansdowne, and she was extremely . . . curious.

"We've been over the *Almanach de Gotha* too many times to count," Mama said in an even tone. "There is simply no one who is eligible or favorable to Louise, and both must be satisfied. This is no fly-by-night decision, Bertie. I've been in counsel with my staff for months now, debating names and dissecting family trees."

Bertie cast a glance in Louise's direction. "I agree that *both* must be satisfied. But we cannot turn our backs on centuries of honor and tradition just because Louise is finicky."

This did get under her skin, and Louise could no longer be silent. "Would you have me leave Mama in the care of our twelve-year-old sister while I live in Denmark or Prussia—miserable for the rest of my life?" A year ago, Louise might not have taken her mother's side so staunchly, but now . . . She couldn't stomach the thought of Prince Frederick or Prince Albrecht. Yes, arranged marriages had always been made for the good of the country—but more often than not, those marriages were miserable.

Although Louise loved Alix dearly and would never want her sister-in-law replaced, her marriage to a man like Bertie had diminished her light and belittled her worth. Bertie's indiscretions had come to light in the past months, and even Louise could no longer deny them. His marriage was simply an institution now. Which was what he was trying to talk the queen into having Louise join.

In this, Mama was standing up for her. She was giving a priceless gift to Louise.

Louise rose to her feet and faced her brother. "There's no chance an heir to the throne will come through me anyway. Mama has three other daughters who have married royalty. Do you really think it matters if I, Louise, fourth daughter of the queen, marries a duke or a marquess?"

Bertie's eyes were hard, his face a mask of disbelief. "You are still a princess. Royalty doesn't marry below our sanctity of station. There's a reason we still follow the law King George III passed in 1772."

"George III made that law because his brothers had married objectionable women," the queen cut in. "Louise's husband will be perfectly suitable."

Louise loved her brother, dearly, but he was too quick to judge, too quick to take offense, and too quick to belittle when he should be looking inward at his own life.

"I cannot marry Frederick or Albrecht," Louise said in a quiet tone. "I would rather remain unmarried, and at Mama's side, for the rest of my life."

Bertie rubbed at his face, then turned toward the window again.

"You and your wife are welcome to join us for dinner, but it is not a command," the queen said, her voice equally quiet.

Bertie's shoulders stiffened. "I will not be in attendance tonight. Meet the marquess if you must, but you will see why taking this path is foolish."

Louise closed her eyes. Perhaps she wouldn't meet anyone she liked, and she'd still remain unmarried. But if this was her chance to try, then she'd take it.

She dressed carefully for dinner, adding myrtle buds to her dress. As she gazed into the mirror, Louise pinched her cheeks, bringing more color into them. She tried to imagine what Henry would see when he looked at her. He was currently the Lord of the Treasure in Gladstone's government. His position intrigued her, and wouldn't it be interesting to talk politics with her husband?

When Louise walked into the drawing room, Leo introduced her to Henry. Louise had heard his looks took after his French mother, and she supposed they did. Henry had dark hair, and his manner was quite French. He stepped forward and greeted her with a kiss to the hand. His words were smooth and flattering, and when the queen entered, he fussed over her quite profusely.

During the meal, Louise asked him about his work for Gladstone, and she was pleased that he was most forthcoming. He didn't hold back his opinions even though she was a woman and the queen was present.

When he took his leave, Mama waited for her pronouncement. How could one really determine much after a single dinner? Regardless, Louise joined Mama in her bedchamber before her nightly ritual.

"What do you think, Loosy?" Mama said as Skerrett combed out her hair.

"I don't mind him," Louise said. "He's intelligent, quick, and fairly handsome. He also looked me in the eye."

Mama nodded, as if these were very important attributes indeed. To Louise, they were.

"He meets my stipulations of coming from a fine family, having a fortune, and working in a fine position," Mama said. "Therefore, we shall inquire if he'd like to join us for another dinner. Then you can get to know him better."

"All right." Louise bent to kiss her mother's cheek. On the way back to her bedroom, she thought of Henry. . . . It was a noble name. A fine name for a fine man.

But whatever hope Louise had built up in her mind about Henry, it quickly bled out the next day when Sybil visited. She clapped her hand over her mouth when she learned who Louise's dinner partner had been.

"You should have told me this was happening," Sybil said. "Henry Petty-Fitzmaurice is engaged to be married."

Louise nearly knocked over the chess pieces they were playing a game with. "*Engaged?* But why would he accept the invitation to dine then?"

Sybil straightened her shoulders. "How discreet has Granville been in introducing these men to the queen? Perhaps Henry didn't know he was being vetted."

Louise scoffed. "Surely he did." Embarrassment collected in her chest. "Do you think he didn't? It would be a relief if he didn't know because then I haven't exposed myself."

Sybil patted Louise's hand. "It wasn't of your doing, but those who the queen has put her trust in."

They both knew that Sybil hoped her father would be reinstated to the inner circles.

Then this type of grievous error wouldn't have been made.

"What shall I tell Mama?" Louise said under her breath. "She will not be happy."

"I'll come with you," Sybil said. "Unless you think it will make it worse."

"That is the perfect plan," Louise said. "Mama can verify with you and not think I'm seeking out gossip."

Louise took Sybil with her to the queen's audience chamber, and once there was a break, they told her about Henry's engagement.

"How could this happen?" Mama said at once. "I've been atrociously misled. I must see Granville at once. And Louise? We must write directly to the lord chancellor. I don't want any of King George III's law to interfere with your choice of a spouse."

CHAPTER 22

"I can quite understand your wish that we should not be absent from England too long, but you must not take too gloomy a view of matters at home. If dear Mama will only open Parliament and say just a few words, that will be a great point gained. . . . When at Berlin, I shall keep my eyes open—that at least I can promise you—and I have no doubt all will end well, and that you will find a good husband, as P.A. [Prince Albert of Prussia] is not absolutely the only one in existence. . . . I suppose you will remain at Osborne till February. I must say I pity you, as it must be very dull there."

LETTER FROM THE PRINCE OF WALES
TO PRINCESS LOUISE, COPENHAGEN, JANUARY 2, 1869

AUGUST 1869
LOUISE, AGE 21

Would she have to live in Scotland once the dukedom passes to him?" the queen mused during an afternoon that had become much too long, in Louise's opinion, as they sat in the library at Osborne during a warm day in August.

Granville stopped his pacing in front of the cold hearth. "The Scottish ancestral home will surely stay in the family, but Louise could choose to live with her husband anywhere in England."

Louise had lost count of the names the queen had gone through in her new book about the peerage. She idly pet Frisky, who had curled up next to her side and was now half-asleep. Mama was finding names and connections that Louise had never known existed in *Burke's Guide to the Peerage and Baronetage*. And poor Granville—yes, Louise had come to think of him as "poor Granville"—had to make discreet inquiries into the selected peerage.

Currently, standing above the rest was John Douglas Sutherland Campbell, who held the courtesy title of Marquess of Lorne and was heir to the eighth Duke of Argyll. Louise already knew John—at least she had as a child. He'd been in the mix of children who'd come to play with her brothers. She remembered his blond hair, blue eyes, and habit of stating his opinions—which were at least intelligent. He'd been knowledgeable about politics and wasn't afraid to express his opinion to any of her siblings. He'd played games with her and her brothers at Windsor before the children's ball that never happened for her thirteenth birthday. Grandmama had died soon after. What was he like as a man though? She'd seen him only briefly in March when she and the queen had visited his mother, the Duchess of Argyll, in her London home in Kensington.

At his mother's, John Campbell had been attentive enough, Louise supposed, and had even showed her some of his brother's artwork. But they'd only talked for a handful of minutes. He was an intellectual—a published author of political articles, as well as a member of the House of Commons. She'd read a couple of his speeches in the *Times*. He likely outpaced her in political knowledge and might even find her dull. A man like him wasn't pining for a marriage to elevate his station in his country of Scotland. He already had status and position by birth.

So Louise wasn't allowing any intrigue or hope to overtake her yet. She was only twenty-one, and she wasn't going to marry the first member of the peerage who wasn't engaged. She was going to be picky, very picky. She wasn't telling Mama that, but now that she had quite a few more options in her choice of a husband, Louise was determined to choose one who'd truly fit her personality and match her interests.

"Lord Lorne will understand protocol and tradition," Mama mused. "As the next chief of the Clan Campbell, he'll be well trained and educated. Besides, his grandmother was the dear Duchess of Sutherland."

"Harriet?" Louise said. She knew this, but now recognized the connections between the marquess and Mama. Louise remembered the Duchess of Sutherland as an older, beautiful woman. She'd known the queen as an infant and had been the queen's Mistress of the Robes at the time of her wedding to Papa. She'd even been in attendance with Mama the day Papa had died. So the young marquess came from a solid and respectable family.

"I remember the first time I met Lord Lorne as a boy," the queen said. "Have I told you the story, Granville?"

He dipped his chin. "I don't believe you have."

Louise hadn't heard it either.

"I met him at Inveraray Castle, which is the Argyll seat in Scotland," she said, her gaze on Louise.

Louise nodded for her mother to continue.

"He was about two, I'm guessing—before you were born, Louise," Mama said. "He was a plump baby, and I'll never forget his strawberry hair and delicate features. He was so merry and sweet that I scooped him up and kissed him." Mama smiled at the memory, and Louise found herself smiling too. "I am sure I surprised his parents, but I went with my impulse."

Granville chuckled. "Your first impression of Lord Lorne must have been right. He comes from a solid family, and they are firmly situated in their duchy. I've never heard ill gossip of Lord Lorne, but I will put out my questions regardless to discover the man he has become."

The queen folded her hands. "Make all haste to discover if Lord Lorne is a man worth issuing an invitation to dinner."

Granville bowed low to the queen. "I will devote all my hours to it. I am related to him on both my Sutherland and Argyll sides."

After Granville left the room, Louise caught herself wondering about John. He was a few years older than she, which made her wonder if he already had a woman in mind to marry. His rank was confining, like hers, and likely his family would be looking for their ducal heir to marry someone of equal rank. A marriage to Louise would put him subservient to her.

"What if Lord Lorne is set on his path and doesn't want to marry a princess who will always outrank him?" Louise said, mostly to herself.

Her mother's eyes snapped. "Any man would be happy to marry a princess, even if he is outranked. It would be a privilege, an honor, and the best way a subject could ever serve the Crown. If the men we are investigating have any fealty, they will be scrambling to get into your good graces."

But Louise didn't want that in her marriage. She understood protocol, but in the end, she wanted a husband who would be an equal to her. In their likes, dislikes, and passions. Any man who agreed to marry her would become part of a complicated system in which his wife would always outrank him, and his mother-in-law would be able to command him at will.

Louise eyed Mama. She'd seen the queen at her worst, her best, her happiest, her saddest—but whatever happened, she was a champion for her children's welfare.

"If the report from Granville comes back favorably," Louise said, "I'm willing to consider him."

Louise went to bed that night, thinking of John.

The following morning when Louise began helping with the queen's correspondence, she discovered that Mama had already sent an invitation to the Duke and Duchess of Argyll to visit at Osborne.

"They will tell their son," Louise said, worry in her tone, "and it will appear as if I'm chasing after him when I don't even know him."

Mama pressed her lips together and glanced over at Granville.

"We'll ask the Argylls to not mention this to their son," Granville suggested.

"There is no point to inviting them for a visit if we can't be open and frank." The queen's brow lowered. "Is that what you want, Louise? To keep hedging and dragging your feet?"

"No." Louise felt embarrassment climb her throat. What if the Argylls were *not* interested in the match, despite Mama's claim that every man in the kingdom should be clamoring?

Louise didn't care to learn the information secondhand, so she told her mother that she wanted to be part of the visit between the Argylls and the queen.

When the Argylls—or simply "the Duke" and "the Duchess," as Louise called them—arrived at Osborne, Louise greeted the Duchess with a kiss on the cheek, then she smiled at the Duke.

"It is an honor to meet you, Your Royal Highness." The Duke took her hand.

He was a wiry man, but his personality was much larger than his size. He was well respected in politics and considered an avid and thoughtful speaker in the House of Lords. In contrast, his wife was quiet and gentile. She was a gracious woman, letting her husband steer the conversation, although she seemed older than her forty-something years. But with having birthed twelve children, it was no wonder.

Over tea in the drawing room, Louise listened as the Duke skated from one subject to another. He had a wide variety of interests—from yachting to bird-watching—all of which fascinated Louise.

"Have you ever been fly-fishing, Princess Louise?" the Duke asked.

Louise sensed the queen's surprise at the question.

"I have not," she said. "But it seems such a lovely way to pass an afternoon that I should like to try it sometime."

The Duke smiled broadly. "We have fine rivers at Argyllshire that you are welcome to visit. I'll be your personal guide."

Louise smiled back. "I should like that very much."

The Duke slapped his knee. "It's settled then. At your earliest convenience, Your Royal Highness."

The afternoon was very pleasant indeed, but it came time for Louise to excuse herself so Mama could frankly speak to them about their son. Louise politely and cheerfully took her leave, thinking to herself that if their son had grown into a man as witty and friendly as his father, she'd accept the match. She paused outside the door, wanting to hear a little of the conversation between Mama and the Argylls.

Within moments, Louise's smile completely faded, and instead of soaring, her heart plunged.

The Duke's voice was loud and clear, and surely carried through all of Osborne, as he said, "John has a great many responsibilities as it is. Taking a wife who is royal will mean that he'll be subservient to his own duties when he has obligations to fill in Scotland."

This was true, of course.

"Then there is the matter of his position as a Liberal member of Parliament representing the constituency of Argyllshire. What happens when his duty there conflicts with attending royal events?"

"He will attend only necessary events," the queen said in a steady voice—a voice that Louise had heard often when she was in discussions with her advisors and she didn't agree with what they were saying.

"Is there no other member of the peerage more suited to take on such a responsibility?" the Duke pressed.

Louise's face heated up. The man was really against this . . . Was it so terrible to marry her, a princess?

"As my heir, John has his future already established," the Duke continued without a word of interruption from the queen or from his wife, for that matter. "A wife will come into the picture eventually. Elizabeth has reminded me more than once that he's plenty in age to choose one, but with your daughter, ma'am—do you not see the complications?"

Louise took a half step closer to the door.

"We are aware royalty comes with complications, I can assure you, sir," the queen said. "My daughter and I have considered several names, and your son meets all the conditions we are seeking. If your son's heart and hand are free, do you think that—above and beyond all the complications and changes—he might consider Louise for a wife?"

Heart pounding so hard, Louise was afraid she'd miss the Duke's reply. It came much quieter than his previous conversation. "Have you considered other men of the peer such as Lord Ailsa or Lord Rosebery?"

"We have gone through the peerage book multiple times. My daughter and I have considered several names, and your son meets all the conditions we are seeking." Now the queen's voice rose. "Quite frankly, your son is the most well suited for this match."

Another space of silence.

"In addition, I have been informed that you don't smoke or drink but run a conservative household. Louise has been raised conservatively as well." Next, the queen pressed the Duchess. "Do you see any possibility, Lady Elizabeth?"

A voice murmured—Elizabeth's—but Louise couldn't make it out.

"Elizabeth is right," the Duke said. "I've voiced my concerns, but the decision is ultimately up to our son. Do I have your permission to speak to him about it?"

Louise brought a hand to her chest. This was happening . . . She closed her eyes, wondering what John Campbell might think of this entire situation. Would he be shocked? Surprised? Put off? Interested?

She opened her eyes as the queen said, "I shall pen a formal permission to discuss this with your son."

Lady Elizabeth's soft tone sounded again.

"I agree," the queen said. "If your son is amenable, then he and Louise need to meet. If they like each other, then things can move forward. If they don't, then that will be that. He can visit Balmoral when we are there this autumn."

It was August now, so autumn was around the corner. And it was time for Louise to retreat to her room—to think all of this over. Not that thinking about it would settle her nerves any. Was she really going to be married? And would John Campbell be the man for her?

The next several days were a blur. Louise knew she was annoying everyone. She baked everything and anything in the kitchen, sometimes using ingredients set aside for other things. She also wrote letters to Leo, Affie, Arthur, and Helena. She didn't write to Bertie, Alice, or Vicky. She knew what their replies would be already. But Sybil would sympathize. She always did.

Days later, a letter arrived from the Duke of Argyll at last, and Louise waited as the queen opened it and read the words. Louise tried to decipher the response by watching Mama's expression, but like the skilled monarch she was, she didn't give anything away. Finally, she set down the letter.

"John Campbell says he feels 'unworthy' of the honor, but he's willing to meet you at Balmoral and see how the two of you get along."

Louise couldn't quite believe what she was hearing. "Is that all? What else?" Surely there was more.

A small wrinkle had appeared at the queen's brow. "The Duke adds that he'd like to see this matter settled soon so his son is not kept in suspense."

"In suspense?" Louise echoed. "How soon is 'soon'?"

Mama pursed her lips. "I don't know. Weddings should never be rushed though."

Helena would agree. Louise had read her sister's letter that morning, urging her to take her time. She absently touched the letter she'd kept in her pocket.

"What's that letter?" Mama asked.

"Helena wrote me," Louise said, "advising me about the Campbells."

Mama lifted her hand. "Well, let's see it."

Louise had no choice but to hand over her letter to Mama. She read through it slowly, her brows arched as she read a few sentences aloud: "You are still young, dear sister. Twenty-one is not so great an age when one has to choose a husband. Especially when you have the choice of the peerage, you'll want to meet as many of them as you can to properly decide. Besides, once you are married, who will attend Mama? Beatrice is still too young to take over."

The queen paused, her gaze lifting to study Louise. "Do you agree with what Helena says in her letter? Is that why you are so subdued about the note from the Duke of Argyll?"

Louise sighed. "I do not know, Mama. One moment, I'm excited about the prospect of finally settling on a husband. The next, I feel that this is all happening so fast. If the Duke wants things settled soon with his son, I feel as though I'm starting out a relationship based on everyone else's timeline. And this is all before I even know the man!"

The queen didn't brush off Louise's worries, even though she hadn't articulated them properly, most likely because she didn't exactly understand them herself. She did want to marry, didn't she? Was it as Helena said? Merely too soon? Why rush? Affie wasn't married yet, and he was four years older than Louise.

"We need a good excuse to tell the Duke that you are no longer interested in his son," the queen said in an even tone. "It will be best if we use your age as the reason, but then you'll have to go a year or more without entertaining any more suitors or else they will find out."

Louise threaded her fingers together. "I don't want to offend them, but I also don't want to stop the investigations we already have going on. In case . . ." She didn't need to finish that sentence.

But the queen was waiting.

"We'll go ahead with the November meeting," Louise said with some reluctance, "but let the Duke know that you want me to be older, and in the meantime, I am still considering others."

Mama gave a brisk nod. "I will then have to tell the Duke that his son is free to marry should he find someone else."

Louise's heart was heavy, but she needed to be fair to John and not have him count on something that might never happen. She would have to find the courage to turn him away when he came to Balmoral.

CHAPTER 23

❦

"Bertie and Alix have been evidently and most successfully worked on by the Hessian relations. I would advise you not to begin the subject again to them unless they do to you, and then just tell them what you think. I do not think there will be any row at all. I really do not see what on earth there is to ferret out. You spoke of dear Mama herself—if she asks you again you have but to tell her what you wish and what you think. I do not believe she can fancy anything so unjust or absurd as that we *should wish to try and* make *you marry anyone you do not like for* wishes *of our own."*

LETTER FROM THE CROWN PRINCESS OF PRUSSIA
TO PRINCESS LOUISE, BERLIN, JANUARY 9, 1869

OCTOBER 1869
LOUISE, AGE 21

Are you nervous about tomorrow?" Bea asked as she rested her chin on her hand, her gaze focused on Louise. At age twelve, her blond curls had mellowed to a darker color, though she still had a cherub face that made her look younger.

Frisky startled awake and yipped, and Louise tried not to flinch. She'd finally distracted herself by reading the first volume of *Little Women,* a novel approved by Mama, in order to stop thinking about the Argylls' impending visit to Balmoral. Time had passed much too fast, and tomorrow, John Campbell would arrive. The Duke had visited the second week of October for a council meeting, and he'd stayed overnight at Balmoral. Louise had felt awkward around him at first, but then their conversation became more natural as they talked about his wife and children. The Duke had presented her with a cross necklace, which Louise found very charming. She didn't know if she'd ever wear it though—not if she wasn't directly connected to the family.

At the very least, the Duke was an entertaining man. He'd told Louise stories that she laughed at, and the bright eyes of the man who might become her father-in-law didn't miss much. "I've been told that you're an excellent sculptress," the Duke had said.

Talking about her art had put Louise completely at ease, but she didn't know if she felt better or worse after he left. The queen had been the one to broach the topic of Louise and John and then later said that Louise wasn't going to marry anytime soon. So what did the Duke think of *her*?

Now she looked at her sister. With all the talk and speculation in the house, Bea had decided that Louise was her favorite subject.

"I'm not nervous," Louise said, petting Frisky so he'd settle back down. "Lord Lorne knows that I want to wait to marry. Our meeting will be cordial, that's all. Nothing to be worked up about." She didn't trust Beatrice to keep anything in confidence, both because of her age and the fact that she was Mama's pet daughter. As the baby of the family, Bea had always been coddled. It might be extra difficult for her to take over as Mama's personal secretary when Louise did marry. Another reason to put off a wedding.

Louise might have been hesitant and tense to follow in Helena's footsteps, but as the months had passed, Louise had grown comfortable in her role. She and Bertie worked well together for the most part when Bertie needed an ally, and Alice and Vicky were distant enough that whatever thing Louise disagreed with them on didn't come to pass anyway. Louise had her own secure and familiar existence. Marriage would change all that she knew and most of what she was.

"Are you going to wear one of your creations?" Bea prodded.

Louise set down her book with a sigh. Focusing was out of the question at this point. She'd head to her studio and work on the clay model she was creating to make a bust of Leo. Or perhaps she'd take a walk and sketch somewhere else, just for the solace. "My creations? Do you mean will I dress normally?" Louise typically might laugh at the inquiry, but she was having a hard time relaxing or enjoying anything.

"Normal for you," Bea said. "I think you like the newspapers to write about you, so you always come up with something different than what's fashionable."

Louise looked down at her current dress with its scalloped overlay and piped hem. When she looked up at her little sister, she said, "Did you ever consider that maybe women are following after *my* fashion and not the other way around?"

Bea wrinkled her nose.

"You're a minx," Louise said with a laugh. "One day, you'll appreciate your older sister's fashion sense."

Bea lifted a shoulder as if she didn't care, but Louise knew that she'd be gleaning every bit of information she could when John arrived.

The following morning, Louise paced the back gardens, walking among the trimmed hedges, not caring that the air was frosty. She smiled to herself as her skirt swished in the silence. She'd given up on bell skirts and wore the style where the volume was directed toward the back of the skirt. She'd also added white lace to the collar and cuffs.

When she heard the sound of the arriving carriage, she hurried into the house, only to be met by Leo, who must have heard the carriage too.

Her brother smiled, his brows lifted in question, but Louise couldn't meet his gaze. "You're nervous," he said as they both walked to the drawing room.

"Not for the reasons you think," she said with an unexpected edge in her voice.

Leo's frown was quick. He was limping again. His limp was always more pronounced in cold Scotland. "He's a decent chap, you know."

"Don't make me feel worse."

"Maybe you'll change your mind?"

"Hush."

He chuckled. They arrived in the drawing room as the front door was answered by the butler. Louise walked to the hearth and gazed into the fire as it crackled. Her heart felt like it had been drawn and quartered. She'd get the greetings over, and then she'd be able to breathe easy.

Why was she surprised when John walked in wearing a kilt? They were now in Scotland, after all. He was taller than she remembered, but maybe that was because the drawing room was smaller than the other rooms in the castle. His smile was quick and his blue eyes sharp, but friendly, reminding her of the Duke's.

His jacket was tailored to his shoulders, the heather-gray color complementing his kilt. John looked like he'd walked straight off the Scottish Highlands—which of course he had.

"Prince Leopold," John said first. "I hope you've been well."

"Quite well," Leo said. "Call me Leo—except when my mother is around. And you remember my sister Louise."

John stepped forward and took her hand. "We saw each other not too long ago." He dipped his head. "Your Royal Highness."

Did he consider nine months "not too long ago"? Instead of the cheerful and casual chatter she'd prepared, something happened to her throat, and she went almost mute. His scent of sage and cedar had reached her. It was nice, subtle. She wondered if he smoked like Prince Christian. Perhaps not—or he would smell like it, right? She pushed the random thoughts away. "Lord Lorne, nice to see you again," she managed to say.

"Call me John, the both of you." His voice was a higher pitch than most men, nearly a nasal quality, but it didn't bother Louise. "Or I answer to Lorne as well. Those stuffy titles are so tiresome. Not *your* titles, of course."

Leo chuckled. "I quite agree, but I am not always able to enforce—"

"Enforce what?" the queen asked, coming into the room with Beatrice. Her gaze landed on Lord Lorne. "Welcome to Balmoral, Lord Lorne."

Everyone turned and bowed or curtseyed to the queen.

Mama in her usual black stood out among everyone in their various outfits of color, yet the somber black also made her look more regal.

"Now, Leo, what are you trying to enforce?"

Louise hid a smile, although her heart was racing something fierce.

"Lord Lorne and I were discussing the formality of titles and whether to use them among friends."

The queen settled on one of the chairs, and Beatrice on another. Looty, who'd trailed in behind, jumped up onto Mama's lap. As she stroked the dog's fur, she said, "Titles are a show of respect and keep everyone and everything in proper perspective."

Louise winced and glanced at John—Lord Lorne—but he only smiled good naturedly. His smile was nice, she decided. Genuine, at least.

"I certainly agree, Your Majesty." John gave the quickest glance at Leo as if sharing some inner dialogue.

Mama didn't shy away from examining the man from head to toe. "Have a seat, Lord Lorne, and tell us the news of your parents. I am fond of them, and I held great esteem for your grandmother the Duchess of Sutherland, who was my Mistress of the Robes."

John dipped his chin and took a seat after he was assured that Louise was seated first. As John spoke, he directed more than one question to Louise, and much to her frustration, she only came up with short answers. Answers that should have been intelligent and charming ended up being singular and dull.

The longer the visit progressed, the more Louise wanted to be out of the room—free from the gazes upon her and the speculation in everyone else's minds. Surely, they were all thinking the same things—was Louise interested in Lord Lorne, and did John find anything compelling about Louise? She wouldn't blame him if he didn't—she could barely string a handful of words together.

When John talked of fly-fishing with his father, Leo jumped in, expressing great interest. They talked about planning an excursion, and

Louise wanted to say she'd love to join too, but she remained mute. The conversation progressed to hunting—something Louise would never participate in—and sailing. She felt queasy thinking about it.

She was more interested when John told Leo about his dogs at his Scotland estate, Inveraray, in Argyll County. Louise should have been able to join in *that* conversation at least, but somehow, she remained wordless.

Although Louise knew the man was a Liberal, she also knew that politics wouldn't be discussed around the queen. Yet Louise found herself intensely curious about John's viewpoints. Was he following his father's allegiance, or was John a man of independent thinking?

Leo was likely hoping she'd show some positive sign toward John, but she only wanted the visit to be over so she could retreat from everyone.

The evening progressed, and after dinner, everyone retired for the night.

Louise felt deflated. Dinner hadn't been much better on her part. Her nerves had intercepted any light or entertaining conversation she might have engaged in.

Finally in her bedroom, she went over the afternoon and evening in her mind. She couldn't pick out one redeeming moment. From her window she saw John depart in his carriage. So . . . he wasn't staying the night after all? Was it because . . .

A tap at her bedroom door cut into her thoughts. It was well after dark, and she wasn't sure who was up or what they wanted.

She opened the door to find Leo, wearing his night robe. Arms folded, he leaned against her doorframe. "Tell me what happened. Was he so awful?"

Louise puffed out a breath, then folded her own arms. "He left. Why?"

He motioned for her to come out into the hallway. She stepped out, and they both leaned against the wall.

"At great cost to his own pride," Leo began in a low voice, "John Campbell asked me if you have another man in mind for your future."

"Of course I don't," she said. "Oh, I don't know. Why couldn't I speak *normally* to him? Why did everyone have to be there to witness it all?"

They both knew why everyone was there. Leaving Louise alone with a man wouldn't be acceptable, not until they were engaged.

"If it had just been me, or one of our other siblings, would you have been more conversational?"

Louise bit her lip. "I don't know. What did you tell him?"

He shrugged. "I told him the truth."

She didn't know if that was good news or bad news. Nudging him, she said, "Which was . . . ?"

"That you aren't ready to marry, but you are staying open minded," Leo said. "And I might have said that others are on their way to visit with you as well."

She closed her eyes. It was true, but she didn't want John to think he was part of some meat market and that Louise was examining all the available cuts before making a purchase. "What was his reaction?"

"He didn't seem too surprised or put off, now that I think of it," Leo mused. "In fact, he asked if you were bending to pressure from the queen. Or the opposite—rebelling against her pressure."

Louise snapped her gaze to her brother's profile, dim in the corridor with the lowered gaslights. "Is that what everyone thinks? That I'm at odds with Mama so I'm refusing the men she suggests?"

Leo leaned on one shoulder so that he was facing her. "All of us must enter arranged marriages that will benefit the family as a whole. It's the nature of being born into royalty. John Campbell knows and understands that. But, like you, he wants more out of an arranged marriage."

Her mouth went dry. "Such as a great love story?"

Leo gave a half smile. "An affinity, I suppose. A friendship. An attraction? These are my words, of course . . ."

She peered at her brother. He was quite wise for a man younger than she. "Is Mama quite upset?"

His brows raised. "You must choose the husband who is good for *you*, Loosy, not Mama."

"I know."

They both knew, but like Leo had mentioned, a balance needed to be achieved.

"I don't want to formally reject him, but I also want to know what he thinks of *me*. With all other issues aside."

Her brother smiled at this.

"Why are you smiling?"

His smile widened. "I don't think you have to worry so much on that account. Yes, any living, breathing man would find you beautiful—because you are. And any living, breathing man would be flattered to be chosen by a princess. But John knows you beyond this rather dismal meeting we all had to endure."

Louise wrinkled her nose. "It wasn't that bad."

Leo scoffed, then chuckled. "It was quite awful, but I have no doubt that Lord Lorne will wholly forgive you if given a chance."

She let the words sink in. If she believed Leo, and she had no reason not to, then John wasn't offended or disgusted or annoyed . . . maybe just frustrated? Confused? Well, she was confused herself. A man as charismatic as Lord Lorne would not hang around forever, waiting for her to make up her mind.

"Loo Loo," Leo said, using her childhood nickname and grasping her hand, "we all want your happiness, no matter what."

She smiled at this, but tears threatened anyway. What and who would bring her the happiness Leo referred to?

CHAPTER 24

"I am glad to hear that you have a proper studio now in which I hope to see a whole collection of your works of art when I return. I must then give you a sitting for a bust for the last was unsuccessful. . . . P.S. No signs of a husband yet???"

LETTER FROM PRINCE ALFRED
TO PRINCESS LOUISE, *HMS SALAMIS*, GULF OF CHILE, OCTOBER 1, 1869

MARCH 1870
LOUISE, AGE 22

Helena flipped another page. "What about Lord Cowper?"

"He's out of the question," the queen said.

Before Louise could ask, Helena turned to look at Mama, who was sitting near the window, sketching something in a notebook. The March evening was descending fast, and the winds had started, screeching their way around Windsor Castle.

"What's wrong with Lord Cowper?" Helena's hand rested on her pregnant belly. She was due in two months.

"Lord Palmerstone is his step-grandfather, and I'll not have that man related to me." The queen didn't even look up from her sketchbook as she added, "Besides, he's thirty-four, and he's been about London too much."

"My husband was thirty-five when we married," Helena said hotly, "and I was younger than Louise is now."

"Your husband is a prince." The queen paused. "Even Louise will agree that Cowper isn't suitable."

Although Helena seemed quite put out by the debate, Louise was used to this sort of discussion. "I have no opinion since I've never met Lord Cowper."

At this, the queen looked up. "You haven't?"

Louise wanted to laugh and say, *How could I? You've never let me go to any balls or parties unless they were sponsored by my brother. And even then, I couldn't dance with a commoner.*

"You must meet him, then," Helena said. "He will be at Marlborough House tomorrow night for a dinner."

The queen folded her hands. "Well, if Louise wants to go, she has my permission."

Louise wasn't sure if she should allow herself to feel elated about this so soon. She'd had her hopes up more than once, too many times to count now, and this might be one more letdown.

But perhaps this meeting would let her get over some of her guilt for what happened with Lord Lorne—how his family had been in discussions with Mama, at Louise's request, and then nothing came of it. Complicating matters was the fact that the Duchess of Argyll had suffered a stroke soon after John's visit to Balmoral. Surely the last thing on his mind was finding a wife.

Louise had been too self-conscious to go with Mama and Beatrice to visit the recovering Duchess. She didn't want to run into John by happenstance. Not after the questions he'd asked Leo about her.

The dinner at Marlborough House was about to begin by the time Louise arrived with Helena and her husband, Christian. They waited near the carriage before entering, while Christian smoked a cigarette. Louise had grown quite used to the pungent tobacco scent that always lingered about him, and most grand houses had smoking rooms now. Perhaps one day, the queen would acquiesce. For now, Helena told her husband to find a room with a chimney whenever they visited Mama.

Louise told herself not to scan the room for any of the men she'd met with over the previous year but, instead, keep her focus on the ladies who stopped Helena for chatter.

"Princess Louise, I'd like you to meet Lord Cowper," Christian said.

Louise lifted her gaze then. Lord Cowper wasn't as tall as Lord Lorne, but he had solid looks. He also wasn't talkative or quick-witted like Lord Lorne. She could appreciate quiet shyness, though. Lord Cowper was a far cry from a Scotsman straight from the Highlands, since he was quite thin—but he had an . . . artistic look.

Perhaps he *was* artistic?

Louise also had no trouble speaking to him, which she considered a good sign. "Tell me of your favorite sculptures." She hoped appreciation for good art was something they might have in common. She was right.

In a mellow tone, Lord Cowper said, "It used to be Boehm, although he was quickly replaced when I visited the sculpture of Her Majesty at the Royal Academy at Burlington House. Which you, apparently, had sculpted. It was truly a masterpiece, Your Royal Highness."

Louise laughed. There was no way he preferred her work over Boehm's.

"One would have to be blind and deaf to not know that Your Royal Highness is a master sculptress," Lord Cowper continued.

Louise grinned. Compliments as of late went straight to her head. Maybe Lord Lorne should have paid her a few. Then they would've had a decent conversation.

"Tell me, then, who your favorite painters are," Louise said. "And please don't test out more of your flattery on me. You've done that enough."

Lord Cowper gave a soft chuckle. His lashes were unusually long, giving his face a feminine appeal. No matter.

"It's no flattery, I assure you. If a complete stranger had asked me the same question, I'd have given the same answer."

Louise had to lean slightly forward in order to catch all of the gentleman's words above the general thronging noise. He was so soft spoken. It was a nice change, she decided, from the posturing and loud opinions she was used to from her brothers.

"Since you insist, I must say I've been entranced with Edmund Niemann as of late."

"Ah, yes," Louise said. Niemann was well known and respected for his landscapes in oil. "May I compliment you on your good taste?"

His smile had a dimple to go with it. "You may."

They both laughed.

The rest of the evening was quite a blur, and the first thing the next morning, Louise reported to Mama that she had found Lord Cowper quite agreeable.

Mama sent Skerrett away immediately, then faced Louise square on. "We will invite him to dinner then. Does tonight work for you?"

Louise's heart might not have plucked in excitement, but she felt a pleasant warmth spread through her. "Tonight will be excellent."

Dinner with Lord Cowper, Helena and Christian, and Beatrice and Leopold turned out to be a delicate affair. Louise couldn't put her finger on what was not quite right. Everyone was cordial, and Lord Cowper shared some humorous stories, drawing smiles and chuckles. This was a nice change since Mama, who more often than not ate in private, had discouraged lightheartedness for so many years. When Louise asked him what his pastimes were, he only mentioned that he enjoyed reading and studying art. Not hunting, fishing, or sailing for this peer of the realm.

"Lord Cowper is so thin," Mama murmured the following morning in the middle of Louise taking correspondence. "Delicate looking. Don't you think, Loosy? Reminds me a bit of Leo. Did he have a childhood disease?"

"How is that something I can ask when I've barely met the man?" Louise said in a stiff tone. Mama was as generous with her criticisms as she was with her compliments. Yes, Louise had noticed the same thing about Lord Cowper, but surely he had the stamina of any man of her acquaintance.

"I'll have Granville discreetly inquire," Mama mused.

It was no use arguing with her. Health was very important to the queen.

"In the meantime, Loosy," Mama said, her focus direct now, "we cannot make Lord Lorne think he has a chance if you are to choose Lord Cowper. It's not fair that he be kept waiting."

"I thought we told him not to wait," Louise said.

"We told him not to wait upon you but didn't tell him that there was no chance."

Louise's stomach felt hollow. She wasn't rethinking her decision about John Campbell, but the timing felt horrible. His mother was still recovering from her stroke. Yet it wasn't fair to him if she was this keen on Lord Cowper. The men were quite opposite of each other, and it was easy for her to imagine a life with Lord Cowper. They'd visit museums together in the day and discuss literature at night. Their conversations would be deeply thoughtful and intelligent. If Mama had overcome her earlier prejudice, that was a good sign indeed.

"Then write to the Duke," Louise said at last. "It must be done."

The queen sent the letter to the Duke, and in a few days' time, his most cordial reply came. Mama was satisfied with it, and Louise was as well. All talk of marriage between the two of them was officially dead. Louise had seen Lord Cowper twice more, both at the invitation of the queen, and each time, Louise felt more convinced that he would be an excellent match for her. She wasn't ready to broach the subject yet or have the queen reach out to his parents. No, Louise wanted their relationship to develop naturally and grow into a mutual affection.

"Your Royal Highness," Lady Clifden said, after knocking on Louise's studio door. Lady Clifden was one of the queen's ladies-in-waiting. "Her Majesty would like to see you immediately in the queen's drawing room."

Louise had started a painting of the grounds of Balmoral, using previous sketches as her guide. She set down her brush, then she removed the smock she wore over her dress. "I'm on my way."

Her pulse fluttered as she hurried to the drawing room. She'd spent all morning with her mother working on correspondence and, from time to time, discussing how to proceed with Lord Cowper. Louise wouldn't deny that she was eagerly looking forward to the next steps.

Mama was holding a letter when Louise entered. "We need a new plan, Loosy. Granville has informed me that further inquiries into Lord Cowper reveal that he's been courting Lady Katie Compton, and they are about to become engaged."

Louise heard her mother's words but couldn't quite believe them. If that was the case, then why had Lord Cowper been so friendly to Louise? Why had he accepted all the invitations and spent so much time flattering her? More than that though, Louise had thought he liked her.

She smoothed her hands along her upper skirt, noting that her fingers were trembling. "Again?" Her voice came out as a choked whisper. "How could no one know this?" She thought of Helena's encouragement and Lord Granville's first letters of approval.

The frown lines between the queen's brows only deepened. "We were too hasty in our eagerness about Lord Cowper. We should have had Granville conduct his investigation before we invested in any conversation with the man."

Louise nodded. She should have been much more careful with her expectations and hopes. When Helena had suggested Lord Cowper, she shouldn't have met him until she knew more about him.

"That's that," Mama declared as if Louise wasn't feeling a painful twist in her heart. The queen opened the *Peerage* book and began to leaf through it again. "We haven't gone through all of the names yet, and surely there are men better and less attached than Lord Cowper. Make a list, Louise. I want Granville to investigate all who we come up with."

Louise's heart felt like lead, and her thoughts went numb.

"Henry Strutt," the queen said. "Lord Hartington. Tommy de Grey. Lord Camperdown."

Louise exhaled. "Maybe we should ask them to join a parade? Or attend a huge banquet all together. Or else there will be a lot of dinners."

"It will only be a lot of dinners if you remain finicky."

Now, Louise felt offended. She hadn't been finicky with Henry Petty-Fitzmaurice and Lord Cowper.

"Lord Ailsa," the queen continued. "Lord Gosford. Lord Rosebery."

Some of the names Louise knew, but now she was more wary than ever.

"Now, that is a good, solid start," Mama said. "Write to Granville and ask him to begin his investigations and report back immediately."

The year of 1870 already felt like a very long year, and it was only March.

"While we are waiting for Granville, we need to stay busy," the queen said after the letter was dispatched. "Come, we are going to Claremont House to choose some paintings to display at the galleries."

It was better to stay busy—that Louise agreed with. So she accompanied the queen to Claremont. The beautiful mansion was the former residence of Princess Charlotte, daughter of King George IV. Louise and the queen spent a nice afternoon walking the grounds and the house, then selecting the paintings.

"Your Majesty," a man said, causing both the queen and Louise to turn to face the messenger. "I've brought word from St. James Palace to inform you that General Grey has suffered from convulsions and had a stroke." He held out a note. "This is from Mrs. Grey."

The queen took the note and read through it, then handed it to Louise.

Mrs. Grey was worried about Sybil hearing such hard news when she was so close to the delivery of her second child. In the letter, she asked if Louise could attend to Sybil but not let her know how serious her father's condition was.

The general must get better. He must, Louise thought.

The queen grasped Louise's hand and told the messenger, "Thank you for bringing us the news. I will have our best doctors sent over."

Louise squeezed her mother's hand. General Grey might no longer be in the queen's inner circle, but Louise was grateful for Mama's generosity toward the man.

When they returned home, she readied herself to visit Sybil. They'd been writing letters regularly, which had mostly focused on Louise and eligible peerage. Now it was time to focus on Sybil's health.

But even the queen's best doctors could do nothing to save the general. Six days after his stroke, Grey died. The weather may have held the promise of warmth and newness of spring, but Louise could only think of the loss to the world. General Grey had been like a father to her at times. He'd never looked down on her and had always given excellent and sincere advice.

On the afternoon following the general's death, Louise settled onto Sybil's bed and grasped her hand. Her friend had violet circles beneath her eyes, and her hands trembled as she clutched at Louise. She understood her best friend's grief firsthand, yet the loss was devastating all the same.

"How did you bear it, Princess Louise?" Sybil asked.

"One day at a time, I suppose," she said. "Sometimes it was one moment at a time." The sharper memories of her father had faded with the years, but she'd never forget the man he was and all that he was passionate about. It was why Louise had taken her study of sculpture seriously—it was something her father revered.

"I wish I had known he was so close to death," Sybil said. "I would have said goodbye to him."

Louise understood this as well. "No one knew he wouldn't recover. I suppose death has its own timeline, and we can only be grateful for the time we do have with someone. The doctors said that even if he'd survived, he would have had a difficult recovery."

Sybil leaned her head on Louise's shoulder. "Little Louise is so young right now that she'll not remember him when she gets older. And the baby too—he'll never know his grandfather." Her voice broke.

Hot tears formed in Louise's eyes. It was the same for her. "Papa will never meet the man I marry or lay eyes upon any of my children."

"Surely my father and Prince Albert are together now, looking down upon us from heaven."

Louise held Sybil's hand tighter. "They were great friends in life and will be so in heaven."

A small sound came from the nearby bassinet. Sybil had wanted the baby in the bedroom with her even though she hadn't fully recovered.

"What will you name him?" Louise asked.

"Charles," Sybil said. "After Father."

"Wise choice," Louise said with a smile. The infant began to fuss. "Do you want me to call for the nurse?"

"No," Sybil said. "Bring him to me. I'm breastfeeding him. Don't tell the queen."

Louise laughed. It wasn't a secret that her mother considered breast-feeding below the station of royalty. She'd been most displeased when Alice and Vicky had breastfed. Thankfully, according to Mama, Helena had the good sense not to.

Louise lifted the tiny infant swaddled in white. He weighed less than a puppy. Before handing him to his mother, she gazed into the infant's murky blue eyes.

"Hello, my precious," Louise said. "I'm Loosy."

"Oh, don't get him in trouble with the queen," Sybil said in amusement. "She won't even allow me to call you anything so informal."

Louise was glad to see some pink had come into Sybil's cheeks. "You can call me Louise or Loosy anytime. I've told you over and over."

Sybil wrinkled her nose. "But if anyone overheard, I'd probably be banned from seeing you."

Louise gave a good-natured shrug. "Perhaps. Now, I think Charles needs his mother."

CHAPTER 25

"Dearest Bertie, I received dear Alix's letter this morning for which I pray thank her, with the extraordinary proposal of Prince Albert of Solms. My two letters of the day before yesterday and yesterday . . . will be the best answer to any of these proposals: viz: that Louise wishes to settle here in her own Country and that I think she is quite right. A Poor, small German Mediatized Prince, one of 6 brothers with no Home or fortune would never do. . . . I can't conceive how he [Albert] could dream of such a thing. He is so besides [German for commonplace]. I will not here repeat what I said in my two letters, but Prince Albert of Solms may be told there is no chance for him."

LETTER FROM QUEEN VICTORIA
TO THE PRINCE OF WALES, WINDSOR, NOVEMBER 26, 1869

JUNE 1870
LOUISE, AGE 22

D uckworth is leaving shortly," Leo said, poking his head into Louise's studio, where she was working on an inscription. His eyes were rimmed red as if he'd been crying, and Louise had no doubt that he had been.

Reverend Robin Duckworth had been Leo's governor for years, and Louise had been grateful for the reverend's good and gentle treatment of her brother. There was no good reason for the queen to dismiss him, Louise decided. But Mama had insisted, saying that Leo needed someone who could better prepare him for adulthood and the future. Besides,

Duckworth was to become the incumbent of St. Mark's Church in Hamilton Terrace. None of Louise's arguments on her brother's behalf had changed the queen's mind.

"Do you have the ring?" Leo asked, walking into the studio.

"Right here," Louise said. "I've finished the inscription." As the sun had begun to rise, she'd gone to her studio to work.

Louise reached for the jewelry box she'd designed—as well as the ring—and built herself. She set the ring inside of the box, making sure it fit. With forty-three stones of rubies and diamonds that formed Robin Duckworth's initials, it was a beautiful piece of jewelry. Added to it were two lapis lazuli, representing Leo and Louise. Now she held it up for Leo's inspection.

He stooped close and read the inscription inside the ring aloud, "Forget us not. Le. Lo. 1867." Leo looked up, his gaze watery. "Let's go say goodbye then."

Carefully she set the ring inside the jewelry box, nestled into a square of velvet fabric. She and Leo walked downstairs, arm in arm, her brother only slightly leaning on her. The summers in England were warm enough that his arthritic legs moved more fluidly.

Duckworth was waiting by his carriage in the early morning light when Louise and Leo stepped outside. He was a striking man with dark hair and dark eyes. His cheerful manner and sympathetic nature had been a good match for Leo during his trying health problems. He'd be deeply missed.

Leo embraced the man, and Louise held out her hand to shake.

Duckworth smiled at her. "Now, Princess Louise, be very picky about who you choose to marry. Remember, you are the prize."

Louise laughed. "Mama won't let me forget. She's invited who knows how many young men to parade at Windsor this season."

Duckworth squeezed her hand gently, then released it. "I have every bit of faith in you."

The sentiment made her sigh, but it was encouraging as well. After delivering their gift to Duckworth, Louise stood with Leo, arms linked, as they watched Duckworth's carriage pull away. The sun had yet to cast heat across the lawns and gardens, so the temperature was still cool and mellow.

"I feel like I'm saying goodbye to Walter Stirling all over again," Leo said.

Louise nodded. "Goodbyes don't get any easier with age. Why can't everything stay the same, always?"

"That wouldn't do us any good either," Leo said. "We must accept goodbyes as part of life."

His voice trembled, but Louise also felt his maturity and strength.

"Now," Leo said in a much clearer tone, leading her around the castle until they stepped onto one of the garden trails. "Which suitor do I get to meet tonight? I will do my best to dissect his personality until I've uncovered each and every flaw."

"Oh, there will be many flaws, I am sure." Louise smiled as she walked slowly, passing rose bushes that had yet to bloom. A few bees were already at work at this early hour. "Mama has allowed lesser ranks to present themselves. And she's replaced her three F's."

Leo's brows popped up. "What are the requirements now? To be breathing and under forty?"

Louise scoffed and kicked at a cluster of pebbles, sending them scattering in front of them. "Don't terrify me. Mama has declared that character and an independent future are all that's needed to marry her esteemed fourth daughter."

Her brother's mouth quirked as he looked over at her. "You mean a man who will heed her every command?"

"Precisely."

"Then should I ask who the newest victim is tonight?"

With a laugh, Louise said, "His name is Henry Strutt. Thirty years old. Father is a baron, but there is plenty of money since the family has a fortune from coal."

"Baron of what?" Leo pressed, his tone suddenly serious.

"Belper." Louise paused before the blooming peonies. Leo stopped as well. She plucked a head off that had wilted, then dropped it in the soil to be regenerated or swept away by a gardener later. "From an old Derbyshire family."

Leo stepped back. A deep frown marred his features. "Derbyshire? If you're to live there, the only decent estate is Chatsworth, and Lord Hartington is the heir. I believe *he's* unmarried."

Louise blinked. "How do you know this?"

"I've looked through the *Peerage* book too," Leo said. "As a good and helpful brother does." He folded his arms. "Actually, Hartington is a great friend to Bertie. I'm sure if you suggest him to Mama, she'll have a fit."

Louise laughed. Any "great friend" of Bertie was surely questionable in the queen's eyes. "I have no problem suggesting him, but it wouldn't be to tease Mama. In fact, Bertie will be over for breakfast, and I can bring it up then. I mean, why would I take Henry Strutt when I could have the heir to Chatsworth?"

Leo grinned. "Then you'll cry off Henry Strutt and suggest Lord Hartington?"

"I will."

An hour later, with Mama, Bertie, Alix, Leo, and Bea all sitting at the dining table, Louise did just that.

Bertie dropped his fork against his plate. The clatter echoed in the room. "Hartington?" He stared at Louise. "You can't be serious."

Mama exhaled, her eyes focusing on Louise. "This is no time to be difficult. You know that Hartington is not suitable."

"How would I know unless someone tells me?" Louise said innocently, her gaze finding Bertie. "Why isn't he suitable, brother?"

"He is . . ." Bertie took a long swallow of the drink in front of him, then set down the glass. "He is enamored of another lady. Her name is Louise as well."

No one at the table seemed to know how to react.

"In fact, she is a married woman, to the Duke of Manchester," Bertie finished choking out.

"Well." Louise breathed in, breathed out. "I still don't want to be second fiddle to the Chatsworth estate by marrying Henry Strutt."

"Henry Strutt?" Bertie turned to Mama. "What is this? You're bringing in the sludge now?"

Mama lifted her chin. "His family is beyond wealthy."

Bertie's expression tightened, and he mumbled something to Alix. Then he looked at Mama again. "What are the other names?"

Louise wanted to shrink in her chair because she wasn't interested in a row this early in the morning between her brother and mother.

The queen didn't seem bothered by the question, however, and smiled. "I'm pleased you're here to add in your opinion. You know quite a bit about the men of the peerage and their *other* interests."

Louise waited for Bertie to become insulted and storm out, but he simply threaded his hands atop the table. "I know some things, and if I can be of use, then so be it."

That had to have been difficult for her brother to say. Last year, he'd been dead set against anyone in the peerage. Now he was offering his advice.

"Lord Camperdown," Mama said.

"His father is mad in the head," Bertie said.

"But if Camperdown isn't mad, then perhaps he's fine," Mama countered. "He has two estates in Scotland."

"Who's next?"

"Lord Ailsa," the queen said. "Although Granville thinks he's too ugly."

Bertie barked out a laugh. "What does Louise think of him?"

"I haven't met him yet."

Bertie went silent at this. "You can be your own judge, I suppose. You'll be the one looking at him every day."

Louise's face heated. Bertie could be so callous, yet she wanted to hear his opinion. She didn't want to be blindsided again.

"Lord Gosford is eligible, but he might be too poor."

"He is," Bertie said.

The queen hesitated. "A fortune isn't everything, especially if Louise likes him."

Bertie tapped the table. "I don't have a problem with Gosford at this point."

Louise exhaled. Did Bertie actually approve of someone?

"Is that all?" he asked Mama.

"No, we are also considering the Earl of Rosebery," she said. "But I've been told he likes to go on the turf."

Louise hadn't ever met a horse racer personally, but if he were to come into the family, the queen wouldn't want her son-in-law involved in something so low class.

"Rosebery might be inclined to give up the turf," Bertie announced. "And adjust his other goals."

Louise leaned forward. "Which are?"

"Well . . . I've heard him say more than once that he wants to accomplish three things in life: win the Derby, marry an heiress, and become prime minister."

The room went silent. Then Leo started to laugh.

Louise knew immediately it was one of his fits, and it wouldn't be stopping anytime soon. She directed a sharp gaze to Beatrice, who sighed and urged Leo out of the room. With his laughter still echoing from the corridor, Louise said, "I want to meet him," the same moment the queen said, "He is out of the question."

Louise and Bertie turned to Mama.

Her face had reddened, and that was never a good sign. With practiced calm, Louise said, "Lord Rosebery clearly has character and an independent future, Mama."

"I am not keen on him," the queen said. "But if you want him invited for dinner, then we will do so. Rosebery and Gosford."

Louise gave a satisfied nod, although her stomach was starting a slow twist. Nerves, she supposed.

Bertie's expression was both thoughtful and triumphant, and Louise didn't know what to make of it. She took her leave and headed up the stairs to her studio.

Everyone was involved with the selection process now, and she had little chance for having any sort of natural conversation with any of the men. They'd be inspected, questioned, prodded, and scrutinized by her entire family.

Leo was waiting inside the studio, his laughing fit faded. He must have known that's where she'd end up. He leaned against one of her tables, his arms folded. "I'm sorry," he said immediately.

Louise shrugged. It didn't matter—not her brother's fits, not Bertie's opinions, not Mama's allowances. What *did* matter was that Gosford and Rosebery would be coming to Windsor this week, and she'd be on display once again. She moved past Leo and began to chisel on a statuette of Sybil.

"I'll be perfectly pleasant to Gosford and Rosebery," Leo added above the sound of her chiseling. "No laughing."

At this, Louise fixed her gaze on her brother. "I wish this husband-finding business was all over with. How am I to have a proper chance of knowing anyone with everyone watching, speculating, and giving me advice? Mama says one thing, Bertie another, and Granville something else. It's maddening."

"I agree. Can you tell Mama that you aren't in any sort of race?"

"That worked last year, and the year before," Louise said. "I'm still in no hurry, but the more people involved, the more rushed everything becomes."

"Everyone wants to please the queen and find her daughter a match."

"Exactly. Duckworth told me to choose well, and that's all I can do, I suppose." She blew off some marble dust, then began chiseling again. "Now, unless you want to model for another bust, best leave my studio."

Leo straightened, saluted her like she was a Royal Navy captain, then walked out of the room.

CHAPTER 26

"In reply to your few words about Louise, I can only say that I must most positively decline to transmit your intentions to the King [William of Prussia]. You will I am sure, understand that any message conveying so unmitigated an affront to the Head of my family from you, cannot go through me. . . . I am well aware that my opinion has since long had no weight with you, and therefore refrain from discussing the subject again."

LETTER FROM THE CROWN PRINCESS OF PRUSSIA
TO QUEEN VICTORIA, GRAND HOTEL, CANNES, NOVEMBER 29, 1869

JULY 1870
LOUISE, AGE 22

"You've met them both," Helena said from her spot on the sofa in the Windsor drawing room, "yet you refuse to let us know whether you like either Gosford or Rosebery." Helena held her sleeping baby, Helena Victoria, who they'd all started calling Thora. At only two months, the infant slept more than she was awake.

Louise moved her gaze from the sleeping Thora to out the window at the trees full of summer leaves. "I don't *dislike* them."

"Mama, how do you put up with this?"

"That's why I asked for you to come," the queen said. "Louise isn't committing to anything. I understand about Lord Rosebery. He is only a year older than Louise, so he's young too. But she's seen Lord Gosford more than once, most recently at Lady Clifden's. She's had plenty of time to get to know that man's character and form an opinion of him."

Louise turned from the window. "Is it too hard to believe I *don't* have an opinion? They were both gentlemen, and I don't dislike them. *That* is my opinion."

Helena groaned. "I don't understand you, Loosy. You have opinions about *everything*. It would be better to say you dislike them, so we can move on."

"It's not that I'm enjoying this," Louise shot back.

The queen cut in. "That's enough."

Both sisters went silent.

Helena adjusted the bonnet about her infant's head. "If you have no opinion of those men, then consider Prince Doppus. He's healthy and an heir to a duchy, so he'll be independent. Since he's a lesser prince, he has no reason to insist on staying in Germany."

"We can hardly consider Prince Adolphus if we've refused Prince Albrecht," Mama pointed out.

Adolphus of Mecklenberg-Strelitz might be a prince, but he was also German, which meant that Louise would have to join him in the court of Strelitz.

"She could have her visits to England written into the marriage contract," Helena continued. "Since it's been so difficult for Vicky and Alice to come to England over the years for any length of time, Louise could insist that she lives in England for most of the year and only spend the Season in Strelitz."

The queen considered this, but Louise knew Mama's pride wouldn't allow it—they'd come too far down the peerage path.

"Prince Adolphus comes from a wonderful family," Helena said. "Queen Charlotte is a descendant of Mecklenberg-Strelitz, and—"

"It's out of the question," the queen said firmly. "Louise, you must spend the next few days carefully weighing Lord Gosford and Lord Rosebery. Tomorrow Gosford will be at Lady Granville's garden party. You need to determine your feelings for him there."

None of this was new to Louise, yet the pressure was unfair. Dutifully, she went to the garden party the next day with Helena and

Christian, and the only thing enjoyable was the opportunity to wear her new hat with ostrich feathers.

"It's lovely to see you here, Your Royal Highness," Lord Gosford said as he took a seat next to her at one of the banquet tables. His rather impressive mustache made him look much older than seven years her senior. He reached for his wine glass and enjoyed a healthy swallow.

Helena and Christian sat on Louise's other side, and she felt their gazes upon her, waiting for her reaction.

"It's nice to be here," Louise said. "I trust you are well."

"Very well," Gosford said with a nervous smile. He looked trussed up from the last time she'd seen him, at Lady Clifden's musicale event. Louise guessed he'd purchased a new suit of clothes. The previous outfit he'd worn had been a bit shabby.

The queen's words echoed in Louise's head about Gosford's dire financial situation. Well, *dire* compared to a royal income, that is. If Louise liked him enough, Mama had said that the money wouldn't matter. Yet Louise couldn't get the issue out of her mind as she listened to Gosford talk about a hunt he was looking forward to in the autumn. His conversation reminded her of something John Campbell had told her about his hunting dogs.

"What type of dogs do you use?" Louise asked.

"Oh," Gosford paused as if he were surprised at the question. "I only have family dogs. My estate neighbor has the hunting dogs." He took another sip of his wine. "I don't have the patience to upkeep hunting dogs."

Looking at him, Louise guessed he was full of patience. Perhaps he was tiptoeing around his financial distress. She had the sudden urge to straighten his cravat. Had it been crooked from the moment he joined the table? She couldn't quite recall, but now it was distracting. That and Mama's complaint from the night before about Gosford's six-thousand pounds a year income that had to upkeep his establishment, of which three thousand went to his mother's jointure.

"Even Lord Lorne has four thousand pounds a year," Mama had

said, then added, "with the prospect of forty thousand pounds a year eventually." The queen had corrected herself then. "But, dear Loosy, if Lord Gosford is the man you wish to marry, then I will accept his financial state."

"I hope all is well here and you are being taken care of, Your Royal Highnesses," Lady Granville said, joining their table. She was only a year older than Louise and had married Earl Granville as his second wife. Her dark hair was piled high on her hatless head, and she wore a perpetual smile. She was originally from the same county as John Campbell, but Louise wouldn't be bringing up that topic.

As the garden party progressed, they were entertained by musicians. Then they watched groups of people playing lawn games. Louise herself didn't join in because the heat was beginning to give her a headache, so she stayed in the shade beneath the striped tent.

"What do you think?" Helena asked in a quiet voice as they sat together once Gosford had left.

"He's rather nice."

Helena puffed out a breath. "Is that all?"

"Yes, that's all." Louise didn't even look at her sister. There was no need to. Nothing in her eyes would give away more because her feelings didn't go any deeper. Gosford was a nice man. There was nothing singular or spectacular about him, and that was all right with her. In fact, it was probably best he didn't have strong opinions about anything. They'd never argue about politics or literature or art. She had enough conflict with Mama and didn't need it in a husband.

"Lord Dalrymple is over there," Helena said. "Do you want an introduction?"

Louise did look at her sister then. "He's younger than me. And shorter. I'd have to stoop in my bare feet."

Helena looked like she wanted to laugh, but she said in a serious tone, "Many marriages are perfectly happy with the woman being taller than the man."

"Whose?"

"I can't recall at the exact moment, but how many times will you be standing together, shoulder to shoulder anyway?"

Louise narrowed her eyes.

"All right, how about Lord Coke?" Helena said. "He's younger too, but he's tall. You'd never have to stoop."

"I'm not marrying a boy," Louise stated.

"I hope I'm not interrupting anything," Lady Gladstone said, approaching. "Your Royal Highnesses," she added with a curtsey. Her hat wavered atop her head. It was missing more than one pin because it was nearly falling off.

"Of course not," Louise said. "Come, sit with us." Lady Gladstone was a refreshing break from all of Helena's quizzing.

Lady Gladstone was married to the prime minister, and she was nearly his opposite in every way. She was chatty and always a bit disheveled, but she laughed at herself, and joined in causes to improve enterprises such as convalescent homes and orphanages. She had a full social calendar and never sat still for long.

"If neither of you are otherwise engaged, I'm holding a breakfast party at Carlton House Terrace in two days' time," she said with a broad smile. "It will start at *noon*."

Louise laughed. "I shall attend."

Helena's look was sharp, as if to reprimand Louise from accepting the invitation so readily. But the queen wouldn't keep her at home—a breakfast party was another social event where Louise might meet her future husband, although the task had turned into somewhat of a farce.

"I must warn you, it will be an eclectic group."

Louise had no trouble with that. She'd heard of the famous gatherings at the Gladstones', and the more she thought of it, the more excited she became. "Will there be many scandalous people in attendance?"

Lady Gladstone's smile was sly. "We'll have the leading statesmen there, as well as churchmen, so things won't get too out of hand. But we always end up with a handful of literary men and artists who provide flavor to our conversations."

"Oh, it sounds wonderful," Louise rushed to say before Helena could put a damper on anything. "Doesn't it sound wonderful, Helena?"

Her sister's tone was tight. "It certainly does. I'll have to consult with my husband before I can confirm."

"Certainly," Lady Gladstone said.

The next couple of days couldn't pass quickly enough for Louise. She'd reported on the garden party to Mama and told her the same thing she'd told Helena . . . that Lord Gosford was rather nice. And he was. So he stayed in the running, and Louise honestly didn't know who was in the lead between Gosford and Rosebery, especially with the latter's talk of racing horses and sporting events. He'd been on the horse-racing teams at Eton and Oxford, so he was certainly keen. Although he knew that marrying a princess would mean giving all that up.

Louise wondered if the man would resent giving up so much for a marriage. Bertie had assured her, though, that he wouldn't.

Rosebery joined them at dinner the night before the breakfast party. He chatted with Leo and Christian quite easily—they talked of horse racing as soon as the queen had left the room. In fact, it was almost as if Louise wasn't in the drawing room with them, for all the attention he paid her. Finally, she began to play quietly on the piano with Helena sharing the bench and turning the pages.

"Are you musical, Lord Rosebery?" Louise asked.

He paused in his vigorous conversation and focused on her as if his eyes needed to adjust to the women's presence in the room. "I appreciate music like any fellow, I suppose. I'm not much of a dancer, though, or, heaven forbid, a singer."

Louise felt Helena stiffen beside her, but Louise only smiled. "We can't all have the same talents, now, can we?"

"Certainly not," Rosebery said, his smile easy, confident. "Although you have quite a share of them."

Louise laughed. "Are you a flatterer, sir?"

He rose then and walked toward her. He did make a fine figure. Perhaps not as tall as Lord Lorne, or with as much swagger—that would always be reserved for a Highlander. But Louise could appreciate Rosebery all the same. The man was sharp-witted, intelligent, and sporting, and now his attention was fully on her.

Helena rose and slipped past him, joining Christian and Leo's group.

"Why don't you play me something?" Rosebery asked.

He was smiling, but Louise sensed it was more of a polite smile than an encouraging one. "Energetic or calming?"

"You choose, Your Royal Highness."

So Louise played a short piece full of life and energy. Still, Rosebery lost interest after only a half-page. Well, most men couldn't be enthusiastic about everything, she supposed.

That night in bed, as she thought over the evening and conversation with Rosebery, she felt less settled than ever. Attending the Gladstones' breakfast party would be a welcome break. Surely there wouldn't be any eligible dukes or princes there to navigate through. Besides, none of her siblings would be going, so Louise would finally be free from their speculating gazes.

The morning of the breakfast dawned bright and clear skied. Louise took her usual ride through the grounds, letting her horse open up. As the mild summer wind teased her hair beneath her hat, she smiled to herself. She'd decided, just this morning, that she would not force herself to like any of the men her family was parading in front of her.

If she liked someone, then she would marry. If she didn't, then it wasn't time yet. She'd continue helping Mama with correspondence, and Beatrice could continue growing up.

With her thoughts easy and relaxed, she enjoyed dressing and donning a hat she'd decorated herself. Arriving at the Gladstones', Louise realized she was late because everyone was already seated for the meal.

"Oh, you've come, Your Royal Highness," Lady Gladstone rushed to say as she rose from her chair. "I wasn't certain if you'd changed your mind. We waited for—"

"No matter," Louise said. "I am frequently late when I don't have Mama's lady-in-waiting hovering over me."

Lady Gladstone looked as if she didn't know whether to laugh or frown. "We're serving eggs benedict today, a recipe all the way from New York. I hope you'll like it."

"I am sure I will."

The conversations about the table hushed, and the men and women all stood and either bowed or curtseyed.

"Please, be seated," Louise said, with a wave of her hand. "I'm a regular guest today."

Several people chuckled, and Lady Gladstone led Louise around the table and made introductions. Louise knew some of them, but she was most delighted to meet those she didn't. Two of the artists and one of the writers were ones Louise already respected and appreciated.

"It's so very nice to make your acquaintance," she told one young man.

The young man with extensive sideburns blushed a cherry red as he bowed low. "You are too kind, Your Royal Highness."

"I am only speaking the truth, sir."

"And this is John Campbell, the Marquess of Lorne," Lady Gladstone continued. "I am sure you need no introduction."

CHAPTER 27

"What Lorne wished the Duke to convey to your Majesty was that provided other views were not already entertained, he would avail himself of whatever opportunities might be offered of making farther acquaintance;— and this is the footing which would be least embarrassing to the Princess—that neither should be considered in the least degree compromised by such acquaintance. The Duke thinks that in seeking this farther acquaintance he does not wish to put himself forward as a suitor, unless and until the acquaintance should lead to a real mutual liking."

LETTER FROM THE DUKE OF ARGYLL
TO QUEEN VICTORIA, OSBORNE, JANUARY 25, 1870

JULY 1870
LOUISE, AGE 22

Louise turned from the artist and nearly bumped into Lord Lorne. He'd risen from where he'd apparently been sitting. His direct blue gaze held hers, and her mind raced with what she should say to the man—after all that had happened . . .

"No introduction needed," Lord Lorne said. "Please call me John or simply Lorne. Everyone does."

Louise hadn't considered what it might be like to see John Campbell again after all the fuss that had been made between them by their parents, followed by their last dismal encounter at Balmoral. Would he be formal? Stiff? Dismissive?

She needn't have worried because John took her hand and kissed the back of it, breaking through any reserves she might have built up. His scent of sage and cedar was present again, and she decided it was pleasant, much better than cigarette smoke or a Prussian man.

"Pleasure to see you again, Your Royal Highness."

She blinked. "And you . . . John. I trust you are well? And your family? How is your mother?" Asking after his family was the safest bet.

She'd forgotten how tall he was and how blond. Without a hat, his blue eyes were even lighter than she remembered. He wasn't wearing his Highland clothing—no kilt today or half-bare legs. But he still appeared commanding in a single-breasted jacket, brocade waistcoat, and trousers—as if he'd been born and bred a duke. Which, of course, he had been.

"Mother has recovered quite well," he said. "She's back to clipping flowers and badgering the gardener. Oh, and having Father turn out his pockets because she's decided on a remodel of the London house in Kensington."

He spoke with such ease and warmth that Louise found herself smiling.

John Campbell smiled back.

And that's when she noticed he'd pulled out a chair, right next to him.

Louise glanced about the table. This was the only empty chair. Had Lady Gladstone intended for her to sit by him . . . ?

"Tell me, how fare Arthur and Leo?" he asked as if she hadn't just been looking about for another place to sit.

The question did not leave room for a one-word answer, and Louise found herself sitting next to Lord Lorne and talking of Leo's recent obsession with chess. She filled him in on Arthur too, who was back on military duty. "We were ever so sorry to see Reverend Duckworth leave, but we sent him away with a ring that I made of jewels—spelling out his initials."

John didn't seem to be looking anywhere else except at her. In fact, he was completely ignoring the partially eaten eggs benedict on the plate before him. A staff member brought Louise her own plate, but she ignored hers too.

"With all of your obligations, it's a wonder you have any free time to be so creative," John said. "Every other day the newspapers are reporting on the activities of the royal family, and your name is always included."

He'd been reading about *her*? "Mother is more amenable to public appearances now, and she's given me more freedoms in order to meet—"

She cut herself off before she embarrassed the both of them.

"Meet more friends?" he asked, covering up her near blunder.

"Yes." She shouldn't be discussing something so private in such a public setting, and especially not with *him* of all people—a rejected suitor. But everyone else around them was involved in their own conversations. "If I'm not with Mama, I'm with my sister Helena—who can invite me along to social engagements since she's a married woman."

John didn't ask her to elaborate. He only nodded. "Her Majesty has brought great comfort to my mother. I do believe they are true friends, and it means so much to have her support."

"Your family has always been dear to mine." Louise's neck warmed as she delivered the compliment. Could John see her beginning to blush? Could anyone else?

John smiled. "The sentiment is mutual, Princess Louise."

Her name spoken by his Scottish accent was somehow charming—she wasn't sure why. But she needed to change the direction of their conversation from becoming sappy with compliments or she'd truly blush.

Thankfully, John did it for her. "The eggs benedict is the best breakfast I've had anywhere."

"Oh, it does look delicious," she said. "I'm sorry if I've kept you from eating."

He chuckled and speared a forkful. "I am eating. You are just more interesting." He didn't give her time to react to the compliment and added, "Leo told me you're quite proficient in the kitchen when allowed to bully your way in."

Louise clapped a hand over her mouth to stop from laughing

aloud—which would certainly bring undo attention. "Leo is a dolt. What else did he say about me?"

"You are not denying your bullish ways?" John's blue eyes flickered as he scanned her face.

"I consider myself merely persuasive and helpful in the kitchen," she said. "The cook last summer at Balmoral didn't know how to make a full English breakfast. I gave him instructions, and he was forever grateful."

At this, John did laugh. Heads turned, as expected, but Louise found she didn't mind too much. Everyone at the breakfast party was having their own lively, enjoyable time.

When there was a break in her conversation with John, someone asked, "Are you the princess who sculpts?" The young man who spoke had been introduced earlier, but now Louise had forgotten his name.

"Yes." Louise turned her attention to the artist. He had an extraordinary, long nose but the greenest eyes she'd ever seen. "And I'm sorry I haven't heard of your work. Tell me about it."

The artist's ears pinked. "I'm studying watercolor. I was at the National Art Training School for two years, and for the past three, I've been an apprentice."

"Very impressive," Louise said. "I shall look forward to seeing your work. You know I spent a few months taking classes at the Institute."

The artist's ears pinked again. "I have heard that—I think everyone has."

"Everyone?" Louise looked at John to find his blue eyes upon her once again.

The edge of his mouth curved. "It was in the newspapers."

"Of course," she said, holding back a laugh. "I'm afraid to learn what else you've read about me or whatever Leo's told you. Perhaps we should make it even, and you tell me something that can't be found in the newspapers."

"How is that fair?" John asked, but his eyes were full of humor.

"It's fair because I say it's fair."

"And I must listen to you?"

"Yes."

John chuckled, then he pretended to think. "Well, I am a hopeless poet, without a publisher. It's no great secret, though, but not interesting enough for a journalist to write about." He took a bite of his eggs benedict. "If I did not have a duchy to inherit, I'd be sleeping on sofas and eating scraps while I pen ostentatious words that would never reach beyond my own scribbled notebooks."

"You shortchange yourself, Lorne," the watercolorist said.

"If you are about to pay me homage, sir, I will not object."

"Your reading the other night about Lord Douglas who was killed on the Matterhorn was quite intriguing," the watercolorist said. "You have a gift of phrases, and no doubt you'll be published eventually."

"The *eventually* is the hard part to swallow—"

"You do poetry readings?" Louise asked.

John's gaze shifted to hers again. "Only when coerced or bribed. There's nothing more humiliating than reading your own work aloud before literary critics, even amateur ones."

"Where are these poetry readings?" Louise was sure they were casual, bohemian affairs, and she could never attend one.

John adjusted the cuffs of his jacket. "Sometimes they are impromptu at other events, sequestered in a library, or sometimes they arise out of a shared meal."

"Do you always have a poem at the ready, then? A book with them all written out?"

John tapped his temple. "They are here, but they are also written out." He reached for his glass.

This fascinated Louise—to have written and memorized one's own poems. "I should like to attend a reading," she declared. "Are there other ladies in attendance?"

John nearly choked on the drink he'd just taken. He brought the cloth napkin to his mouth, then swallowed. "There are no ladies in attendance, at least not yet."

"Well, perhaps that can be changed?"

John's eyes crinkled at the corners. "Perhaps."

Though they both knew it was impossible for a princess to attend a soiree of poetry reading, for the moment, they could both pretend.

More people joined in their conversation, discussing poetry and literature. It appeared that others had heard or read John's poems, and that only made Louise more curious about his work.

The talk soon turned to the Prussian conflict with France. The newspapers had been full of the growing animosity and threats of war between both countries. Louise was tired of the divisions in her family over who to support, the Prussians or the French.

"I am sorry if this conflict is dividing your family loyalties," John said quietly during the vigorous discussion at the table.

"My brother-in-law Christian wants to enlist in the German army," Louise said under her breath. "Mama has dissuaded him. She wants our family in England to remain neutral."

"How are your sisters who live in Prussia doing?" John asked.

"They support their husbands—how could they not?"

John's nod was solemn. "And what about you—do you have a preference?"

"I only want the threats to stop and for no war to happen," Louise said. "But that's not practical. France has already mobilized its army, and Prussia will be next. The Prussians are always in hot water with one country or another. But Bertie's wife, Alix, wants the Prussians to be annihilated." She grimaced. "I probably shouldn't have said that."

"I won't tell a soul." John winked. "Are all Danes sympathetic to France?"

Louise didn't know what she thought of John winking at her, but he'd asked her a question. "I wouldn't know. I've sent a letter to Florence Nightingale to find out how I can help with the wounded if there is a war. On both sides."

"*Both* sides? That's magnanimous of you."

"Miss Nightingale founded the National Society for Giving Aid to the Sick and Wounded in the War. They are completely neutral and send supplies to both sides." She sighed. "So, you see, my summer will be full of collecting supplies for bandages and other things and sending off boxes for the wounded. I might not have time to come to one of your poetry readings, even if women were allowed at such events."

John's smile slowly grew. "It will save you from donning a disguise, I guess. Perhaps I can send some poems along for your boxes. I'm sure reading poetry will cheer the injured soldiers."

Louise matched his teasing smile. "I've no doubt."

Her light mood hadn't waned by the time she returned to the palace. Oh, she kept it to herself, but inside she was smiling. And humming. To add to her cheerfulness was a letter addressed to her from Florence Nightingale. In it, Louise found the instructions she needed. She immediately started writing letter after letter, seeking donations of old sheets and linens and other necessities.

Over the next few days, she continued writing letters in her spare moments, requesting donations. When Leo found her in the library, she was on her final letter of the day. "Beatrice says you are trying to save the world one letter at a time."

"If that is what it takes," Louise said, sealing the letter. She rose to her feet. "What are you doing right now?"

"Nothing . . . unless—"

"Come with me," she said, "We're helping the staff make charpie."

"Bandages?"

"Of course," Louise said. "Then we'll send the younger members out to gather thistledown to stuff pillows."

"You're going to turn this place into a work factory, sister."

"There's a war going on beyond our borders," Louise said, sizing up her brother. He was a man who'd never qualify as a soldier, but his heart was big enough to help behind the scenes. "We can't ignore the suffering."

Leo saluted. "Yes, ma'am." Then he fished a letter from his waistcoat pocket. "Before you go down and give everyone their marching orders, I have something for you. At least I think it's for you. I don't imagine that Lord Lorne would send Beatrice a poem, and more doubtfully Helena."

Louise eyed the folded paper in his hand. "What are you talking about?"

"Lorne sent me a letter, mostly conversational, and then he said, 'I've included a poem for your sister.' No other explanation." Leo stared at her, and Louise stared right back. "Is there something you aren't telling me or, better yet, Mother?"

"Let me see the poem." Louise reached for the paper, but Leo held it out of reach.

"Tell me why Lord Lorne is sending you a poem," Leo said.

"It's John. He goes by John, you know."

Leo's brows lifted.

"All right. He was at Lady Gladstone's breakfast party the other morning." Louise shrugged like it wasn't anything to speculate over. "We talked about his poetry, and so maybe that's why he sent something over. He couldn't write directly to me because . . . well, speculation again."

Leo lowered his arm. "You're flushed, Loosy. Have you had a change of heart toward John?"

"My heart is the same as it always has been." Louise snatched the paper from Leo's hand.

He let go easily with a laugh.

She crossed to the window, her back turned to her brother, and unfolded the note. Across the page were several scrawled lines. She took her time reading, even though Leo was still in the room.

She could hear John's tone of voice and inflections as she read about Lord F. Douglas's demise in Switzerland. His writing had a pleasing cadence. *Well done,* she thought.

She folded it and tucked it into her dress pocket. Then she turned to Leo. "Ready?"

He studied her face, his eyes full of questions. But instead of asking her anything more, he said, "Ready."

As they walked out of the library together and down the stairs, she saw Leo smiling to himself. At least now she knew her brother's opinion of John Campbell.

Mama had been in full support of donating supplies to wounded soldiers, so she had no trouble with the household staff putting off other tasks and helping Louise tear old sheets and linens that had been gathered throughout the palace. Boxes of donations had come in as well—the fruit of her earlier letters.

As the staff members gathered, Louise told everyone, "Whichever side of the war you are on, we all need to help with the wounded soldiers. I don't care if they are French or Prussian—they are all men who need us." She spoke mostly for the benefit of Fräulein Bauer and Herr Sahl, who hadn't held back their triumph when Prussian victories were brought by telegram. The French governess, Mademoiselle Norèlle, had felt picked on, and a few times, she hadn't appeared for meals.

Sybil showed up to help as well, bringing with her more supplies. After they'd been working the better part of the afternoon, Sybil said quietly to Louise, "I've never seen you so cheerful while working on something other than art."

"This is for a cause I believe in," Louise defended.

"Ask her about poetry," Leo murmured from where he sat folding bandages.

Sybil's eyes brightened. "Do tell. I'm all ears."

CHAPTER 28

———— ❧ ————

"Lord Granville presents his humble duty to Your Majesty. He ventures to think Your Majesty has taken the honorable and kind course with regard to Lord Lorne. Lord Granville will lose no time in obeying Your Majesty's command, and he has no doubt that although the young man may feel a little present mortification, both he and his family will perfectly appreciate the considerate manner in which Your Majesty and Princess Louise have acted and that there will be no diminution of the deep and affectional loyalty which they feel towards Your Majesty."

LETTER FROM LORD GRANVILLE
TO QUEEN VICTORIA, 16 BRUTON STREET, MARCH 12, 1870

SEPTEMBER 1870
LOUISE, AGE 22

You must come to Balmoral at the end of September," Louise told Sybil as they shared tea in the drawing room of her London home. "Bring your babies to keep the both of us busy. In fact, maybe I'll sleep in your cottage so I can avoid who I must avoid."

Sybil laughed. "And who is that?"

"All the men who Mama is going to parade in front of me."

"Oh, now you have me curious. Who are these men? Any of them handsome and wealthy?"

"Do not tease," Louise said. "The invitations have gone out from Lord Granville, on behalf of my brothers, as if they can't write their own invitations."

"Tell me *who* before I combust with curiosity," Sybil cut in.

"You might ask who *isn't* coming," Louise said. "That would paint a better picture." She sighed, then leaned forward. "First there's your brother, Albert, who is perfectly fine. But the other names are quite suspect, and I think I can guess Mama's motivation. Lord Rosebery, Henry Fitzroy, Lord Stafford, and Lord Lorne. Pray tell, how is this going to look when so many of England's eligible bachelors are not participating in the Season but are instead sequestered at Balmoral together?"

Sybil's eyes widened. "Goodness. That is quite a feat. It would take a queen to pull it off."

"That's a terrible joke," Louise said, but a small smile emerged.

"The queen found out then about your breakfast conversation with Lord Lorne?"

Louise sighed. "She did, and the information went straight to Granville. I'm surprised there hasn't been an article in the *London Times*. It's John's fault though. He should have never sent that poem to Leo." She tapped the rim of her teacup. "Perhaps he *wanted* to get Leo involved."

Sybil's brows shot up. "How did you come about calling Lord Lorne by his given name?"

Louise shrugged but remained silent.

"All right, I suppose you don't have to tell your closest friend everything. And perhaps you are right about the Marquess of Lorne sending a poem so that you might consider him in a different light. Do you suppose he holds affection for you after all?"

"*After all?*" Louise smirked. "I'm the one who turned *him* down, and believe me, I am glad for it. He's much better as a friend than a potential husband." She picked up her teacup and took a sip.

Sybil leaned back and studied Louise. "Are you sure?"

Louise scoffed but decided it was time to drop the subject of John Campbell. "Now, how are your children? Shall we visit them in the nursery?"

"They would love that," Sybil said.

Louise popped up, ready to be distracted from the event that would bring so many eligible men to Balmoral at the same time. Perhaps Mama was onto something. It would be much easier to compare the men when they were all in the same room. But Louise didn't know if she was up to the task of having all eyes upon her, like a bird in a pretty cage.

Three weeks later, that was exactly how Louise felt. Sybil hadn't been able to come to Balmoral after all. The "friends" of her brothers had all arrived, save for Lord Lorne, who'd come later. The men had spent several days hunting and fishing, only intermingling with the women in the evenings. But even those short visits had been overwhelming for Louise. She was already at the point of fleeing to her studio and losing herself in something other than conversation that was being dissected by every member of the household within hearing distance.

At the moment, Louise sat across from Lord Rosebery, playing chess as the evening sun faded behind the horizon. The staff had already lit the gas lamps throughout the room. Louise was soundly beating Rosebery, but he wasn't entirely focusing on the game. No, he was speaking to Henry Fitzroy about a pair of horses he'd recently bought.

"Are these new horses for racing?" Louise asked.

"They aren't racing horses," Rosebery clarified. "I've given up racing and all the activities surrounding it." Something was off about his tone, though, and Louise noticed again how different he was around his peers compared to when the queen was in the same room. Then without another word to Louise, he continued his conversation with Fitzroy.

Across the room, Helena played the piano. Her children had gone to bed. Christian was chatting with Lord Stafford and Arthur. Leo sat in one of the overstuffed chairs, his eyes half closed.

Mama had gone to bed already since she'd awoken early that day, worried about her two sons-in-law fighting on the Prussian side of the war. France had declared war in July, and the next day Austria had declared their neutrality. Now it seemed most of the victories were Prussian.

Louise wished again that Sybil had been able to come on the

excursion. As it was, Louise been writing her friend every day, sending long and detailed missives. She eyed the company as she waited for Rosebery to make his next move on the board. Lord Stafford had been polite but so quiet that Louise felt like she had to poke him in the side to get him to make a sound. Albert Grey was younger than she, and his boyish quality reminded her of one of her younger brothers. Fitzroy was amiable but seemed more eager to speak to Rosebery than to her.

Lord Hatherley, the lord chancellor, was speaking with Henry and Mary Ponsonby. Henry Ponsonby had become Mama's private secretary a few months ago. Lady Jane Churchill wandered over in their direction, and Louise suddenly wanted out of the chess game. She was bored of hearing Rosebery and Fitzroy chat about the horses she was quite sure they were still racing.

Someone knocked at the front door, and Louise straightened in her chair. Who was here at this late hour? The conversations hushed, and Helena stopped playing the piano as everyone's ears tuned to the butler answering the door.

Louise wasn't sure how to define the feeling that swept through her when she recognized the voice greeting the butler. Lord Lorne's voice was distinctive, not only for his Scottish accent but also because of the higher pitch.

Immediately, she felt Helena's gaze upon her, but Louise kept her attention on the chess game. It was her turn to make a move.

"I apologize for my late appearance." Lord Lorne's voice was much closer now. He'd entered the drawing room.

Louise's neck felt prickly and warm. She should rise to greet him, act as a hostess, but for some reason, she stayed rooted in her chair.

John Campbell was making his rounds, warmly greeting everyone, shaking hands, and apologizing over and over. He was getting closer, and Louise wouldn't be able to stare at the chessboard much longer.

Lord Rosebery rose to his feet along with Fitzroy. At that point, Louise looked up.

John was wearing a kilt. Of course he was. They were in Scotland,

and he was Scottish. His blond hair touched the edge of his collar—it was shorter than the last time she'd seen him. He wore the Clan Campbell tartan colors of blue, green, and black.

"Your Royal Highness," John greeted, his blue eyes cutting to hers without hesitation. He stepped closer and bowed over her hand, but he didn't kiss it as he'd done at the Gladstone breakfast. For this, Louise was grateful. She suspected that her cheeks were already rosy enough.

"Welcome to Balmoral," Louise said, miraculously untying her tongue and speaking with complete normalcy. "If you are hungry, I can send for something . . ." Everyone was watching and listening, but she could only focus on his blue eyes that had crinkled at the corners with his smile.

"I am not hungry," John said. "Thank you for the offer, Princess Louise. I was going to sleep in my carriage if the house was dark, but it appears there is quite the party going."

"A half-asleep party," Louise said. "Unless you care to read or play chess? I've nearly beat Rosebery here."

John studied the board. "You have the upper hand, that is certain."

Helena began to play the piano again, and Louise recognized the tune to "The Campbells Are Coming."

"Ah, is that my welcome song?" John walked toward the piano and sang the rest of the song as Helena played.

Louise couldn't help but stare. John wasn't shy about his musical ability; he didn't need to be. He was a fine tenor.

> *Upon the Lomonds I lay, I lay,*
> *I lookit down to bonnie Lochleven*
> *And saw three perches play-hay-hay!*
> *The Great Argyll he goes before,*
> *He makes the cannons and guns to roar,*
> *With sound o' trumpet, pipe and drum,*
> *The Campbells are coming, Ho-Ro, Ho-Ro!*

The song lasted only a moment longer, and when Helena played the final notes, John said, "Well done, Your Royal Highness."

Helena smiled up at him. "I should be complimenting you, sir. I wasn't sure if I had the rhythm right."

"I've never heard it played better."

Louise walked to the piano and joined in on the next song. She stumbled over some of the words, but that was half the fun. A few others wandered over, and pretty soon it was like a musical event. Louise laughed through half of it, especially when John led everyone in the chorus as if he were a maestro.

Before he'd arrived, she'd been ready to retire. But now, she didn't want the evening to end. Mama had been right. Having John in the same room as the other men only made him more appealing. Not that Louise could change her mind, since that would throw both families into a tailspin; she was only making an observation. But she couldn't deny that John was by far more interesting than any of the other men present.

After the songs had ended, John sat across from her at the chessboard. As the other conversations faded away, Louise asked, "What do you think about the petitions going on for women's right to vote?"

John made his next move on the chessboard. "It's long overdue. England is behind other countries in women's suffrage. We need to progress if we're to keep a respectful foothold in the world."

Louise was so stunned at his directness that she didn't have a reply. She was only glad that he'd spoken softly enough that others in the room hadn't overheard. His opinion was so decided, so matter-of-fact. "Indeed." She made her next move. Her voice might have been calm, but inside, her heart was leaping.

Rosebery could keep his horses. Lord Stafford could stick to his silence. Fitzroy could follow after his idol Rosebery. And Albert Grey could return to the schoolroom. She was fully intrigued by John Campbell. He was a man of reason, through and through.

The following morning, Louise arose early, her mind full of thoughts and questions. Mostly about John. There was no mystery about his family. His parents were well known to her family, and the queen was close to the Duchess. John's family was large—twelve children, five brothers and seven sisters—and she wondered about the dynamics of his siblings.

Was he a kind brother? One who teased? A man who was always too busy for trivial family matters? All of those questions would have to wait. When she reported for breakfast, she discovered that the men had gone stalking for grouse.

Mama was in conference with Mary Ponsonby and Lady Jane, probably discussing the various "suitors for Louise." Last night as she was heading to her bedroom, Lady Jane had remarked, "Lord Lorne stands heads above the rest of the men, don't you think, Your Royal Highness?"

Louise had only said, "He is very amiable."

Now, dressed and ready for the day, she sat at the window seat of her bedroom and sketched the wooded hills of Balmoral. She entered in some depictions of the men stalking. The man wearing a kilt, his hair flowing to his collar, was definitely a born Highlander. She turned the page of the sketchbook and drew from memory those who'd crowded around the piano last night. A tap at her bedroom door brought her out of her memories.

Helena came in, carrying six-month-old Thora. "You are hiding out, I see. Everyone is talking about Lord Lorne, you know."

"Which is why I'm hiding out." Louise set her sketchbook down. "Perhaps I'll spend the day with Thora." She reached for the baby, kissed the top of her head, then cradled her close.

Helena perched on the window seat and gazed across the grounds. "The men will be returning soon for luncheon, and then several of the guests will leave."

"Oh?" This surprised Louise. "Who?"

"Why, all your suitors. Except for Lord Lorne, since he's just arrived."

Louise pursed her lips. "He will surely notice their departure. You know what the pressure did last time, and now . . . I don't want that to happen again."

"Because you like him after all?"

Louise lowered her gaze and placed another kiss on Thora's head. "He is very agreeable."

"And handsome?" Helena pressed.

"What does handsomeness have to do with a happy marriage?" Louise's neck warmed. Lord Lorne might not be the most strikingly handsome man of the peerage, but his charisma and intelligence were far more valuable to her.

"There's no harm in having a handsome husband," Helena said with a knowing smile.

Louise laughed at this, then she sighed. "I think the marquess and I are getting on so well because we've already canceled any progression toward marriage. Everyone is watching and speculating now that we've had some friendly conversations. Can't we talk without all of the fuss?"

Helena's brows arched. "Mama has schemed for you to accompany the riding party this afternoon, so you can talk without fuss then."

Louise rested her chin atop Thora's head. "This whole process is both taxing and embarrassing."

"I'm truly sorry." Helena rested a hand on her arm. "Everyone wants the best for you. No matter what you decide, I'll support you and your laird."

Louise kicked Helena. Not hard.

Helena laughed. "You'd better start your preparations, sister. Lunch is soon, and you haven't even dressed. You are the attraction of the year, you know."

"Maybe I'll skip lunch and give everyone a chance to discuss me."

Helena took Thora from Louise's arms. "You wouldn't dare. Besides I think you're looking forward to seeing a certain Highlander." She'd crossed to the door, then sent a smirk to Louise.

"See if I don't appear," Louise called after her.

Her attention was distracted by the arriving hunting party outside her window. She moved to the side so she wouldn't be spotted if some-one happened to look up to the second-floor window. She picked out John easily. He was wearing a tartan again, despite the cold of the morn-ing. He and Rosebery were deep in conversation. Arthur was chatting with the other men. Leo must not have joined them. Had he had a bad night, then?

Louise dressed quickly, not admitting to herself that she cared how she looked this particular day, and headed to the library, searching for Leo. He was reading on the sofa, Frisky next to him, taking a nap. At her entrance, the dog raised its head and trotted over to Louise.

She bent to scratch the top of Frisky's head. "What's this, brother? You're lazing about while the men do the real work of hunting for sus-tenance?"

Leo's lips quirked as he set down his book. "If chasing a few grouse on foot constitutes work, then I'm guilty for being lazy. I'm not inter-ested in getting briars and thistles stuck on my clothing."

Louise laughed. "You are spoiled."

He wrinkled his nose, but he didn't laugh like he should have.

"What's wrong?" she asked. "Are you ill?"

"I didn't sleep well, that's all." He paused. "How is *your* headache?"

She shouldn't have been surprised that her perceptive brother had remembered her complaint from the previous morning. "It's gone. For now."

"Does its absence have to do with the arrival of a certain marquess?"

"You're worse than Helena," Louise said. "And I've already had an earful from her. The only reason I tolerate her is because her children are darlings."

Leo shrugged, his smile now in place. "You're very good at deflect-ing conversations, sister. The marquess likes you, Loosy. I can tell. Even if he hadn't sent you that poem, last night things were very obvious."

"*Things?*"

"A man knows when another man is interested in a woman."

Louise went quiet at this and let her gaze stray to the library door.

Somewhere in the house the men were preparing for the luncheon, and then most would be leaving. John would be staying, and maybe . . . maybe . . . She sighed and looked at her brother. "I don't know what to do, Leo. He's a fine man—there is no denying that. But he has been put off once before, and I'd hate to—"

"Just be yourself," Leo said. "If you are yourself, and he is himself, then you'll know. You'll *both* know."

Louise swallowed back her next words of doubt. "I hope you're right."

"Once those other men leave, you'll have fewer people vying for your attention," Leo said, "and perhaps you'll discover what answers you're seeking."

"Perhaps."

Things didn't quite happen as Leo predicted. Instead, Louise overheard a conversation between the queen and Lord Lorne coming from the drawing room. It was after luncheon, and indeed the other men of the peerage had taken their leave. Louise had been polite and friendly to all, but Lady Churchill had been correct. John stood heads above the rest in quality and appeal. "Did you read Lord Granville's letter?" the queen asked Lord Lorne.

Louise paused before the doorway, keeping out of sight. She'd nearly walked into the drawing room but then stopped when she saw the queen sitting with Lord Lorne.

"I did receive the letter, Your Majesty," Lord Lorne said. "I am not sure why Granville wrote to tell me how to behave around Princess Louise. Has my behavior been indecent in the past?"

"Oh, nothing like that," the queen said. "But I want you to appeal to Louise and that means not being too loud or overtaking the conversation like some men do. She's a princess and should be given deferential treatment."

"Of course, ma'am," Lord Lorne murmured. "I believe I have always done so and will always do so when I see her. But please tell me why Granville wrote to me of this matter."

243

"Because you were coming to Balmoral, and Louise is here." The queen paused, and Louise could only guess what was going through John's mind. "I want her to change her mind about you."

Louise stifled a groan. If only she could see John's face. Or perhaps not. It was probably one of concealed surprise and discomfiture. The silence stretched, and Louise worried that the pair of them could hear the rapid tapping of her heart.

"If I am not myself, ma'am," John finally said, "then how will Princess Louise, or anyone else for that matter, get to know me?"

"We all have different sides to our character," the queen said matter-of-factly in a tone that Louise was well familiar with. "I am asking you to use your quiet side, sir."

John must have agreed, as all peers do when given requests by the queen, because he was quiet during the luncheon. Gone was his easy conversation and witty charm from the night before.

And it made Louise furious.

She thought she did admirably well hiding her frustration, but she was sorely tempted to plead a headache—it wouldn't be a lie—and stay home from the afternoon's riding excursion.

But she didn't because she decided to ask John about his conversation with the queen. That would settle his character once and for all. Would he confess? Would he smooth over what had really been said? If she were to marry him—not that she was considering it—she needed her future husband to not withhold anything from her.

CHAPTER 29

"Madam, May I ask Your Royal Highness to accept the Cross which I now send, made of the Iona Stone. This cross is out of a piece which I picked up in Iona last September and which was the only specimen which I have ever seen of sufficient size for such a purpose. Professor Maskelyne of the British Museum does not seem to be sure what the mineral is—whether a soft jade, or a soft serpentine. It is half transparent when held up to a strong light."

LETTER FROM THE DUKE OF ARGYLL
TO PRINCESS LOUISE, APRIL 26, 1870

SEPTEMBER 1870
LOUISE, AGE 22

If there was one thing that put Louise at ease besides being in her art studio, it was riding a horse. She enjoyed riding by herself the most since she didn't have a need for conversation. Yes, there was always someone to accompany her, but her lady-in-waiting knew enough to not bother her with chatter.

Lady Churchill, Arthur, Mary Lascelles, Lord Chancellor Hatherley, the Ponsonbys, Lord Lorne, and Louise all set off together in the warm afternoon. The wind was tame, and for that Louise was grateful. The ride was more leisurely than she preferred, but the number of people warranted it, and she couldn't very well ride ahead of them all.

At first, she rode with Arthur, and as the ride continued toward the River Dee, the horses became more spread out, and pairings developed.

The Ponsonbys rode side by side, while Lady Jane and Mary Lascelles stuck together, conversing about something or other. Lord

Hatherley trotted his horse alongside Louise. He was talkative and full of compliments—so much so that Louise sent a questioning gaze to Mrs. Ponsonby. It was as if Lord Hatherley were trying to get into her good graces for some reason. Did he have something he wanted her to talk the queen into?

Thankfully, Mrs. Ponsonby must have spoken to her husband because Henry soon rode up to join them and asked Lord Hatherley a question about Scottish law. That was all it took to fully divert Lord Hatherley's attention.

Louise almost laughed aloud.

She increased her pace and was on her way to catching up with Arthur when she noticed another rider beside her.

"That was a clever escape, Your Royal Highness," John said.

"Was it that noticeable?" She glanced over at him. He made a fine horseman.

John looked behind them, then his blue gaze settled upon her again. He was in his element, out here in the wilds of Balmoral. He rode easily, the reins loose in his hands, his back erect, yet his body moved confidently in control of the horse beneath.

"To me it was," he said, "but I don't think anyone else was paying such close attention." His gaze moved over her, and Louise didn't know if she should be flattered or annoyed at his unconcealed perusal. "You get this crease between your brows when you're not pleased with something."

Louise raised a gloved hand to her forehead. "I do?"

One corner of his mouth lifted. "You do. Now, what was Lord Hatherley saying that bored you nearly to your death?"

Something warm bubbled in her chest. "How about I tell you all about our conversation after you tell me what Mama said while she had you sequestered in the drawing room."

That made all humor disappear from his eyes.

Louise waited, wondering if he'd avoid telling her directly, change the subject, or brush it off as if it were nothing.

In a quieter voice, he said, "She requested that I not talk very much around you and not take the lead in conversation."

Louise blinked. This was precisely what she'd overheard. "I don't understand why Mama would dictate what you can or cannot say to me or when you must speak. I'm not a schoolgirl."

Again his gaze assessed her. "No, you're not. But Her Majesty believes that you don't hate me as much as you used to, and that if I make enough of a good impression, you'll add me back into your lineup of suitors."

She gaped. "I don't hate you——" She clamped her mouth shut.

John Campbell was smiling.

And she was blushing. She had to think of something to say—to cover up how this man's boldness was affecting her. How had she entirely changed her opinion of him from the year previous? "The queen will be most disappointed that you are not being quiet at all this afternoon."

John chuckled. "Like I told Her Majesty, if I am not myself, then how could anyone know whether he or *she* liked me?"

His words were so full of innuendo that Louise feared her heart might beat out of her chest. She tried to look anywhere but at him. He filled her vision anyway, despite the expanse of the wild countryside. She needed to ride faster, harder, let the wind tug at her clothing and hair. It was the only way to clear her mind of encroaching, and somewhat ludicrous, thoughts.

She cast him a sideways glance. "You make a fine form on a horse, Lord Lorne," she said, using his more formal title on purpose, "but how are you at racing?"

His brows arched, and his blue eyes glimmered at her challenge. "I can compete."

"Then I shall meet you at the valley's edge." Louise slapped the reins of her horse and nudged the mare with her heels. Soon she was passing everyone, including Arthur. Sailing ahead, she leaned forward, keeping her gaze centered even though she heard pounding hooves behind her. Then to the side of her.

John had caught up.

She knew the stable horses well enough to know that he could easily pull ahead of her if he wanted to. Perhaps he knew that as well. But he didn't advance. They rode at a breakneck speed, matching stride for stride, until they reached the edge of a valley.

No one else joined in the race, which didn't surprise Louise at all.

When Louise reined in her horse, she was well out of breath. John hadn't even broken a sweat. But his hair was windblown now, which seemed fitting since darker clouds had gathered. And with the incoming clouds, the temperature dropped. She and John were fully out in the open, in view of the others, yet she'd never been so alone with him. Or with another man, for that matter. She could say anything, and not a soul in the world would hear it save for John.

"You could have easily beat me." Louise eyed the man atop his horse.

The reins were loose in his hands, his smile relaxed. "I wanted to race *with* you, not *against* you."

The words were like poetry, but this was not the time to think of that. So he was a poet and quite good with words—that shouldn't be turning her thoughts inside out.

The silence between them stretched. It wasn't an awkward one, not like things had been between them the year previous. The silence felt warm, if something like that were even possible. She focused on the approaching riders.

"Tell me, Princess Louise," John said. "Is it too presumptuous for me to ask for a tour of your art studio?"

She snapped her gaze to him. He was much closer than she realized, and perhaps she did see a bit of perspiration on his forehead and on the hollow of his neck, where his shirt had opened from the wind. "There's not much to see," she said. "I keep most of my work at Windsor or Osborne. Here, I have scraps I'm working on. A few sketches. A half-finished painting that I've lost ambition for."

"I've seen your work, you know," John continued before she could exclaim her surprise, "at the Royal Academy at Burlington House."

When he said nothing more, she said, "Well. Are you going to tell me what you thought?"

A single brow arched. "Are you going to tell me what you thought about my poem?"

He was teasing her, baiting her . . . She took a careful breath. "The poem was . . ." She searched for the proper words that would be kind but not too complimentary. "Well done."

John gave a curt nod. "You've kept me in suspense for months only to tell me my poetry is *well done?*"

"You have been in suspense?" For some reason, her breath went shallow. Maybe it was due to the fact that John was closer now. Still feet apart, but closer. The blue of his eyes wasn't easy to describe, nor would they be easy to paint. She'd have to use more than one color.

"I have been in very great suspense," he said in a soft tone.

She didn't look away from his direct gaze. "All right. I loved the poem. Now can we move on from the topic?"

His smile was slow, then grew wider.

"Wait." Louise's breath scattered. "Have you really been wondering what I thought?"

He didn't hesitate. "Yes, and I am now greatly relieved to hear that you loved it."

Her heart rate should be back to normal by now, yet it was far from that. "It's your turn to tell me what you thought of my sculpture."

John lifted his chin and gazed at the clouds now racing across the graying sky.

"You have to *think* about it?"

His mouth quirked. "No, I am narrowing down all the compliments I have in mind."

The riders were getting closer now, making leisurely but steady progress.

Finally, John looked at her. "Surely you know how talented you are, Princess Louise, but I shall add to the accolades if I may."

Warmth shivered along her arms. "You may."

With a light chuckle, he said, "It is clear that not only are you skilled and well tutored, but you have an excellent eye for shape and form."

Louise had been complimented many times, and the most-dear compliments to her had been the queen's, until now. "Well, then . . ." She paused. "Perhaps I'll give you a tour of my studio after all."

"I'd love nothing better."

She barely heard his voice because he'd spoken so softly and because the sound of horse hooves had grown louder. They were once again surrounded by people and chatter. All privacy was gone.

Louise's mind kept repeating her conversations with John over and over as they continued to ride along the trail next to the River Dee. Eventually the clouds grew heavier and darker, forcing the riding party to return to the castle before the first raindrops fell.

The queen joined them for dinner that night, and the conversation was mellow and pleasant. Lord Lorne wore a black-velvet tunic embroidered with silver fish—another Clan Campbell symbol. He was definitely displaying his station and heritage for all to see. And true to his word to the queen, he didn't lead any conversations or talk all that much.

In fact, when Arthur asked John how his horse did in the faster ride earlier that day, John deferred, "You should ask Princess Louise. She knows all the horses at Balmoral much better than I."

Then he winked at her.

Louise flushed. She worried someone might have seen the wink. And she was right. At the other end of the table, Leo was making a valiant effort not to laugh. She would have glared at him if so many guests hadn't been at the table. Thankfully, he'd grown out of the uncontrollable laughing fits, so he was able to muster some control.

She knew exactly what John was doing—keeping quiet and demure for the benefit of the queen—but it had become something exaggerated now. Mama had asked for a report that afternoon when Louise had returned from riding, and she'd stayed as neutral as possible, saying that Lord Lorne was "very agreeable."

The queen hadn't hidden her frustration very well, but at least she'd said, "Whatever decision you make, you will have my support, Loosy."

Dr. Norman Macleod, who would be preaching at Crathie Kirk the next day, visited after the dinner hour when everyone had reconvened to the drawing room. Helena and Christian had already excused themselves, and shortly after greeting Dr. Macleod, the queen also retired for the evening. Louise found the evening most fortuitous because John knew Macleod, since he had been the one to confirm John. They chatted at first from familiarity but included others in their conversation. Louise was content to listen, happy that Mama's presence wasn't silencing John.

"It's such a lovely evening," Mary Ponsonby said, settling close to Louise. "And so lovely to be in such good company."

Louise smiled. "Very good company. I've been quite entertained by the conversations tonight."

"Oh, have you?"

"I find that I'm impressed by John having his own opinions. He's educated on many different topics. It's refreshing."

Mary's brow lifted. "You mean you tired of Rosebery's constant talk of horseflesh?"

"You noticed that too?"

Mary laughed quietly, and the two women fell silent again. Content to sit and listen to the discussions among the men, Louise didn't feel left out as John's gaze frequently shifted to her.

Perhaps she'd play chess or the piano later. Or perhaps she'd watch the colors change outside as the evening descended. The rain had come and gone, and the evening sunset glowed orange and gold through the separating clouds.

She hadn't been fond of Balmoral as a girl, with all repetitive tartan patterns in the furniture, carpets, draperies, and bedding. Not to mention the number of deer-head trophies, with their dead, beady eyes looking down upon everyone. Right now, though, the drawing room and company were perfectly cozy and perfectly interesting.

CHAPTER 30

⚜

"Princess Louise was charming last night, and won the hearts of everybody. H.R.H. had Lord Ilchester on her side, and Lord Rosebery opposite, the table being very narrow there was some general conversation. The latter seems anxious to put himself 'sur les rangs'. Lord Dunglass is pleasing, not good looking, and engaged but not to Lady M. Scott, but to Miss Grey, Lord Grey's niece. Lord Dalrymple (pleasing but young) never took his eyes off the Princess, but was too shy to speak. So was Mr. Compton and Mr. Robartes. . . . Lord Granville does not think much progress was made last night, but it will not be without use for the future, in encouraging young men to approach the Princess."

LETTER FROM LORD GRANVILLE
TO QUEEN VICTORIA, LONDON, JULY 9, 1870

OCTOBER 1870
LOUISE, AGE 22

The tour of her art studio occurred after Sabbath services the following day, and it took twice as long as it should have since Leo, Arthur, and Lady Jane had accompanied Lord Lorne. Louise hadn't planned to go into a lot of long explanations. They'd surely get bored.

Yet John asked plenty of questions, which told her that he was truly interested in her work and not just being polite, as so many others were. Although they were not even speaking directly to each other half the time, Louise felt that something between them had shifted. It was like she could read his expressions. She could guess what he was thinking or wanted to say, without him saying a word at all.

She was aware of so much about John Campbell.

As on the other days, he wore a kilt, this one with darker shades of blue and green—perhaps she shouldn't be noticing, but she had.

"Have you ever thought about doing a sculpture for the gardens?" John asked, while holding Frisky, who'd taken a great liking to him. "Something outside that can be admired freely?"

"Not particularly." Louise reached over and patted Frisky on the head. "Though I'm not opposed to it."

"If you did, what materials would you use?"

"Marble, surely," Louise answered.

"The bust she did of me was wonderful," Lady Jane broke in with a smile.

The studio felt cramped with so many people stuffed inside of it, plus a dog, so Louise was grateful when Lady Jane suggested, "We should enjoy the fair weather in the gardens, before any surprise rainstorms crop up."

They walked through the gardens, and the men talked about fly-fishing on the River Dee. Louise remembered when the Duke had told her she was welcome to fly-fish anytime at Inveraray.

"I will have to join you another time," John said to Arthur and Leo. "I am leaving in the morning."

Louise knew this, but hearing it said by John struck her unexpectedly with a desire to rush to him and beg him not to leave so soon. Lady Jane and Mary Lascelles would be leaving in the morning too, but Louise didn't have the inclination to beg *them* to stay. The more the men's conversation progressed, the more she wanted to tell John not to leave quite so soon. There was too much to do. They could go riding again. He could fly-fish with her brothers. Roe deer were aplenty if he cared to hunt.

The rest of the afternoon and evening, Louise felt like a clock was ticking down, and there was no way to stop it. She would see John again—their families would always be connected—but she didn't know when. Months could pass, and then where would she be? Where would *he* be?

Would Louise at some point cave under the pressure of the queen's lineup of suitors and choose one? Someone she hadn't met yet? Or would she wed one of the men who'd been at Balmoral that week?

After dinner, when everyone had moved into the drawing room, John settled across from Louise at the chess table.

"Do you play much chess with your family?" she asked.

"Winters are long in Scotland."

"England too."

They shared a smile, but Louise quickly straightened her features. She didn't want her family to pounce on her again about what she thought of John.

Helena struck up a slow tune on the piano while everyone else lounged and discussed everything from the Franco-Prussian War to the recent wreckage of the *SS Cambria*—a British steamship that had sunk off the Ireland coast. Nearly two hundred lives had been lost.

A time or two, Arthur or Henry Ponsonby asked John for his opinion on something, which he quicky and decisively gave. But then his attention would be back on Louise and the game.

"Did I ever tell you about my scandalous visit to Elizabeth Garrett?" Louise wasn't sure why she wanted John to know about her illicit visit. Would he take her side or the queen's?

His gaze locked on her face. "Dr. Elizabeth Garrett?"

"Yes." Louise was impressed that he knew who she was.

"Do tell me more."

She wasn't sure if he was teasing, but his blue eyes seemed lighter. "I visited her by showing up on her doorstep. Mama found out and was furious. Forbade me from such scandalous activity again."

John watched her closely. "And what sort of activity were you conducting that was so scandalous?"

"Well, first of all, I should have asked for the queen's permission."

John nodded for her to continue.

"And the scandalous activity was asking Dr. Garrett a host of questions, I suppose." Louise shrugged. "I was curious about her education and what obstacles she faces as a female doctor."

"Which," he said, "I am sure are immense."

"Yes." She sighed. "Many people won't even let a female doctor attend to them. She had to be trained in France."

"A shame." John moved a chess piece.

He'd spoken so casually that Louise wasn't sure she'd heard him right.

"Do you think women should be allowed into medical school in England?" She held her breath because the answer was suddenly very, very important.

John didn't even look up from the board. "England, Scotland, Denmark . . . every country should allow women into medical school." He lifted his eyes suddenly. "Women are more than capable, don't you think?"

Louise blinked hard because her eyes were burning. "I do." Her voice was rough with emotion, and she focused on the chess game—giving herself time to calm her heart rate.

They made the next few moves in silence. When she'd soundly won the game, and he was dominating the second, she asked, "I know you plan to leave Balmoral tomorrow. Is it because you have pressing matters to attend to elsewhere?"

John paused before picking up the next chess piece. "Not extremely pressing."

"If you were to delay, perhaps a day or two, would the matters keep?"

John slowly lowered his hand, his gaze not leaving hers. "They would certainly keep."

Louise allowed a small smile to escape. "It's your turn, Lord Lorne."

"So it is, Princess Louise." He looked at the chessboard again and made his move. "Checkmate."

The following morning, Louise found Mama at breakfast and noted that she must have had another restless night of sleep. Dark circles rimmed her eyes, and her hand trembled as she reached for her teacup.

"Are you well, Mama?" Louise sat next to her with a plate of eggs, sausage, and black pudding.

"There was another telegram last night," Mama said. "The French armies have recruited five hundred thousand more troops."

Louise fell silent. How long would this war continue between the French and the Prussians? How many lives would be lost before it ended?

"Do you have anything cheerful to distract me from my two sons-in-law leading armies?" Mama asked.

Louise looked up from her plate. "Perhaps." She couldn't hold back a smile.

The queen's brows arched. "Does this have to do with Lord Lorne? Before Lady Jane left this morning, she said that you and the marquess had several nice chats. He really is a well-behaved young man, Loosy."

Louise's pulse quivered now. "Might you ask Lord Lorne to stay another two nights? There are ever so many things to do still, and I am sure that Arthur and Leo will be delighted."

Mama smiled wider than any time in Louise's memory. "Will *you* be delighted as well, my dear?"

Louise knew her next words would precipitate a bevy of letters between the queen and Granville. And once that happened, there was no going back. So be it.

"Yes, I have enjoyed Lord Lorne's company," Louise said. "Much more than I thought I would considering last year's events."

Mama watched Louise closely. "Tell me, Loosy, has your opinion of him quite changed then?"

There was no use denying it. "Yes, it has."

The queen tilted her head, her tired eyes no longer weary but full of life. "I will invite him to stay longer."

Louise felt like she might burst inside. "Thank you."

Would John agree? Of course he would. The *queen* would be asking him.

And that was how Louise found herself on another horse-riding excursion that afternoon. John had accepted the invitation to stay another two nights. This time they rode to Dhu Loch. The party was much smaller, consisting of Lady Ely—the queen's lady of the bedchamber—and Lord Hatherley, as chaperones to Louise and John. The queen had taken Beatrice, Helena, and Mary Ponsonby along the south side of the River Dee.

John had turned down the invitation to fish with Leo, Arthur, and Christian. Louise tried not to read anything into that. They stopped for tea at one of the bothies, a small shelter for hikers, and then continued their excursion on foot. Walking to the Upper Loch of Loch Muick, Louise and John soon put distance between Lady Ely and Lord Hatherley, leaving them well behind.

Louise didn't feel like walking slow. She'd brought her small sketchbook and planned to sketch the fantastic views. The afternoon was absolutely heavenly, with the crispness of autumn in the air, vibrant red- and orange-colored trees surrounding them, and in the distance, the first snowfall upon the mountain peaks, which promised a strong upcoming winter.

John easily kept up with Louise's brisk gait. She was no stranger to walking or riding and was far from the type of female who preferred to sit and embroider. Even her art kept her active and fit—sculpting was no easy feat.

"You hike like a Scotsman," John said.

"I'm the one out of breath, not you." Louise glanced over at him with a smile.

His blue eyes were on her.

She swallowed and looked forward again. Too late, though; she stumbled and sent a few rocks skittering.

John grasped her elbow, and when she steadied, he let go.

"Thank you," she said. "You jinxed me."

John chuckled. "I apologize for my observation then."

"You are forgiven."

His eyes twinkled with humor. As they began hiking again, he stayed nearly at her elbow. Louise was grateful for the crisp air because it kept her heating neck cooler than it would have been.

John slowed his step and stopped. Curious, Louise paused and turned to face him. Beyond, the hills rolled for miles, the trees soaked in autumn gold, orange and reds. It was really quite breathtaking. John looked portrait worthy—a Highlander overseeing his loch. But mostly, Louise noticed his eyes. It was hard to look away from him when he was gazing at her with . . . Interest? Fascination? Attraction?

"You surprise me, Princess Louise."

"In what way?"

"Your request that I stay on longer at Balmoral."

Louise shouldn't be shocked that he knew the request had come from her. "Did the queen inform you?"

"About your request? No. That was courtesy of Leo."

She hissed through her teeth. "That blockhead brother of mine."

"He's not so bad," John said, taking a step closer. "It was very useful information."

"How so?" The warmth that had prickled her neck spread to her collarbone, then settled into her chest.

"I have been in Balmoral for a few days only, but it has renewed my hope . . ." He cut himself off, then started again. "Last autumn I was convinced you thought little of me. You said almost nothing, and I believed it was because you were uncomfortable and against any union between us."

Since the breakfast at the Gladstones', Louise had learned that John was extremely direct—a refreshing change from the other men she'd considered as suitors.

"I *was* uncomfortable," Louise said. "I have little trouble keeping up a conversation, but I felt put on the spot and spied upon by every person in the room."

The edge of his mouth lifted. "A situation that I wish could have been less formal. But no matter. Time is a great equalizer and reveals greater truths. I hope the passage of time has been in my favor."

Louise folded her arms, not because she felt cold, but because she needed to put pressure on the fluttering in her stomach. "Time has been good for me as well."

Somewhere below them, Lord Hatherley and Lady Ely were still hiking, but they were not yet in view. Louise felt quite alone with John, and she was perfectly happy to be. Out of all the places she could be, she wanted to be here, right now, with John Campbell. She wanted to hear what he had to say with the wilds of Scotland spread before them.

"Seeing you wear the Argyll cross has made me both pleased and curious," he said.

Louise touched the necklace at her throat. A year ago, the Duke had presented her with the necklace, but she hadn't worn it until this day. This morning, she'd removed the locket of Papa's hair that she wore most days. She wanted to wear the cross in front of John, perhaps *for* John. But not until this moment, did she realize what message she might be sending to the man now gazing at her. And, she realized, it was a message she wanted to send. "Your father's gift was generous."

"You wear it very well," John said. "I've never been more pleased to see a representation of my family."

"I'm grateful for such a gift."

"Is that why you're wearing it then, because of my father?"

Louise was truly called out. But she didn't mind. "The Duke might have given it to me, but I'm wearing it because I thought *you* might appreciate it."

John's blue eyes darkened. If only she knew what was going through his mind.

"I am honored, Your Royal Highness," he said at last. "I hope that means you'll reconsider who is a worthy match for you and that consideration might extend to me, although we both know that I am completely unworthy of you."

"You have never been unworthy, John." Her cheeks were surely pink now. "I did not know you last autumn. How could I trust you to respect me if I made up my mind without knowing you? I asked for time, and that is what I needed. But I also didn't think it fair to keep anyone waiting month after month, especially you."

The wind stirred about them both, rippling Louise's sketchbook and ruffling John's hair.

"I wouldn't have had it any other way," he said softly, "because it made me realize how deep my feelings for you run and how much I truly want to marry you."

Louise stared at the man before her. The tapping of her heart rose to full staccato now. "Are you proposing, John Campbell?"

John sank to a knee and looked up at her. "With all my heart." He exhaled in a way that despite his steady gaze, told her that his heart was beating as fast as hers. "Your Royal Highness, Princess Louise, will you marry me?"

She might not have expected this hiking excursion to involve a marriage proposal, but her mind was as clear as the autumn air. If he'd asked last year, her answer would have been quite different. But the maturing relationship between them gave Louise no hesitation now. With a tremulous smile, she said, "Yes."

John blinked as if he wasn't sure he'd heard right. "Yes?"

She nodded, and he moved to his feet in an instant. Grasping her hands, he drew her closer. He hadn't been out of breath hiking to the Upper Loch, but now, his breathing seemed quite shallow. "Only say *yes* if you think you can love me and we can care for each other the rest of our lives."

She tightened her grasp on his warm and sturdy hands. "I believe I've already answered that."

He chuckled and drew her so close that she wondered if her first kiss would be overlooking the Upper Loch.

John merely looked into her eyes, his gaze steady and sure, full of promises. "You have made me the happiest of men, Your Royal Highness."

The warmth in her chest expanded to every limb. "If we are to marry, you can't keep calling me *Your Royal Highness*."

"What am I allowed to call you?"

"You decide," she said.

His smile emerged. "Does the queen have to approve?"

Louise looked down at their hands. She'd never held a man's hands before. It was an unexpected thrilling sensation. She threaded their fingers, hers cool and delicate, his warm and strong. Being this close to John Campbell was sending darts of fire straight to her center. "My mother is not the one you'll be married to, John."

He chuckled, and the warmth of his breath touched her skin. He was close enough that she could smell his scent of sage and cedar.

"Yet, you must know that Mama will try to mold you to fit her expectations." Lifting her gaze, she met his clear, blue eyes. "You will not just be marrying me. You're marrying into a complicated family and a royal dynasty with traditions and expectations."

"That may be so, but you forget, I have eleven siblings. And you know the personality of my father."

"That is very true," Louise said with a laugh. "At least you won't be able to say I didn't warn you."

His eyes didn't lose any of their enthusiasm. "Whatever we have to face, or whatever adjustments are needed, it will all be worth it." Slowly, he brought one of her hands to his lips and pressed a lingering kiss there.

If only this moment could last much longer, with only her and John Campbell, without all the interference or cares that combining their families would bring. But she agreed with him. They could face things—whatever they might be—together. They'd be stronger as a pair.

The wind had turned cool, but she didn't feel any of its bite.

"I have been most impressed that you have educated opinions," she said. "They will be sorely needed if you are to stay your own man. Mama will want us living close to her, you know, but I want to live as a married woman in my own household. Making my own decisions, running the staff how I see fit, and ordering around my husband."

John's eyes crinkled at the corners. "You shall have your own house-hold, my dear Louise."

He had called her *Louise*. Simply her first name. It was a novelty, and she was beyond pleased. Oh, Mama wouldn't like it, but as for Louise—she loved it. "Do you promise?"

"I do. And we will help Her Majesty with whatever is needed. Don't worry, we will make our way together from now on. We are returning to the old ways, you see. It is providence that Scottish nobility should join with the sovereign's family."

"Well, then," she said, her hands still entangled with his, warm and secure. "What happens next?"

"You must tell the queen—she needs to be the first to know."

Louise nodded. He was right. "Perhaps we can stay out here a little longer though."

"There is nothing I desire more, but we are out of time for that." He nodded toward the base of the hill.

Louise caught sight of Lord Hatherley and Lady Ely, still at a fair distance. She reluctantly released John and stepped back. It wouldn't do for there to be rumors or gossip before the queen heard the news.

John didn't move back though. Instead, he offered his arm. Louise hesitated, then took it, sliding her fingers about the crook of his arm. If only for steadier footing as they walked back to where they'd left their horses.

On the ride to Balmoral Castle, as Lord Hatherley led the conversation, Louise didn't speak a word to John Campbell. She didn't need to. His gaze upon her, an intensity that made her knees feel like water, told her everything she needed to know.

CHAPTER 31

"I cannot go to bed tonight without telling you that I give my ready consent to what Louise has informed me of—and earnestly pray for God's blessing on you both. I know that my dear Child will be safe in your hands and I trust that you will protect and guide her and be that support which every Husband ought to be. Your very high character gives me every confidence and I doubt not that you will, with your kind heart, good sense and devotion to her overcome the difficulties which will naturally be unavoidable in a marriage with one of my daughters."

LETTER FROM QUEEN VICTORIA
TO LORD LORNE, BALMORAL, OCTOBER 3, 1870

OCTOBER 1870
LOUISE, AGE 22

Louise watched her mother walk back and forth on the tartan-printed carpet. Louise had just told the queen of Lord Lorne's proposal on the loch and of her acceptance. They'd returned as the sun had set, and now it was nearly dark outside.

When Mama stopped, she faced Louise. "This is so sudden, Loosy. I knew you were talking and getting to know each other, but a *marriage* proposal? I can't quite wrap my mind around it. He did not seek permission from me first. Did you not think of that?"

"You are the first person he said we should tell," Louise said, a frown marring her brow. She didn't expect these concerns from Mama. Not when she'd been delightedly pushing them together the past several days.

Mama crossed to the sofa where Louise was sitting. She sat and they grasped hands. "You are sure? You are not settling because you are tired of the parade of suitors?"

"When Lord Lorne asked me, I knew my answer immediately."

The queen's gaze bore into Louise's. "I believe he will make a good husband. The best that can be found today."

Louise nodded. She thought so too. She considered him a good and decent man. A kind and thoughtful man. Mama seemed to be with-holding something. "But?"

"There are no buts," Mama said. "Lord Lorne is a fine man, and I could not respect his family more. I've told you before that I only want your happiness. If he is the man who will give you that, then I will give you both my blessing."

Louise took a deep breath. "He is the man I want to marry. A year ago, I simply wasn't ready. I needed to meet more people and to mature before knowing what and whom I wanted."

Mama squeezed her hands. "Then let it be so. I will tell Granville after Lord Lorne has told his parents."

"I believe Granville will be greatly relieved."

Mama's smile was tender. "I am most happy for you, darling Loosy. You and your laird will have a wonderful future together. I will miss you dreadfully, even though you'll be staying in the country. You know how hard change is for me."

"I know, Mama," Louise whispered. She leaned forward and embraced her mother.

Mama might be the most powerful monarch in the civilized world, but she was also a mother who worried and cared about her children. A wife who had to carry on without her beloved husband. And a woman who was constantly in the spotlight.

"I don't know if I can attend dinner without bursting about the news," Louise confessed.

Mama chuckled. "You must, my dear. We will let everyone know at the proper time, but for now, you will have a lovely secret to keep close."

It certainly felt lovely. Like a weight had been lifted in the best way. Lord Lorne—John Campbell—was a man she could envision herself with. Walk through life together, hand in hand, come what may.

An hour later, Louise changed into a more formal gown, although she still wore the Argyll cross that now represented her future family. Perhaps she'd never take it off. And she'd been right. Dinner was torture without anyone knowing about her engagement. Mama was very solicitous to John and drew him into conversation multiple times.

When he looked her direction, Louise couldn't help but smile. After the second time, she had to stop meeting his gazes. Her brothers were too astute. She caught Helena watching her closely, and from that point on, she kept up a conversation with Lady Ely.

As if they'd preplanned it, John joined Louise at the chess table after dinner. Helena played a handful of merry tunes on the piano. Her brothers and Christian chattered about fishing and hunting. At one point, they tried to talk John into going fishing with them the following day.

"I have other matters to attend to with my father," he said simply.

"Is he coming to Balmoral?"

"No, I will be visiting him."

Leo looked over at Louise, but she refused to add any more information.

None of them suspected, did they? She made her next chess move, and soon, the men were talking about something else entirely. But John wasn't paying attention to them.

"What did the queen say?" he asked in a quiet voice that only Louise could hear. "She was very talkative to me at dinner, and it was plain that she knew. I hope she approves."

"Of course she approves." Louise slid her foot beneath the table to tap his. "How can you even think she wouldn't? It was quite obvious that she arranged this whole week at Balmoral with the intent of bringing you to my attention."

"Oh?"

Louise tapped his foot again, then smirked. "She wanted me to see how you compared to the other men and hoped that I would notice your superiority."

John straightened his shoulders and grinned. "And did you notice?"

"Hush," Louise said. "Someone will overhear us."

He pretended to consider his next chess move. "Now that some hours have passed, and you've conferred with the queen, are you still amenable?"

Her eyes flew to meet his gaze, and a storm of panic stirred in her stomach. "Are you?"

"More than ever."

She couldn't explain the relief she felt. "I feel the same."

"Truly?"

She didn't miss the hope in his voice. "You are gunning for compliments this evening, Lord Lorne."

This time, his foot nudged hers. "What do you say to a short engagement? Is Christmas too soon to marry?"

Louise brought a hand to her mouth to stifle her startled laugh. She turned it into a short cough, then said, "Much too soon. You forget who I am."

John's eyes were a darker blue tonight, yet they still shone as bright as ever. "I'll never forget who you are, Your Royal Highness."

"Louise," she whispered.

His brows shot up. "Do I have permission from the queen?"

"No," she said. "And you'll not likely get it, but I'd like you to call me Louise. Unless you want me to call you Lord Lorne?"

"You may call me John, or Lorne, or *husband dearest.*"

Louise coughed-laughed again. She took a sip of the water at the edge of the table.

"How about January, then?" he pressed.

She met his gaze. "May."

His brows furrowed. "You cannot be serious. Six months might as well be six years."

She arched a single brow.

"All right. February? That should be plenty of time to arrange all of the pomp and circumstance and heaven knows what else."

She leaned closer and moved a chess piece out of turn because he was taking so long. "You have much to learn, sir."

He moved her piece back to where she'd started, then moved his own piece. Leaning back in his chair, he folded his arms. "March."

She pretended to consider. The queen would be declaring the wedding date anyway, but March was definitely foreseeable—after the deeper gloom of winter was over. "All right, March. But after my birthday."

"The seventeenth, right?" His mouth quirked.

This time, she kicked his shin.

John didn't even flinch. "Oh, that's right. The eighteenth. How could I forget?" He winked. "Your turn, Your Royal Highness."

She made her move, a poor one it turned out. John won the game fair and square, but she didn't mind. She'd beat him next time. There would be plenty of evenings to play chess with the man who would be her husband in a few months. Perhaps March was too long to wait after all.

The following day, after Lord Lorne departed, Louise sequestered herself in her studio. Her siblings popped in from time to time, but she kept herself busy drawing birds and modelling them into clay.

In the afternoon, she rose from her workbench where she'd been sketching and walked to the small window. Gazing at the hills and the loch, she imagined the sequence of events that were possibly taking place at that very moment. Perhaps John would change out of his traveling clothes before meeting with the Duke. No, John would stride into the house and right into the Duke's study, where the man would probably look up from some estate paperwork he was reviewing. Without much preamble, except for maybe a very brief greeting, John would announce that he was officially engaged to her—Princess Louise.

The Duke would be stunned at first, and then as the news settled, he'd be elated. He'd walk around his giant desk that had been hewn from a large tree and embrace his son. The two men would slap each other on their backs, and perhaps the Duke would wipe a tear or two from his eyes. His oldest son and heir would be marrying a princess of England, bringing more prestige and honor to their name and family and ensuring a legacy for the next Duke of Argyll.

Together the men would pay a visit to the Duchess, and she would be joyful and insist on returning to Balmoral and speaking to the queen. But mostly, she'd want to congratulate her future daughter-in-law, and the two women would sit together, planning the most exquisite wedding.

Louise's imagination was vivid and hopeful, but the reality turned out quite different. The Duke did indeed come to Balmoral. Alone. Mama had requested it. She wanted to discuss the marriage contract and all the specifics without the interference of other family members, and that included the bride and groom.

Not even John would be arriving for another two days, and Louise was in agony over it. She wanted to ask him personally how the conversation had gone with his father. Now she felt like she was in a fishpond where everyone could look and point and talk about her, but who could *she* talk to? Arthur had returned to his military duty, and Leo was battling a serious cough that had gone to his chest. Helena had returned to England to tell Bertie and Alix the news in person, and so Louise felt like she was ambling about in a nearly empty castle—devoid of allies.

If only Sybil had come. Louise wrote a series of letters. One to Sybil, confessing all. One to Bertie, sharing the announcement in a diplomatic yet charming way, hoping he wouldn't put up a fuss about Lord Lorne. One to Vicky and then to Alice. Mama had already written to them, breaking the news and hoping their criticism wouldn't be heavy. Discussions about Louise marrying a commoner were one thing, but now that it was a reality, everyone would have an opinion. Next, she wrote to the Duke, telling him to ask for her the moment he arrived at Balmoral so that she might talk to him first.

But Lady Ely told her the queen had sent a note to the Ballater station so that upon his arrival, the Duke would know that his first audience would be with the queen. Louise didn't want that to happen because then she would have no chance to hear about John firsthand. Besides, Mama would begin the wedding plans and marriage agreements before Louise could add her opinion. Once Mama approved of something, it would be too hard to change. So it was imperative that Louise speak to the Duke first so he would know what to request from the queen.

When Louise heard the sound of the carriage, she sent Lady Ely to place a note on the Duke's table in his assigned bedroom. Mama had gone to visit the parish church, Crathie Kirk, in her carriage, but she would be returning soon.

She hurried to the library to wait for her guest, but as the minutes passed, she continued to wait. "Can you inquire as to the delay?" Louise asked Lady Ely, while the two of them pretended to read while not actually reading a word.

"They've sent for Mama." Beatrice came into the room. "She will see him first since she's the queen."

Louise wanted to box her sister's ears, but she remained sitting stiffly in her chair. "Thank you for letting me know, Bea."

Beatrice gave a half curtsey, then walked out of the room with a triumphant smile on her face, as if it had given her great pleasure to deliver such news.

Lady Ely offered Louise a sympathetic smile. "You will see the Duke soon enough, and Lord Lorne will be here in two days' time."

"I know," Louise said. "I need to learn better patience." Inside, she was fuming though. She didn't want to confide in Lady Ely—it would get back to her mother—but she hated to sit in the library while her fate was being planned.

If only John were here. He'd find some humor in it and make her feel better. Or perhaps he'd insist they all meet together and not suffer in anticipation while the queen and the Duke had their tête-à-tête. It wasn't that Louise relied on John—they were barely engaged—yet she knew the void that she felt right now would be filled if only he were here and navigating this with her.

So, Louise waited. She waited for the queen to return. She waited for Mama and the Duke to speak. She waited to be summoned.

Louise had nearly picked apart the seam on her skirt by the time she was sent for. Now, instead of confident and excited, she felt nervous and timid. Too much time had passed, and her anticipation had built up and then crashed down.

The Duke stood as Louise entered the drawing room. He wore the Clan Campbell colors, and his hair, long like John's, though a burnished red, was combed away from his face.

"Princess Louise." The Duke walked forward, then pulled her into an embrace, surprising her. "Her Majesty gave me permission to embrace my future daughter-in-law."

The queen was smiling, and Louise decided all was well and that she could relax.

The Duke drew back. "I'm sorry the Duchess could not be with me, but she is most pleased about the engagement. She sends her love and congratulations."

Louise nodded, her chest expanding with warmth. "I am pleased to hear it."

"John told me that you have been wearing the Argyll cross," the Duke continued. "It suits you well."

She smiled and touched the necklace at her throat. "Thank you for such a kind gift last year. I didn't know when you presented it to me how important it would become."

With the queen looking on, the Duke spoke many platitudes, but all the while, Louise was curious as to what had been settled upon. And what she needed to prepare herself for.

CHAPTER 32

— ❧ —

"How very kind of you to write to me yourself, and to wish me joy of this most happy event. How lovingly you speak of my becoming a daughter of yours; believe me how truly I shall love you and the dear Duke and strive to be a comfort and happiness to you. You can guess how proud I already feel of Lorne, and how I shall love and respect him. I hope this sudden news has not been too much for you. I hope it will not be very long before I see you, and can by word of mouth assure you how anxious I am to do all that will be expected of me."

LETTER FROM PRINCESS LOUISE
TO THE DUCHESS OF ARGYLL, BALMORAL, OCTOBER 7, 1870

OCTOBER 1870
LOUISE, AGE 22

Y ou have clearly captured my son's heart," the Duke said as he sat with Louise in the library the following day. Finally, they'd been allowed to have a private conversation.

"He surprised me with his timing of the proposal," Louise said, "but I knew my answer straightaway."

The Duke chuckled.

From a corner of the room, Frisky rose from his nap and trotted over to Louise. She scooped up the terrier and gave him a good rub-down. She had yet to learn what the queen and the Duke had agreed upon for the marriage contract and other arrangements. While Mama had been all smiles and sweetness yesterday, this morning she'd been very quiet at breakfast. Louise hadn't dared ask what was wrong because she was afraid the queen may have been displeased with something the

Duke had said or done. It would all be worked out before John came to Balmoral anyway—at least Louise hoped. She didn't want her mother to find any new criticisms to dwell upon.

"You are all John has talked about," the Duke continued, "and it does my own heart good to see that not only are you a charming young lady, but you are very aware of the complications that such a union will bring."

Louise set Frisky to her side. He curled up next to her and fell back asleep. Apparently the conversation about her future wasn't all that interesting. "I am sure that John and I will have many things to discuss."

"The bloom of first love wears off quickly, and what is more important in a marriage is that your values and characters align."

"I agree," Louise said, although she was starting to feel nervous. It was as if the Duke were trying to warn her about something. If so, what? "We are certainly no strangers to each other, and the respect we have for each other's families will also create a stronger foundation."

The Duke considered this, then he smiled. "You are a bright young lady," he said. "Very talented and intelligent. I can see why my son has claimed you as his own." His voice fell then. "But we must speak of the obstacles and risks of this union, my dear."

Louise nodded, for what else could she say? Once again, she wished she had John at her side. "It would be the same with any man I married, I suppose."

The Duke slapped a knee. "And so it would. Marrying into a royal family might seem like a fairy tale to those who do not understand the complexities. Now, there is the matter of what a man calls his wife—which most would agree is by her first name."

Louise swallowed. She'd discussed this with John—had he already brought it up to his father?

"I asked this of the queen last night," the Duke said. "She is adamant that my son call you Princess Louise at all times. Even privately."

Was this the explanation for Mama's dark mood that morning? None of her other in-laws called their spouses by their titles. But they were royalty, so they were on equal footing. "Ah, I see."

The Duke grimaced. "You see the situation now?"

"I don't think John will like that, but I suppose he'll get used to it?"

The Duke adjusted his tartan and leaned forward. "Here's the thing, my dear. John might be a commoner to you, your family, and England, but in Scotland, he's the Marquess of Lorne and will be the ninth Duke of Argyll upon my death. He has made it very clear to me that he'll call his wife by her first name without any preemptive title."

Louise stared at the Duke. "He told you this?"

"It's very concerning to him," the Duke said. "Which is why I approached the queen about it in advance of the marriage contract."

"And she is opposed?"

"Extremely."

Louise looked down at her clasped hands. She'd clamped her fingers so tightly together that they were white at the edges.

"You have a decision to make, my dear," the Duke said in a quiet voice.

Louise lifted her head to meet her future father-in-law's gaze. "John and I already agreed that he must call me Louise, so Mama will have to live with that."

"Well." The Duke's eyes crinkled as his smile emerged. "My son will be very happy to hear that."

She eased her hands apart and wiped her palms on her skirt. "What else must we discuss, sir?"

The Duke dipped his chin. "Now, this is a more serious matter. The queen has offered to honor John with British peerage. I understand Her Majesty's reasoning. She wants to elevate his rank in England and give him a seat in the House of Lords. This would remove his close association with Prime Minister Gladstone and the Liberal party and make him politically neutral."

Louise suspected this might happen. Mama had given Christian a military title as major general in the British army upon his marriage to Helena. "Does John know about this yet?"

"He doesn't, but he will as soon as he arrives in Balmoral," the Duke said. "If John accepts the title, then he'll no longer be considered a commoner in England. But he's done nothing to earn the British dukedom, and his pride, and my pride, won't allow that. Receiving this court favor will also curb his independence, and he'd have to give up his political convictions. Even though your mother is the queen of England, and the title will be seen as an honor by the public, it will be stripping my son of who he is at the core."

Louise didn't know what to say. She didn't want John to regret anything or to have to give up his political convictions and pursuits in order to marry her. But if he refused, would Mama give her blessing to the union? With her pulse throbbing, Louise asked, "Do you think John will accept the peerage title?"

"If he does, he'll have *me* to answer to," the Duke said. "He's my first son and holds all the birthrights. In Scotland he is lord and laird. In England, he might not be peerage, but at least he can maintain his Scottish pride and heritage."

Her throat hurt from being so tight. This was all true, and any commoner who married her—a royal princess—would be facing the same decisions and complications. It wasn't a simple matter for a man to make such a sacrifice, especially if he was ambitious, or even if he was in love. Louise didn't know if John was either. Oh, he might be entranced by her—but love would have to be developed.

Would the queen's insistence at giving John a British peerage title be the division that would break them apart? The thought of her engagement being broken only made Louise surer she didn't want to lose John. It was a strange thing. They'd been engaged only a few days, and they'd been apart in the last year much more than they'd been together, but the thought of rescinding all that they'd built together made her stomach turn upside down.

The Duke was watching her carefully. Waiting, she realized.

She swallowed, then slowly, carefully said, "If John doesn't accept the peerage title, I will stand by him. As his wife, Mrs. Lorne, the Marchioness of Argyll."

The Duke's brows popped up. "You are willing to upset the queen?"

Louise nearly laughed. "Mama and I have disagreed plenty, but there is one promise I must have faith in. She told me she wanted me to be happy. And if my husband is happy, then I shall be happy."

The Duke moved off the sofa and knelt on one knee. With a hand to his chest, he said, "Your words have honored my son and all of Scotland, and most importantly, they have honored you."

It wasn't hard to settle on a course of action when she had the impassioned Duke speaking to her. But once she faced Mama, the pressure would be quite heavy.

Louise spent the better part of the afternoon walking the grounds of Balmoral. Lady Ely walked with her, wisely staying silent as Louise focused on her own inner thoughts—reflecting on every conversation, every word, every action, that had taken place between her and John. She had to put faith and trust into her feelings for him, which had not ebbed. If anything, she felt more drawn to him. The man, even if he rejected the British peerage title, would be giving up plenty in order to serve as husband of a royal princess.

Perhaps by the time he arrived at Balmoral again, his head would be quite turned the other way. Disastrous things had happened before. Broken engagements and broken hearts. Would that be Louise's story? To have finally found a man who wanted to take her to the altar and to whom she was willing to pledge her heart and soul, only to have centuries of tradition stand between them?

Louise pressed her sketchbook against her chest as she walked along the River Dee. The rush of the water wasn't soothing like it normally was. It seemed to only speed up her pulse and drive more worries into her head. At one point, she paused and looked across the river. The sun was still hours from setting—today had been the longest day of her life.

"How many hours until sunrise?" she asked no one in particular.

But Lady Ely answered. "I believe twelve hours, Your Royal Highness."

Twelve hours until the new day. The time would pass, but it would do so slowly.

"Do you know if the boxes for the injured soldiers are all filled?"

"They are not."

"I shall help then. More hands will make the work lighter." Louise turned and strode back to the castle.

With the help of Bea, who'd taken a great interest in the war in recent weeks, they finished packing all the boxes for the wounded soldiers.

Dinner had been another quiet affair, with Mama subdued. At least Louise was no longer in the dark about what the Duke and the queen had discussed. Louise couldn't help but be proud that the Duke and John had their own convictions and opinions. She wholeheartedly agreed with the Duke; his son and heir must retain his honor in his birthright and dukedom. As for Louise, she was more than happy to move outside the circles of strict tradition and formalities. She wanted to participate more in causes and make a difference in people's lives.

With the Duke's bubbly conversation with the Ponsonbys, and the queen's near silence, Louise tried to keep her end of the conversation congenial, without saying anything she knew could irritate her mother further.

It was with great relief that Louise climbed into her bed that night because when the sun rose again, it would be the day of John's arrival at Balmoral. She could only hope that his opinions of her would not change with all the fuss.

She would know, the moment she saw him. She'd know if he'd stick with her no matter what they faced.

Louise spent the morning in the back gardens, sketching whatever she could see from the gazebo. She felt too antsy to work her sculpture, confined indoors. Ignoring the cold, she hoped the stiff breeze would help keep her thoughts clear. As it was, time dragged by the minute, and her nerves were too rattled to wait where she could hear John's carriage arrive.

She didn't want to watch him alight and greet his father. She didn't want to be the third, or fourth, or fifth party in the drawing room when he was presented to the queen. Louise wanted to be alone with him, to look into his eyes and know his feelings. To know if marriage to her would be worth whatever sacrifice he'd have to make.

Sketching right now was only a way to pass the time. Nothing she was creating would amount to much, if anything. She drew John atop a horse. She drew him in the gardens talking to the Duke. She drew him with her brothers Leo and Arthur as they stood about in the drawing room discussing the war. She drew him playing chess. Sitting across from her.

Turning page after page, as the breeze fluttered the edges of the sketchbook, she soon had a collection of discarded sketches. Ones that would be tossed into the fire. No one needed to see her tumultuous emotions spilled in gray graphite onto white paper.

"It is a fair likeness, although my hair is shorter."

She snapped her head up. John stood, feet away, inside the gazebo. His tartan was green, blue, and black, and he wore a deep green jacket over his shirt. His blue eyes were gray in the shade of the gazebo, and they were focused on her. She couldn't read his expression though. Her heart was beating too fast at the sight of him to try to figure out his thoughts.

Louise closed the sketchbook with a snap, blocking out her frenzied drawing from view. "How—how long have you been here?" she asked, nerves climbing her throat.

"Here in the gazebo? Only a moment, but long enough to see that you are troubled. Or at Balmoral? An hour. Long enough to be concerned that you didn't come to greet me."

The breath rushed out of Louise, and to her horror, tears filled her eyes. Crying shouldn't happen, *couldn't* happen. She blinked rapidly and stared down at her fingers gripping the sketchbook as if it were a life raft keeping her afloat in the middle of the sea.

"Louise."

Her given name upon his lips should have comforted her, but it didn't. It only made her heart sink more. What if she lost him? Just when she'd found him?

John crossed the gazebo and gently pried the sketchbook from her hands. She thought he was going to leaf through it. Instead, he set it on the bench and encased her hands in his. Then he slowly drew her to her feet. "Tell me what's wrong. Why are you out here alone in the cold?"

She blinked back her tears and lifted her chin. "Your father told me what you said."

He tilted his head, his forehead creased. "Yes, he informed me."

Her hands were already warming inside of his. Louise hadn't realized how stiff her fingers had become. "I don't want you to regret marrying me. It's not fair for you to have to change so many things."

John gazed at her, and she gazed right back. She waited for the agreement in his blue eyes, but it didn't come. "I wouldn't have proposed if I hadn't already considered all the changes," he said. "Marriage takes change, no matter what. I simply have a few more on my plate than the typical marquess."

Could she believe his words, or were they just platitudes? "The Duke said if you take a British peerage title, you'll lose your independence in political circles."

"Correct."

"And you would sacrifice that?"

"Not if I don't have to," he said. "I will turn down the queen's offer unless it becomes an unsurmountable hurdle in marrying you."

"So if she insists, you will take the title?"

John nodded, but the edges of his mouth had lifted. Why was he smiling? His father would be furious if he gave up his political career and took a British title, and in years to come, John might regret it.

"The bigger question is *yours,* dearest Louise."

His endearment made her breath go shallow. "How so?"

"Are you willing to be my marchioness?"

She knew what he was asking. Was she willing to enter into a marriage with a commoner—a marriage in which she would be equal to his station, at least in Scotland? She'd already told the Duke her answer, and that hadn't changed. "Yes."

His smile widened. "Then there is no cause for tears, right? You shall be my darling Louise, and I shall be your dearest husband. That is all that matters. The world, the newspapers, the queen, the Prince of Wales, your Prussian brothers-in-law, and everyone else can call us whatever they want. But from my viewpoint, you will be my wife, and no one else can interfere with that."

The tears were gone, replaced by relief.

"So, you see, this is *your* decision, my love," he murmured. "I've already made mine."

She saw it then. What she'd been waiting for. The conviction in his eyes—not of a temporary declaration—but of something deeper. A devotion that went to his very center. A commitment filled with a river of words that didn't need to be spoken.

"I've already made mine as well," she whispered, "dearest John."

He released one of her hands, then slid his thumb along her jawline. His touch sent a warm tremor through her body, and all cold fell away as he leaned down and whispered, "I am very glad to hear it."

His fingers lifted her chin, his touch light and warm on her skin, and she was sure either her heart or her breathing had completely stopped. His scent of sage and cedar was dearly familiar now. As he erased all distance between them, she closed her eyes, wondering if *this* would be the moment.

It was.

John kissed her. One hand linked with hers, the other beneath her chin.

Although only his mouth was pressed against hers, every part of her body flared warm. Her free hand curled around the lapel of his jacket, and she felt his smile against her mouth as she drew him nearer. He tasted of the cool Scottish breeze, yet he was so solid, warm, and . . . *hers*.

When he broke off the kiss, she wasn't ready to let him go, and she buried her face against his neck. Wrapping her arms about his waist, she was gratified when he enveloped her in his embrace, secure and sure.

"No more tears, dearest Louise," John whispered against her hair. "My heart is yours."

CHAPTER 33

Not home to land and kindred wast thou brought,
Nor laid 'mid trampled dead of battle won,—
Nor after long life filled with duty done
Was thine such death as thou thyself had'st sought!
No, sadder far, with horror overwrought
That end that gave to thee thy cruel grave
Deep in blue chasms of some glacier cave,
When Cervins perils thou, the first, had'st fought
And conquered, Douglas! for in thee uprose
In boyhood e'en a nature noble, free,—
So gently brave with courtesy, that those
Old Douglas knights, the "flowers of Chivalry,"
Had joyed to see that in our times again
A link of gold had graced their ancient chain!

"Lord F. Douglas Killed on the
Matterhorn, Switzerland, 1865," by John Campbell

MARCH 1871
LOUISE, AGE 23

Louise didn't know if she had ever felt happier. The Franco-Prussian War had ended in January—with a Prussian victory that had been brutally swift—and she'd be marrying John George Edward Henry Douglas Sutherland Campbell in three days.

The wait had been difficult, but she'd filled page after page writing to John when he wasn't in her presence. She'd hurt her knee and had it splinted for a while. Mama had refused to let John come and visit her while she was convalescing—her reasoning being that *she* wanted to spend the time with Louise and not compete with her fiancé. So John received long, detailed letters instead. And he'd returned the letters most ardently.

Today was her twenty-third birthday, and she was delighted that John and some of his family would be arriving at Windsor. She'd met several of them, of course, but not all. But she wasn't nervous about it since she was feeling secure in John's affections.

No matter what obstacles they faced, Louise felt confident in her future with John, especially since time was the great equalizer for the queen. She hadn't yet given John permission to call Louise by her first name, and he'd been calling her Princess Louise in the queen's presence. So far. But Louise was certain that was going to change on March 21, the date of her wedding. And she couldn't be more thrilled. Mama didn't even believe in kissing before marriage, and so that was information that Louise had kept strictly to herself—well, Sybil knew.

"There you are, Your Royal Highness," Sybil said, as if Louise had conjured her from her thoughts.

The March day had turned out fair, and Louise sat in a favorite garden nook with her sketchbook—although she wasn't drawing.

"You've come early."

"No, I am on time," Sybil said. "It seems you are late in getting ready."

Louise frowned, and her gaze shifted to the sky. The day had progressed faster than she'd expected. "I don't know where my mind is. I'll probably put something on backwards."

Sybil laughed. "Do you need help?"

"Yes," Louise said.

Once they reached her bedroom, Louise found a letter from Vicky waiting for her.

Sybil saw her hesitate before opening it. "Does she still oppose?"

Louise had confided in Sybil about the letters from Vicky on the subject of her marrying Lord Lorne. Vicky was not happy that Louise had not only turned down the Prussian prince but was now marrying a commoner.

If Bertie could come around and be supportive after all the complaining he'd done, then Vicky—in her distant Prussian kingdom—could too. Alice had also wanted Louise to marry a Prussian prince, but she'd only written letters of sweetness and support.

"Maybe I'll wait until after the wedding to open it," Louise said. "She'll be here soon anyway, and I can hear all her opinions in person."

Sybil nodded. "Once the Crown Princess sees how happy you are, she will realize it was the best decision for you."

Louise opened the gummed seal with a sigh. "The entire country of England is celebrating, so why can't my sister be happy for me?"

"For once, I agree with the press," Sybil said with a smile.

Louise scanned her sister's elegant handwriting. "Vicky has resorted to quoting her father-in-law. She says that the king of Prussia is most displeased that Princess Louise has chosen to lead a quiet life with a commoner instead of taking a position at the Berlin court by marrying his nephew."

"Ah." Sybil winced. "That's quite direct. And from a king too."

Louise folded the letter and handed it to Sybil. "Take it. Burn it. I don't want to see it again."

Sybil tucked it into the pocket of her dress, then put on a bright smile. "See what?"

Louise smiled, although inside, her stomach had balled up like yarn. She shouldn't have opened the letter in the first place.

Soon Louise was dressed and primmed. No matter what the feelings of her siblings were about John, she was determined to make this year's birthday enjoyable. She was much too old for a children's ball, and because the wedding was so close, the birthday gathering would be kept to a small number. No matter.

Mama was in a festive mood, and that made all the difference. This morning at seven o'clock, the band of the Second Life Guards played pieces from her favorite music beneath her bedroom window. Then in the afternoon, at one o'clock, the Royal Salute was fired in the Long Walk, followed by the ringing of the bells at St. George's Chapel.

Louise had felt well and truly honored.

As Sybil put the finishing touches upon Louise's hair, she said, "The crowds at Windsor are increasing by the day. Everyone is looking forward to the wedding and hope to catch a glimpse of the bride and groom."

"I read the papers this morning," Louise said. "I do hope that Lord Lorne isn't accosted."

"If anything, the marquess will be reminded of how enthusiastic everyone is."

"Can they share some of that enthusiasm with Vicky?" Louise quipped.

"Well, you are twenty-three now, quite the woman with her own mind and wishes." Sybil paused. "Are those carriages I hear?"

"I can't look. Will you look for me?"

Sybil chuckled. "Don't tell me you are nervous to see your beloved?"

"I will be nervous until we are well and truly married," Louise said. "Beyond the ceremony even. After our first night as husband and wife, only then will I believe that nothing will stop our wedding."

Sybil crossed the window to look out. "I've never seen so many Campbells in one place."

Louise popped up from her chair. "What? How many?" She arrived at the window to see that there were indeed at least a half dozen Campbells stepping out of carriages. They all wore Campbell colors, as if to drive home the idea that though they might be united with the royal family at Windsor, they were Scottish through and through.

"Oh, goodness," Sybil whispered. "Is that the Prince of Wales's carriage?"

Louise watched in disbelief as Bertie's carriage pulled behind the Campbell carriages. He'd vowed not to see Louise until her wedding day. She didn't want any sort of row between Bertie and John—or the Duke for that matter; he was the more vocal one.

While in Balmoral, Louise had received a disheartening letter from Alix in response to the announced engagement. Her words had been cold, disappointed, although she'd ended the letter with a promise of support. That hadn't extended to her husband, at least not at first.

Upon Louise's return to Windsor, Bertie had confronted her and Mama. He'd first criticized Lord Lorne for his near-engagement to another woman, Lady Victoria Ashley-Cooper. Thankfully, Louise already knew the story from John's own words—it had been one-sided and driven by the lady's mother.

In fact, when Louise had written to John of her brother's complaint, he'd said he expected nothing less from the Prince of Wales. So Bertie had dug deeper, saying that the queen's future son-in-law's political convictions put the Crown in the dangerous position of being too closely affiliated with a party. John was the Liberal member of Parliament for Argyllshire, and the Duke was a cabinet minister.

This had all been discussed with the queen, however, and deemed acceptable since he was a commoner.

Bertie, finally defeated, went silent.

"What is he doing here?" Louise asked Sybil, who had no answer. At least he'd brought Alix. Bertie would be better behaved with his wife present. Alix climbed out of the carriage with assistance. She was pregnant again, and the swelling of her feet and ankles required the use of her cane.

"Perhaps he's come to see the Liverpool merchant for himself," Sybil quipped.

Louise laughed. Bertie's earlier complaints had included that Louise would be marrying into a family that were connected with trade workers. One of John's brothers was a merchant in Liverpool.

"Well, whatever Bertie says tonight," Louise mused, "it can't be worse than the letter from the queen of Holland."

Sybil turned her head. "Is this new? I haven't heard."

"Prepare yourself to hear an insult about your beloved Princess Louise," she said with dramatic effect.

Sybil smirked.

"The queen of Holland declared that I am stooping and entering a *mésalliance*." Louise shrugged. "She's not specifically wrong in her statement, but I still take offense to her tone."

Sybil reached out a supportive hand. "I'll take offense with you, Your Royal Highness."

Louise embraced her friend. "What would I do without you, Sybil? I'd have gone mad over my impassioned family's declarations and ultimatums if it hadn't been for your friendship."

Fortunately Bertie did behave himself, but only just. He spoke very little, in fact, and that was perfectly fine with Louise. She caught his glower more than once, but what could she do? Ask the Prince of Wales to smile more? She also sensed that the Clan Campbell was holding back their lively personalities. She'd met enough of them to know that they were big talkers and easy to get along with. Yet, at her birthday dinner, they let the queen lead the conversation for the most part.

A few splinter groups held their own quiet conversations, the men mostly talking about the upcoming hunting season. Louise listened halfheartedly to the Duchess, Helena, and Sybil, while sharing stolen glances with John—who wasn't paying attention to his group either. Long before the dinner hour was over, she was tired of all the people, even if it was her birthday.

It wasn't until they reconvened in the drawing room after birthday cake had been served and Louise had politely opened the gifts from the Campbells—though she'd told them not to bring a thing—that Bertie and Alix excused themselves.

After they left, Louise felt relieved. Both that her brother had come in the first place and that he'd now left. Thankfully no one had talked politics, or the night might have gone much differently. Frisky found her through the maze of people, and she picked him up.

"Have you been reading the newspapers, Your Royal Highness?" John asked when they finally had a moment to stand together.

Louise lifted a brow. "About . . . ?"

John smiled and patted Frisky on the head. "You. Oh, and me too."

"You've achieved your lifelong dream," she teased. "You're finally featured in the dailies."

John laughed.

A few heads turned, but only friendly smiles were offered.

When they turned away again, John's blue eyes shifted back to her. "Frisky is the most well-traveled dog I know. Does he go with you everywhere?"

"He does."

Frisky agreed with a yip.

John grinned. "I know not all of your siblings are enraptured with me as their almost brother-in-law, but what is that compared to the rest of England? Crowds gathered at the railway station today hoping to catch sight of the groom, but I was able to give them the slip."

"Indeed." Louise smiled. "I am sure the papers will be full of the evading groom tomorrow." But she wasn't able to stop her sigh.

Never one to miss much, John said, "What? Have you received another letter from the Crown Princess?"

"How did you guess?"

"How did I *not* guess?" John countered. "She writes you every week." He paused. "And she will arrive tomorrow to give her opinion in person, I am sure. Has she changed her mind yet about me?"

"Not quite." Louise was trying not to let that thought ruin her birthday celebration. "Her letter informed me of the thorough disappointment from the king of Prussia." She leaned close and lowered her voice. "He's most displeased, you know, and he considers my marriage to anyone who is not Prussian as a hostile act against Prussia, right on par with how the queen sold arms to France in the war. How dare I choose a commoner over his royal nephew? I'm snubbing the opportunity to hold a position at the Berlin court. What do you have to say to that, sir?"

John's blue eyes gleamed. "If I may be so bold, while we are discussing our ancestry . . . my forefathers were kings, and the Hohenzollerns were *parvenus*."

Louise couldn't stop the smile spreading across her face. "I think I might love you for saying that, Lord Lorne."

The room seemed to go very still. No one had overheard them, but John's eyes had fixated on her. Slowly, he lifted her hand and pressed a kiss on her skin, just above her gloves. "It is a good thing that we are getting married this month then, my dear, and not the dreadful May you first suggested."

If they hadn't been in a drawing room full of people, Louise would have pulled the man into her arms and kissed him soundly. She set down Frisky, who'd suddenly become wiggly.

"How is your knee doing?" John asked.

Louise wanted to swat his arm, but she refrained. "You don't need to ask me any longer about my knee. It's perfectly healed."

"I am pleased to hear it." He winked.

She smirked.

"Prince Arthur informed me that Mr. Reibolds has agreed to accompany us on the honeymoon since Her Majesty brushed off Monsieur Kanné."

Oh, that. Louise fidgeted with her gloves. Mama was against their honeymoon plans, which would take them on an adventure throughout Europe. Because of the recent war, the queen believed that everything was inaccessible and Louise would be attacked from all corners. Since John had refused to change their plans, Louise had come up with the idea of inviting the courier, Monsieur Kanné, to accompany them.

"Loosy," the queen said, cutting in as if she'd overheard the conversation from where she sat across the room. "We must discuss the honeymoon before Lorne and the Duke depart tonight."

Louise nodded and tried to conceal her growing frustration. She'd already explained their plans to Mama. They would not be changing their minds.

So it was with some reluctance that Louise reconvened to another drawing room and sat with John, the Duke, the Duchess, and the queen to discuss the safety of traveling through countries that had recently been involved in war.

"You cannot wander about a war-torn Europe and expect to sight-see," Mama said, her gaze upon Louise, although she was talking to everyone in the room. "I have also spoken to Lord Granville, and he agrees with me. A princess should not be traveling abroad at a time like this, and Lord Lorne is not accustomed to all that's required for your comfort and safety."

Louise felt John bristle beside her. She wanted to tell him not to react strongly. It was always better to listen to Mama and then later, much later, bring up alternate solutions gently. Their current plan was to spend four days at Claremont House, then return to Windsor before their early-April departure to Europe.

"Princess Louise will be safe with me, Your Majesty," John said, his tone light but laced with firmness. "We won't be changing our honeymoon plans. We will travel incognito as Lord and Lady Sundridge."

Louise drew in her breath, anticipating the queen's response.

"Prince Arthur has arranged for Mr. Reibolds to accompany us for safety measures," John continued. "Since you have already informed us that Monsieur Kanné would not be available, I trust this will alleviate your concerns."

The queen's brows lifted. Her gaze cut to the Duke, who was smart enough to not take either side in the matter. He only clasped his hands together, and the Duchess kept her eyes lowered.

The queen again looked at John. "Monsieur Kanné is available after all—that is, *if* you insist on your plans."

"I insist, ma'am," he said without any hesitation.

The Duke cleared his throat as a sort of warning, but the words had been said. It was a wonder to Louise that Mama allowed this Scottish noble to speak so frankly to her. Yet that was his way and always had been.

"There is one more thing, Mama," Louise said, hoping that her timing wasn't ill-mannered. Both the Duke and Duchess looked at her with interest. "We will be passing through Darmstadt. May we have permission to visit Alice and her family?"

Louise might be marrying a commoner, one who did not have to seek a parent's permission in all things, but she didn't have the luxury.

"I will think upon it," the queen said.

"There is actually a second matter I'd like to discuss, ma'am," John said, reaching for Louise's hand and linking their fingers.

Mama certainly didn't miss the intimate action, and the Duchess drew in a sharp breath, then cut a glance at the Duke. He gave no indication that he knew what was coming, and Louise couldn't possibly guess what John was about to ask. They hadn't discussed any other requests to make of Mama.

"Once we are married, I will be calling your daughter by her given name," John said. "She'll be Princess Louise in all public events, but around my family, your family, and when it is only the two of us, she will be my Louise."

No one in the room seemed to move or breathe.

Louise was afraid to see Mama's expression. It was a long, long moment before she spoke. "The Duke and I have had this discussion already, Lorne, and I was under the impression that he agreed that the princess's title should always take precedence. In every situation. Public or private."

The Duke's face flared pink, but to his credit, he kept his chin lifted, his gaze steady. "Yes, we did have that discussion, Your Majesty. But my son is his own man, and in this situation, he has made up his own mind."

Mama's stare was quite fierce as she kept ahold of the Duke's gaze. "You support your son in this?"

The man gave an audible swallow, and Louise was pretty sure all warmth had drained from the Duchess's face.

"I do," the Duke said at last.

Louise felt the breath whoosh out of her, and she realized she was gripping John's hand rather tight.

The queen didn't move, didn't blink. Beyond the drawing room doors, indistinct sounds could be heard of people moving about the palace and conversations continuing in the other drawing room. But inside this room, time seemed to have halted.

Mama's gaze broke, and she slowly turned her head. Her blue eyes weren't blazing though—they were . . . conflicted? Finally, her words came. "In private only, Lorne. And no one else may have that privilege. Not your siblings or your parents."

"Yes, ma'am," John said humbly.

But Louise heard the triumph in his voice, and it traveled through their linked hands and straight into her heart.

CHAPTER 34

—❦—

"On waking I could hardly believe this trying day, which seemed so far distant had really come at last! It was dull early but it soon began to get very bright.— Dear Louise came as usual to breakfast which she took with Leopold, Beatrice & me & was quite calm, but not very well, having got a fresh cold & sore throat, with which she has been so troubled of late.— Crowds beginning to assemble and bustle everywhere.— Louise gave me a little locket to put a piece of her wreath in.— The sun came out brilliantly & the day became beautiful."

QUEEN VICTORIA'S JOURNAL, MARCH 21, 1871

MARCH 1871
LOUISE, AGE 23

Why today, of all days?" Louise murmured as she stood before the mirror on her wedding day. She was dressed, veiled, and bejeweled. A vision of a bride, but her complexion was pale. She'd awakened with a headache, an earache, and definite signs of a cold.

Lady Jane had brought a restorative tea earlier, and it was all that Louise could depend upon for now. She'd sent a note to John, telling him that she had the beginnings of a fierce cold, and did he want to change his mind?

He wrote back immediately to say he'd bring the bishop of London into her bedroom and perform the ceremony in their nightclothes if necessary.

Louise had been smiling since. Well, at least when she wasn't bemoaning her symptoms.

The day had begun early with masses of people arriving at the Windsor Castle grounds. From her window's viewpoint, the crowds extended as far as she could see. The reports in the newspapers the past week had left her feeling both exhilarated and overwhelmed. All those who had been critical of her marriage to the Marquess of Lorne should read today's papers and see the celebration and support.

It seemed that all of England had turned out.

She and John were the darlings of the country, said to be living out a true love story, and they were single-handedly turning the hearts and minds back to the monarchy. Louise analyzed the idea of a "love story." Perhaps it was. The only thing she knew for certain was that John was the man for her. Louise hoped this very public wedding would be a good omen of things to come—a sign that the royal family would be less secluded and more accessible to its subjects.

She and John had managed to work out any conflicts so far, small ones as well as larger ones. Surely that was a sign Providence smiled upon them. Last month, the papers had been critical of Mama's appearance to open Parliament. Naysayers had claimed she only opened Parliament when she was about to ask for dowries from the taxpayers. But the queen had prevailed, the dowry had passed Parliament, and now the celebrations were underway.

All of her siblings would be present, save for Alice, who was pregnant with her fifth child. Louise hoped that Vicky and her husband would keep their harsher opinions to themselves. Perhaps this wedding could herald in goodwill among the siblings permanently.

"You are a vision, Your Royal Highness," Sybil said in a soft voice as she attached the train to the wedding dress.

Louise's wedding gown was made of white silk with Honiton lace on the flounces. Trimmed with white heather, orange blossoms, and myrtle, she could have easily had a garden ceremony. The white heather was for luck, and the myrtle was for her father's Germany, as well as the Campbells.

Upon her head, she wore a wreath of myrtle and orange blossoms she'd crafted herself. She'd also designed the short wedding veil of Honiton lace. Arthur, Leo, and Beatrice had given her three diamond brooches shaped as daisies, and she used them to hold her veil in place.

The gift from John was her most treasured though—a bracelet of sapphire, diamonds, and pearls that could be worn as a pendant. She'd added it to her diamond necklace so that the gift could be on display. As a final touch, she wore two bracelets—an emerald one given to her by the Prince and Princess of Wales and a diamond bracelet inherited from her grandmother, the Duchess of Kent.

John's kinsmen would be wearing Campbell-tartan kilts, but John himself would wear the uniform of the Argyllshire Artillery Volunteers.

And Louise couldn't wait to see him.

"Ready?" Sybil asked softly as she rose to her feet.

Louise met her friend's gaze in the mirror. "I'd better be. There are a lot of people out there waiting."

Sybil only smiled and reached for Louise's hand. The two friends squeezed fingers, then Louise closed her eyes. She thought of her father and wished he could be here to walk her down the aisle and give her away. Instead, it would be her mother. Perhaps, though, Father was watching from his own place in heaven.

With a smile, she opened her eyes. She was ready.

A knock sounded at the door, and Lady Jane walked in, dressed in her wedding finery. "Lovely, just lovely, Your Royal Highness. I've come to tell you that Lord Lorne and his escorts have left for the church. The rest of the royal family will leave soon."

"Very well," Louise said and walked toward the door.

The Campbell children were gathered at the end of the long corridor as she'd requested. She smiled and welcomed each of them as she passed by. She would be their aunt, and she was looking forward to getting to know all of them.

The members of the royal family were soon ushered into carriages while Louise waited. She would go last, escorted by eight bridesmaids—all unmarried daughters of the peerage—who would carry her train. Her chief bridesmaid was John's sister, Elizabeth, or Libby, as everyone called her.

The Prince of Wales, Prince Alfred, Uncle Ernest—all wearing their military uniforms—stepped out of the green drawing room, with the queen at their side. Bertie bent to kiss Louise on the cheek, followed by Uncle Ernest, then Alfred.

"You are a vision, my dear Loosy." Mama wore her customary black but had added the blue sash of the Order of the Garter and crimson rubies at her throat. "I am both joyful and sorrowful today. I am giving you up, and you will no longer be my little girl."

Louise squeezed her mother's hands. "I will always be your daughter, dear Mama."

Louise's heart floated as she stepped outside. The view at ground level was much more daunting than from her bedroom window, and the masses of people gathered at Windsor, with lines of policemen in front of them, were awe-inspiring.

Cheers went up, and Louise stood, gazing about and smiling.

She didn't care to be gawked at, but her wedding day was an exception. This day was for the public, and for family celebration, and she and John didn't expect any private moments anytime soon. Keeping that in mind would help her enjoy each and every moment.

When she was settled on the velvet bench in the carriage, after Lady Jane and Sybil both fussed over her wedding dress and veil, the queen came out of the palace and climbed into the same carriage. The distance to the church wasn't far, but the five carriages made a slow procession along the crowd-lined road.

At the end of all this, her groom would be waiting at the altar.

It had been over three hundred and fifty years since the daughter of a monarch and a British subject had been allowed to marry, and protocol had to be created anew. It was decided that John wouldn't enter the chapel until all the royal family had been seated.

Sitting across from her, Lady Jane said, "Did you know they had to give out tickets so that uninvited guests wouldn't try to enter?"

Louise almost laughed at this, imagining any of her royal relatives draped in diamonds and sapphires being held up and questioned as to their invitation. She peered out the window, marveling at the crowds. There stood a long row of boys from Eton in their smart uniforms, likely there because the man to marry the princess had attended Eton.

At last, it was time for Louise to step out of the carriage. The bridesmaids were waiting outside the door to lift her train. Louise had designed the bridesmaid dresses of white glacé silk, trimmed in satin. The tunics of gossamer were decorated with red roses, heather, and ivy, and the floral wreaths upon their heads matched the decorations of their dresses. Each bridesmaid also wore a locket of blue and white enamel inscribed with "Louise 1871."

A bridal bower had been created at the church in case the princess should need to adjust her dress, but she didn't sense anything wrong. Besides, the wait had been long enough. She lined up with the queen and Bertie, then stepped up to the West Door which had been covered with a heavy crimson drape.

As Louise walked inside, she felt like she was standing on the edge of a cliff—exhilaration mixed with trepidation. The entire chapel glowed with the early-afternoon light coming through the stained-glass windows, bouncing off the luxurious silks and satins and jewels of the congregation lining both sides of the wide aisle. All heads turned, gazes upon her. Trumpets played, announcing her entrance.

The church filled to capacity was a grand sight to behold, and she was humbled to know that over two hundred were in attendance—her family members and other royal guests, the queen's household, representatives of foreign governments, the clergy, government officials, and all the attendants to the royals, along with other invited guests.

At the pinnacle of it all, where the long aisle ended, stood John Campbell.

"Thank you, Mama," Louise whispered before she began to walk, the queen on her right and Bertie and Alfred on her left.

Louise knew the program, the songs that the choir would sing, the words that would be spoken by John Jackson, bishop of London, and the vows that would be uttered. But she didn't think of any of that because her focus was on John, dressed in his formal Royal Argyllshire Artillery uniform, waiting for her. Although his kinsmen wore kilts, John was in full dress uniform of navy trousers with a gold stripe running down the length, and a navy jacket with a gold and red collar, then edged with red and gold at the cuffs. Hanging from his side was a ceremonial sword.

He stood unmoving, his gaze upon her, waiting patiently. Despite all the attention, his expression was neither sheepish nor cocky. He was simply . . . her marquess. Each step brought her closer, and she walked with practiced grace, the bridesmaids following behind, holding up her train. She felt the smiles and the gazes, but she didn't meet anyone's eyes.

John's blue eyes were upon her, direct and warm. And that was all that mattered.

Mendelssohn's *Athalie* surrounded them, filling the chapel. As they arrived at the altar, the queen presented Louise, then stood aside as Louise faced John.

His eyes searched hers as if to ask if she was well. She gave him a small nod, and he returned it with an imperceptible smile.

As the bishop of London began the formal ceremony, Louise kept her gaze on her almost husband. The directness of his blue eyes told her that he trusted her, that he was here willingly. She wanted him to know that she was too.

Their vows were simple, straightforward, and when they'd finished, the bishop pronounced them married. The royal salute fired outside the church, its tremendous sound reverberating through the walls and echoing in her heart.

She was married. At last.

The queen kissed her cheek in congratulations, then John stepped forward to politely kiss the queen's hand. He drew Louise's hand close, his fingers a steady pressure upon hers, and placed it atop his arm. They walked up the aisle, together this time. The organ played the energetic *Occasional Oratorio* by George Frideric Handel, and Louise's heart soared with the notes.

Instead of traveling in separate carriages, Louise now rode in the same one with John and his parents.

"You are a lovely bride, Your Royal Highness," the Duchess said.

The Duke wiped his eyes and couldn't stop grinning.

The crowds were cheering so loudly that she couldn't have spoken to John if she'd tried. He grasped one of her hands, and with the other, waved at the people.

Louise did the same. Waving and smiling. This much enthusiasm was usually reserved for a monarch, yet today, she felt like she was the queen of the entire world.

Back at Windsor, Bertie directed everyone into the drawing room. "The queen has a presentation to make."

Louise found Mama inside, and Bertie and Alix stood on one side of her. Alix's exquisite dress was of blue satin. Behind her, a train of velvet, edged in lace, extended from the dress. Her headdress dominated all others in the room—made of feathers, pearls, and diamonds. She leaned on her cane, her pregnancy obvious. Louise had heard she'd fallen while getting out of the carriage. Thankfully she seemed fine now. Only her siblings and their spouses were there, along with officials.

"I will be presenting the Order of the Thistle to Lord Lorne," the queen said.

Louise looked over at her new husband. This was completely unexpected, and now the queen had put him under pressure in front of everyone. Would he object? The others might not notice the faint flush along his neck.

The Order of the Thistle was the highest knighthood one could receive in Scotland. It was founded by King James VII of Scotland and represented the order of chivalry. Louise fully prepared herself for him to reject the queen's offer, but instead, to her surprise, and perhaps the queen's as well, John stepped forward.

"Thank you, Your Majesty. I'll receive it with great honor."

After the ceremony, Arthur stepped forward and embraced John. "Welcome to the family. It's too late to back out now."

Everyone in the room laughed, and then Louise watched as all of her family members embraced John one by one, welcoming him to the family. By the time he turned back to her, her eyes had filled with tears. John pulled her into an embrace, startling her, and likely the queen too. All of their shared affection had been out of her family's views. But John had now broken through that barrier too.

"Now, might we move on to the wedding cake?" Leo quipped.

CHAPTER 35

———◦◦◦———

"Louise was very pale, but looked very handsome & graceful in her white satin dress, with beautiful Honiton lace (my gifts) & orange blossom, myrtle & white heather, the veil to match,— a very long train trimmed the same. At ¼ to 12 we started, only dear Louise driving with me, sitting opposite. My Procession consisted of 5 carriages. We drove down the hill, where lots of people stood, including Eton Boys, in at the St. George's gate, driving under the low arch of the cloisters, up to the great door."

QUEEN VICTORIA'S JOURNAL, MARCH 21, 1871

MARCH 1871
LOUISE, AGE 23

Y ou're bringing the dog?" John asked from where he stood next to the carriage with his parents.

She'd changed from her wedding dress into an elegant day dress, and they were about to be sent off for their honeymoon. The herbal tea she'd been plied with earlier had also made her feel better, and for that she was grateful. Of course they weren't going alone—Mama had insisted that upper staff accompany them on the two-hour ride. Colonel McNeill would be traveling with them, and Lady Jane would be waiting at Claremont to attend to their needs and keep them company. Louise didn't think she needed anyone else's company but her husband's on her honeymoon, but she'd decided not to make an argument of it.

"Frisky isn't just any dog," Louise said. "He's been my friend for ages, and he'd be mightily depressed without me."

John's expression was hard to read, but when Louise stopped before him, he merely pet the small terrier. "I hope you didn't give him any wedding cake."

"Now why would I do that?" Louise teased.

John shook his head, a half smile on his face. "I have no idea, but he won't be happy with anything less at Claremont if you had."

The wedding cake had been shaped like an elegant tower, and at five feet tall, it was a work of art, decorated with cherubs, flowers, and vases and topped with a classical female figure. Leo had had more than one piece, Louise had noted.

The rest of the family began to arrive to bid farewell. Most of the wedding guests had already left on a specially ordered train to take them to London. Louise hugged each of her siblings fiercely—Leo, Alfred, Vicky, Helena, Arthur, Beatrice, and finally Bertie. Next, she hugged her nieces and nephews—lastly the oldest, Willy, a tall lad of twelve now, who would be the Emperor of Prussia one day. He wasn't a cherub toddler anymore, but Louise still felt a strong connection to him.

"Safe travels," she told Willy after embracing him and kissing his cheek.

"Safe travels, Auntie Loosy," he said with a smile.

The front doors opened, and John grasped her elbow. "Ready, darling?"

Now that the formal ceremony and wedding meals were over, she was more than ready to begin life as a married woman. Wedding guests had lined the path to the carriage, and they threw handfuls of rice and satin shoes at the bride and groom. Louise laughed and ducked her head as the rice pelted her shoulders and collected in her hair. John Brown held a new broom that he'd throw after the carriage, in Highland tradition. Beyond the drive, there were still crowds of people at Windsor, watching their exit.

As John handed her into the carriage, she said, "I thought everyone would have gone home by now."

John chuckled as he settled right next to her, then he reached for her hand. Colonel McNeill, their escort, climbed into the carriage, and despite his presence, John didn't let go of her hand.

"You look quite the confection, my love," John whispered in her ear.

She let the words slide all the way to her heart as she tightened her hold on his hand.

Once they made it down Windsor Hill, they traveled along the road, past homes and buildings, finding the streets lined with people.

"No one has anything else to do today?" Louise asked with a laugh.

"Nothing more important. You are a princess, my dear," he said. "And a royal wedding is not an everyday occurrence."

"Yes, but I don't remember any of this with my other siblings' weddings," she said. "There were some crowds when Alix arrived, but I was kept at Windsor, so maybe I didn't understand the extent of it."

John squeezed her hand. "Look. It's raining flowers."

And it was.

From the balconies and upper windows, people tossed out flowers as the carriage passed by. Louise stared at the flowers in wonder. They were dotting the street, making it seem as if they were driving through a garden.

Once they cleared the main parts of the city and were no longer driving through crowds of cheering people anymore, Louise turned to John. "Were you waiting long at the altar?"

"At least an hour."

She elbowed him. "No, really. How long? The carriages were all backed up, and I was worried you thought I'd changed my mind."

John brought her hand to his lips and pressed a kiss there. His blue eyes were intent on hers, saying more, desiring more. But they were still in a carriage, and although Colonel McNeill was looking out the window, he was plenty alert. No afternoon snooze for this man. They couldn't exactly have a private conversation, and Louise was certain that John was addled by that, but to his credit, he didn't complain.

"It was only ten minutes or so," he said. "But it felt like much longer since everyone was watching me, probably trying to figure out why their lovely Princess Louise had chosen me of all the men in the United Kingdom."

"No one was thinking that." She tilted her head. "Well, maybe two or three."

John threw his head back and laughed. When he straightened his features, he said, "Certainly more than three, my love."

Arriving at Claremont felt like Louise was stepping into another world. The sweeping grounds of rolling lawns, trees surrounding a pond, and flowers blooming everywhere made the place feel like a private country estate. The house itself was a regal two-story mansion with four proud pillars at the front entrance. Louise let Frisky out of the carriage to explore a little before she and John climbed the twenty steps to the front entrance, where they were greeted by Lady Jane.

"Dinner will be ready soon, Your Royal Highness," Lady Jane said after a curtsey. "I trust that the journey was comfortable."

"Very comfortable," Louise said.

"Very long," John said at the same time.

Lady Jane smiled knowingly, then waved them into the house. "I'll show you two around the place while your luggage is taken to the bridal suite. Then I can help unpack your things, Your Royal Highness."

"That would be wonderful, although I don't mean for you to go to all this trouble, Jane."

"It's no trouble."

"I didn't know Claremont had a bridal suite," John said as they followed Lady Jane.

"It doesn't," Louise said, "but one has been especially prepared for us."

Lady Jane took them through the elegant house, with its colorful patterned carpets, and a plethora of paintings hanging from the walls. The arched doorways opened to rooms of floor-to-ceiling windows and recessed ceilings.

They walked up the steps and along the corridor, heading to the bridal suite. Lady Jane said, "The carpet is new and was woven especially for your visit."

When Lady Jane opened the door to the suite, Louise gaped. The carpet had been woven into an orange blossom pattern. Fresh roses had been set about in vases upon side tables, and the room smelled like a garden.

"It's beautiful," Louise said.

"Exquisite workmanship." John crouched to run his fingers along the design. He looked up at Louise. "Perhaps I can help you unpack."

His gaze slid to Lady Jane, who'd already opened a trunk that sat at the foot of the bed.

"It's no trouble," Lady Jane said. "I'm here to assist."

John rose to his feet and crossed to her. "If we need something, Lady Jane, we'll be sure to call for you."

Lady Jane met his steady, direct gaze. "Of course, Lord Lorne." She cast a glance at Louise, who merely nodded, although she was surprised at John's interference.

John walked to the door and held it open. Lady Jane wasted no more time and hurried out of the room. He closed the door with a quiet click, then turned the lock.

"I hope her feelings are not offended by your dismissal," Louise said as John walked back to the open trunk.

"We'll see her soon enough at dinner, and I'll apologize if necessary," John said. "But I don't think it will be necessary. Surely she, and all of the other staff here, realize we are on our honeymoon and are not to be hovered over. I'd prefer it if they not disturb us at all."

Louise had no way of concealing her blush. "What if we get hungry?"

"Then we will dine with the others. Or if we are too occupied, you could fix us something in the kitchen later? I haven't forgotten hearing about your cooking skills." He lifted his gaze, a soft smile on his face as he studied her. He still stood by the double-sized bed—the bed, Louise realized, she was now authorized to share with her husband.

She drew in a breath. "Do you really know how to unpack a lady's trunk? Is this a skill I don't know about?"

"You can tell me where you want your things, and then you'll know where to find them." John lifted out a shawl. "I am sure you won't be needing this since I'll keep you plenty warm. Shall I put it in the bottom drawer of the bureau?"

When he turned to open the drawer, Louise hurried to his side and snatched the shawl. "I don't want it in the bottom drawer to be forgotten. It's my favorite shawl."

His lips curved as he reached for the shawl, but she tucked it behind her and backed up.

John's brows lifted as he stepped close. She moved back again, until she was pressed against the bureau. He moved closer still until she was trapped between him and the bureau. If heat had flooded her cheeks before, now it flooded her whole body.

"John, what are you doing?" she breathed.

"Helping you unpack by getting your shawl put into its right place."

She handed him the shawl. "Fine, take it. But give me a little room here."

John took the shawl, tossed it on the bed, then crowded her again. He rested his hands on her hips. "Louise."

She bit her lip and looked up at him. "Hmm?"

His smile was slow. "Thank you for marrying me."

"You're welcome."

He chuckled. "How does it feel to be my marchioness?"

She let her smile emerge. "Quite nice, Marquess."

He returned her smile then closed the distance completely and kissed her. Slowly this time. They didn't have to fear being walked in upon since a locked door separated them from the rest of the household.

Louise returned the kiss, more fully than she ever had before. She didn't know much of what happened between a husband and wife, but she trusted John, and that was more important to her right now.

In the distance, a bell rang. When it rang a second time, Louise pressed a hand against John's chest. "Is that the dinner bell?"

He lifted his head. "There's a dinner bell?"

"It's better than knocking on our door, I suppose?"

John sighed and leaned his forehead against hers. "You're hungry, I'm assuming."

Louise patted his chest. "I am, and so are you. Let's go before they start to gossip about us."

"I don't care about gossip, dear Louise." John moved in for another kiss.

Louise only allowed the kiss to be brief. "Come on, husband. We are being discreetly summoned."

He straightened, then stepped back. Extending his hand, he brought hers to his lips. "I think this has been the longest day of my life."

Louise laughed and curled her fingers into his. She led him out of the room, with its luxurious carpet, and they joined Lady Jane and Colonel McNeill in the dining room, where china and crystal gleamed in the gaslight. The conversation was light and easy as they chatted about the wedding festivities. They talked much longer than Louise expected, and she was wondering when it would be polite enough to excuse herself with John.

Her unexpected yawn took care of that.

"You must be exhausted, Your Royal Highness," Lady Jane said. "I'll help you prepare for bed."

"Thank you," Louise said. "That would be wonderful."

She didn't know when John would retire for the night or how long she'd wait for him. She walked with Lady Jane to their suite. Nothing was unpacked after all. John had removed only the shawl, and it was hanging halfway off the bed, so now she had to find her nightclothes.

Once she'd changed and Lady Jane had turned up the gas lamps, Louise sat at the boudoir, and Lady Jane began to unpin her hair. She continued to talk about the marvelous events of the wedding, but Louise was barely listening. Her friend and lady-in-waiting was only trying to keep things light and comforting, when all the while, Louise was wishing that John would appear. She didn't like this anticipation, this unknown.

Someone knocked softly on the door, then opened it. Without turning her head, Louise could see through the mirror that John had entered. Lady Jane was still working on getting Louise's hair undone, and she hadn't pulled on a robe yet.

"Lord Lorne," Lady Jane said. "I'm helping Her Royal Highness prepare—"

"I can manage from here," John said.

He wasn't looking at Louise, not yet, keeping his gaze on Lady Jane.

"Of course, sir," Lady Jane said. "I could finish her hair if you'd like."

"We'll see you tomorrow," John said, his tone kind yet direct.

As Lady Jane left the room, John locked the door behind her, then he turned, his gaze meeting Louise's in the mirror.

"More talents?" Louise said above the zipping of her pulse.

He hadn't changed into nightclothes, not yet, and that's when Louise remembered his trunks were in the same room as hers.

John only smiled and walked to where she sat at the boudoir. Resting his hands on her shoulders, his gaze continued to hold hers in the mirror. "I was hoping Lady Jane would be in here for only a few moments, but as the clock ticked the hours away, I decided I had to intervene."

"*Hours?*"

"Felt like hours." He leaned down and kissed the back of her neck.

Warmth seared through Louise, and she drew in a shaky breath. "John . . ."

"Yes, my love?"

Her pulse thrummed harder. "Thank you for marrying me."

He smiled, then straightened and, quite deftly, removed the rest of the pins from her hair. Then before she could use the hairbrush herself,

John picked it up and gently ran the brush through her light-brown locks.

She watched him in the mirror as he concentrated on his task, as though he were aiming to displace every lady-in-waiting she'd ever had work on her hair.

"You have some rice in your hair," he murmured.

She laughed, though it came out as a nervous sound. He tossed a couple of rice pieces onto the boudoir.

"I don't think I've ever seen you with your hair down," he said after several more moments of brushing.

The touch of his fingers sliding through her hair made her skin hum. "If you had, it would have caused quite the scandal."

He lifted his eyes to meet hers at that, and the edge of his mouth curved. "And now?"

"And now . . ." This stalling was agony. She reached for the brush, pulling it from his hand. "I think that's enough brushing for now."

She rose to her feet, her limbs feeling a bit unsteady. She turned to face him. He might've still been in his Argyll uniform, but without anyone else in the room with them, he was far from formal. Placing a hand on his chest, she said, "Is this what you're sleeping in?"

He looked down at his uniform, then met her gaze with smiling blue eyes. "I hadn't planned on it."

"Do *you* need help changing, Lord Lorne?"

"Most definitely. Do you think you can manage, my love?"

She drew in a breath. "I can."

CHAPTER 36

"I would rather you had not met her so soon [after the wedding], for I know her curiosity and what is worse and what I hardly like to say of my own daughter. . . . I know her indelicacy and coarseness. . . . Don't let Alice pump you. Be very silent and cautious about your 'interior.'"

LETTER FROM QUEEN VICTORIA
TO PRINCESS LOUISE, APRIL 28, 1871

MARCH 1871
LOUISE, AGE 23

The tapping on the door weaved in and out of Louise's dream like fine thread in a tapestry.

"Is someone knocking?" she whispered. She'd been married for two days now, and she and John had little cause to leave their suite except for meals.

"Ignore it," John said, his chest vibrating against her cheek.

She'd curled next to him, her new favorite sleeping position. She understood now why mothers were so protective when it came to letting their daughters spend time with men.

If Louise had known that sharing a marriage bed was so enchanting, she would have married ages ago. She smiled at her scandalous thoughts. She was a wife now, and she had never felt a bond like this with another person. Even the thought of her and John being in separate rooms sent an ache into her heart. She assumed this intense feeling would pass, but for now, she was going to revel in it.

"What are you smiling about?"

Nothing got past her John. "You," she said.

The next knock was louder and wiped the smile from Louise's face.

"Your Royal Highness," came Lady Jane's voice through the door. "Her Majesty has arrived at Claremont."

Louise bolted upright in bed. "What?" she gasped. She grabbed for her robe that was on the floor. Drawing it on, she hurried to the door and cracked it open. "What is Mama doing here?"

Lady Jane stood a few feet from the door, her face decidedly flushed. "Her Majesty said she's come to ensure that you are well."

Louise closed her eyes. Behind her, John rummaged around, likely getting dressed. "Tell her we'll be down shortly."

Lady Jane curtseyed, then turned away. Louise shut the door and leaned her forehead against it.

"We should have gone straight to the train station and headed out of England," John said, right behind her. He ran his hands down her arms. "But since we cannot, we will dress and greet your mother."

Louise turned and buried her face against his chest. He'd slipped on a shirt, and the fabric was cool against her heated cheek. "Mama will scrutinize me from head to toe. She'll want to know if you've made me happy."

John's hands moved up her back. "What will you tell her?"

She sighed against him. "I will tell her that I am the happiest I've ever been."

He kissed the top of her head. "I think I need to be part of this conversation."

Louise drew away from him. "Well, you are my husband, and we must do all things together now."

"I agree." John leaned down and kissed the tip of her nose. "Now, let me help you with your clothing so we don't keep Her Majesty waiting."

Louise and John found the queen settled in the drawing room, tea spread before her. This was a good sign, Louise decided, because it appeared that she wasn't staying the night but would be returning to Windsor today.

"My darling Loosy," Mama said when Louise entered. "How is my beloved daughter?"

Louise curtseyed, then bent to kiss her mother. "I am well."

Mama made no secret of examining her while keeping their hands clasped. "Are you still feeling ill?"

"I just had a pesky cold," Louise said. "John has taken good care of me though."

At that point, the queen finally turned her attention to John. He bowed deeply and said, "It's a pleasure to have you at Claremont, Your Majesty."

She held out her hand, and he bent to kiss it. Then she folded her hands in her lap and leaned back to survey them both. "I have been worried about you up here by yourselves. There are so many things going on at Windsor, and everyone misses Louise."

Louise wanted to argue, but she wouldn't do so in front of John. Everyone knew—the entire country, in fact—that Louise was on her honeymoon, and they supported it.

But Mama seemed to be in her own world now that she'd seen that Louise was perfectly well. "You have many official duties to attend to, my dear. Duties that your husband will be supportive of, I am sure."

"Of course, ma'am," John murmured.

His response wasn't necessary, for the queen continued to speak. "The Emperor Napoleon has arrived and needs our compassion. He's looking forward to being received by you."

Louise only nodded. She wanted to say something about how it was fortunate he hadn't attended her wedding, with his sworn enemy's family there—which happened to be the queen's own son-in-law.

"I will do what I can before we depart for Europe," Louise said matter-of-factly. "Everything else will have to wait until my return."

Frisky ran into the room before Mama could bemoan the honeymoon once again. The terrier offered the needed distraction, and soon the queen's mood seemed much lighter. When she left, hours later, Louise didn't know whether she needed to apologize to John or not.

He'd been perfectly amicable toward Mama, like he always was, but she wanted to know his thoughts—his true thoughts.

Once they were alone again, after having dinner with Lady Jane and Colonel McNeill, Louise said, "At least Mama did not stay overnight." She was standing before the window, watching the setting sun cast its net of gold and orange across the parkland. John came up behind her and slipped his arms about her waist.

She leaned back, letting the warmth of his arms encircle her.

"She's a mother who worries about her daughter," John said in a gentle voice. "Although she does go to quite the extremes sometimes, I can't fault her for the love she has for her children."

"How are you so wonderful?" Louise said.

John rested his chin atop her head. "Keep thinking that, dear Louise. The longer you are blind to my faults, the better."

She turned in his arms to face him. "You know what I am most excited about?"

"Our honeymoon throughout Europe, where you'll see world-famous sculptures?"

"No," she said. "I mean, I am very much looking forward to that, but I can't wait until we visit your Scotland home and I can learn more about your origins. I carry your name now, you know, and it will be my home too someday."

John smoothed a bit of hair from her face with gentle fingers. "They will love you. Everyone will. You're vibrant and beautiful, and I'll have to keep locking doors to secure us some privacy."

"We're used to that already, are we not?"

John lowered his forehead to hers. "I wish we could bypass Windsor altogether. I don't imagine I'll have much time alone with you there."

"I wish we could too," she said. "But the plans are set, and anything different will cause too great of an upheaval." She pushed up on her toes and kissed him on the cheek. "Thank you for your patience."

"I am happy to be patient, my love, but I'll need more than a kiss on the cheek as compensation."

Louise laughed, then she kissed him on the other cheek. Only when he drew her tight against him did she kiss him fully.

Windsor was exactly as John had predicted. They might have shared a bedroom, but they rarely saw each other except for at meals. Mama kept Louise so busy working as personal secretary again that she missed one of the Drawing Rooms held at Buckingham Palace in which many had come to see the new bride.

Louise was allowed to attend the opening of the Royal Albert Hall in South Kensington, and she loved having John at her side now. Still the focus of the news reports, the wedding and the white dress she wore were described in newspapers the following day.

The day of their departure to Europe was crisp, and Bertie showed up to accompany them to the train station. Louise supposed that it was his way of offering peace with John. It also helped with Mama, who had declared that it was a sad day and that Louise leaving would create a terrible emptiness in her life.

Once inside the carriage, Bertie kept up a jovial chatter, reminding Louise of how her brother used to be before so many other things had weighed their family down. He'd been such a good friend to her in their youth. All the complaints about John seemed to have faded away, although Bertie appeared to be assessing the man.

"Now, when you return, don't let Mama monopolize all of your time," Bertie said as they drew near the train that would take them to their first connection in Dover. The smell of cinders was sharp in the air, mixed with sooty steam. "You and Lord Lorne will be invited to many events now, ones that Mama refuses to attend any longer. It will be nice to have another royal representative I can rely on."

"What about Helena and Christian?" she asked. "They're perfectly capable."

Bertie shook his head, but he was smiling. "Who do you think I'd rather introduce as my sister? Lively, beautiful Louise or quiet, dull Helena?"

Louise smirked. "Helena might be quiet, but she's far from dull."

"Says you."

"John, tell my brother that he can't disparage one of his sisters."

Bertie raised his hands. "I'm not disparaging anyone. I'm merely paying you a compliment and speaking the truth at the same time. Lorne, may I not compliment my sister?"

"Certainly, Your Highness," John said. "I have seven sisters of my own."

Bertie gave a satisfied nod and peered at Louise. "Besides, the entire country is enamored of your Scotsman."

John barked a laugh. "Simply because I'm a commoner like them. They've known nothing about me and never cared one whit until I became engaged to your sister."

Bertie turned his astute gaze upon John. "Well, let's hope they still like you when all the shine wears off and we see what you're really made of."

"Bertie!" Louise shot out.

But John only chuckled. "I have nothing to hide. Like you said, I'm a Scotsman, and what you see is what you get."

Bertie narrowed his eyes, but they gleamed with approval.

Louise recognized the endorsement at once. She reached for John's hand and clasped his fingers. He squeezed back.

At the station, once out of the carriage, Louise embraced her brother. "Tell your wife to take care, and we'll pray that her baby is delivered safely." Alix's sixth baby wasn't due for another couple of months, and Louise would likely still be gone when the child was born.

"Thank you, Loosy," he said, his smile easy. "Safe travels to you and your Scotsman."

Leaving the country with her husband by her side was a new experience for Louise. She'd always been in the presence of her other family members, and even though the couple had their escorts, she felt a new freedom. One that she enjoyed immensely.

Both of them wrote their family members letters about their progress on the trains as they traveled through Ghent and Cologne. When at last they arrived at Darmstadt, Alice met them, and Louise was able to introduce her husband to her sister.

They couldn't stay long because the next train was about to arrive, and Mama had given strict instructions to Louise not to make the visit long or stay overnight.

As they settled into their next train compartment, Louise scooted to the end of one bench and put up her legs. She wouldn't fully admit it, but her knee had begun to ache the past few hours.

John settled himself on the bench across from her in order to give her more room. "Can you share with me why Her Majesty doesn't want you spending much time with Alice?"

Louise sighed and looked out the window. She should be able to discuss this with her husband, right? "Alice is very involved in matters pertaining to women's health. She's been researching gynecological matters and has done nursing work in Darmstadt. Mama thinks that my sister will ask me a host of questions about my own person, as well as influence me to become a supporter of women getting medical degrees."

John frowned. "I know you support women's further education, but are you allowed to become involved in matters outside the royal interest?"

Louise had long buried any hope of doing so, ever since she'd been forced to return Mrs. Butler's book and sit back as she watched Sybil and Henrietta involve themselves in suffrage meetings and gatherings. Louise had consigned herself to writing letters to solicit donations and making bandages.

"Mama doesn't support women's suffrage, and she won't hear of her daughters doing it either."

"Except for Alice?"

Louise smiled. "Mama's long arm of influence is perhaps not quite as long as she wants."

John smirked. "I come from a family full of sisters who are all accomplished, and I am sure if they had more options, they would excel. I'm a Liberal for a good reason, not because of my father, but because the progression of human rights, and women's rights are part of my core beliefs."

She was keenly interested in his opinion; suddenly this was a very important thing to find out about her husband. "Do you think women are levelheaded enough to vote?"

"*Levelheaded?*" John chuckled. "If that's the requirement for voting, then most men should be exempt. I've never met a woman who couldn't grasp political issues and what it means for her family's future. So yes, I am supportive of women voting."

Louise smiled, feeling relief to her very toes. "I agree."

"Yet you can't openly support it because of the queen's opinion, and it's too political for the royal family to be a part of?"

"Correct." She sighed and looked again toward the window and the passing hills and distant mountains. "But the two reform bills passed last year give me hope for the entire country. The Married Women's Property Act and the Education Act are both steps in the right direction. I too want all children to have access to education—it will only elevate our nation. And women should be able to study at a university, any subject." She cut herself off. Perhaps she'd gone too far, too fast. "Is this shocking to you?"

When she dared meet his gaze, she found him watching her carefully. She wondered if he could read straight into her thoughts because he said, "Surely there are many causes you might become involved with that wouldn't irk your mother yet would help those you want to help?"

She only nodded because she didn't know how to reply.

John leaned forward, resting his elbows on his knees. "I have been married to you only a short time, Louise, and engaged to you months more, but I've observed many things. You are well liked and well respected by everyone you meet. When you walk into a room, it's as if it comes alive. I see how men and women look at you. You draw them to you. You make them happy. You make them want to be stronger and better."

Louise had never trusted such compliments coming from others since most of them were mere flattery. But with John, it was different. Yes, he was her husband, but he was also an outsider—he hadn't been raised royal and conditioned to be at her beck and call.

"My dearest one," he said softly, reaching across the space between them and taking her hand in his. "I see it in your eyes right now. You have dreams that you need to fulfill. And since you're now my wife, I want to help you as a supporter of education for the poor, health reform, and women's suffrage."

If Louise's knee hadn't been aching something fierce, she might have leapt across the compartment and hugged the man. For now, she drew his hand to her lips and pressed a kiss there.

CHAPTER 37

⸻

"The name 'Hospital' was derived from hope and every hospital ought to be a centre of hope to sufferers. We want to build up all these children to become strong, healthy citizens. That is a privilege everyone has a right to."

SPEECH BY PRINCESS LOUISE AT THE FOUNDATION-
LAYING CEREMONY FOR THE KENSINGTON DISPENSARY
AND CHILDREN'S HOSPITAL, NOVEMBER 2, 1926

APRIL 1871
LOUISE, AGE 23

Only a few days into the honeymoon, Louise received a telegram with the most dreadful news.

"What is it?" John asked, coming to her side where she'd sunk on the hotel room sofa.

Her throat had swollen with emotion. "It's Bertie and Alix . . . Their baby was born premature, and—" She handed over the telegram to John and buried her face in her hands.

The poor, innocent child was born early, like his oldest brother, except this child—christened Alexander John Charles Albert—had not lived for more than a day.

John read the telegram, then set it aside and pulled Louise into his arms. "I am so very sorry," he murmured against her hair.

Louise wrapped her arms around him and cried against his shirt. She wanted to be with Alix and Bertie. Her mind kept turning over the experiences that Alix must have gone through. The early labor. The pain

317

and fear. Then the dreadful news of a son who wasn't thriving, but failing.

"I wish I could do something," she whispered against John's chest. "I can't imagine their pain right now. Poor Alix. Poor Bertie. Poor little baby." She started crying again, and John only held her closer. Behind her initial shock and sorrow, a part of her wondered about her own motherhood. So many women dealt with such sorrows—would she be one of them?

"Do you want to return?" John asked. "We can put off traveling through Europe for another time."

Louise exhaled. Her thoughts were too heavy to make such a decision at this moment. "I don't know, my dearest. I don't know."

The next morning, Louise still felt weighed down, although writing letters to both Bertie and Alix helped. She also sent a heartfelt letter to Sybil, who was pregnant with her third child, due in a couple of months. Louise implored her to take care of herself and get lots of rest. Louise's swollen eyes were a fright that morning, and John fetched a cloth and wet it with cold water.

Life was unexpected, and death even more so. She could only appreciate each day and care for her loved ones. While Louise leaned against her husband, the cloth over her eyes, she said, "I want to stay. Show me Florence and the places you love, like we talked about before."

John caressed her arm. "Are you sure?"

She nodded and whispered, "Yes."

Their honeymoon had been planned to span two months, but it felt like only a few short weeks. The highlight had been Florence, where John had spent the winter of 1867, and he took her around to his remembered haunts. They spent their days wandering through galleries, examining paintings and sculptures, eating at cafés, and deciding what to buy for their home together. They found art pieces, terracotta busts, and venetian blinds, but mostly they learned about each other's tastes, likes, and dislikes.

In Florence Louise had her first experience staying in a hotel and walking streets incognito. Soldiers in uniforms drifted about, as if they weren't quite ready for the war to be over. Mostly they flirted with shop-girls and maids. Strangers jostled her in the crowds, having no idea who she was. Louise found it vastly amusing, and she also enjoyed their next adventure in Venice. The city was utterly charming. It was only over-shadowed by her heart aching for Alix and Bertie's loss.

As their honeymoon began to draw to a close, they had more and more discussions about which charities they were interested in support-ing. Louise only knew that she wanted to find a way to help women and education. Perhaps time would be in their favor, and Mama would warm up to advancements in education and health. Besides, John had brought up a good argument one night over dinner as they sat at a Venice café, overlooking the canals. If other countries, such as France and America allowed women to become doctors, then England would look like the elderly uncle who refused to leave his country estate when progress was knocking right at his front door.

"Bringing together innovation and advancing commerce was your father's vision, was it not?" John had said. "Prince Albert was the master-mind behind the Crystal Palace, and look what that did for the world— brought hundreds of countries together and thousands of brilliant minds into the same location. What is more fantastic than that?"

Louise had stared at him in wonder.

"I've read the archives of the newspapers leading up to that time," John continued. "They were full of criticism and mirth. Many predicted the Crystal Palace would be a failure."

"But it wasn't," Louise murmured.

"It was a major success," John said with a nod. "And even today, it's considered one of your father's greatest achievements for all that it accomplished, near and far."

But planning out an ideal future in beautiful Italy, away from the reality of the pressures from family, was a far cry from implementing the projects they wanted to undertake.

"There's no rush to do anything immediately," John had told her, more as a warning. He'd learned quickly about her impatient nature. He was the patient one in their marriage, mostly.

It was with these thoughts that Louise arrived with her husband in Kensington at the Argyll House in early June. Louise's first moments were surreal. She was truly a married woman, and she would be living on her husband's family property. She'd no longer reside under the queen's roofs except for visits.

John gave her the grand tour of the spacious house, with stained-glass windows overlooking the two staircases, a lovely library, and charming drawing rooms.

Louise asked him, "How long has this house been in your family?"

"Father purchased this house in 1853." John kept ahold of her hand as they walked some of the acreage of Campden Hill.

Her husband wasn't as fond of long walks as she was, but he indulged her plenty. "This area is lovely and feels like we are in the country, even though we're so close to London."

"Locals consider it a village since we are so removed from the noise of traffic and congestion."

And it was like a village, Louise agreed. The four acres of beautiful land spread out before her, filled with old oaks, May trees, chestnuts, sweeping lawns, lovely gardens, and plenty of birds.

"This will be the first night you'll have spent in England in a non-royal home," John observed.

Louise looked up at him. They were holding hands, standing before the lawn area where John said the family held summer teas and Sunday gatherings.

"I'm looking forward to it," she said. "And getting to know your family better."

"They are eager to spend time with you, especially my mother and sisters."

Louise smiled. In truth, she was a bit nervous. Would she match up to the kind of wife they hoped their brother would have?

"Will you be all right with a single footman and maid?" John teased.

"If I have more needs, then I'll ask my husband. He should be around here somewhere."

"If you see him, let me know." John's blue eyes glimmered. "I've got other duties to attend rather than showing a princess around this estate."

Louise laughed and turned toward him. Looping her arms about his neck, she reveled in this instant of joy with her husband. Their private moments would be few and far between if she were to guess. The Argyll family was a large brood.

John drew her close and kissed her softly. "You're welcome to put anyone in their place as you see fit. I won't stand in your way."

"I don't think that will be necessary," she said. "I know that I must take the initiative because of my status, but I want to be considered one of the family. A daughter. Your wife. Plain and simple."

John wrapped a tendril of her escaped hair around his finger. "You could never be plain or simple, my love."

"You know what I mean."

His gaze held hers. "I must tell you something before the chaos of my large family dictates our days and nights."

Louise lifted her brows. She didn't think it was bad news because his eyes were smiling, yet his tone had been somber. "You can tell me anything."

"I love you, dear Louise," he said. "I want you to know that. We are young in our marriage, but I am ever so happy that you chose me."

Louise gazed at this man who she knew would continue to make great adjustments to be in a union with someone of the royal family. But she'd been a witness to his courtesy, his respect, and his patience time and time again. She could honestly say that this man's heart was pure and honorable.

"I am so happy you proposed," Louise said in a quiet voice. "When you asked me to marry you, I knew without a doubt that my answer would be yes. I believed I could find happiness with you, and that has proved to be right."

John scanned her face in the manner she had grown used to. He watched her, studied her, and wanted to understand her. She felt the same about him.

"Do you think you'll ever come to love me?" he asked.

The hope in his voice made its way into her soul. It wasn't really a question she had to scramble for an answer to. John was an intriguing man, a generous man, and the thought of not being married to him was something she couldn't bear to consider. Perhaps that meant she loved him. "I think it's too late for that."

His brows dipped, and a frown line crossed his forehead. "What do you mean?"

"It means that I already love you." She wondered if her heart might leap straight from her chest.

John kissed her then.

Not everything was perfect in their marriage—that Louise knew. But there were perfect moments, and this was one of them. So she relaxed into his arms, opened to his kiss, and let her heart soar as high as it would go.

Unfortunately, they could not tarry because his family would soon be searching for them. They joined the Argylls on the south veranda, which was like an outdoor drawing room but more comfortable. The veranda was dotted with flowers, potted plants, woven chairs, and a bevy of dogs. John had insisted that Louise bring Frisky so that he could have other dogs to play with.

Everyone rose to greet Louise, and she was kissed and embraced by the Duke and Duchess, followed by John's siblings. Their children were present too. It was summer, and her own family was at Balmoral on holiday, and as at Balmoral, she had expected the children here to be with their governors or governesses. Instead, they intermingled with the adults as though they were perfectly welcome and perfectly comfortable, and apparently they were.

The casual family gathering reminded Louise of Sybil Grey's family cottage at Osborne and how they didn't have to stand on ceremony. It was cozy, with children and dogs, plenty of food, and the discussions surprised Louise. Apparently, John and the Duke weren't the only Liberals in the family.

They discussed everything from Parliament passing the Bank Holidays Act, which created four holidays in England and five in Scotland, to how the Universities Test Act removed the restriction of only members of the Church of England being able attend the universities of Oxford, Cambridge, and Durham.

Louise was pleased that not only were the children not excused, but a few of the older ones weighed in with their opinions, which she found quite intelligent. She understood now why her husband would be so supportive of social change. It was obvious that he'd been bred with open discussions with all viewpoints.

When the sun began to descend, the family moved inside to the white-and-gold drawing room. As Louise walked with John, she said, "Are the children always part of the family this way?"

"It's the weekend, and on Monday, they'll have more structure." John interlaced their fingers. "The children will have their lessons, and I'll need to begin at Parliament soon." He stopped with her outside the drawing room so that they'd have more privacy. "If you don't mind me starting on Monday, that is."

John was essentially asking her permission. He didn't need to, but maybe he felt he did?

"Of course. I will find ways to occupy my time, I am sure. Or maybe I'll join you in Parliament."

John only smiled. "That would be something." He kissed her cheek, then led her into the drawing room.

Over the next days and weeks, Louise settled into a happy routine with her in-laws. She and John would set up their own household soon enough. But right now, it was time to become better acquainted with everyone.

When John started attending his Parliament meetings, Louise visited Sybil.

"Are you very happy?" Sybil asked one afternoon.

"Very," Louise said. "My life is busy and full, and I have an attentive husband." She eyed her friend's swollen belly. "Perhaps next year, I'll join you as a mother."

Sybil beamed. "Oh, that would be great fun. We shall swap toddler tantrum stories."

Louise laughed.

"Tell me of your life as a marchioness." Sybil reached for her teacup.

"When Parliament adjourns, we'll be traveling to Inveraray," Louise said. "I'm both nervous and excited. Everyone will be watching me and talking about me."

"You're used to that already," Sybil said. "They'll find you wonderful."

Louise lifted a shoulder. "I'd rather be incognito most of the time, you know, but it isn't to be."

"No, it's not." Sybil sipped at her tea. "Now, what will you do with all your spare time?"

Louise threw up her hands. "Spare time? I have very little since John and I have decided that once we set up house, we're going to look into becoming patrons of worthy causes."

"What? That's wonderful." Sybil's brow crinkled. "I'm surprised you have permission."

"I don't—at least not yet," Louise said. "But now that I'm a married woman, I can do so much more with a husband's support. I plan to continue sculpting as well, and John is supportive of that."

Sybil's smile was full. "I'm so happy for you, my dearest."

CHAPTER 38

"I am all impatience to hear how you get on *in your new home, for it will be stranger to you than* anything else yet. Pray *don't rush about London, as you always used to do! visiting and going to exhibitions, shops and studios, without ever getting fresh air and exercise which you know always ended in making you quite ill. Pray be prudent and reasonable. And don't ever go out (when Lorne is* not *there) without some lady or other."*

LETTER FROM QUEEN VICTORIA
TO PRINCESS LOUISE, BALMORAL, JUNE 12, 1871

AUGUST 1871
LOUISE, AGE 23

This article is saying the 'Royal Mama' isn't coming to Inveraray after all." John held up the latest newspaper.

Louise looked over from her open trunk. John still liked to dismiss the staff who could attend her, insisting he could help the princess. They were in the midst of packing at the Argyll House before setting off for Scotland. "That's what the telegram said from Helena this morning as well."

A six-day celebration of their marriage had been planned by the Inveraray township. Louise had been to celebrations and events before, but not a six-day-long one.

Since the queen was going to attend part of the festivities, the entire township was being whitewashed and the Duke had overhauled the castle and erected a pavilion in order to house a ballroom. A porch had been built over the main entrance to the castle in case of rain. The Duke had gone to extremes with preparations, and now the queen wouldn't be attending after all. She'd suffered from a bee sting in early August and was still experiencing aftereffects.

"Will your father be upset?" Louise asked. "I know that he's made so many changes, including reserving his own stables for Mama's horses."

John set down the paper. "He'll grumble, but he'll survive. As long as we don't cancel the whole thing. Do you think it should proceed without dear Mama?"

Louise smiled. John had taken to calling the queen "dear Mama," and she'd seemed to like it. "We should proceed. Soon it will be winter, and then what? No one will be excited about our marriage anymore."

John laughed at this, then he sobered. "No one will ever tire of you, my love. But truly, I hope your mother will heal fully. She's a bit important in the world."

"She's assured me she's mending, but it's not fair for all those at Inveraray to keep being put off."

With a nod, John said, "Then shall I pack your shawl or leave it here?"

"Pack it."

Louise wrote one more note to Sybil before joining in to help her husband. She wished her best friend well in her upcoming childbirth—which would happen while Louise was in Scotland.

As she and John left England, she continued to marvel at how much her life had changed after her marriage. No wonder Mama had told her it was all right to put off such a decision when Louise was so undecided the year before.

When they arrived in Arrochar, a tiny village in Loch Long, the Duke joined them aboard the steamer after it docked. "Thank the heavens you've arrived at last. I've been feeding hordes of people waiting for the celebration to commence. My inn, the Argyll Arms, is teeming with guests, and there've been yachts and steamers coming in by the day with supplies and passengers."

Despite this complaining, he welcomed Louise with a hearty

embrace, then a kiss on the cheek. "Welcome, daughter. Or should I call you Your Royal Highness?"

Louise grinned at the man, even though she was a bit travel weary and her seasickness had made her stomach hollow. "I haven't had a father in a long time, and I'm honored to be called daughter by you."

"You're a good daughter," the Duke said, emotion coloring his voice. He presented a Campbell tartan to her, woven into a shawl, and John helped her drape it over her shoulder and fasten it above her hip. She welcomed the added warmth since she'd worn a summery white dress of muslin with blue bows and sash. Her bonnet of lace was also trimmed in blue. Fine clothing for a warm day, but today was anything but warm.

"Come, my dear Louise." The Duke smiled. "Come see your welcome."

Louise thought the wind and rain might have prevented any sort of elaborate welcome at Loch Long, but she was wrong. They disembarked the steamer where a guard of honor lined the pier as a bagpiper played "The Campbells Are Coming." John, wearing his Campbell kilt, grasped her hand as they stood in the fierce wind that clawed at their hair and clothing.

Louise was presented with multiple bouquets, and several speeches were given. She tried hard to follow the thick accents above the sound of the wind. Finally they were allowed to enter the waiting carriage and gain some protection from the rain. The Duke followed in a second carriage.

She stopped counting how many times her stomach plunged to her toes as they traversed the humpback bridge dividing the counties of Dumbarton and Argyll, then climbed the steep pass of Glen Croe. She'd been seasick on the steamer, and now, the steep climb wasn't helping any.

"You can close your eyes if you want to," John said into her ear.

"I already am."

John chuckled and pulled her closer. "We'll be there soon, my love." They were 860 feet above sea level, and at the summit, while the horses were being changed, John pointed out a white stone with an inscription.

"*Rest and Be Thankful*," Louise read. She looked at John. "I feel like I've barely escaped with my life."

He smoothed a finger along her cheek, examining her face. "Did you have any doubt we'd make it this far?"

"I suppose if you can do it, then so can I."

His smile emerged. "That's the spirit, although I am truly sorry that you've felt off."

All too soon, or none too soon, they loaded into the carriage again and started down the twisting road into Inveraray.

It was some time before they rounded the head of Loch Fyne, so Louise focused on John's warm, strong fingers wrapped around hers as her stomach flipped this way and that.

"There she is."

Louise followed where he pointed, and she caught her first glimpse of the small bay. Decorated yachts and smaller boats filled the space. The township of Inveraray sat on the left, and the gray castle with its imposing turrets rose on the right.

"What's that?" Louise pointed to a watchtower on the summit of the hill rising behind the castle.

"The hill of Duniquaich. The watchtower was built to warn us of attack by enemies."

Louise felt like she'd stepped into another time, another era. The wooded hills extended beyond Inveraray, circling the township like a protective glove.

As they approached Frew's Bridge, the yachts fired a welcome, and people started coming out of homes and shops. They were already cheering and waving by the time the carriage reached the main road. Their carriage slowed to a crawl, its four horses moving through the crowds swelling by the second.

"I've never seen so many people at Inveraray," John said with a shake of his head. "I believe people have traveled from all over Scotland to welcome you. I told you the Scots would be happy to see you, my love."

As for Louise, her heart had lodged in her throat. She was close to crying. She didn't want to be a sniveling bride, so she smiled widely and waved. The rain was only a sprinkle now, thank goodness, but the well-wishers were still getting wet.

"Do they not want to wait for the rain to pass?" Louise said.

"They might be waiting an entire year if we let the weather dictate our lives." John squeezed her hand. "Almost there. Mother is waiting."

The Duchess stood with other family members who Louise knew from Argyll House, but there were plenty of extended relatives she had yet to meet. She could hardly believe that these were all her new family members. It was as if her world had increased by tenfold—no, a hundredfold.

When they reached the porch in front of the castle, John jumped out first and extended his hand. The Duchess moved forward to greet Louise with a kiss, and the Duke joined them all on the porch.

"Where's Provost MacArthur?" the Duke asked.

It was some moments before the man could work his way through the crowd. Then he delivered his speech of welcome to Louise.

She listened carefully, following his thick dialect, honored and delighted to be welcomed so sweetly. After she thanked him, John led Louise inside. He had to change into his uniform, and then it was his duty to inspect the Argyllshire Volunteers and to present them to Princess Louise and the Duke.

"It's still raining—do you mind?" John asked once he was dressed in uniform.

Louise pulled her tartan closer. "Of course not. I'm protected."

John smiled, and she smiled back. Soon, they were in the rain while John went about his duties, walking along the line of men in their uniforms, nodding to each.

Later, after tea had rejuvenated them, Louise joined the Campbells in the saloon where they presented her with the clan wedding present of a lovely diamond and pearl necklace with a pearl locket and pendant bearing the Galley of Lorne. Sir Donald Campbell of Dunstaffnage read a formal address from a roll of parchment, the borders illustrated with the Scottish thistle and English rose, intertwined with orange blossoms.

Louise was prepared with her reply. She was fairly sure that her words sounded too stilted and formal. But John only smiled, and the Campbells greeted her as if she were already a part of them.

Over the next few days, Louise's head spun with all of the activities and celebrations. The Duchess threw a ball where Louise put to practice all the country dances and reels she'd learned at Balmoral. On the third day was the regatta, which turned out to be a bit of a failure since the yacht race had only two entries. But John's brothers had fun placing bets on the eight fishing boats racing for port during another fierce rainstorm.

Finally, the sun came out at Inveraray, and Louise received the joyous news that Sybil had given birth to a healthy baby girl. They were naming her Sybil Evelyn de Vere Beauclerk, after her mother. Louise was ecstatic but wondered why Sybil hadn't written her. The telegram had come from Helena instead.

Worry niggled at the back of Louise's mind, but her days and evenings were so full that she didn't have time to analyze why she'd be worried. Within a few days, surely Sybil would write herself. Louise wrote her own note of congratulations and posted it. Soon they'd travel to Kintyre, the home the Duke had given them as part of the marriage settlement.

One early morning, Louise joined John and the Duke on a fly-fishing excursion. They chose their salmon fishing rods first, and Louise tramped through the underbrush toward the loch, wearing one of the Duchess's tweed jackets. Old Sandy McKellar, the Duke's fisherman, joined them at the loch.

McKellar was a man of few words, but his square face and thick brogue was charming. John showed Louise how to cast the fishing rod, but she was all thumbs the first few times, so McKellar took over. Within the first hour, Louise had triumphantly caught both a grilse and a sea trout.

On the way back, John insisted on carrying the basket full of fish since he didn't want Louise's knee to start acting up.

"You are spoiling me, husband," she teased.

John pulled her close with one arm and kissed the side of her head.

Louise batted him away. "You smell like fish."

He chuckled. "As do you, my love."

Louise was more than proud to join the ranks of the Campbell fisherwomen. She decided that she'd have her own tweeds made so that she'd be ready for future excursions.

The weeks spent at Inveraray were full of charm and adventure, but Louise still worried about her friend Sybil. Louise hadn't received any replies to her letters. Before they made the sea voyage to Campbelltown, Louise received the most distressing telegram from Helena. She was grateful that she was sitting down and alone with John when she read it.

Sybil Grey Beauclerk, Duchess of St Albans, Louise's closest friend since the age of sixteen, had died of puerperal fever on September 7, only a few weeks after her daughter had been born. The fever related to childbirth was feared among all women, and Louise could barely comprehend that her confidante and lovely friend was gone. Forever. She would be forever twenty-two.

"What is it, my love?" John asked, his voice sounding far away because of the hammering in Louise's head.

This time she couldn't even speak the words. She handed him the telegram with a trembling hand, and he read it silently. He wiped his eyes and knelt beside her. "She is free from her pain now."

Puerperal fever would have kept Sybil in agony all this time, and no one had written to Louise of the situation. She'd been so caught up in her new surroundings and new family, she hadn't pressed Helena for more information.

"Her babe is healthy, yes?"

"I haven't heard otherwise," Louise whispered.

John drew her hands into his, clasping her fingers in warmth, then kissed each of hers. His blue gaze steady on hers, he said, "Sybil will always live on through her children, and *we* will never forget her."

Louise's tears finally came, but they were not great wracking sobs like they had been when she'd learned of her little nephew's death. This grief was too large to comprehend fully yet.

"We will return to England right away," John said. "You can be with her family and bring them comfort. Meet her young daughter."

Another weight moved through Louise. Sybil's husband, William Beauclerk, was now a widower with three young children. "I do not wish to interfere with the Grey family arrangements," Louise said. "Surely they are being put into place as we speak, and my arrival will require protocols to be adjusted for." She didn't know how her mind was so clear right now when her body felt like it was in another world.

John watched her closely. "Will you regret not going?"

She exhaled. "I don't know. Perhaps? But my place is here, with you. Royalty attending Sybil's . . . funeral . . . will put undue burden on a grieving family." It was all true, no matter the pain it gave Louise to stay so far away from her beloved Sybil.

John nodded. "Should we postpone our plans and stay in Inveraray a while longer?"

"No." Louise wiped at her tears. "I only need today. And you." She moved into his arms and closed her eyes. Breathing in his scent of sage and cedar and nestling against the solidness of his body was calming.

"I will sculpt a bust of her," she whispered. "I have sketched her many times, and everything else will be from memory."

"I am sure the family will be honored with such a gift."

Louise nodded, but she felt so very, very tired. "I'll write of my condolences to Mrs. Grey, but I'll wait until after the funeral to suggest my offer." Her eyes began to water again. "What if . . . what if when we have children, I develop such a fever?"

John squeezed her shoulder. "I don't have an answer, dear Louise, but I do believe God is watching over all of us, all the time, whatever happens. We miss our lost loved ones dearly, but it's up to us to continue on in their honored memories. I'll be here with you every day and every moment."

He was right, and she took solace in his words, although she wouldn't fully accept them until much later. Right now, though, she was grateful for the time and space to grieve the loss of her dear friend.

Over the next few days, Louise felt fragile. Her emotions were constantly on the surface, but John watched over her carefully, staying in tune to when she became overwhelmed and encouraging her to take time for herself. Louise began to write down her memories of Sybil and determined that the next time she visited Windsor, she'd collect all of the letters she'd received from Sybil over the years.

One event that Louise couldn't miss was the tenantry ball, where over seven hundred people showed up. She was able to muster up smiles and graciousness for all those she was introduced to. Although she felt as if her heart had split into jagged pieces, she knew she was in the right place, doing what she needed to do. Sybil had been so happy about her marriage, and Louise was intent on living her life to make her best friend proud from where she was watching in heaven.

"I think we should travel a day ahead of schedule to Campbelltown," John told her on one of their final evenings at Inveraray. "You became seasick on the journey over, and I want you to have time to recover before we are surrounded by celebrations again."

Louise agreed, and they arrived in Campbelltown after a calm evening. The community was small, but the people had gathered in droves. They lined the roads, waving their handkerchiefs and tossing flowers, reminding her of when she and John had left Windsor on their wedding day. Even the church bells rang as they crossed the town boundary.

The carriage traversed the nine-mile journey to the south coast. The winding lanes and beautiful rising hills captured Louise's attention. "It's like a tropical island," she marveled, unable to decide which window of the carriage to look out of. "A hidden gem. Absolutely breathtaking."

The beaches of clear, sparkling sea were complemented by lush farmlands, rolling hills, and quaint hamlets. Once they reached Kintyre, where their new home, the Macharioch House, was, they stopped at the small parish church.

"This is completely charming," Louise said as they climbed out of the carriage.

John grinned, then kissed her swiftly, despite being in full view of the public.

A tenant read a formal welcome, and then Louise and John were led into a dinner at the Home Farm. The food was enjoyable, and the company even better. It was strange to think that Louise had been missing out on such experiences her whole life—a community that was open and friendly and full of humor and genuine affection. They accepted her instantly, without question.

"What do you think, my love?" John asked the following morning as they strolled about the grounds, arm in arm.

He'd warned her of the neglect of the place. Without a permanent tenant, only basic upkeep of the house had been done, and that hadn't been much at all. But Louise wasn't daunted in the least, and she didn't mind putting her dowry to good use—for the establishment of her new family. "This is such a beautiful estate that it will be a pleasure to put in some improvements."

John reached for her hand. "And what might those be?"

"Well, we need to hire an architect." Louise looked up at her husband. "George Devey will do, should he accept the position. He specializes in houses and cottages."

John only nodded.

"We need to modernize the house by adding bathrooms, and I have plenty of ideas myself for the landscaping." She drew John to a stop. "The sea is beyond all of this underbrush, but it would be lovely to see it from every room."

John gazed at their surroundings. "I agree."

"Here." She withdrew her small sketchbook from her pocket. Right there, she drew the semblance of a garden layout. "This could be a walkway to the beach, lined with fuchsias."

"I love it," John said, sincerity in his tone.

He'd been watching her carefully for days, since the loss of Sybil, and Louise realized he was worried about her grief. It had ebbed somewhat, although her eyes still stung when Sybil came to mind. But this beautiful location, which represented a new beginning in her life, was already a balm. Sybil had lived a good life. She'd brought three children into the world, and now her suffering was over. Louise needed to be grateful for the time she'd had with her friend.

"I've decided on our charity," Louise said suddenly, turning to her husband.

The sea breeze was light this morning, stirring his hair.

With John's light blue eyes upon hers, she said, "I want to be a patron and supporter of a school for girls who can't afford a boarding school. This school program will be a day school that offers more than just classes on manners and domesticity. The girls will learn science, mathematics, art, and music. They will be educated at a higher standard so that they can prepare and qualify to enter into universities. My aim is to honor Sybil St Albans." She turned to face the sea and gazed across the blue-and-green water that sparkled beneath the Scottish sun. "It is time."

"I agree, my love." John slipped an arm about her shoulder, and Louise leaned against him.

For a brief few moments, there was nothing interfering with her dreams. She could see the future clearly. Surely more sorrow and setbacks would befall them, but with John at her side, and her father and her best friend looking down upon her from their places of rest, Louise felt at peace. "Thank you," she whispered, her words carried on the wind.

John didn't reply, but he didn't have to.

Perhaps she was thanking her husband. Perhaps she was thanking her mother, who gave her life. Her brothers, who loved her. Her sisters, who challenged her. Her friend Sybil, who taught her how to serve others. Her father, who'd dedicated his whole being to his family.

She was part of them all, and as long as she embraced all of her pieces, she'd weather whatever storms came her way. Foul or fair. Long or short. Health or sickness. Happiness or disappointment.

It was time to return to the house now. Letters had to be written. Plans put into place. Hopes to be dreamed of.

And life to be lived.

AFTERWORD

᪥

Louise once told her great-niece Maria Cristina, who was Beatrice's granddaughter, "It was always my greatest pity not to have any children and I'm happy when I see them" (Hawksley 321). Oh, the pain of a heart's hope not realized. Although Louise was not able to have children, most likely due to the meningitis she contracted at sixteen, and despite her numerous treatments at spas in Germany, she was beloved by her many nieces and nephews.

Like all marriages and relationships in general, Princess Louise and John Campbell had their own difficulties. Not having children was a great loss to Louise and also to John, since the heir to the dukedom did not pass down his direct line but instead went to his brother Archi's son, Niall Campbell.

After Sybil Grey St Albans's death, Louise's offer to sculpt a bust of her dear friend was rejected by the Grey family, specifically by Albert Grey. Edgar Boehm was hired instead. So Louise created a medallion of Sybil's head for Mrs. Grey. The medallion is currently on display at the church at Bestwood St Albans (Wake 160–61).

John was offered a British peerage title multiple times by Queen Victoria, but he repeatedly and firmly turned it down (Wake 134–35). He didn't want anything to interfere with his political convictions and influence as a Liberal or his strong loyalty to the Argyll family.

In 1878, John Campbell was offered the governor generalship of the Dominion of Canada, which was Britain's viceroyalty (Packard 187–88). Having the queen's son-in-law in such an assignment created a valued representation of Queen Victoria in Canada, and of course, the presence of Princess Louise was an added boon. The couple embarked on the five-year assignment, sailing for Canada in November 1878 (Packard 190). Unfortunately, in February 1880, Louise suffered a sleigh accident; their sleigh overturned, and she was dragged about one thousand feet (Packard 208). This resulted in a head injury that plagued Louise the rest of her life, causing severe migraines.

Regardless, John Campbell and Princess Louise made many important contributions to Canadian society, including founding and supporting academies of arts and sciences. Lorne authored several works of prose and poetry, highlighting the beauty and his love for Canada (see "John Campbell, 9th Duke of Argyll, Marquis of Lorne Collection," Lord Durham Rare Books, https://www.ldrb.ca/pages/books/7949/john-george-edward-henry-campbell-campbell-marquess-of-lorne-9th-duke-of-argyll/john-campbell-9th-duke-of-argyll-marquis-of-lorne-collection). Other notable published works by Lorne include his book of poetry, *Guido and Lita—A Tale of the Riviera*; a rewriting of the Psalms, called *The Books of Psalms Literally Rendered into Verse* (Packard 185–86); a biography of Lord Palmerston (Packard 280); and a biography of his mother-in-law, titled *V.R.I. Queen Victoria: Her Life and Empire* (Packard 330).

Louise became a lifelong advocate for education, women's rights, and other charities. She founded the Ladies' Work Society, which taught employable skills to women who'd fallen into hard circumstances. She sponsored educational organizations such as the Girls' Public School Day Company, which she became president of and grew to establish thirty-three schools for girls (see "Princess Louise's Charitable Work," *Every Woman Dreams* [blog], August 24, 2017, https://reginajeffers.blog/2017/08/24/princess-louises-charitable-work/; and "Girls' Day School Trust," Wikipedia, https://en.wikipedia.org/wiki/Girls%27_Day_School_Trust). Added to these were numerous endeavors, including serving as patron of the Kensington Dispensary and Children's Hospital, earning her a namesake in a facility called the Princess Louise Hospital for Children. She was also made Honorary Freeman of the Royal Borough of Kensington in 1928 (Packard 336).

Louise's care and compassion toward soldiers continued throughout her lifetime. Following the Great War, Louise was bestowed the honor of Dame Grand Cross of the British Empire by her nephew, George V, for her contribution to the war effort. She was also appointed colonel in chief of the Argyll and Sutherland Highlanders (Packard 335).

John's death in 1914, at the age of sixty-eight, ended several long years in which Louise stuck by her husband's side as his mind faltered, possibly from Alzheimer's disease. John contracted pneumonia and never recovered. Louise's tribute to her husband of forty-three years appears as a verse upon his sepulcher, concluding with: "Labouring to make the Empire Nations one / His best was given to serve his country's cause / Loving, high-souled, and valiant, he now lives / In death, as in earthly days, Beloved."

Princess Louise spent her final years living in either Rosneath or Kensington. Toward the end of 1939, trenches were dug outside her Kensington Palace windows in preparation for the Second World War. But she wouldn't live to see them used. Her health took a downward turn in late November (Packard 337). In her will, Louise had instructed that if she died in Scotland, she wanted to be buried next to her husband at Kilmun, but if she died in England, she wanted to be buried next to her parents at Windsor (Wake 412).

True to her atypical nature, Louise had decided to be cremated after reading about it in a pamphlet. Her request was fulfilled after her December 3 death, and her ashes were sent in a coffin, which also contained her wedding and engagement rings, to Windsor for her funeral. Louise outlived six of her siblings and was survived by Arthur and Beatrice. The funeral was quiet and small for a royal princess, due to the burgeoning war, but it was attended by her royal family and her Argyll family, the Campbells (Packard 338).

Princess Louise, Duchess of Argyll, carved her own path through life, even until the very end. She arranged her own funeral music so that her favorite hymns would be sung—"Abide with Me" and "God Be in My Head." Her funeral concluded with pipers playing "Flowers in the Field" (Wake 412). A fitting tribute for a woman beloved by so many and for a life well lived.

CHAPTER NOTES

❧

CHAPTER 1

Epigraph: Queen Victoria, journal, April 2, 1848, pp. 116–17, QueenVictoriasJournal.org (UK); http://qvj.chadwyck.com/marketing .do (US).

Endearments were frequently used among the royal family, and Louise called her father "dear Papa" (Wake 48). Nicknames were also prevalent, and Princess Louise had her share of them, including Loo Loo, Little Miss Why, Lou, and Loosy (Packard 35). Lord Lorne began calling her "Dearest Alba" at one point, perhaps because her third name is Alberta (Longford 249). Prince Albert used pet nicknames for Queen Victoria, including Gutes Fräuchen, Liebes Fräuchen, and Gutes Weibchen (a full list can be found at "Queen Victoria's Pet Names, Titles, Nicknames & Aliases," Helen Rappaport, https://helenrappaport .com/queen-victoria/queen-victorias-pet-names/).

Queen Victoria kept a lifelong diary, starting when she was thirteen years old. The pages amassed to 140 bound volumes, at least originally. She asked her daughter Princess Beatrice to edit her journals following her death. Princess Beatrice did, but more than editing was done, and some of the passages were completely rewritten (see Elizabeth Jane Timms, "Queen Victoria in Her Letters and Journals," Royal Central, August 7, 2018, https://royalcentral.co.uk/features/queen-victoria-in-her -letters-and-journals-106936/).

When Prince Leopold was born, Queen Victoria described him in her journal: "a pretty child with large blue eyes, a very marked nose, a small mouth, & nicely shaped head with more, & darker hair than Arthur had.

He fills out daily" (Zeepvat 7). He was the smallest baby born to Queen Victoria, and when he was only a few months old, bruises began to appear on his body. Prince Leopold was diagnosed with hemophilia. This set the tone for the rest of his life and led Princess Louise to become interested in medicine and natural cures for illnesses (Packard 42).

CHAPTER 2

Epigraph: Queen Victoria, journal, March 25, 1861, pp. 76–77, QueenVictoriasJournal.org (UK); http://qvj.chadwyck.com/marketing .do (US).

Queen Victoria was opposed to royal mothers breastfeeding their children, so she hired wet nurses. In addition, the wet nurse had to "remain standing while feeding any royal child, obviously in recognition of the infant's exalted station" (Packard 20–21).

Before the death of Prince Albert, he organized and supervised the education of their children. Once the responsibility fell upon Queen Victoria, one thing she didn't allow was novels, which she considered "unsuitable books" (Wake 49). I don't know if Bertie ever gave his sister a novel, but Princess Louise got into trouble for reading novels at age fourteen. A book such as *A Woman in White* by Wilkie Collins was considered a sensation novel (see "Sensation Novel," Wikipedia, https://en.wikipedia.org/wiki/Sensation_novel). When the queen discovered that the French governess Madame Hocédé had given Princess Louise and Princess Helena novels to read, the governess was dismissed. Princess Louise lied to try to protect her governess, so the queen believed that the governess's influence had "done Louise a terrible deal of harm, made her deceitful and has disobeyed orders" (Wake 50).

With both parents having artistic talent, Princess Louise was naturally influenced by them, and she began her first art lessons at age four. Prince Albert became interested in etching and modelling and subsequently hired tutors. A series of professionals were brought in to tutor the royal family, including Princess Louise. Although the art endeavors of a royal daughter were never meant to be compared to those of the masters, Princess Louise's talent became undeniably stellar. Her early tutors included Edward Corbould and William Leitch, followed by many others of note (Wake 57).

CHAPTER 3

Epigraph: Longford, *Darling Loosy: Letters to Princess Louise 1856–1939*, 87.

Queen Victoria and the royal family lived mostly at Windsor and Buckingham. Eight of her nine children were born at Buckingham (see "Where Did Queen Victoria Live?" *Endymion* [blog], May 20, 2019, https://robertstephenparry.com/endymion/where-did-queen-victoria -live.html). Christmas was always spent at Windsor during Prince Albert's lifetime (Wake 40). Princess Louise spent months of work pre-paring Christmas gifts for her family members and all those in her circle. Homemade gifts she created included cross-stitch, crochet, illus-trated poems, drawings, and albums of pressed leaves or flowers (Wake 39).

Princess Louise dealt with many health setbacks, as most children did during this era, including scarlet fever, measles, and chicken pox. During an autumn stay at Balmoral, Princess Louise began to suffer from debilitating headaches. The first doctor consulted diagnosed her with neuralgia, and when the symptoms didn't ease, another doctor was sent for. Dr. Sieveking diagnosed her with tubercular meningitis (Wake 59). Of this period, Sybil Grey said, "She can't ride, fond as she is of it, for it shakes her so. She can't draw though there is nothing she likes so well, nor read. No noise. Scarcely the rustling of a silk gown can she bear nor the light either" (Wake 58).

CHAPTER 4

Epigraph: Queen Victoria, journal, December 24, 1856, p. 272, QueenVictoriasJournal.org (UK); http://qvj.chadwyck.com/marketing .do (US).

Prince Albert brought a brightness to the Christmas season with his festive enthusiasm, which affected the royal family and beyond. He oversaw the tree decorating at Windsor Castle "with wax candles and sweets such as barley sugar and sugar plums. These were actually caraway or aniseed comfits, covered with boiled sugar and crafted into the shape of a plum" (see "How Did Queen Victoria and Prince Albert Popularise Christmas?" English Heritage, December 2, 2016, https://blog.english-heritage.org.uk/how-did-queen-victoria-and-prince-albert-popularise-christmas).

Yet during the years before his death, Prince Albert suffered from neuralgia, toothaches, insomnia, and depression. He also received tragic news that his two Coburg cousins, King Pedro V and Prince Ferdinand, had died of typhoid, an unfortunate precursor to Prince Albert's own demise (Wake 42). In mid-November 1861, Prince Albert caught a cold after attending an event at Sandhurst. This began his health's sharp decline, which unfortunately coincided with Bertie's affair with Nellie Clifden (Wake 43). Prince Albert contracted typhoid, and during this era, there was a very low chance of survival.

Prince Albert's letter to his son Bertie is a sober reminder of a father's disappointment in a son and reads, in part, "No forgiveness can restore him to the state of innocence and purity which you have lost, and you must hide yourself from the sight of God" (Wake 43).

CHAPTER 5

Epigraph: Zeepvat, *Queen Victoria's Youngest Son: The Untold Story of Prince Leopold*, 49–50.

Princess Louise was known for making remedies throughout her life for various illnesses, likely instigated by her brother Leopold's serious illness (Wake 363). The recipe in the story that Princess Louise tries for her ailing father is found in *Domestic Medicine,* 133.

CHAPTER 6

Epigraph: Longford, *Darling Loosy: Letters to Princess Louise 1856–1939,* 88.

During the week leading up to Prince Albert's death, the younger children were kept from their father, for fear of spreading the infection. This included Princess Louise, which meant the last time she saw him alive was on December 14, when he was literally on his deathbed and couldn't acknowledge anyone in the room. Princess Louise was sent off to bed and found out the following morning that her dear papa had passed away at 10:15 p.m. the night before. When she, Prince Arthur, and Princess Beatrice were taken to their grieving mother's bedside, Princess Louise burst out, "Oh! Why did not God take me. I am so stupid and useless" (Wake 44).

Women didn't typically attend funerals, being considered too delicate to expose their grief in front of others, so Queen Victoria didn't attend her husband's funeral, and neither did Princess Louise. The Prince of Wales and Prince Arthur were the only members of the immediate family who attended Prince Albert's funeral (Wake 46).

CHAPTER 7

Epigraph: Queen Victoria, journal, December 18, 1862, pp. 324–25, QueenVictoriasJournal.org (UK); http://qvj.chadwyck.com/marketing.do (US).

The royal family dressed in the height of fashion. Women's dresses in the 1860s had tight bodices with high necks and buttons down the front. The skirts were bell shaped in the early part of the decade, and lace was worn at the collar and cuffs. A popular women's hairstyle included hair parted in the middle, then pulled into a low chignon, complete with ringlets or loops over the ears.

Men's clothing comprised single-breasted, semifitted jackets or coats and, beneath, single-breasted waistcoats. Collars were starched, and cravats or neckties were worn. Men's hair was commonly parted in the middle. Side-whiskers, beards, and mustaches were also fashionable. (See "History of Fashion, 1840–1900," Victoria and Albert Museum, http://www.vam.ac.uk/content/articles/h/history-of-fashion-1840-1900/.)

CHAPTER 8

Epigraph: John Campbell, "Song," 1882, in *Memories of Canada and Scotland: Speeches and Verses*, available at https://www.gutenberg.org/cache/epub/7212/pg7212.html.

To reduce the number of names that start with the letter "L," I refer to Helena by her real name instead of her nickname, Lenchen. I also call Prince Louis IV by his German name, Ludwig, to avoid confusion with Princess Louise.

The beach at Osborne and the Swiss cottage were delightful adventures for the royal children. When Princess Louise was six years old, the Swiss cottage was completed and became a playhouse for the children. The cottage included a working kitchen and dining room, in which the sisters learned to bake and cook, and they would often present a meal to their parents. Outside, the children were encouraged to hunt for items for a natural history collection. Each child had their own garden plot where they learned to nurture and grow vegetables, fruit, and flowers (Hawksley 32).

CHAPTER 9

Epigraph: Longford, *Darling Loosy: Letters to Princess Louise 1856–1939*, 89.

Vicky (the Princess Royal) and her husband, Fritz (the Crown Prince of Prussia), were against Bertie marrying Princess Alexandra of Denmark as a result of the Three Years' War, or the First Schleswig War. The Danes achieved victory when the Prussians were pressured into withdrawing by other international powers, and the Danes won control of the duchies of Schleswig and Holstein (see "German-Danish War," *Britannica*, https://www.britannica.com/event/German-Danish-War).

CHAPTER 10

Epigraph: Longford, *Darling Loosy: Letters to Princess Louise 1856–1939*, 90.

Princess Louise had no privacy growing up. Of course, Queen Victoria wanted to know what her children were doing—especially since she was so busy and couldn't attend to them. So Princess Louise knew that everything she did and said had the potential to be reported on. This was one reason she truly relished having Sybil Grey as a close friend and confidante. At last, Princess Louise could talk to a friend who wouldn't turn around and inform the queen (Hawksley 66–67).

CHAPTER 11

Epigraph: Longford, *Darling Loosy: Letters to Princess Louise 1856–1939*, 90.

Over eighty thousand people greeted Princess Alexandra of Denmark when she arrived with her family on the royal yacht in Gravesend to begin her union with the Prince of Wales. After all, Alix would be England's future queen—many decades later. The country had been mourning the death of Prince Albert for over a year, so the people were ready for something good to celebrate. The Danish family was welcomed by pretty maids with flowers, and as the family traveled to their destination, they found the streets decorated with banners, lanterns, and flowers (Hawksley 60–62).

CHAPTER 12

Epigraph: Hawksley, *Queen Victoria's Mysterious Daughter*, 69.

Princess Louise didn't care much for Balmoral as a child. She once wrote to Prince Arthur that their brother Leo had another case of rheumatism in his leg and had to be carried up and down stairs. The doctor claimed the rheumatism had come from wearing a kilt in bad weather—which the queen had insisted on (Hawksley 69). To add to this, the following year in 1864, Princess Louise contracted tubercular meningitis while staying at Balmoral. Her headaches were fierce and required her to stay in a darkened room. It was months before she recovered well enough to attend a ball at Marlborough House to celebrate Bertie and Alix's wedding anniversary (Hawksley 71–72).

CHAPTER 13

Epigraph: Longford, *Darling Loosy: Letters to Princess Louise 1856–1939*, 91.

The Drawing Room was a court event that Queen Victoria maintained, despite her mourning. Drawing Rooms took place in the throne room at Buckingham Palace and were ceremonies in which the Victorian debutantes would wear long dresses, long white veils, and tiaras, and would be presented to the queen. When Princess Louise would attend, she'd stand for hours with the other royals, but it was one social event she was allowed in the early years after her father's death. Eventually, Princess Louise was allowed to attend a court ball, although she was only allowed to partner with another royal in a dance, she wasn't allowed to waltz, and she was forbidden to dance the supper dance (Wake 68–69).

CHAPTER 14

Epigraph: Longford, *Darling Loosy: Letters to Princess Louise 1856–1939*, 92.

Bertie was long blamed for his father's death by Queen Victoria. After his love affair with Nellie Clifden, Prince Albert traveled in damp weather to chastise his son; the queen believed her husband wouldn't have fallen so ill if he hadn't gone to speak with Bertie about his misconduct. As a widow, Queen Victoria instead turned to her daughters for help. She excluded Bertie (who would be the future King Edward VII) from involvement in affairs of state. He was over fifty years old when he was finally made privy to cabinet proceedings (see "Edward VII," *Britannica*, https://www.britannica.com/biography/Edward-VII).

John Brown was a great friend and helpmeet to Queen Victoria, but her children and others didn't like or trust him. Brown started in service to the queen at the end of 1864 at Osborne, and a few months later, in February 1865, she gave him a permanent appointment. He became known as the Queen's "Highland Servant." More Highlanders joined the queen's household, including Archie Brown in July, who became a valet to Prince Leopold. The queen found the Highlanders loyal and defended them when others criticized their methods (Zeepvat 70–71).

Although Prince Albert had been dead four years by 1865, Queen Victoria was still reluctant to appear or participate in any public events. She relied heavily on her daughters for support instead of her heir, the Prince of Wales. The growing republican movement in England and the many wars abroad put more duress upon Queen Victoria. This led her to accept Prince Christian as a suitor for Princess Helena, despite her oldest son's opposition to the match. The Prince of Wales refused to meet Christian at first, and it took his sister's appeal, along with General Grey's interference, for Bertie to back down and keep the family peace (Wake 62).

CHAPTER 15

Epigraph: Packard, *Victoria's Daughters,* 115.

Although Queen Victoria highly approved of hiring Walter Stirling to work with Prince Leopold in the beginning, when Stirling didn't get along with the Highlanders who worked for the queen, things drastically changed. In a letter to Major Elphinstone, Queen Victoria wrote about Stirling's behavior: "It will never do to speak harshly and dictatorially to Highlanders. . . . Their independence and self-respect and proper spirit . . . makes them resent that. . . . A young officer accustomed to order about soldiers may not understand the peculiar nature of these people" (Zeepvat 77).

The first mass women's suffrage petition was brought to Parliament by Dr. Elizabeth Garrett and Emily Davies. On June 7, 1866, John Stuart Mill MP presented the petition to the House of Commons. The petition had to be concealed under the stall of an apple seller in order to prevent too much unrest. And although the petition was voted down, it was a major step toward eventually replacing the word *man* with *person* in the Second Reform Bill (see "Presenting the 1866 Petition," UK Parliament, https://www.parliament.uk/about/living-heritage/transform

ingsociety/electionsvoting/womenvote/parliamentary-collections/1866
-suffrage-petition/presenting-the-petition/).

CHAPTER 16

Epigraph: Longford, *Darling Loosy: Letters to Princess Louise 1856–1939*, 93.

Prince Leopold was an avid chess player, and in February 1874, he was elected to be a member of the University Chess Club at Oxford. He also belonged to the Bullingdon Cricket and was a founding member of the University Musical Club (Zeepvat 159).

Princess Louise's artistic talents extended to jewelry making and design. One item she created was a beaten-silver cross (Wake 79). She also designed a gem-studded ring that was a farewell gift to Robin Duckworth, who served as Prince Leopold's governor (Wake 117).

CHAPTER 17

Epigraph: Longford, *Darling Loosy: Letters to Princess Louise 1856–1939*, 94.

After some persuading, when Princess Louise expressed interest in sculpturing, Queen Victoria commissioned two sculptresses to train her. The first was Susan Durant, and the second, Mary Thornycroft (Wake 89). Eventually, the queen allowed Princess Louise her own space for a studio. In 2021, I asked the curator for Osborne House to send a description of Princess Louise's art studio: "It is a small room, very much like one of the bedrooms. It is on the same corridor as Louise's bedroom. It is nothing like what one would think of as a typical studio with lots of big windows. It must just have been used occasionally for small projects."

If Prince Albert had lived longer, perhaps he would have encouraged his daughter in the art of sculpting more so than Queen Victoria did. The queen, like many others of her era, thought the work unnatural and unsuitable for a princess. Yet, time wore on her, and eventually, Princess Louise impressed the queen when she sculpted a bust of Prince Arthur for the queen's birthday in 1867. She thought the quality was good enough to be displayed at the Royal Military Academy at Woolwich (Wake 90).

Over time, Princess Louise's heavy involvement in art began to soften Queen Victoria's staunch rejection of so many things she'd loved before her husband died. By 1868, the queen allowed Princess Louise to organize amateur theatricals, and this led to her playing the piano and singing. Eventually, the queen joined in, singing once again (Wake 92–93).

The incident of Queen Victoria saying that any society lady who advocated for women's voting deserved a good whipping reflects her true opinion. Ironically, although queen, she believed a woman's place was in the home, subservient to her husband (Packard 129).

CHAPTER 18

Epigraph: Longford, *Darling Loosy: Letters to Princess Louise 1856–1939*, 95.

Attending a public art school was a novelty for a royal princess, and Princess Louise became friends with those outside her royal circles, such as Henrietta Montalba. Henrietta went on to become a professional sculptress. Unfortunately, Princess Louise wasn't allowed to attend the National Art Training School as regularly as she'd like since the queen had many demands on Princess Louise's schedule (Wake 92).

Henry James O'Farrell shot Prince Alfred in 1868. O'Farrell supported the Fenian movement, which stemmed from the Irish demand for independence and their grievances against British rule, such as the missteps during the Irish Potato Famine (Hawksley 94–96).

CHAPTER 19

Epigraph: Longford, *Darling Loosy: Letters to Princess Louise 1856–1939*, 101.

Queen Victoria was known for going silent on a family member when she disagreed with them. At times, Prince Albert was reduced to sending her notes in order to communicate with her. When Beatrice chose a husband whom Queen Victoria didn't approve of, the queen didn't speak to Beatrice for six months. Not until the couple agreed to live with her after they were married did verbal communication resume (see "Queen Victoria: The Real Story of Her 'Domestic Bliss,'" BBC News, January 1, 2013, https://www.bbc.com/news/magazine -20782442).

Elizabeth Garrett was the first female doctor in England, although she had to receive her training and degree in Paris, France. When Princess Louise heard about Dr. Garrett, the princess wanted to meet the doctor. Princess Louise believed that if women could be nurses, they should be able to train as doctors too. The Victorian opposition to the idea stemmed from the belief that women were supposed to remain pure and innocent. Because Princess Louise knew her mother didn't support women's suffrage, the princess paid a surprise visit to Dr. Garrett's residence in London in order to meet the woman (Wake 97–98; Packard 130).

CHAPTER 20

Epigraph: Longford, *Darling Loosy: Letters to Princess Louise 1856– 1939*, 104.

Artist Edgar Boehm arrived in England in 1862, but it wasn't until 1869 that he met Princess Louise, when she sat for an equestrian statuette. The queen agreed that Boehm could give Princess Louise some sculpting lessons, and he taught her to sculpt in bronze, as well as produce more realistic drapery of clothing in her sculptures (Wake 104–5).

The queen of Holland was very interested in Princess Louise marrying her son, Prince William of Orange. Queen Victoria was heartily opposed though since the prince had been previously considered for Princess Alice in 1860 but was found unsuitable. In addition, it was rumored that he had a *demi-mondaine* in Paris (Wake 100).

Out of the thirteen princes considered marriage material for Princess Louise, only seven were eligible, but they were slowly weeded out when obstacles arose. One such case was Prince Albrecht, nephew of the king of Prussia. Princess Royal Vicky was determined to cast Prince Albrecht in a favorable light to Princess Louise. He was wealthy, good, kind, and handsome, despite being a giant of a man with a large head. Yet as appealing as his pedigree might have been, he refused to reside in England, which was a deal breaker for Queen Victoria. She wasn't about to send another daughter off to the Prussians (Wake 101). In addition, Princess Louise was set against marrying a Prussian prince, not only because she didn't want to live in Prussia but because she found them "boorish and boring, and that they smelt bad" (Hawksley 73).

CHAPTER 21

Epigraph: Longford, *Darling Loosy: Letters to Princess Louise 1856–1939*, 105.

Queen Victoria declared that marriageable candidates for Princess Louise must come from a respectable family, possess a fortune, and have a fine position—called the three F's. The first man who met these qualifications was Henry Petty-Fitzmaurice, the fifth Marquess of Lansdowne (Wake 105–6). This began a long string of suitors that would soon fall away or be rejected for one reason or another.

CHAPTER 22

Epigraph: Longford, *Darling Loosy: Letters to Princess Louise 1856–1939*, 105–6.

To find Princess Louise a husband, Queen Victoria set aside the *Almanach de Gotha* and replaced it with *Burke's Guide to the Peerage and Baronetage*. This became the starting point for the queen in searching for eligible young men who met the requirements of the three F's. Things weren't that simple, of course, and the queen objected to characteristics or circumstances as they arose; for instance, Lord Douglas attended the wrong church, and Lord Cowper was too old at thirty-four (Wake 114). Eventually, the three F's were replaced by the streamlined guideline of having a good character and an independent future, which opened the doors for more eligible suitors (Wake 118).

CHAPTER 23

Epigraph: Longford, *Darling Loosy: Letters to Princess Louise 1856–1939*, 106.

After the fiasco of discovering that Lord Lansdowne was engaged, the name of John Douglas Sutherland Campbell, the Marquess of Lorne, was suggested. He had many attributes in his favor, and he came from a family that had long been associated with the royal family. He'd known Princess Louise as a child, and better yet, he wasn't attached (Wake 106–7). In the story, I commonly refer to the marquess as John Campbell instead of his other known names of Lorne or Ian, in order to differentiate between him and other characters in the book.

In August of 1869, the queen met with John Campbell's parents, the Duke and Duchess of Argyll. Interestingly enough, the Duke was not thrilled at the prospect of his son marrying a princess. His son had a bright future mapped out as the future ninth Duke of Argyll and the chief of the Clan Campbell, and marrying into the royal family would put him on a very different path (Wake 108–9).

CHAPTER 24

Epigraph: Longford, *Darling Loosy: Letters to Princess Louise 1856–1939*, 111.

Queen Victoria hated smoking and forbade it in her homes. When Prince Christian married Princess Helena, he had to find alternatives for his tobacco habit. He would blow the smoke into the chimney in whichever bedroom he was staying in under the queen's rule. When she discovered this, she had them use a "cubbyhole in a distant part of Windsor Castle, which they had to reach by crossing open courtyards in all weathers" (Packard 234–35). Later, when Prince Henry of Battenberg (Liko) married Princess Beatrice, the two smoking in-laws were able to convince the queen to assign a larger chamber, with furniture and a billiards table, for a smoking room (Packard 235). Princess Louise became a known smoker as well, but always away from the presence of the queen (Longford 110).

The death of General Grey was a hard loss for Princess Louise since he'd been a father figure to her and he was the beloved father of her best friend, Sybil. Grey held the position of secretary to Prince Albert from 1849 to 1861 and secretary to the Queen from 1861 until his death in 1870. Even though he was currently on the outs with the queen, she sent over her doctors to attend to him. Still, General Grey died six days later. During this time, Sybil was in confinement, about to deliver a baby (Wake 116).

CHAPTER 25

Epigraph: Longford, *Darling Loosy: Letters to Princess Louise 1856–1939*, 111.

Historians theorized that Princess Louise might have had a school-girl crush on Robin Duckworth, who'd worked for the family since 1866 as an instructor and later as governor to Prince Leopold. Duckworth was charming, charismatic, and a talented singer. Biographer Jehanne Wake theorized that perhaps Princess Louise compared the men paraded in front of her to Duckworth. Regardless, Queen Victoria had him dismissed around this time on account of Leo's health (Longford 19), and Louise and Leo created a stunning ring as a farewell gift (Wake 116–17).

CHAPTER 26

Epigraph: Longford, *Darling Loosy: Letters to Princess Louise 1856–1939*, 113–14.

Two standout suitors in the peerage were Lord Gosford and Lord Rosebery. Each of them was invited to dine with Princess Louise, but she refused to commit herself to one over the other. Queen Victoria had some complaints about Lord Gosford because she thought he might be poor. But Lord Rosebery favored the turf—horse racing—and another mark against him was his friendship with the Prince of Wales. This only lowered the queen's opinion of him (Wake 119). At this point, it seemed that everyone was involved in choosing a husband for Princess Louise, and it was surely disconcerting to have all eyes upon her and judgements passed swiftly around.

The Prince of Wales didn't want his sister Princess Louise to marry a commoner. When Prince Adolphus of Mecklenberg-Strelitz was brought up by Princess Helena, Queen Victoria's pride wouldn't allow the union because Prince Adolphus was a lesser prince than Prince Albrecht—whom they'd already written off. Besides, Princess Louise would have to join him in the court of Strelitz, and even if visits to England were written into her marriage contract, that still wasn't good enough for the queen (Wake 120).

CHAPTER 27

Epigraph: Longford, *Darling Loosy: Letters to Princess Louise 1856–1939*, 117.

One of Princess Louise's heroines was Florence Nightingale, who started the National Society for Giving Aid to the Sick and Wounded in War. This was a neutral agency, which helped soldiers on both sides of conflicts. Princess Louise eagerly spent time collecting old sheets and materials to make charpie. She also created pillows from thistledown to be sent to hospitals (Wake 122–23).

CHAPTER 28

Epigraph: Longford, *Darling Loosy: Letters to Princess Louise 1856–1939*, 119.

The Gladstones held breakfast parties at their home at 11 Carlton House Terrace. The breakfasts took place at noon and included an eclectic group of friends and family, statesmen, churchmen, writers, and authors. Lady Gladstone invited Princess Louise to one, and this is where she met John Campbell again. Perhaps because they weren't surrounded by the usual royal snoops, they were able to have a more relaxing, natural conversation (Wake 121).

CHAPTER 29

Epigraph: Longford, *Darling Loosy: Letters to Princess Louise 1856–1939*, 122.

John Campbell—Lord Lorne—was described as having a fair complexion with bright-blue Campbell eyes. His hair was yellow gold, which he wore long. His build was slim, and his voice had a high, nasal quality. While visiting Balmoral, Lord Lorne wore distinctive Clan Campbell clothing, including a black velvet tunic covered with embroidered silver fish (Wake 124).

CHAPTER 30

Epigraph: Longford, *Darling Loosy: Letters to Princess Louise 1856–1939*, 127.

The wreckage of the steamship *SS Cambria* was a tragic event in which all passengers and crew, save one, perished. The *Cambria* had been approaching the coast of Ireland when it hit stormy weather and struck the rocks. The lifeboats were lowered, but they capsized ("Cambria Passenger/Cargo Ship, 1869–1870," Wrecksite, https://www.wrecksite.eu/wreck.aspx?63263).

CHAPTER 31

Epigraph: Longford, *Darling Loosy: Letters to Princess Louise 1856–1939*, 128.

In quite the power play, Queen Victoria and Princess Louise both wanted the chance to speak to the Duke of Argyll on his October 13, 1870, Balmoral visit. Once Princess Louise learned of his impending arrival, she was determined to speak to him about marriage arrangements before she was left out of any major decision-making. The Duke was planning to meet with the queen first, but then he found a note from Princess Louise asking to speak with him before the queen returned from an afternoon drive. The Duke had a decision to make, and finally went with obeying the queen's request. Once Princess Louise was allowed into the meeting, the Duke secured permission to embrace his future daughter-in-law (Wake 128–29).

CHAPTER 32

Epigraph: Longford, *Darling Loosy: Letters to Princess Louise 1856–1939*, 128–29.

Queen Victoria's mood swings were apparent to those in her close circles. In one example, she was elated during the Duke's visit to Balmoral to discuss marriage arrangements between her daughter and John Campbell. But then the queen spoke to no one during dinner on the last night of the Duke's visit (Wake 129).

CHAPTER 33

Epigraph: John Campbell, "Lord F. Douglas Killed on the Matterhorn, Switzerland, 1865," in *Memories of Canada and Scotland: Speeches and Verses*, available at https://www.gutenberg.org/cache/epub/7212/pg7212.html.

The Prince of Wales had three main concerns over Princess Louise's choice of a husband in John Campbell. First, Bertie cited that Lorne had been nearly engaged to another woman. When that was proved false, Bertie complained that Lorne's political persuasion—which he refused to turn away from—would make the Crown seem as if it was identifying with a political party. In addition, Bertie didn't like that Lorne's family was full of men employed as trade workers, stockbrokers, and bankers (Wake 132). In response to all of this, Queen Victoria decided to create a British peerage title for Lorne. This would mean that Lorne would be removed from the House of Commons and would then have a seat in the House of Lords. In this way, Lorne would be raised above the commoner status and be separated from the Liberal party. Lorne refused the peerage title, and Princess Louise supported that refusal (Wake 134–35).

Princess Alice was supportive of Princess Louise's choice to marry a commoner, but the Princess Royal Vicky wasn't nearly as amenable. She wrote to her sister and said that even the king of Prussia was very disappointed that Princess Louise would turn down marriage to his nephew and a position at the Berlin court (Wake 131). Another royal figure who weighed in on Princess Louise's choice of husband was the queen of Holland, who said that the match was certainly a *mésalliance* (Wake 132).

The Franco-Prussian War divided loyalties in the royal household, including Princess Louise, although she was more sympathetic to the French (Wake 123). During her courtship with John Campbell and beyond, events often centered on what was going on in other parts of Europe (see "Timeline of the Franco-Prussian War," http://francoprussianwar.com/timeline.htm).

CHAPTER 34

Epigraph: Queen Victoria, journal, March 21, 1871, pp. 65–66, QueenVictoriasJournals.org (UK); http://qvj.chadwyck.com/marketing.do (US).

The marriage settlement for Princess Louise, approved by Parliament, was the same as Princess Helena's. The income was four thousand pounds per year, along with the public provision of six thousand pounds per year. This was in addition to her thirty-thousand-pound dowry (Wake 137).

On her wedding day, Princess Louise suffered the beginnings of a cold. She'd awakened with a headache and earache, but the event would not be delayed (Wake 141). Princess Louise had designed her own wedding gown, and although Queen Victoria wore her usual black, she added color through the blue sash of the Order of the Garter. Princess Louise wore gifts of jewelry from her siblings and from her future husband (Wake 141; a full list of wedding guests can be found at Susan Flantzer, "Wedding of Princess Louise of the United Kingdom and John Sutherland Campbell, 9th Duke of Argyll," Unofficial Royalty, 2019, https://www.unofficialroyalty.com/wedding-of-princess-louise-of-the-united-kingdom-and-john-sutherland-campbell-9th-duke-of-argyll/).

Until Princess Louise, the last time a marriage between a princess and a British subject had been officially recognized was 1515, when

Princess Mary (King Henry VIII's sister) married Charles Brandon, first Duke of Suffolk. In 1772, King George III passed a law, called the Royal Marriages Act, that prescribed under what conditions a member of the royal family could marry a commoner (Wake 106).

Even though John Campbell had turned down a British peerage title, he accepted the Order of the Thistle from Queen Victoria. This was the highest chivalry knighthood one could receive in Scotland (Wake 142).

CHAPTER 35

Epigraph: Queen Victoria, journal, March 21, 1871, pp. 66–67, QueenVictoriasJournals.org (UK); http://qvj.chadwyck.com/marketing .do (US).

The drive to Claremont House didn't afford any privacy for Princess Louise and her new husband since they had a royal escort with them inside the carriage. Once they arrived at the house, Lady Jane Churchill and Colonel McNeill were there to greet and attend to the couple. A room had been adapted into a bridal suite for the newlyweds, complete with specially woven orange-blossom carpet (Wake 145).

CHAPTER 36

Epigraph: Longford, *Darling Loosy: Letters to Princess Louise 1856–1939*, 147.

Two days after Princess Louise married, her mother showed up at the Claremont House to pay the newlywed couple a visit. The queen wanted to make sure all was well in the brand-new marriage and insisted they soon return to Windsor so that Princess Louise could continue as personal secretary until her official departure on her honeymoon (Wake 146). In addition, the queen wanted Princess Louise to meet the newly arrived Napoleon III, who had taken exile in England after being released by Bismarck following the fall of the French empire (Hawksley 133).

During Princess Louise's interim stay at Windsor, there was quite a backlog of the queen's correspondence to deal with. In addition, Princess Louise was too busy to attend a Drawing Room where others expected her to appear, but she and her husband did make it to the opening of the Royal Albert Hall (Wake 146). On April 3, the Prince of Wales accompanied the newly married couple to the Charing Cross station. There, they boarded a train to Dover. Princess Louise had secured permission from the queen to pay a short visit to Princess Alice in Darmstadt. Queen Victoria didn't want the two sisters to spend too much time together for fear of Alice discussing her nursing work and having influence over Louise (Wake 148). The queen also feared that Alice would ask Louise personal questions about being married (Hawksley 135).

Two important pieces of legislation passed in 1870: the first Married Women's Property Act and the Education Act. As a supporter of women's rights and children's rights, Princess Louise was still confined to her role as a representative of the Crown, and she dared not go against her mother. Because of the Princess of Wales's poor health, Princess Louise was happy to accompany her brother Bertie to official functions in order to expand her interests and influence (Hawksley 118).

Princess Louise was likely drawn to John Campbell even more because he was a strong supporter of women's education and feminist ideals. Both John and Louise were passionate about improving education, health, and poverty in Britain (Hawksley 135).

CHAPTER 37

Epigraph: Wake, *Princess Louise: Queen Victoria's Unconventional Daughter*, 403.

John Campbell's father, the eighth Duke of Argyll, purchased the Argyll House in 1853. He was very impressed with the remote feeling of the house, which was set apart from the bustle of traffic. He loved the old oak trees, gardens, and variety of birds on the grounds. When Princess Louise arrived with her husband, she had brought along her own footmen and a maid, but her first experiences living among the

Argylls would have been very different than her royal upbringing (Wake 150–51).

CHAPTER 38

Epigraph: Longford, *Darling Loosy: Letters to Princess Louise 1856–1939*, 151.

John Campbell took to calling Queen Victoria "Dear Mama" or "Madam" (Wake 154). When Queen Victoria planned to visit Inveraray with the Argylls, the town prepared for the great event. The castle needed improvements, such as a pavilion, erected to act as a ballroom, and a porch, constructed over the main entrance. Unfortunately, the queen was stung, fell ill as a result, and had to put off the visit. But Princess Louise and John decided to go anyway since so many preparations had already been made (Wake 154).

The stone with the inscription "Rest and Be Thankful" still exists atop the pass of Glen Croe (Wake 156). Once Princess Louise reached Inveraray Castle, in a poignant moment, Clan Campbell presented her with a wedding gift of a necklace of diamonds and pearls. A pearl locket hung from the necklace, and below that, a pendant bore the Galley of Lorne in sapphires (Wake 157; see also "Jewel History: Royal Wedding Presents [1900]," The Court Jeweler, December 14, 2017, https://www.thecourtjeweller.com/2017/12/jewel-history-royal-wedding-presents.html. For a picture of the necklace, see "Lorne Jewels," object no. EDIN059, Historic Environment Scotland, "https://www.historicenvironment.scot/archives-and-research/archives-and-collections/properties-in-care-collections/object/the-lorne-jewels-20th-century-modern-edinburgh-castle-10251).

Princess Louise fell in love with the new lifestyle she was exposed to and the resulting freedoms, especially compared to her austere and sheltered upbringing. She delighted in family togetherness, and when the Duchess of Argyll died, Louise was the one who encouraged her husband and his siblings to give their father's new wife, Amelia Anson (Mimi), a chance (Wake 265–66).

But when the second wife died and the Duke married for a third time, to Ina McNeill, the siblings could no longer countenance their father's choices. The situation became so dire that upon the Duke's own death in 1900, John refused to visit his father in his last days or attend his funeral. Louise tried to convince her husband. She even had her brother Bertie, the Prince of Wales, plead with John. But the third duchess had dug her claws in too deep, dividing the family completely asunder. McNeill even insisted on burying him at Westminster Abbey and not where the Duke had dictated in his will. His body lay in holding until Queen Victoria at last intervened, and the Duke was buried at Kilmun. Louise attended the funeral incognito, but still the duchess noticed her, and she left the chapel immediately (Wake 327–29).

Readers might encounter some of the rumors surrounding Princess Louise, which have been discussed and debated by various historians. The rumors include that Louise had an affair with Edgar Boehm or Walter Stirling or even Reverend Duckworth. Another rumor grew out of this one—that she bore an illegitimate child. Biographer Lucinda Hawksley discusses this in depth in her book *Queen Victoria's Mysterious Daughter* (75–87). In studying the timelines, as well as reading the biography of Louise's brother Leopold (*Queen Victoria's Youngest Son: The Untold Story of Prince Leopold*, by Charlotte Zeepvat), who was the student of both Stirling and Duckworth, I wasn't able to find anything beyond theories to take up this angle in the novel.

As the early years of Princess Louise and John Campbell's marriage passed without a pregnancy, Louise took added measures to ensure that she was of healthy body. Although John was tender and supportive, she wanted to improve her health in all ways possible. This began a chain of events over the next twelve years of Louise and John traveling to bathhouses in Germany, such as Kissingen, Homburg, or Marienbad, in order to achieve a cure for her barrenness. Louise also met with doctors and the top specialists at the time, and the resounding conclusion was that Louise suffered from meningitic complications, and the by-product was infertility. John was never examined (Wake 195–96).

That Louise didn't become pregnant created another rumor that John Campbell was homosexual. Hawksley compiles some of these speculations in her book (124–25). My historical novel covers only the first few months of Louise and John's marriage, but their letters to each other show their obvious devotion. In addition, the compassionate way Louise nursed John in his later years and how John always cared for Louise and put her health above all else firmly convinced me that the ninth Duke of Argyll was a faithful and devoted husband until the end.

SELECTED LIST OF PRINCESS LOUISE'S ART

Princess Beatrice, 1864. Marble, Royal Collection Trust

Prince Arthur, 1869. Marble, Royal Collection Trust

Prince Leopold, 1869. Marble, Royal Collection Trust

Queen Victoria, 1887. Bronze, Leeds Museums and Galleries, Temple Newsam House

Self Portrait, n.d. Terracotta, National Portrait Gallery, London

Memorial to Mary Ann Thurston, Kensal Green Cemetery. Thurston was a nanny to Queen Victoria's children, 1845–1867

Memorial to her brother-in-law Prince Henry of Battenberg, Whippingham Church, Isle of Wight

Memorial to the colonial soldiers who fell during the Second Boer War, Whippingham Church, Isle of Wight

NOTABLE CONTRIBUTIONS
BY PRINCESS LOUISE

Ladies' Work Society (LWS), which provided employment for impover-
ished gentlewomen
Princess Louise Scottish Hospital for Limbless Sailors and Soldiers
(name later changed to Erskine Hospital)
Lady of the Royal Order of Victoria and Albert (First Class)
Companion of the Order of the Crown of India
Member of the Royal Red Cross
Royal Family Order of King Edward VII
Royal Family Order of King George V
Dame Grand Cross of the Order of the British Empire
Dame Grand Cross of the Venerable Order of St. John
Dame Grand Cross of the Royal Victorian Order
Dame of the Order of Queen Saint Isabel
Honorary Colonel, Fifth Princess Louise Dragoon Guards
Colonel-in-Chief, the Argyll and Sutherland Highlanders
Colonel-in-Chief, the Argyll and Sutherland Highlanders of Canada
Colonel-in-Chief, the Princess Louise Fusiliers
President of the Women's Education Union, from 1871
Patron of the Girls' Day School Trust, 1872–1939
Patron of the Ladies Lifeboat Guild, Royal National Lifeboat Institution,
1923–1939

NOTABLE TITLES OF
JOHN CAMPBELL, MARQUESS OF LORNE

Fourth Governor General of Canada

Ninth Duke of Argyll

Earl Campbell and Cowal

Viscount of Lochow and Glenisla

Baron Inveraray

Member of House of Lords

Head of Clan Campbell

Keeper of the Great Seal of Scotland

Lord-Lieutenant of Argyllshire

Master of the Royal Household in Scotland

Admiral of the Western Coasts and Isles

DISCUSSION QUESTIONS

1. What are some things about the royal family that surprised you?

2. What do you think about the way spouses were chosen for Queen Victoria's children and about how the process was different for Princess Louise?

3. What health difficulties did Princess Louise or other family members experience that you felt went untreated?

4. Regardless of Princess Louise's independent thinking, why do you think she really didn't want to marry one of the eligible royals?

5. How do you think family dynamics, her being the fourth daughter and sixth child, played into Princess Louise's personality?

6. What impressed you most about Princess Louise, and what traits did you not expect?

7. If Princess Louise had been born in a more modern era, what do you think she would have been involved in? How far do you think her talents would have taken her?

8. Why do you think there was such a disparity between those who believed in women's suffrage and those who didn't?

9. Why do you think Queen Victoria was so against women's suffrage when she herself was a powerful monarch?

10. What is your overall impression of Princess Louise, Queen Victoria, and their family?

SELECTED BIBLIOGRAPHY

Buchan, William. *Domestic Medicine: Or, a Treatise on the Prevention and Cure of Diseases by Regimen and Simple Medicines.* Boston: Otis, Broaders, and Company, 1848.

Cadbury, Deborah. *Queen Victoria's Matchmaking: The Royal Marriages That Shaped Europe.* New York: Public Affairs, 2019.

Dennison, Matthew. *The Last Princess: The Devoted Life of Queen Victoria's Youngest Daughter.* New York: St. Martin's Press, 2008.

Dolby, Karen. *My Dearest, Dearest Albert: Queen Victoria's Life through Her Letters and Journals.* London: Michael O'Mara Books, 2018.

Hawksley, Lucinda. *Queen Victoria's Mysterious Daughter: A Biography of Princess Louise.* New York: Thomas Dunne Books, 2017.

Longford, Elizabeth. *Darling Loosy: Letters to Princess Louise 1856–1939.* London: Weidenfeld & Nicholson, 1991.

Packard, Jerrold M. *Victoria's Daughters.* New York: St. Martin's Griffin, 1998.

Queen Victoria's Journals. QueenVictoriasJournal.org (UK); http://qvj. chadwyck.com/marketing.do (US).

Stamp, Robert M. *Royal Rebels: Princess Louise & the Marquis of Lorne.* Toronto & Oxford: Dundurn Press, 1988.

Wake, Jehanne. *Princess Louise: Queen Victoria's Unconventional Daughter.* London: Collins, 1988.

Zeepvat, Charlotte. *Queen Victoria's Youngest Son: The Untold Story of Prince Leopold.* London: Lume Books, 2020.

ACKNOWLEDGMENTS

⸺⸳⸾⸳⸺

When beginning the research for this book, I knew it would take a significant amount of time to pull together the events and details of Princess Louise's life. I bought several biographies, and as I began to read through them and annotate, I felt immensely grateful for the historians who spent years researching and compiling information. I didn't have their expertise and resources, so their work became my support. The primary sources that I read, cross-referenced, and annotated were books by Jehanne Wake, Jerrold M. Packard, Lucinda Hawksley, and Elizabeth Longford. Their book titles are in the bibliography. Other authors were also helpful in double-checking details and discovering answers to my many questions.

I reached out to others for help with very specific questions, such as the Osborne House curator, Laurie Bester (descendant of Eliza Collins, who was a nursemaid to Louise. Eliza was married to Rudolph Lohlein, a valet to Prince Albert, and later, literary secretary to Queen Victoria), the Instagram account "Queen.Victoria.Roses," Andy of Edinburgh Cab Tours, and Nichole Van, who helped me with some research.

My sister Julianne helped me with typing up my annotated notes so that I could cross-reference all of the books. When I found out the number of hours it took her, I was glad she'd agreed to help me. Later, she also read the manuscript and offered some great feedback, which my readers will definitely benefit from.

Julie Wright was another reader of the manuscript. I think she became just as caught up in the saga of the royal family as I did, and we had several conversations about the royal family. Julie is a fantastic author and an even better friend.

My agent, Ann Leslie Tuttle, read the manuscript before we submitted it to Shadow Mountain. I always appreciate her editorial notes and comments on both smaller details and bigger-picture issues. Many thanks as well to Jen Geigle Johnson and Rebecca Connolly, friends and fellow authors, who were my sounding board on many decisions I had to make on the spot.

I'm grateful for the faith that my publisher Shadow Mountain has in my projects, and I believe they are some of the best people on the planet to work with: Heidi Gordon, Lisa Mangum, Chris Schoebinger, Troy Butcher, Callie Hansen, Ilise Levine, and Alison Palmer.

Many thanks to my family, including my husband, Chris; my children, Kaelin, Kara, Dana, and Rose; my parents, Kent and Gayle Brown; and my father-in-law, Lester Moore. I feel blessed to add one more name this year—my grandson, Ezra Moore. The circle of life is such a blessing, and spending months learning about Princess Louise and her "darling boy" Lorne has taught me that despite trials and extreme challenges, relationships are what we will take with us beyond this life.